Advance Praise for

THESE BLOODY GAMES WE PLAY

These Bloody Games We Play is the revenge story of the century. Plan on dropping everything, because once you pick it up, you won't want to put it down.

–Lauren Bayliss Schuldt

This was an absolute blast to read. There were triggers but not so much that I needed to stop reading. This author really was able to convey the anger and pain these two women endured.

—Josette Thomas

This book is proof, yet again, that Wofford Lee Jones is an excellent writer. A very satisfying, thought-provoking, dark, disturbing story; exactly what I like to read."

—Laurie Griffith Jones

Jones shocks in this story of twisted games and brutal revenge. In a tale that's definitely not for the squeamish, *These Bloody Games We Play* explores the ugliest sides of both childhood and adult trauma. A psychological thriller that attempts to explain the reasons behind extreme actions and atrocities committed by humans against fellow humans. The character development is rich and the reader feels the pain that each of the main players goes through. We also feel the rage. There are some truly cringe-inducing scenes in this book and Jones' descriptive prowess is as detailed and grisly as always. This is a bold and powerful statement on today's society and is the best book I've read in some time.

—D.A. Schneider author of
Salvation **and** *Whiskey and Cigarettes*

Jones has crafted another dark and disturbing tale of vengeance that will have you rooting for the main characters all the way to its bloody conclusion!

—Evan Bond author of *Charred Remains* **and** *After Death*

THESE BLOODY GAMES WE PLAY

A Battle of the Sexes Novel

Author of Hell Night in Hopewell and Lethal Doses

Wofford Lee Jones

These Bloody Games We Play
Wofford Lee Jones
Print Edition

ISBN: 978-0-9990925-8-3 (Paperback)

Visit the author at www.woffordleejones.com.

Cover design by Wofford Lee Jones
Manuscript formatting by www.damonza.com

OTHER BOOKS BY THIS AUTHOR

NOVELS

Soul Dreams
Off the Beaten Path
Hell Night in Hopewell
Lethal Doses

ANTHOLOGIES

Bag of Bones – 206 Word Stories
(featuring *A Comforting Touch*)

GORE
(featuring *Don't Turn Your Back on Halloween*)

GORE 2 - Ghosts
(featuring *Last Call*)

GORE 3 - Monsters
(featuring *Midnight Snack*)

Winter of the Raven
(featuring *That Cold Cursed Winter Moon*)

GORE 4 - Demons
(featuring *Spirits in Old Hopewell*
and *Nocturnal Rites*)

The Raven Collection
(featuring *Crowfoot Smile*)

TRIGGER WARNINGS MESSAGE

I have mixed feelings about trigger warnings. If you read the trigger warnings, it could be a spoiler, or spoilers, for something that happens within the book that you would otherwise not be expecting. I know traumatic events happen to people, and not having trigger warnings could bring up unwanted memories from a reader's past. So this is my solution. On the book's last page, I have added all the possible trigger warnings within this story. You can find them there.

I will stress again—these warnings contain spoilers. The listed words and phrases are insightful to this book's full story. But I would rather give you a chance to prepare yourself for what's to come rather than subjecting yourself to something you would otherwise not want to experience. Whichever the case, I hope you do not have an adverse reaction to this story. It is always my hope that you thoroughly enjoy my dark tales.

DEDICATION

This book is dedicated to all those who have been abused at some point in their life.
I hope this story gives you some peace.

And for Laurie; always for Laurie.

PART I

UNSPORTSMANLIKE CONDUCT

CHAPTER ONE

CELESTE BAKER WAS in her own little world as she walked up the sidewalk to her car. She shook her head in frustration about the early-morning court proceedings that had gone awry.

The way her firm handled that court fiasco, she knew she would be handing in her two-week notice tomorrow; that is if she could get a friendly resignation letter written that didn't burn the bridge to the law offices of Spencer, Broadbent, and Hathaway.

She certainly didn't want to show up in a courtroom a few weeks from now with them bitter at her for quitting, but she was done working for someone who kept deviating from the agreed plan. And working with Barry Sloan, the attorney she was assigned to, well, anytime something blew up in Barry's face, he blamed someone else.

It will probably be me this time. He's such a presumptuous piece of shit.

She always thought if Barry could quit worrying about when the firm would make him partner, they would've already won the case and be on to the next one.

Asshole.

Celeste's heel hooked into a wider sidewalk crevice, causing her to stumble for a moment. The interruption pulled from her wandering thoughts. She glanced down at her navy high heels as they whisked back and forth on the sidewalk. She was careful not to step on any more sidewalk cracks. God, she didn't need any more bad luck today. And—the distant childhood nursery rhyme briefly flitted through her mind—she certainly didn't want to break her mother's back.

Celeste knew this area well, as she walked it daily. Her surroundings were quite familiar to her. Providence Avenue was one of the primary side streets here in Silver Ridge, a two-lane road, just wide enough for cars to drive up and down, and spaces to park on either side. There were only a few passing cars on this street, but plenty of automobiles lined the road with few spaces left. The sidewalks lining either side of the avenue allowed pedestrians access to any of the shops and restaurants.

Celeste usually glanced at the windows to see if there was anything of interest in the clothing shops, but not today. Her mind was elsewhere, pondering what career change she should make.

Tall, thin trees with clustered branches had been planted near the curbs; they were evenly spaced up and down the sidewalks on either side of the street.

What she hated most about this avenue was that the tall buildings lining either side turned the street into a wind tunnel. A strong gust would blow down now and then, and Celeste would bow her head to shield her face against the warm summer wind.

"Spare a little change, ma'am?"

The male voice came from her right and nearer to the ground.

Yanked from her meandering thoughts, Celeste gave a small, startled hop away. "Jesus! You scared the hell out of me," she said, placing a hand on her chest. She spoke a little more harshly than she'd meant.

The man didn't seem to notice her clipped response. Instead, he smiled. "My apologies, ma'am. Some change?"

Her first thought while glancing down at the man seated on a jutted-out stoop near an alleyway was to say 'no' and continue on her way. Because first of all, she rarely helped the homeless; you never knew what they used the change for. Secondly, they didn't want change; they wanted the green stuff. They could buy more drugs or booze with it. And thirdly, he'd scared the shit out of her. But then she noticed the man had kind, stunning eyes with an intense gaze.

Beautiful eyes were a weakness for Celeste.

Seeing he had her attention, if only briefly, the homeless man gave her another reluctant smile and shook his paper coffee cup. The few coins already in there rattled around in the bottom.

He was a good-looking man, handsome, and a little on the rugged side.

Why is this guy not able to find work? He looks healthy enough. Strong. Striking even.

His dark hair was tousled but not unkempt. His tanned skin didn't seem dirty, and his camouflage jacket looked worn but certainly not filthy from days and nights on the street.

She looked back into his eyes. She liked them; oddly, she was drawn to him, which made her want to help him. Perhaps he'd caught her with her guard down, her mind wandering, and not paying attention to her surroundings.

He could've just gotten back from another tour, she thought. She had no idea if they were even doing tours or if a war was still happening. She didn't keep up with the news in her busy life. He could have PTSD, which hindered him from holding down a job. She felt terrible for even assuming that as a possibility.

Since she had stopped, she chose to give him something. To continue on without giving him anything would've made her look like the biggest bitch ever to walk this avenue, and she didn't want him thinking that of her. She took her wallet from her purse and flipped it open.

He said, "Thank you, ma'am. Anything you can spare will be helpful. Anything at all."

He sounded so appreciative.

From the corner of her eye, Celeste noticed him look away from her and glance up the sidewalk. His knee was bobbing up and down with anticipation. Or was that nervousness? *God knows I would be embarrassed to beg for money if it came down to it.* Turning her attention to her wallet again and wanting to get out of here—*Dammit! No singles*—she reluctantly snagged a five-dollar bill.

He shook his coins again.

I'm hurrying as fast as I can, buddy, she thought harshly in answer to his impatience.

Putting away her wallet, she stepped close to him and stuffed the bill into his paper coffee cup.

"Thank you," he said with an extra helping of vocal gratitude. He was beaming as she stood again.

Such a beautiful smile to go with those eyes. Wow, he takes excellent care of his teeth for a man down on his luck. "You're welcome. Best of luck to you, sir," Celeste said. She moved away from him, but there was a blur of motion as he quickly rose to meet her.

Celeste took a startled step back, but he had already grabbed her arm and squeezed it tight, pulling her into him. She caught a strong whiff of coffee breath as he exhaled. His other arm snaked around her shoulder, constricting her to him in a tight grip. Hip to hip with him, she now felt a sharp pain in her side.

Did he stab me?

The shock of the moment hit her first. It wasn't a deep cut, just a tiny nick with the tip of the blade to let her know he meant business. She was about to protest his advancement, but he was already talking to her. The gentle, somewhat pleading voice from before had changed into a fast, firm, low, commanding tone. "Don't make a fucking scene. Don't make a goddamn sound, and don't try to run. If you do, I'll cut you deep. Do you understand?"

Already locked in frozen panic, all Celeste could do was give him a shaky nod.

"Good. Look down at my hand."

Celeste slowly looked down. He moved his hand away from her side and rotated it enough to show her the knife he held. Her breath hitched as she stared at the four-inch blade. It was the cause of the sharp pain she'd felt in her side moments ago.

He turned their bodies away from the main sidewalk and pointed them toward an alleyway. To anyone nearby, it would look like a lover wrapping his arm around his girlfriend and whispering something lovey-dovey in her ear.

He continued, "If you make any sudden moves, I'll slide this blade into you as deep as I can. You picking up what I'm putting down?"

She nodded quickly. "What do you want?"

"I want you to take a little romantic walk with me into that alleyway." He gestured with his knife, then placed it back on her side. Another prick of pain to show he meant business.

Celeste was terrified of the knife and of what it could do to her, but she instinctively resisted. In a fearful whisper, she said, "No." Realizing the inevitable might happen, she pulled away.

He tightened his grip and pulled her back into him. He pressed the knife harder into her side as he hiss-whispered, "What did I say? Are you hard of hearing? Do not fuck with me on this."

She felt its point cut through her clothes and puncture her skin again. Not far, just enough to hurt. She understood he could quickly shove it in, all the way to its hilt. She immediately relented and stiffened at the possibility that it would all be over if that blade slid into her side.

"Okay-okay-okay-okay," she said in a panicked whisper. "I'll go."

"Smartest decision of your life, bitch."

Celeste glanced frantically along the street. They were alone as far as she could tell—not a soul in sight, at least on this side of the road. *Shit.* She'd have to get out of this herself. But how? What *could* she do?

As they entered the alleyway, Celeste was punched in the nose by an invisible wall of stench. She felt her body instantly slathered in filth simply by walking through the warm, dirty air. All the delis, diners, pizza joints, and bars were connected to this back alleyway maze. Each eatery had garbage cans, and those trash receptacles had been used for too long. They were grime-coated with spillage residue from trash bags that had burst on unlucky workers with the unfortunate job of trash duty. The miasma of the stagnant, rotted food wafted over them as they moved deeper into the alleyway.

These alleys were damp, with condensation dripping from the bottom of numerous window air conditioning units that ran continuously. In addition, a constant *plink-plink* of dirty liquid dropped from leaky piping, running along the outside walls.

"You can have all my money," Celeste said, "Even my purse. It's… it's a Louis Vuitton, and… and my wallet is a Hobo. They were both expensive. You could make some good money for them if you pawned them."

"Shut up," he snapped. He was looking around like a frantic weasel. "Walk faster." He sped up their movement and pressed the blade into her side.

"Please don't kill me."

"I said, shut the fuck up, bitch. Can't you follow simple instructions?"

They turned a corner in the alleyway; he abruptly uncoiled himself from her and pushed her up against one of the moist walls. Celeste's head banged off the brick surface. It hurt like hell, though it wasn't hard enough to daze her. His hand was immediately around her throat in a tight grip, and he moved close to control her movements.

Water dripped on the backside of her head from something above. It ran down through her hair onto her back. It felt like a slimy earthworm sliding down her spine; her body involuntarily shivered in disgust.

"Please, don't kill—"

"Goddammit!" he said in an agitated whisper. With his knife hand, he jerked her purse from her arm and flung it away. Her purse hit the asphalt and its contents skittered across the pavement.

"I said I'm not going to kill you, and I don't want your goddamn handbag." To emphasize his point further, he moved his knife back to her side, threatening to stab her deep. He looked all around the alleyway, paying more attention to his surroundings than her.

"What are you looking for? What do you want?"

He focused on her again, leaning in close and looking directly into her eyes. The eyes she previously thought were kind had now turned cold and filled with malicious intent. He held up his knife so she could see it. Celeste's eyes widened at how huge and dangerous the blade looked. She closed her eyes against the sight of it.

Her body froze even more when she felt his knife touch her cheek. He slapped the flat side of the blade against her cheek, then began to slowly and delicately stroke her face. A lover's caress. A steel-bladed kiss.

He answered her question as he traced a path down her neck, between her breasts, lightly scraping the knife down the length of her torso to the space between her legs. "I want your most-prized possession, bitch. You're going to give me a slice of that sweet pussy, or I'll take it from you."

Celeste's eyes opened in shock and revulsion. It was one of the vilest statements she'd ever heard. A frantic panic set in and began to build. *NO!* she screamed inside.

"You can either have the four inches of my blade," he said with a raised inflection as he pressed it against her again for emphasis. She flinched as the blade's point pricked her skin again. Then, he flipped the knife around to gesture at his crotch with the blade. "Or you can have the ten hard inches God gave me." He gave a half-hearted chortle at his statement.

She brought her knee up into his crotch, but he anticipated her movement and sidestepped her lashing out at him.

"What did I say, bitch?" he spat in a whisper-yell.

Suddenly fear and instinct snapped her body into motion, and she was moving. She brought her arm up fast and hard. It broke his remaining grip on her neck; his arm flew away. Hyped up on adrenaline, she flung her arm blindly and hit his wrist firmly, driving his arm away from hers. She caught a glance of the blade leaving his hand. She grabbed his jacket and pulled him forward, bringing her knee into his crotch again. This time she made hard contact with the center of his being. She heard a whoosh of air leave his mouth, and another breeze of strong coffee breath blew past her nose as he doubled over.

She turned to run, to get out of there, but felt a hard tug on her jacket, and her body snapped back to him.

What the fu–

Celeste whipped around toward him and just had time to register the incoming fist that slammed flush across the left side of her face. Her cheek exploded, and she dropped to the filthy concrete.

"Oh, fuck! You cunt-bitch!" he said, seething between clenched teeth. He cradled his crotch in his hands. Then he was on her, clambering over her body as he grunted through his pain. His hands were everywhere at once.

Even though she was dazed and confused from the punch, she heard fabric ripping and felt fetid air on her exposed abdomen. His hands were on her breasts, searching, feeling, touching, grasping, and examining. Her bra was jerked apart by violent tugs; her breasts were exposed to his greedy mouth. She felt the coarseness of his half-beard scratching at her tits like sandpaper as his tongue, a fat slug, skimmed over her nipples, leaving a slick residue in its wake.

Celeste's head was still spinning and aching from the punch that almost put her lights out. She returned to her senses when the realization stunned her that she was being raped. This sudden awareness of the possibility of being killed before or after this assault caused her breathing to intensify. The inhalation of air brought the reek of the alleyway storming into her nose and mouth, making this experience exponentially worse.

Fear poured into her body, and tears began to flow out of her. They clouded her eyes, making the figure towering over her blur into an alien-like creature. Celeste swiped at her eyes to clear her vision, but more tears took their place.

His arms were two long appendages forcing her down, controlling her. She slapped and punched at them, but he batted her hands away, giving her a hard punch or a violent slap to subdue her. His fingers were like ten fast-crawling insectoid organisms that scuttled over her body. She grasped at them, desperate to fling them away, but those fingers turned into claws that latched on to her arms, subduing her. His sweaty hands began to crawl south over her skin. She felt her skirt ripped apart; accompanied by a tearing sound. The cloth gave with one tug, and after two more hard yanks, she felt her legs become further exposed. With a third and final violent jerk, her skirt came apart and flapped open.

"Jackpot!" he said as he looked down at her panties. "Ooh, matching bra and panties. Did you get all dressed up for me? You could've just not worn any, and it would've saved me the trouble of having to rip these from you. But *you* know how much I like to hear the sound of fabric ripping, *don't you*?"

His hands were already inside her panties and pulling up on them.

She writhed beneath him on the filthy asphalt, bucking at him to push him off her, urgent to get away from this violation into her aura. She kicked out at him and connected with something, but it wasn't enough to deter him.

One of his hands spread wide across her lower abdomen, pushed down hard as his other jerked up on the thin, lacy fabric. The fabric was nothing and tore away easier than her bra.

Celeste was wholly exposed to him. His fingers were already stroking her womanhood violently, desperate to feel, touch, invade. His other hand forced her legs apart.

Celeste's mind locked down to the fact this was happening to her. She tried to block it out as she continued swimming up from the spiraling darkness of that well-placed punch. She wiggled as she pulled herself away from him.

"Where are *you* going?" he teased. "The party's just starting. I can't let you go without any of my party favors. You'll like my really *big one*."

She was desperate to escape; she turned over and used her forearms to army-crawl away from him, but this did nothing but reveal her bare ass to him.

"Oh yeah, baby. Look at those fuckable goods," he said. He grabbed her ankles and held her from traveling any further. "I didn't know you liked it in the ass, but if you want me to put it there, I can oblige."

Celeste looked back over her shoulder and saw him rise to his knees. He unbuckled and unzipped his pants, then pushed them down low on his thighs. Celeste saw a disgusting, engorged member and shuddered at the sight of it. She knew immediately that nasty *thing* was not going inside her.

I'll grab it; goddamn it! I'll grab it and twist it completely off. The knife! Where the fuck is that knife? She glanced in the direction the knife had slid after it had left his hand. She didn't see it, but she searched. *I'll rip that thing from his body before he puts it into me.*

Her thoughts spun through her panicked mind when he grabbed her ankles again and jerked her back close to him. Pain engulfed her mind and body. Her eyes enlarged as she felt the skin of her knees curl away against the rough, uneven, damp, and grime-coated pavement they were dragged across. Her mouth formed a silent 'O', the pain so immense she couldn't utter a sound. His hands slapped hard against her hips and latched onto her thighs with a violent, vice-like grip. He jerked her back against him even harder. She looked down and saw two red lines, as though a paintbrush had slathered red strokes, away from where she'd initially knelt to where he'd just pulled her.

The pain in her knees was excruciating, crippling, but the subsequent pain she knew she would feel would be his member sliding between her—

"Hey asshole!" a voice yelled. "What the fuck do you think you're doing to her?"

"Get lost, fuckface," the rapist said. "This is my piece of ass, and I'm about to fuck the shit out of it."

"Get your goddamn hands off her, shithead!"

There was a hard slap from behind her, then the rapist gave a surprised, "What the fuck?"

The attacker's weight was lifted from her body. Celeste's mind still threatened to black out, but she glanced around through her haziness.

The stranger grabbed the man's camouflage jacket and jerked him backward and away from her. The rapist stumbled back; he fought to pull his pants up, but the stranger wasn't giving him time to do so. The new guy had already stepped in and punched the rapist, dropping him to the pavement while he continued futzing with his clothes. This gave the rapist enough time to pull his pants the rest of the way up. He rotated backward from the newcomer, stood quickly, and squared off with him.

The rapist sprung forward, but the new guy blocked the attack and fired back with a few solid punches, each finding its mark. This new guy rocked his world. The rapist attacked him again and got one sucker punch in, but the stranger threw a flurry of close-quarter punches and then gave him a quick side kick that dropped him to his knees.

Now pissed, the rapist charged the stranger again. Celeste's savior sidestepped away, but grabbed the attacker's jacket, rotated him, slammed him up against another wall, and peppered him with punches to the face and torso.

The rapist came off the wall, lunging full throttle at the new guy. The full-on frontal assault pushed the stranger back, then the rapist was gone, fleeing for his life. He shot down another connecting alleyway and around the corner with the new guy in close pursuit.

As Celeste's assailant turned the corner, her savior yelled after him, "If I ever catch you, you asshole, you're fucking dead!"

Celeste rolled over, sat up, and pulled her discarded skirt back over her middle. She wrapped what remained of her blouse and jacket over her breasts and buttoned the few remaining buttons with shaking hands.

Then, a voice spiraled back to her as a figure knelt by her side. "Hey, are you all right?" A hand touched her back.

Celeste, not fully there mentally and thinking it was her rapist again, cried out in alarm. She lashed out, slapping his arm away. "Get the hell away from me. Don't fucking touch me."

"Hey, no… no, wait," the newcomer said in as soothing a voice as he could. "It's just me. It's okay." He was a little out of breath from the fight.

Celeste still was not trusting and leaned away. She held her hands out in front of her in self-defense. She tried to slide away from the figure, to put as much distance as possible between them and her attacker.

"Um, I'm the guy who helped you. I ran that other guy off. I tried to stop him, but he was too fast for me. Here, take this."

She glanced up again and saw a careful and slow movement. The guy was taking off an article of clothing.

He held the jacket up to her as a peace offering. "I'm going to put my jacket around you, and then I'll back up and give you some space, okay?"

Celeste considered it for a moment. Her trust was depleted, but she had seen him fight and chase her attacker off. Finally, she nodded acceptance of his jacket.

It gently encircled her shoulders, then the man stepped away as promised.

Celeste was ready to get the hell out of there; she made a motion to stand but couldn't manage on shaky legs and abraded knees.

The man moved quickly to her side, and his hands were on her arm.

Startled at his sudden movement, Celeste yelped and lashed out at him again. "Get the fuck away from me." She moved to run, but her legs dropped her back to the asphalt again—more pain in her knees. Tears welled up within her again, and she fell to the pavement.

The man stopped and held his hands up. "I'm sorry. I'm sorry. I just wanted to help you stand. I didn't mean to scare you. I want to help. That's all."

Celeste wept for a few moments.

The man's gentle voice came back to her. "Will you allow me to help you up? I mean you no harm."

Celeste nodded and began to stand.

The man stepped forward hesitantly. "Please don't be alarmed."

She felt his hands gently take her arm, one above the wrist, the other above the elbow. She allowed him to help her stand, but she was rigid and still on guard. She didn't like him touching her. She didn't want him to be close, but she needed help.

He whispered comforting phrases like, "Shhh-shhh-shhh, everything is going to be all right now," "nothing is going to harm you," and "that guy is gone now." His words did help to soothe her fragile nerves.

Eventually, he moved to the side and walked with her back up the alleyway she had been forced down at knifepoint. As they walked, he told her he was going to grab her purse. She nodded and leaned on the grimy wall for support. Celeste didn't like that it was dirty, but that was the least of her problems.

He moved away slowly. He picked up her purse and the spilled contents; then, he was at her side again. "Here's your purse," he said.

Celeste made a move for it.

"That's okay, let me carry it for you. Just letting you know I had it. I picked up everything that was on the ground. I hope I grabbed everything."

Celeste mumbled, "I don't care. I want out of this place."

"Sure. Of course. That's understandable. This place is disgusting."

In an exhausted voice, she said, "Thank you for helping me. I don't know what would've happened… had you not come along."

"Don't think about that," he said. "I'm just glad I could help." He left the statement hanging out there in the stench of the alleyway and then changed the subject. "We need to get you to the police so you can file a report."

"No," she said hastily. "No police."

"What? Why not? You were assaulted."

"Yes, I was, but I wasn't… raped." She could barely say the vile word and couldn't look him in the eyes. "It was close, yes, but, well, you stopped that. The cops will have nothing to go on." Her voice was shaky as emotion tainted her words and threatened to destroy the dam holding back the tears she desperately wanted to release. "I want to get home, take a long hot shower, sleep for a very long time, and forget this shit ever happened."

"You don't want to get the guy who almost raped you?"

She looked up harshly at her Samaritan and said, "I want to permanently remove the guy's dick from his body. God knows he doesn't deserve to have it."

She was exhausted; she looked away and continued walking. "He's long gone by now. They'd never find him, and we'd just have to spend hours going through paperwork. Right now, I want to go home. So please, let me do that."

"Of course, whatever you want. Would you mind if I walked with you, you know, to keep you company, to make sure you get there, okay?

"I don't care. My car is about a block up the street."

"Then I'll make sure you get to your car. Is that all right with you?"

"Sure," she said; then, "Thank you."

They turned and walked together in the direction of Celeste's car. They walked in silence, not knowing what to say. Eventually, her guardian said, "I don't know what to do in a situation like this. Please let me know what I can do to help."

"Okay," she agreed. "I don't really know myself. This has never happened to me."

"Hey, so my name's Dillon. Dillon Carmichael." He held his open hand out to her.

She saw his hand but didn't take it, but she said, "Hey, Dillon. It's nice to meet you." She finally managed to take his hand with the one that wasn't holding her skirt together and gave it an awkward shake.

"Not the best circumstances," he said in a lame attempt at slight humor to bring down the seriousness of the situation.

Celeste didn't laugh. She stared dead ahead, focused on getting to her car. Sensing he wanted a response, she said, "The worst."

"And you are?" he asked, trying to coax her name from her.

"Celeste."

"That's nice. Does this Celeste you speak of have a *last* name?"

"Baker." Her answer was curt, robotic. Not offering any more information than she had to.

She looked ahead, not wanting to look at him or anybody else on the sidewalk. She could feel blood running down her legs from her cheese-grated, scraped knees. She diverted her face away from anyone who passed, not wanting to see the condescending looks she was sure she was getting.

One random person on the sidewalk asked, "Hey, is she all right?"

The man said, "She will be. She just had an accident. Don't worry about it. I'm helping her."

"Are you sure?"

Her guardian didn't answer but helped move them further up the sidewalk to Celeste's car.

She knew she looked disheveled with her torn clothes, bleeding knees, and damp, mussed hair. She was certain she was a frightful sight and wanted to be anywhere but here.

"Would you like me to follow you in my car to your house?" he asked.

"No!" she said quickly and a little harshly. *God, no!* she thought. She dropped the harshness. "That's all right. I can manage from here."

"Okay. Sure. I just thought I would offer. Can I do anything at all for you?"

"No. Coming along when you did, pulling him off me, fighting him—it was more than I could ask or even hope for."

"Good. I'm glad I was there to help you. This could've been very tragic."

"This is me," she said, pitching her purse onto the trunk of her tan Subaru Crosstrek. With her free hand, she pilfered through the bag's contents to ensure everything was accounted for. Surprised to find all the items, she grabbed her keys, tucked her purse under her arm, and unlocked her car. She opened the passenger side door, dropped her bag onto its seat, then slammed it again. She walked around to the driver's door, opened it, and was about to get in when she heard her name.

"Celeste," Dillon called.

She stopped and looked back at him over the roof of the car. He was looking at her expectantly.

"What?" she asked, agitation creeping into her voice again. She didn't have time for idle chit-chat.

"Um, I don't know. Is that it?"

"Is *what* it?"

"I was just wondering if there was a way I could get in touch with you. You know, to check on you to see if you're okay."

She snapped in frustration. "What do you want from me, huh?"

Dumbfounded, he just stood there with a stunned expression on his face. He didn't know what to say.

Celeste continued, "Look, I'm going to be fine. I don't know what else you want from me. I've already thanked you for saving my life. Thank you. There, I did it again. Was that heartfelt enough for you this time? What else am I forgetting? Do you want my number to call me to check up on me? I don't feel comfortable giving it out because of what just happened. You'll just have to understand that. Do you want my address? Why? Do you want to become pen-pals or something? I'm not ready to write letters to you or anyone else." She was on the verge of tears again. "I just want to get home, get a goddamn shower, and go the fuck to bed. Is that too much to ask?"

"Well, excuse me for caring," he said. "Yes, maybe I would like your phone number to call you because I want to check on you and see how you're doing. I know this was a pretty traumatic event for you, and I don't think you should go through it alone. I don't know how many friends you have or if you would even talk to them about what happened to you. I think you should. Maybe, later on, I would be willing to listen if you wanted to talk to someone. That way, no one else would have to know about this, and you could keep your dignity."

Celeste gave him a drop-dead and go-the-fuck-to-hell look.

He held his hands up to stop her from thinking the wrong thing about his choice of words. He continued quickly, "Not that I think you have lost any *dignity* from what happened, but I think you need to talk it out because I think this will eat you up. Maybe some group therapy counseling might help you. I don't know."

Listening to him gave her a moment to calm herself, and in a firm tone, she said, "Thank you for your concern, Dillon, but I can manage just fine from here." She moved to step into her car.

"Well, if I'm never going to see or hear from you again," he said, quickly grabbing her attention. "You mind if I get my jacket back? It was kind of expensive."

The realization made her snap her head to the side and look down the length of her body. She was still wearing his blazer around her shoulders. She closed her eyes as frustration crept over her. She shook her head against the thought of not giving it back to him. Celeste quickly shrugged it off her shoulders and reluctantly held it out to him.

Dillon approached her from around the front of the car, moving to the open door between them. Celeste flinched back slightly at his advancement. He noticed and held his arms up gently to show he wouldn't harm her. He took it gently and folded it over his forearm, then said, "Um, wait, just a second."

She breathed an agitated breath that he noticed.

"I'm sorry. I know you want to get out of here, but I would never forgive myself if I didn't do this. I feel led to." He pulled his pen and a folded piece of paper from his shirt pocket. He leaned over and scribbled something on its surface. As he stood again, he ripped a section of the folded paper off and handed it to her; then, he stuck the pen back into his shirt pocket. "I know you think you can get through this on your own. But if for some reason you feel like you can't, call me. You may not want to give me your number, but I have no problem giving you mine. Call me if you need someone to listen."

Celeste took the ripped section of the paper and glanced down at it. He had written his first and last name—Dillon Carmichael—along with a ten-digit phone number.

Dillon continued, "If you don't want to talk to me about this, I hope you talk to someone. Take care, Celeste. I wish you the best of everything this world has to offer." He turned, walked back to the front of her car, cut in front of it, and moved back to the sidewalk again. He turned away from her and continued up the sidewalk.

Celeste stood there momentarily, staring at the back of his head. It had been such a weird exchange. It was nice of him to care but odd in the vast, dark shadow of what had just happened. The event was creeping back into her mind; she pushed it away again.

She wanted to be away from the alleyway stench and Dillon. She slid into the driver's seat, stuck her keys in the ignition, and cranked her car. She quickly checked the traffic, pulled into the road, and drove up the street. As she passed him, she gave a short wave and saw him give a wave back to her. And that was it. It was over. The whole shitty turn of events was now over.

Celeste began crying as she turned on the neighboring street and toward home.

Sean Asherton—the man who had just lied to Celeste Baker that his name was Dillon Carmichael—didn't glance back, but he knew Celeste was observing him. He could feel her eyes boring into him. He finally heard her car door shut. After a few seconds, he listened to it start; then she pulled out of the space it occupied. As her car passed, he glanced her way. She gave him a non-committal wave, to which he replied with an upraised hand. He assumed she saw it or hoped she did, anyway.

When Celeste had turned off this avenue onto another street and was gone, Sean stopped near a storefront window and slid his sports jacket back on. While he stood there adjusting his long sleeves, another man in a camouflage jacket left the shadows of another nearby alleyway, walked up, and stopped next to Sean. They stared at their reflections together.

Thomas Bonnomer—the man in the camouflage jacket—jokingly said with a little bit of attitude, "You were late today, Sean. I was about to dive in and go balls deep. Talk about life's little disappointments."

Sean turned slightly and gave Thomas a sly smile. "Sorry I had to interrupt all your fun."

Thomas gave a devilish smile and a guttural chuckle at his statement. "It's okay, man. The game might not work as well if I had raped her."

"True," Sean said, then glanced back over and looked closely at his face. "Sorry about your eye. I got a little carried away in the fight earlier. You okay?"

Thomas sloughed it off as though it were nothing more than the inconvenience of a mosquito bite. "Ah, yeah. I'm fine. It sold the moment of you saving her sweet ass a little better."

"Didn't mean to make contact. That must have hurt."

Thomas sneered back over to Sean. "No sweat, buddy. I'll get you back on the next one."

They stood there for a moment thinking back over their alleyway scuffle.

"You better watch your ass with this one," Thomas said. "She's all about destroying a man's junk. That knee to my nuts fucking hurt. My balls are still aching."

"Yeah, she mentioned removing your goods when I was helping her."

"Be careful with her. That's all I'm saying. You going to play her?" Thomas asked expectantly.

"I'm certainly going to try, but it all depends on her and if she calls me. She has my number."

Thomas laughed, "You mean she didn't give you her number to discuss this tragedy?"

"Not this time. But what difference does it make? I didn't see Angel Domingo throwing *her* number at *you* when it was your turn to rescue her from me."

"Touché," Thomas said.

Sean looked again in the direction of where Celeste had turned off. "She'll call me. It's just a matter of time."

"Well then, I guess the game is on," Thomas mused.

"Oh yeah, it's definitely on," Sean confirmed.

CHAPTER TWO

THE FOLLOWING MORNING, Celeste Baker awoke thirty minutes before her alarm went off. It was still dark outside, and the mundane droning of a few insects near her bedroom window continued to serenade her.

When she woke, she wasn't groggy to where she felt sleepy and wished to return to dreamland; she just opened her eyes and stared at the ceiling. She thought it strange that sleep had immediately left her body, and she was instantly alert. She suddenly had the ominous feeling something terrible would happen to her, then that thought led to the memory of what happened in the courtroom yesterday. She groaned as she relived the highlights of that ordeal.

Oh God, what a shit show.

She knew it wasn't going to be a great day at work. There was no way around it; she and her boss would have that dreaded discussion about Barry Sloan. It wasn't something she would enjoy.

Then, the even worse memory of her attack and almost rape by some money-pilfering, homeless man steamrolled through her mind, body, and spirit, flattening everything inside her all at once.

It was all a ruse to get me back there. Why didn't I embrace my bitchiness and pass him by?

The recollection came down in full force, and all she could do was roll to her side, pull her legs up close to her chest, and relive the horrifying event. When she bent her knees, the excruciating pain of them being dragged across the rough, uneven pavement lit up her body again. She stretched them back out. The bandages she'd added to her knees before going to bed felt like they were stuck to her wounds. She was going to have to clean and rebandage them.

No high skirts in my future for a while.

Celeste settled in to snooze some more. She now begged sleep to come again so that she could put off thinking about the horror from yesterday a bit longer. Unfortunately, rest didn't come, and she cried silently until her alarm went off. She slowly sat up, kicked her legs gently over the side of the bed, careful of her bandaged knees, and silenced her alarm.

She sat on the edge of the bed and breathed deeply as she massaged her fear-tightened chest and mentally tried to calm herself. Long, slow four-count breaths in and out. She was groggy now, so different from when she awoke clear-minded thirty minutes earlier. Her mentality had plummeted in that half an hour, and she imploded.

The easiest thing for her to do was not to go to work today. She quickly justified that trying to heal herself from the traumatic event was more important than going to work to discuss the courtroom hell she experienced yesterday. That had already been settled in her mind when she'd turned over and tried to force herself back to sleep. She knew staying out of work wouldn't go over well with everyone at the office, but she didn't care. They would think she was avoiding work issues. If they only *knew.*

The best thing she could do now was to take another long hot shower, doctor her wounds, call into work, and tell them her plans.

In the bathroom, Celeste stripped out of her shorts and the baggy t-shirt. Leaning down into the shower, she caught a glimpse of herself in the full-length mirror that hung on the back of the bathroom door. She stood again and approached her naked reflection. She leaned closer and looked at her face.

She tested the tender purple and yellow coloring on her cheekbone from where that asshole had clocked the shit out of her. She winced.

Damn, he got me good.

The homeless man with his beautiful eyes swam out of her memory. She closed her eyes and forced him to disappear from her thoughts.

I'm not going to think about him or that situation.

She opened her eyes again and turned to the side with the minor stab wounds where the knifepoint had given her a few cuts. They weren't too bad, but it had hurt when it happened. The blood had clotted pretty quickly. It was her knees that were utterly fubar-ed. The first layer of skin was gone, but there were deeper grooves where sharp edges from the uneven concrete had peeled off more of her skin. She was surprised her knees hadn't been scraped to the bone.

Thank God I still have some left to work with, she thought. "Goddamn asshole," she said.

Even though new blemishes were on her body, the more hideous wounds that were now etched into her psyche would take much longer to heal, if ever.

Celeste returned to the shower, rotated the knobs even more to the hottest setting, and stepped in.

Ahhhh, yes. That feels so good.

The hot water ran down her legs and crossed over her knees. She grimaced at the sharp pain of the heated liquid running over the tender areas. She braced herself against the shower walls as she steeled herself against the hurt and let it happen. She knew it would only help.

She stood there for a long while, letting the hot water relax her body. She tried to force the event from her mind, but the nearly scalding water cascading over her knees kept the sexual assault in the forefront of her mind. There was no forgetting it.

She showered slowly, lathering several times to wash the imagined grime from the alleyway and the event from her body.

After her shower had washed away her grogginess, Celeste dressed in some comfy clothes—as she liked to call them—SpongeBob SquareP-ants socks, baggy lounge pants, and a loose Star Wars T-shirt featuring Chewbacca that stated in big letters: I Speak Fluent Wookie. But the most crucial thing (drum roll, please) no bra. That was taking 'comfy' to its highest level.

Since she had a few pairs of lounge pants, she took scissors to the ones she was wearing and cut the legs off right above the knees. She didn't want the fabric to rub across her knees and irritate the wounds. She needed to let her injuries air before adding more Neosporin and new bandages.

Celeste grabbed her purse and rummaged through it to find her cell phone. She located it and pulled it out, but as she did, her eyes fell upon a scrap piece of paper with a name and phone number written on it. She pulled it out and laid it on the counter.

She reread the name, "Dillon Carmichael." She saw the ten-digit number below his penned name. "Fuck. I was a real asshole to him. All he wanted to do was help me."

She stopped talking to herself, but her mind continued to beat herself up as she stared at the paper. *He did help me. He saved me from getting raped in the worst possible way and in one of the worst possible places. That fucking alleyway. Disgusting. He probably saved my life. Who knows what might have happened if he hadn't come along and stopped—She stopped the visual there. She wouldn't let her mind make things worse than they already were. I owe him big time.*

She picked up the number and cell phone simultaneously and dialed the numbers. She was about to hit send but then stopped herself. She backed the digits off the screen, then placed the paper and phone on the counter again.

No, I don't want to talk to him or anyone else. I want to deal with this situation myself, as I told him I would. I'm a big girl. I'll handle this shit.

"I'm not handling it so well right *now*, but I will. I'll handle it in time and in my way."

Celeste called her work number instead. She waited for the receptionist to pick up; the receptionist did not. Celeste left a brief message stating that something happened yesterday and that she was taking a personal day and then hung up.

"If they want to think that *something* was what happened in the courtroom, let them think it." *It may even help me out when I get back to the office and explain my side of the story. But I'm not going to tell them that I was almost raped. How would they look at me at work if I did that? Dear God, may this info never get out.*

The memory of her almost-rape weighed heavily on her mind throughout the morning, and thinking about it exhausted her. She found herself landing on her couch each time to dwell on it. There were times when the moment seemed to close around her, and all she felt like doing was curling up into a tight ball and watching anything play out on the television. Mindless stimuli.

She finally flipped the remote to one of those channels that play music. She chose one with the heaviest music she could stand—not the deep register, demon possession, sounding like someone gargling razor blades and summoning Satan, anger management music—just one that had a little bit of screaming. She made it loud enough to hear throughout the house. As her mind played out the sexual assault on a continual loop inside her mind, the bands assaulted her body with a pounding from the drums, guitars, and voice. And other than ordering some food through a food delivery service, she remained on the couch for the majority of the day, reliving the horrific event and crying through the hurt and the pain of yesterday's incident. Eventually, she drifted off into a deep sleep.

❧

Celeste jerked awake as a fist grew huge in her eyesight and connected with the side of her face.

She was facing the couch cushions. She realized she never went to bed, then she grasped why. The memory was right there with her, as vivid as when it happened. She breathed a sigh of relief that it was only a bad dream, trauma from two days ago. The assault was now coming to her in fragmented waves.

The sound of her business suit ripping.

The horrendous smell of the alleyway.

The vile statements her attacker had used.

The greediness of his hands skittering over her body.

The pain of his fist pounding her into an almost blackout.

The feeling of embarrassment of being stripped naked.

The rich pain of her knees sliding across the uneven pavement.

She involuntarily shivered as the phantom pain lit up her body from the memories. She closed her eyes against them.

The fragments melded together, and the event played over and over in her mind. She couldn't shake it, and that pissed her off.

She lay on the couch and prayed for sleep so she could forget everything. That prayer wasn't answered.

Celeste knew she couldn't lay around and lose another day to this shitty life event, but she couldn't motivate herself to get started. She didn't know how to begin. It was like the trauma was weighing her entire body down.

The situation with work broke through the vivid memory, which pissed her off even more.

Barry Sloan, another asshole to deal with, she thought. *Nope. Maybe another day.*

She rolled over and found the television was on, but the sound had been muted. She must've muted it sometime during the night to get some sleep. She flipped the television off.

Celeste found her phone and checked to see if she had any messages. Maybe one from work or one from family. But no, there were none, which made her feel all alone. Even though she knew no one—other than Dillon and the asshole who had assaulted her—knew about what happened, it still didn't change the fact that she felt abandoned.

She called into work again before anyone got to the office, and left a message that some things had come up and she was taking a couple of days for herself. She gave no other details and hung up. Once that was done, relief flooded her body that she had faced such a simple task. Just going through the motions of leaving a message and facing the guilt for bailing on work because of this seemed like a monumental feat to her. But it was done, and she didn't have to worry about work for a few days. She would see where she was mentally and go from there.

I have to give myself some time.

Celeste moved to the bathroom because she wanted another hot shower. She still felt the grime of the alleyway on her skin. The stench had permeated her nose, or it could be a sense memory from the nightmare. Either way, the power of the showerhead and the hot water, the lathering of her body wash, did wonders for her. Taking deep inhalations of the soap to get the stench out of her nostrils helped calm her spirit and put her in a better mental state, even if it was on a small scale.

After the shower, she checked her mini stab wounds and her knees.

The stab wounds were getting there, healing slowly but surely. Her knees were raw, ravaged, and still insanely fucked up. She doctored them again with ointment but didn't put a bandage over them. It seemed like that hampered their healing.

She made shorts from another pair of comfy pants and pulled on a Wonder Woman T-shirt. "What would Wonder Woman do?" she asked herself. "Well, first of all, Wonder Woman wouldn't freeze like I did. She would've fucked that guy over. She would've strung him up in the alleyway, called the cops, and left him with a note pinned on his camouflage jacket that read: I AM A RAPIST! I NEED TO BE LOCKED UP SO THE WOMEN OF THIS CITY ARE PROTECTED FROM ME!"

She liked that. It was a ray of positivity that shone through the darkness of the incident. That thought made her smile.

She didn't feel like food but forced herself to eat a toasted bagel with strawberry cream cheese and drink some orange juice. It did make her feel better.

Celeste moved back to the couch, turned on the television, and began channel surfing. It felt good to be free from going to work or having any commitments. She didn't have to deal with anything or anyone but this plague of mental funk from that atrocious event.

All I need is a little bit of time.

There was nothing on; there were so many infomercials or commercials about high blood pressure medicine or something that would help with your diabetes. She opted for the show *Law and Order: Special Victims Unit* and braced herself for what was to come. She had seen this show a few times, and anytime she had ever watched it, it was about a woman—or women—being raped. Celeste's thought process was that since her near rape kept running through her mind, hopefully overstimulating it might cause it not to play out as much. She had no idea, but maybe it would help.

She watched a few episodes, and each was one rape after the other. A bunch of fraternity boys raped a girl. A serial rapist preyed on undocumented immigrant women. An ADA who had worked in sex crimes was raped and murdered. Two underaged models were raped and killed. The detective's raced to find a rapist targeting Asian women… the rapist's defense was that he inherited the "violence gene" from his father, who was also a rapist.

It was all too much for Celeste, and she finally flipped the channel to try and find something less stressful.

She landed on a channel playing the 1983 Clint Eastwood/Dirty Harry movie, *Sudden Impact.*

"Another rape movie? Jesus Christ, is that all there is? Just shows about rape. Rape this. Rape that. Rape. Rape. Rape." She hated what she had just said. That four-letter word was worse than "fuck"—the word considered to be the worst four-letter word.

She realized it was sort of like the thing with cars. You don't notice how many cars of a particular model there are until you decide to purchase one; then you see it everywhere. Same thing with rape. Now that she was a victim, she saw it everywhere. If she turned on the news, no doubt there would be some story about rape and its victims.

She knew the storyline of *Sudden Impact.* A rape victim goes about enacting revenge on the men who raped her. Since it was an older movie, she decided to watch it but fell asleep shortly after it started. She was awakened by gunfire, sat up on the couch again, and watched Clint do his thing.

As she watched, her mind was doing two things at once. She was paying attention to the movie, but she was also reliving her traumatic assault. Hate consumed her. A loathing for the guy who had molested her, groped her, felt her up, stuck his tongue in her mouth, and slid his fingers over her vagina and breasts. His examination of her. All those moments consumed her with hate and rage. It was an unbridled fury, seething beneath her skin, threatening to explode.

The hate took her mind to some dark places, accompanied by even darker thoughts.

Could I do that? If I could find this guy and get my hands on him, could I take revenge for what he did to me?

No answer came to her.

What if I went through with it and did get my revenge and kill my rapist? Would that make me feel better or worse than I am now that I had taken his life? Is it better to deal with the pain of my sexual assault? Or would it be an even worse feeling dealing with the guilt of killing a rapist?

Answers to these questions weren't forthcoming. She didn't force the issue; she just let her mind ask its questions.

What would his punishment be? No doubt he's done this before. Maybe. Probably. Thank God for Dillon and that he came along when he did.

She turned and looked over the back of the sofa. From where she was, she could make out the piece of paper on the counter. She didn't go to it and call the number, but just looking at it and knowing it was there seemed to calm her. She turned back around and stared at the figures on the television again.

What if my attacker had raped a woman before me? But let's say that woman hunted him down and ended him. What if my rape—can I call it that? Did he rape me? It was certainly close and definitely felt like rape. Either way, if my sexual assault had never happened, would that have helped me?

Fuck yes! Of course, it would've helped me!

That thought caused her to stand and pace in front of the television.

If someone had taken him out, I wouldn't be in this situation. But I would have no way of knowing I was saved from an attack, rape, or whatever the fuck it is. I wouldn't be frozen here in my house, afraid to do anything. I wouldn't be mentally reliving everything that happened two days ago. I'm just going over it in my mind. I can't think of anything else but fucking this guy up. Oh, how I wish someone could've taken this guy out before he got to me.

So why would you not do this for another woman who could be hurt in the future?

That thought stopped Celeste in her tracks.

This guy is still out there; he will do it again. Why would you not take him out of the equation for other women to feel safe? Sure, they will never know. You won't even know whom you are saving; it would be impossible to know. But if you know beyond a shadow of a doubt that a rapist wouldn't be harming one, five, ten, or twenty women, why wouldn't you step up to the plate and remove him from existence?

Celeste threw her head back and shook it, as though recoiling from a punch to the face. These were some heavy thoughts to consider.

&

On the morning of the third day, Celeste wanted to hit something. She was livid, even angrier than before. *How dare someone take something from me? Sexual gratification at my expense.* The questions she had pondered yesterday had settled into her psyche; they were a part of her now. Not totally committed to ending the life of a rapist, but consideration of it was constantly there. She didn't care about his well-being. He'd fucked her up mentally, and she wanted to fuck him up too. She needed to expel some of this hatred into something.

Her mind went to her gym. They had a punching bag there. That was all she needed. She wanted to pummel the shit out of it until it busted open, and whatever was on the inside was poured out, or she punched it off its hanger, if possible.

She wore baggy sweatpants to cover her knees to avoid getting weird looks at the gym. A sports bra and a T-shirt that read, "I can't wait till tomorrow because I get better looking every day" completed her gym attire.

Celeste looked in every direction from the moment she left her house till she got to the car. She immediately locked all her car doors.

At the gym, she parked as close as possible to the front entrance. She got out, locked the doors behind her, and checked her surroundings inconspicuously as she made her way inside.

She had a focused determination. She started slow but quickly worked her way up to beat the shit out of the face of the man who had assaulted her in the alleyway. Punch after punch was satisfying as she added force behind each of them. She hit him square in the nose. She was out for blood and wanted to see blood cascading from the image she projected upon the punching bag.

And while she pummeled away, a thousand fragmented thoughts sifted through her mind.

You had no right. That was my body. You took the center of my being. You took everything from me. You stole my trust. I feel like I am less of a woman because of your greed. You've violated my soul. I feel like I will never get rid of this feeling of grime that is on me. I'll never be the same again. I want you removed from this world. I want to take everything from you that you took from me. I want to steal your trust. I want you to feel what I did in that alleyway.

She was exhausted, and her arms were fatigued. Sweat dripped from her body, and her hair was matted and sticky. She drew back and threw a final punch; the thought came with it: *I want you dead.*

Her arms were thrumming. She felt as though they were made of putty and could do no more. She gathered her things and left the gym.

She stopped by a restaurant, ordered something, and returned to her house.

After grabbing a cold bottle of water from the refrigerator, she saw the piece of paper with Dillon Carmichael's name and number. She pulled it in her direction and spun around so it was right side up and facing her.

As she devoured her take-out, she focused on the scribbled name and numbers on the paper. And decided to call him after she finished eating. Maybe he could offer her some support as he'd suggested.

By the time she finished eating, she had talked herself out of calling Dillon.

I made significant progress in the gym today. It's going to take small steps, but I'm getting there. I can do this by myself. I don't need anyone other than myself to make it through. I'm the only one who can find me in all this.

After lunch, she took another shower, scrubbing hard to remove the imaginary alleyway filth from her skin.

The shower helped her relax. Because of all the exertion, Celeste felt extremely tired, dropping her to the couch, where she slept most of the day.

Waking up later in the day, she moved from the couch to her bathroom, where she got ready for bed, then curled up in a tight ball and slept long and hard.

CHAPTER THREE

On the morning of the fourth day, Celeste awoke with an abundance of energy. It was enough to motivate her and get her off the couch easily.

The day started as all the others had this week with a shower and getting dressed. Eating some breakfast soon followed.

Walking down the hall from her bedroom and observing the living room as she made her way to the kitchen, she noticed just how far she had let her house go. She'd been bumbling around for a few days since the incident. She had to do something about that.

Celeste busied her mind and body as best she could with mundane tasks around her house, like general cleaning, vacuuming, dusting, and washing a few dirty dishes that were starting to build up in the sink. She would start doing one chore, and then the memory would sneak up on her again, forcing her to take a break on the couch to sit or lie down for a bit. Those moments caused her to waste most of the morning. Eventually, she would motivate herself once again and continue cleaning until her house was perfectly, completely, compulsively spotless.

Numerous fragrances left her place smelling clean and fresh. Orange furniture polish from her dusting, the pine scent of Pine-Sol from mopping the hardwoods, and the lilac fragrance of a powder Celeste shook out on the rugs and carpet before she vacuumed. The smell was redolent of her childhood home; she felt good about what she had accomplished under the circumstances.

At least the whole morning wasn't wasted on my pity party, Celeste thought, then she smiled and sang softly, "It's my pity party, and I'll cry if I want to. Cry if I want to. Cry if I want to. You would cry, too, if it happened to you." She smiled first, then laughed at how accurate the change of the song lyrics was.

During the morning, as she forced herself to complete her chores, her eyes played over the piece of paper glaring at her from the counter. She had already punched the numbers in to call Dillon several times, but she always chickened out at the last second.

After opening and reading some neglected mail, Celeste discarded the envelopes in the trash. Since it was bordering on full, she decided it would be her final chore for the day. She grabbed the handles of the trash bag, pulled it out of the can, and placed it on the floor. To close it properly, she had to press down on the top pieces so the drawstrings could close around the top and no waste would spill out onto the floor. When she pressed down on the contents, an air pocket of fetid air whooshed up and out from the bottom—food scraps she'd thrown away a day or two before—and punched her in the face. Smelling the aroma seized her body with a gripping panic. She was transported back to the filth of the alleyway. She gagged at the stench assaulting her nose and immediately turned away. She held her breath as she fought to tie the handles of the trash bag, then leaned it against the counter.

Celeste immediately went for her purse, jerked it open, and found the plastic bag that held all of the essential oil vials she carried with her. She pulled the bag apart, grabbed one of the small bottles, unscrewed the lid of the lavender, stuck the opening under her nose, and breathed the scent in as she moved to the living room and settled onto the couch. With each long sniff of the lavender, she calmed to a normal state.

The scent of the trash, combined with the remembered alleyway smells from a few days ago, had penetrated her core. That horrible incident threatened to land Celeste on the couch for the remainder of the day, a few days, or even the rest of the week. She forced herself to move back to the counter, grabbed the paper, quickly dialed the number, and forced herself to wait. After three rings, a man's voice came on the line.

"Hello. This is Dillon."

At the sound of Dillon's voice, Celeste almost jerked the phone from her ear, ended the call, and pitched her phone across the room. His voice startled her at first, although nothing was threatening in his tone; instead, it calmed her.

"Hello? Is… anybody there?"

Celeste stood frozen where she was, listening to a growing silence on the other end of the line.

"Celeste?" Dillon asked.

"Yes?" Her reply was instantaneous and automatic. Her response to him speaking her name scared her, and she whispered, "Oh God." Embarrassed, she pulled the phone away from her face, shook her head, and mumbled a pitiful apology. She was about to kill the call but heard Dillon's voice call out.

"Wait-wait-wait, Celeste. Don't hang up. Please!"

Celeste slowly put the phone back to her ear.

"Celeste?" Dillon asked again, unaware he had caught her before she'd killed the call.

"How? How did you know it was me?"

"I didn't. Maybe it was just intuition about what happened a few days ago. You've been on my mind. You said you could handle it. I guess maybe I had my doubts. I secretly hoped you couldn't handle it and would call me. Besides, you're the only woman I barely know who wouldn't say anything when she calls me."

Celeste smiled, then gave a soft chuckle at that.

Dillon continued, "I take it you're not handling it as well as you'd hoped, huh?"

Celeste was silent.

"Celeste, it's okay. You can talk to me. Don't be afraid."

"Yes," she said. "The past few days have been pretty fucking rough for me. I've pretty much stayed at home away from everyone and everything. It's not like me."

"You want to talk about it now… on the phone?" Dillon asked, but then very quickly added, "Or maybe you would like to get out of wherever you live and meet face to face somewhere and talk. My morning happens to be open. Nothing on my agenda for today. Well, I take that back. I do have a client to meet, but that's later today, around 3:30."

Celeste hesitated. *That is incredibly kind of him to offer. He has been nothing but a gentleman since we've met.* She was thinking of what would be best for her. She looked around her house; she'd been here too long and needed to get out.

"Celeste? You there?

"I'm here. Just thinking."

"Thought I lost you there for a moment."

"Could we meet?" she blurted out. "If it's not too much trouble. Being with someone right now might be the best thing for me. God, that sounds so pathetic."

"Stop it," he soothed. It wasn't condescending. "It's not pathetic at all. Don't beat yourself up like that. I would be happy to meet you. It's no trouble at all. Do you want to meet and talk over food or coffee, or what are you craving? Your choice."

"I don't know," Celeste said, frustrated she couldn't make one simple fucking decision. "Maybe some comfort food. Something that isn't necessarily good for me, I think, would taste the best. Do you know of any places that have good cheeseburgers and fries?"

"Jasper's Ale House on Montpellier Street has the best burgers and fries. Want to meet there?" Dillon asked.

"Sure, that sounds good. Twelve-thirty good for you?"

"I was going to suggest twelve-thirty," Dillon said. "Then you can tell me whatever's on your mind. I'll be happy to listen and offer any advice; that is, if you want my advice. Or I can sit there and listen and not say anything if that is more what you need."

"I appreciate that. We'll play it by ear. I'll see you in about an hour."

"Sure. See you then."

Celeste ended the call and ditched her cell phone on the counter. She placed her hands on its surface and took a few deep, calming breaths.

Why in the hell did I do that? I must be out of my gourd.

That had been hard for her; that one phone call seemed to take the equivalent of a full day's work out of her body. Not that she had tremendous stamina, but now she suddenly felt frail. Maybe another shower would do her some good. She had worked hard all morning and knew she wanted to look her best when she met Dillon.

She shook her head at that strange thought, and as she moved to the bathroom again, she wondered, *What the fuck am I thinking? Look my best. I'd want to do that if I were meeting with one of my girlfriends. It's not like you're going on a date with the guy, Celeste. That's the last thing you need in your life.*

CHAPTER FOUR

Jasper's Ale House looked more prominent on the inside than on the outside. This anomaly was due to it being an older-style house where, over the years, additional rooms had been built onto the backside of the original home. Each room added to the unique structure and took on a more modern build, look, and feel.

Upon arrival, the hostess told Celeste her guest was already waiting for her in the blue room.

Celeste followed the waitress from the foyer to the red room, then into the green room, the orange room, and finally into the blue room at the back of the establishment. The color of each room had artwork and tablecloths to match the walls.

As Celeste followed, she heard soft rock playing at an unobtrusive, low volume and the tiny clink or scrape of silverware on the plates of people already dining. Each room had a different blend of aromas she passed through—an appealing mixture of seasoned chicken, fish, and steaks, with a variety of vegetables.

Celeste saw Dillon sitting alone in the blue room, already nursing a Coors. He waved her over.

As Celeste approached, she noticed his courtesy in standing to meet her.

That was sweet, she thought. *And unexpected. Such a gentleman.* Then she took a mental snapshot as she assessed him all at once.

Dillon was tall, well-groomed, with dark-brown hair and lovely, tanned skin. He had a dark hint of well-maintained stubble. She liked that. She could tell he was lean and muscular with nice arms. *Shit, he probably goes to the gym more than I do. Fuck! Such a handsome guy.*

She suddenly didn't feel worthy of meeting with him, like he was more handsome than the other guys she'd gone out with.

What is wrong with me? This isn't about going out with him. This isn't a date; that's not why he's here. I probably don't even register on his radar as someone he might go out with if that were an option. That's not why I'm here either.

Or is it?

On the day of the assault, she had barely given him a passing glance because of the circumstances.

The hostess indicated her table, waited for her and Dillon to be seated, told them their waiter would be with them shortly, and exited quietly.

"I hope you don't mind," Dillon began, "but I went ahead and ordered you a beer. I don't even know if you drink beer, but on the off chance you do, I thought it could start taking the edge off what's bothering you. Hope that was okay."

Celeste glanced at the beer, then nodded to Dillon. "That was very thoughtful. I do need a beer. Maybe a couple." She picked up the longneck, held it toward him, and said, "Here's to you, heroic moments of saving damsels in distress, and thinking ahead."

Dillon grabbed his bottle again and clinked it against hers. "I'll drink to that."

They took long drags from their bottles; Celeste's a little longer than Dillon's. It was a welcome chill that washed down her throat. She set her bottle on the table and said, "Yes, I do drink beer. That was just what I needed."

Their waiter approached, they exchanged pleasantries, and he took their orders; Dillon, the For the Halibut sandwich with fries, and Celeste, The Dirty Bird Cheeseburger with fries. Then, the waiter left them to their conversation and beers.

After a long pause, Dillon leaned forward and searched Celeste's face.

"What?" she asked.

"Nothing. Sorry, I was looking at that bruise near your eye. We have almost matching shiners. He got me good, too."

"Such a fucking asshole. Mine has faded some since then. Thank God."

Dillon placed his arms on the table. "Talk to me. What's on your mind?"

Celeste looked down at her hands, instantly embarrassed that she was meeting a stranger to discuss her sexual assault. She suddenly wished she hadn't called him. "This is… awkward."

Dillon continued, "I know. Guess I wanted to say you can trust me and talk to me about it if you want. I'm here to listen."

"Now?" Celeste asked, then looked around the room, hoping no one was sitting close enough to eavesdrop. "You want me to talk about it now?"

Only one other couple was sitting in the blue room, on the other side, far enough away to where they wouldn't hear Celeste if she decided to talk.

"Why not? Now's a perfect time," Dillon said. "We might as well get it out of the way. Rip that Band-Aid right off. Not that I'm rushing you to talk about it. But lunch will be more enjoyable for you if you do. You can get some of that off your chest. You started clamming up on me earlier because you didn't want to talk about it. So, let's get it out in the open; then, maybe you can relax a little. Hell, you might even enjoy yourself."

Celeste smiled at his statement. "Thanks. I appreciate that. I didn't feel right in sharing all of a sudden."

"That's understandable." He leaned in closer and lowered his voice. "You were assaulted, and I'm sure it's embarrassing to talk about it. You feel, like, maybe, what's the point? We both know what happened, right?"

"Yeah, something like that." She was quiet for a few seconds.

"So?" he urged.

Oh, what the hell. Celeste thought. *Maybe he's right. What other reason did I have to meet Dillon today but to talk about what happened? Indeed, I didn't unconsciously call him to hook up with—*

"Try this on for size," Dillon suggested.

Thank God. Where the hell was I going in my mind? Celeste said, "Try what?"

"See if this works for you. Pretend I'm the guy who attacked you a few days ago."

"What?" she said, a little startled at the request. She glanced around again to make sure no one was in earshot.

He held up a hand, giving her a calming motion, and continued explaining. "Pretend I'm *him*, and whatever anger that's going on inside that beautiful head of yours, just let it out."

Beautiful, she thought, picking up on that one word. "What?"

He gave her a 'come over here' motion with both hands. "Let me have it verbally as if *I* was the asshole who assaulted you."

"Pretend *you* are the *guy*?" Celeste questioned to see if she had heard Dillon right.

"Sure. And to make this more effective, let's give that guy a name. Something like, oh, I don't know, Aaron, maybe?"

"Aaron?"

"Yeah, just an arbitrary name. I just pulled it out of my ass." He moved his hand quickly to underneath his chair and gave a fake grimace as though he was pulling the suggestion out of his butt; then he released the invisible name of Aaron into the air. He pointed to the hidden name. "Voila! Aaron."

Celeste laughed at his gesture, then Dillon joined in along with her.

"Sorry, that was crude, but I'm glad it made you laugh." Becoming serious, Dillon continued without missing a beat, "Tell *me*, *Aaron*, how you feel about what happened to you by what *he* did to you."

When Dillon said that, Celeste became very serious and locked eyes with him. "Okay, *Aaron.*" She said his name with an immediate, hateful intensity that raised Dillon's eyebrows with interest. She was now all tight lips and clenched teeth. "If you're sure. I'll tell you exactly how I feel. You are, without a doubt, the biggest motherfucking cunt I have ever met. There will never be anyone beyond *you* who will rank lower than the vile piece of dog-shit scumbag you are. I think you're the most cowardly son of a fucking bitch on the face of the goddamn earth. Who the fuck do you think you are to come after me? What is it about *me* that you felt you had the freedom to try and stick your dick into me? Huh, motherfucker?"

Dillon pointed at her and waggled his finger. "Good, that's good. Solid. Go deeper with your feelings. Let them out. Let me have it. Let *Aaron* have it. I want to know exactly what you think about him."

With this encouragement, Celeste continued, "With every fiber of my being, I hope Karma comes back on you with a ten-ton vengeance. I wish I had a voodoo doll with your name on it so I could stick numerous pins in it, and I wish the voodoo worked. Most of those goddamn pins would be shoved straight into your crotch because I sincerely hope, pray, and wish on the highest power in the universe that you get some awful disease or dick cancer and that it slowly eats away everything down there that you're so fucking proud of. I pray something nasty happens to your little twig and berries because you certainly don't deserve to continue living with those things attached to you."

Dillon swallowed hard, then whispered so as not to interrupt her line of spoken anger, "Now, really, let me have it."

"You know what I'm going to do to you if I ever get you in a room alone?"

Dillon said nothing but leaned closer. Intrigued, he raised his eyebrows again in amusement. He nodded as a way to get her to continue.

"If I ever have the opportunity, you can bet your ass that I'm going to cut your cock and balls completely from your body. And I'm going to let you bleed out because Karma might be too slow about taking that body part you need to be separated from."

She was silent and continued to search Dillon's eyes.

When Dillon felt like she would say no more, he nodded, then asked, "That's extremely dark, Celeste. How did that feel?"

Celeste took a deep breath as she sat back in her chair; she hadn't realized she'd slowly leaned forward with each threat spoken to this imaginary 'Aaron' character. She had only breathed shallowly as she vented. These new deep breaths felt rewarding. Then, Celeste took another long drag of her beer and said, "Wow, that felt amazing. I feel so much better."

"I'll bet you do. You have a lot of harbored anger inside you. I think you should continue to do that. Get that hate out of your system. Don't let it fester inside you. And please don't take any of your anger out on me. Jesus Christ. That was hardcore."

She was all of a sudden embarrassed. "I know, that was so bad, wasn't it?" She covered her face with one of her hands and gave a sheepish laugh.

"Hey," he said, reaching for her. He pulled her hands away from her face. "Don't you ever regret voicing your true feelings. You have to get all that off your chest. Keep that feeling of confidence… and, um… *barbarianism*, if you will?"

Celeste laughed at his choice of words. "I can't promise anything. But I'll try."

Their waiter came back and sat each dish in front of them. He asked if everything looked okay and if they needed anything else, to which they answered yes and no. The waiter excused himself, and they began eating.

CHAPTER FIVE

"So, TELL ME about you," Dillon said before taking a bite of his fish sandwich.

"What... do... you want to know?" Celeste asked, not knowing where to start.

"Oh, I don't know. What do you do? You know, job-wise? You looked nice that day I was able to help you, even though that guy, you know, *Aaron...* he did a number on your clothes." Dillon paused, waiting for a quick laugh from Celeste—she didn't laugh—then continued, "He ruined your nice, navy business suit if I remember correctly. I could tell it was probably an expensive outfit."

"You remembered what I was wearing?"

"Well, yeah, you were barely wearing it."

She flashed a look of confusion his way; embarrassment mixed with a slight touch of anger washed over her. Celeste felt vulnerable again, exposed. She self-consciously pulled the long light sweater she'd chosen to wear over her outfit just a little bit tighter. In her mind, that thin layer acted as a shield to deflect his comment and conceal her even more. Her shoulders slumped and turned inward.

Dillon caught her sharp movement and glanced at her but found her look indiscernible. "I'm sorry; that was incredibly insensitive of me. It was a terrible attempt at humor. It was a bad way to relay I noticed how attractive you are. It won't happen again."

She harrumphed and took an angry bite out of her cheeseburger. She chewed a few times, then said, "Better not."

There was a slight amusement in her actions. Dillon knew she was somewhat humored, but he also took her statement to heart.

Dillon stuck a fry into his mouth and continued, "I always pay attention to the fine details. Your clothes made me think that maybe you work for a bank or as an executive in one of the high rises in the city?"

"Close," Celeste said. "I started at Spencer, Broadbent, and Hathaway law offices not long ago."

"Oh, a lawyer. That's interesting."

"No, not so much a lawyer," Celeste corrected. "I'm a paralegal who wants to get her chance at being a major player in the courtroom someday. I've been going to evening classes at the university a few nights each week. Classes focused on just that: courtroom proceedings and linguistics. I'm also studying a few other classes about the law to help me along. It's just a matter of time before I get my big chance in court. How about you?"

"Sales." There was no thought in his answer. He shotgunned the word out of his mouth.

His quick answer seemed weird to Celeste. A look of distrust crossed her face; something seemed off about his answer, but then that thought left her mind as Dillon continued.

"The company I work for has products that help people invest for their future, like retirement, their kids' colleges, other savings plans, blah-blah-blah; boring shit like that. I'm sure you've heard it all before. You being an intelligent female, you probably already have extensive portfolios in place."

"Yes, I do," she lied. "So, you're an investor."

"No, not so much an investor," he said, taking on the phrasing she'd used on him. "Just a guy who has the means to help my clients save money in the right places and the right ways. We help them get those needs taken care of early on, so they have peace of mind they'll have a future when they get to it. The bad thing about it is the company is moving upstate. I'll have to move upstate in a couple of weeks."

"You're moving?" The sudden statement caused her upbeat mood to plummet.

"Yeah, eventually, whenever they tell me about that. I feel it's going to be pretty soon, though."

Celeste had no idea why she was so disappointed by the possibility of him moving away. She barely knew this guy, and as far as she knew right now, she wouldn't see him anymore after this lunch. After all, they were only meeting so she could vent about what had happened a few days ago, nothing more. Or had she forgotten about that? They'd already discussed the event earlier before the food had been served. She didn't know if they would talk anymore about it. She didn't know if she wanted to. She had to admit she was enjoying this time with Dillon. But now, with this moving news, she felt a slight panic and knew an end to their time together was fast approaching.

They ate in silence for a short time, enjoying each other's company and savoring the delicious food and tasty beer. Celeste mulled the news of Dillon's soon-to-be departure into the upstate—a good ways away, she assumed. She didn't know how she felt about that other than she didn't like it. And she really didn't understand why she didn't like it. This guy was so calming and mentally helpful, not to mention crazy attractive. It was a shame he would be out of her life so soon. She just wanted to spend more time with him. And why she was having those thoughts, she had no clue. They shouldn't even be entering into her mind. After what she'd been through only days ago, she felt guilty for entertaining the idea that there could be anything there, even on the slightest level.

And when does this 'wanting to spend more time with him' stop? She didn't know, but she pushed that question out of her head.

"Did I say something wrong?" Dillon asked.

Celeste looked over to Dillon, running his statement over in her mind. Realizing she was being silly, she said, "No, of course not." Then, sheepishly, she looked back at her food again and said, "I never really gave you a correct thank you for what you did the other day."

"Yes, you did. You thanked me."

"I did," she agreed with a deep-thought nod. "But I was rude about it, and for that, I'm sorry." She placed a hand on her chest and looked directly into his eyes. "Sincerely, Dillon. Thank you for rescuing me from that *Aaron guy*. I have no idea what the outcome would've been like had you not come along. I am thankful for you."

The phrase 'Aaron guy' was spoken with much hate, but there was a quick, amused smile after it. A call-back to Dillon jokingly naming her attacker.

"Even though it's been a few rough days dealing with what happened to me, you saved me a lot of pain and misery and beating myself up about what might have happened if he had been able to follow through with what he started."

Dillon placed his hand over Celeste's, the one resting on the table close to him. "Hey, it's okay. I know how appreciative you are. I can feel the gratitude. I'm so glad I was there and was able to stop something so horrible from happening. I wish I could've caught that asshole for you so he could be prosecuted. Hey, maybe then you could've had your day in court with him."

"Oh, I'm going to have my day in court with him… one day. Someday," Celeste promised. Her statement was said with much humor in her voice. It was a loose comment that held much doubt because she knew she would probably never see that dickhead again in this big city. But her statement was filled with a promise because there was always that chance encounter she might see him in the most random places. And if that ever happened, he had better fucking watch out. "I remember what he looks like," she said, tapping her temple with a finger. "I'll never forget his face."

"Well, in that case, I hope you two meet again very soon. I wish I could make that happen for you."

When the waiter saw them wrapping up, he dropped back and deposited the ticket in a black, leather bill holder. He told them it was only for their convenience and not to feel rushed to pay.

Celeste reached for the holder and then grabbed her purse.

"What are you doing?" Dillon asked.

"I'm paying for our meal," Celeste stated as though he should've known.

"You don't have to do that. I was expecting us to split it. Or I was going to pay for it outright."

"Always playing the hero. You saved me the other day. Take a break for today, and let me at least treat you to your meal."

"Ooh, that makes this our first date."

Celeste paused from looking down into her purse. She looked up at Dillon and laughed outloud. "First date? Is that you attempting humor again, or are you being serious?"

"Sure," he said, smiling and not answering either of her suggestions. "If we had paid separately, then it would just be our meeting, talking, and having a nice lunch. But since you're buying, it's officially our first date." He added a charming smile, hinting he was only joking.

Is there a seriousness behind his words? Celeste wondered. She considered his words and shrugged her shoulders, deciding to go with it. "Not a bad first date, in my opinion."

"I agree. I did enjoy our time together. I didn't think you were looking for anything further than this meeting. I thought we were meeting to talk about the incident. I didn't think you wanted anything other than friendship out of this, uh, you made that very clear back then"—he threw a thumb over his shoulder indicating the time of the incident—"and I understand that. Now, you're paying for my meal."

His tone led her to believe he was only joking. She pulled out her wallet, grabbed the correct amount of cash plus a tip, and stuck it inside the leather holder. She said, "You're putting way too much thought into this. I'm going to pay for our meal because I feel it's the least I can do other than thank you verbally. So we can call us even."

The waiter returned and took their bill holder, to which Celeste told him she didn't need any change. The waiter thanked them, gave a hint of a bow, and retreated.

Dillon continued, "Forgive me if I'm too forward here, but you would be a major catch if you were looking to further our time together. I would jump at that chance."

Celeste gave another quick bark of laughter as she reached for her purse. "Me, a major catch? Ha, yeah, right?"

"Don't say that. You are. You don't see how beautiful you are, but I do."

Dillon's statement made her pause. She looked over at him, a little shocked at his forwardness. "You think I'm beautiful?"

Dillon held her gaze. "I do. You may not see it, but I certainly do."

All she saw was honesty in his eyes. She hung her head. "It's been a long time since I've heard a statement like that."

"I'm sorry. Maybe I'm being too forward. I shouldn't have said that."

"No. You *should have* said that. It's something I needed to hear."

"I would say it plenty more times. But it is something you need to start believing."

"That's true. I know, and I will."

"Good. I hope so," Dillon said as he grabbed his beer and took one last drag. "You ready to get out of here?"

"I believe I am."

They made their way back through the colored rooms to the entrance of Jasper's and exited.

"So, what do you want to do now?" Celeste asked, panicking they were about to say their goodbyes. She didn't know what should come next, and the question flew out of her mouth.

Dillon looked over at her, a little confused. "Do? Now?"

"Oh, sorry," Celeste said, shaking her head at her suggestion. "I was assuming you might want to hang out with me some more today." Her comment was sarcastic and more of a slam on herself.

"I mean, I could. But I thought perhaps you've had enough of me for one day."

"No, on the contrary. You put me at ease. The panicked version of me has calmed down. I just wanted to keep that calmness going, I guess."

"Sure. I understand. What did you have in mind?"

"Don't know, but maybe… drinks back at my place?" Her voice went up an octave higher, her mind thinking she wasn't good enough, beautiful enough, or sufficiently sexy for him to want to spend his time with her. She pressed on, talking too much. "I don't live too far from here. And I do have drinks other than beer that are just a bit *stiffer*." She laughed at her choice of words.

Celeste, what the hell are you doing? she asked herself. *Not the best idea you've ever hatched. You sure you want to be back at your place, alone, with this guy?*

Dillon smiled and laughed also. "Stiff drinks in the early afternoon. I'm game." After he spoke, he snapped his finger and pointed it in her direction. "But I can't get drunk. I have that client meeting at 3:30. I mentioned that earlier on the phone. But between now and then, I have time for *whatever*."

Celeste smiled and said, "That's okay. Are you sure you don't have to prepare for it?"

"No, not at all. All those meetings are the same. I could give you the spiel and see if you wanted any mutual funds for your retirement." He didn't wait for an answer but held his hands up, signaling that he was joking.

"Hard pass on that, but thanks."

They both laughed hard at her statement.

"Smart girl," Dillon said.

"My car is over here. Just follow that tan Subaru right there," she said, pointing to her car.

"I can do that." He pointed at a silver car with black effects. "That Charger over there is me. I'll try and keep up."

CHAPTER SIX

Dillon and Celeste were in her spotless kitchen in less than fifteen minutes, pouring repeated shots of Jameson.

Celeste was relieved she'd forced herself to give her house a cleaning overhaul this morning. She would've hated for Dillon to see her home the way it looked before she tackled those chores. She had let it go for too long, but she was proud everything was in its proper place now that she had a guest. Dissipated from its earlier potency, the light scent from miscellaneous cleaners still smelled pure and lingered throughout the rooms.

The Jameson, flavored with subtle hints of vanilla and honey, was neat and smooth. After the fourth shot, Celeste's legs gave out slightly; she did an awkward shuffle sidestep. She grabbed the counter and held on to it, fearing she would end up sprawled out on the floor.

Dillon saw the slump in her body, quickly rounded the counter's edge, and threw one hand behind her back to steady her. He grabbed her arm that was closest to him with his other hand. "Hey, careful. You okay there?"

She nodded, gazing up into his eyes. "Ah, yeah. I think so. Don't think I should've taken that last shot."

He continued, "I think you should cut yourself off from alcohol at this point. Let's cool it on the shots for now."

"That thought did just cross my mind," Celeste said. She raised a hand and pointed at herself. "I'm a little drunk." She gave a nervous titter.

"Yeah, that's not obvious at all," Dillon mimicked back in the same tone and inflection she had used but pointed at her instead of himself as Celeste had done.

Celeste smiled. A single thought spiraled through her mind as his hand pressed into her back. *I'm nervous,* she admitted to herself. *Still nervous. Those shots didn't help. Like, what are you going to do now? Sit on the couch and talk? Watch a movie together? You only have so much time before he leaves. You need to slow everything way down.*

Celeste looked up into his handsome face again, which was now close to hers. He was peering down into her eyes. There was a sexual intensity she couldn't deny. Being this close to him, Celeste saw his broken Christmas light eyes; sharp, bright, and dangerous. She saw his gaze flicker between looking deep into her eyes and back to her lips. His eyes sparkled with lust, a hint of seduction was in them and on his curved lips.

Dillon glanced to the side of her face and saw a light bruise still evident high on her cheek. He said nothing about it but leaned in and kissed it gently. He moved away from her bruise and gazed into her eyes once more.

She said, "I know I will probably regret this in the future. But I may regret it more if I don't."

"Regret what?" he whispered knowingly.

The only answer he received was Celeste moving forward to attack his lips with her own.

The kiss between them was open-mouthed, breathy, and filled with urgency. Their tongues danced over each other's, and their arms wrapped around each other's bodies.

Dillon took both sides of her light sweater and gently peeled them back away from her. The sweater fell away from her shoulders and slid to the floor. One part of her armament was gone.

To compensate for this exposure, Celeste's arms circled Dillon's back, pulling him closer to her, protecting herself with him. One of Dillon's hands snaked around to the base of Celeste's spine, and he pulled her pelvis toward his. Dillon's other hand slid around to the back of her neck, then into her hair. He cradled her head with his strong hands and intertwined her hair around his fingers as he pushed her head forward and kissed her harder.

They took turns sucking each other's tongues; it was playful at first, but then a more profound passion took hold. Celeste sucked Dillon's tongue with long strokes of her lips, hinting the same attention would eventually be applied to another member further down his body.

As Dillon pulled Celeste harder into him, she felt his growing erection through his jeans. Her pelvis began to gyrate, promising they would ride each other's bodies very soon.

Dillon walked forward as he guided her backward into her living room. Celeste knew where he was going and moved with him. She trusted he knew the right direction to the couch and wouldn't let her trip and fall to the floor.

As they moved, Celeste pulled his T-shirt up. Dillon released her body just long enough for her to jerk his shirt over his head, then his muscular arms surrounded her and pulled her into him once more.

Dillon's hand slid from the back of her head down to the front of her chest and over her left breast. There was no tentativeness about it, just firm handfuls of examination.

"Oh, Jesus Christ, Dillon. That feels so fucking good," Celeste whispered. "Please, don't stop."

He continued to squeeze, rub, and massage her breast. He tweaked her nipple between his fingers. Then, he slid his hand over and gave the same treatment to her right one. He finally grabbed the bottom of her shirt and pulled it up. She instinctively raised her arms above her head. Then the shirt was off and flung away.

Dillon said, "My God. Now, that's sexy."

Celeste had no idea what he was talking about and looked down. *Is it my boobs? My bra? My boobs in my bra? What?*

He was staring directly at her breasts, admiring them.

Then she remembered she'd put on a matching bra and panty set just in case things got heated between them. It was a far cry then, but now she believed it was also wishful thinking from the back of her subconscious mind. She even admitted to herself that she felt a little thrill at the rebelliousness of it, that if the situation presented itself, she would follow through in having a sexual relationship with Dillon and not let what happened to her dictate her future happiness. She remembered the fabric of her bra was somewhat see-through. There was nothing like a little obscurity to make whoever was staring want to see everything. It was a sexy little combo pair that teased, and she thanked God she'd rethought the underwear thing because this set complimented her body so well.

Dillon massaged her breasts again, and they both felt how erect her nipples were through the sheer cloth that separated the skin-on-skin contact. Then his lips covered one of her nipples, sucking it hard through the thin fabric. He playfully held her nipple between his teeth and flicked it with his tongue before he moved over to her other breast and gave it the same orgasmic teasing.

Celeste felt Dillon's hand snaking up her spine. His fingers grabbed hold of her bra strap; there was just a hint of a squeeze, and he had unclasped it.

Okay, that was smooth. This guy knows what he's doing. He's experienced. He's probably been with so many women.

Her thoughts dissipated as he pulled her bra from her shoulders and pitched it over his own. He immediately went back to work sucking the nipple of one breast again as he tweaked the other between his fingertips.

Celeste felt his fingers unfasten and unzip her jeans. His hands were on her thighs, gripping the fabric and peeling it down her long legs.

"Be careful," she said in a breathy whisper.

He paused for a second, not knowing what she meant.

"My knees. From the attack. My biggest injury."

He continued, but this time, he was extra careful. A few more cautious tugs and her jeans were off her body.

Celeste saw her knee bandages and relived the mental pain as that moment returned to her mind. She grimaced.

Dillon saw her stiffen and looked down at her bandages. He moved his fingers lightly over her knees, barely touching the applications. He leaned down and carefully kissed around the bandages on each leg in a couple of places. "I hate this happened to you. I wish I had gotten there sooner to save you from this pain."

"Me too," she said, a little aggression painting her voice. She pressed forward, bringing on a more cheerful tone. "Listen, I don't want to talk about it because I don't want that shit to ruin this beautiful moment. Please keep doing what you are doing."

"Are you sure?"

She nodded emphatically, "Yes. Please."

Celeste had no more finished that statement than she had her legs splayed open by his hands and his head buried between them. He licked and sucked at her womanhood through her sheer panties.

Jesus God, this guy isn't asking for permission for anything. He's just going for it. And thank God he is because he is amazing at it.

Dillon sucked and licked the crotch of her panties until he could taste the sexual juices seep from her. Eventually, he grabbed her panties, pulled them aside, and licked her hard, focusing solely on her clit.

As Dillon peeled her panties down her legs, pure elation and ecstasy possessed Celeste's body. She was turned on, and her body continued to ramp up to orgasm detonation.

Dillon focused directly on her clit button and continued to add pressure and speed from his tongue as he flicked and licked her further into ecstasy.

Celeste was lost in the moment's passion and couldn't figure out what to do with her hands. One second, they were gripping the cushions in reach; the next moment, they were gripping the back of the couch as she held on for the ride of her life. A few seconds later, Celeste threw her arms forward, grabbed handfuls of Dillon's hair, and pulled his face harder into her pussy, urging him to lick her furiously.

Dillon obeyed, continuing with more vigorous and faster tongue strokes, ramping up the pressure and intensity. Celeste's feet and lower legs slowly pumped small circles above his head as she rode the euphoria spreading from her vagina into every part of her body.

Celeste chanted, "Jesus-Christ-fucking-hell-Jesus-Christ-fucking-hell-Jesus-Christ-fucking-hell," over and over and over. She knew it didn't make any sense, but she didn't care; her body was about to blow all cylinders. Then, finally, the climax she had been waiting for rippled through her body. She was thrown into uncontrollable shudders she'd never before experienced. Aftershocks pulsed within her vagina, making her body shiver with delight.

A satisfied grin spread across her face, and she stretched in response to her body's delight. "Oh, Jesus Christ, Dillon. What the fuck did you do to me? Where the hell did you learn to do that?"

"I learned it from you," he said.

She shook her head. "What?"

"I just listened to your moans. You told me everything you wanted me to do. I just paid attention to what your moans told me."

"Really? Good God in Heaven. No one before you has ever listened to me as you did. Jesus Christ. Why do I keep saying 'Jesus Christ'?"

"Yeah, I'm not Him. I'm just Dillon Carmichael."

They laughed.

"Take your pants off," Celeste said. "I want to do the same thing to you. That was unbelievable."

"Okay. If you insist."

"I do." She snapped her finger as though commanding him. "Now strip."

"Yes, ma'am."

Dillon stood, unbuckled, unclasped, unzipped his pants, and let his jeans drop to the floor.

Celeste's eyes brightened at the sight of his hard-on bulging within his jockey shorts. He pulled the waistband of his shorts away from his throbbing member, pulled them down as far as they would go, and let them drop to the floor. Then he stepped out of his jeans and underwear and moved closer to Celeste.

Celeste's eyes danced over Dillon's nakedness with lustful abandon. She knew he worked out; she had already appreciated his slim waistline, forearms, biceps curvature, and broad shoulders. She had a hint of his physique on the day she was attacked and earlier today, on their first date, through his clothes, but now, looking at him after those various layers were removed, he was a fantastic sight to behold. He was a beautiful man; he wasn't stacked like one of those heavy-lifting, body-building meatheads in the gym. Instead, he was lean, one who lifts but also does plenty of different aerobics and even throws some yoga into the mix to gain that extra-toned look.

And abs, she thought, smiling. *This guy has some killer abs.*

Celeste could count on one hand—and maybe a few digits on the other—the number of guys with whom she'd had sex. Unfortunately, none of them had defined abdominals. She reached for them, unable to stop herself. At first, she just placed her hands on his abs; then, she slowly ran her fingers over them. She smiled at how sexy they felt.

She sat there on the couch admiring his body as he stood before her, slowly stroking his engorged member.

Celeste looked up at him and said, "What?"

"I'm watching you enjoy this moment."

"You going to stand there all day and jerk yourself off? Or will you let me do that for you with my mouth?"

"I'm warming it up for you." He smiled. "I'm also waiting to find out what you wanted and felt comfortable doing."

"Come here, and I'll show you."

Dillon obeyed.

Celeste slid to the edge of the couch, spreading her legs wide to get closer to him. She was at the perfect height to take him directly into her mouth as he stepped toward her. She tested his girth and then his length as she wrapped her mouth around his swollen cock. As she took a little more of him into her mouth with each slow and steady stroke of her lips, she slid her hand between her legs and began to finger herself.

She felt his hands rest on the back of her head and slowly guided her forward as he started to face fuck her. Dillon didn't force her to deep-throat him in any way, he just gently and delicately held her head, and she moved back and forth to the rhythm of the blowjob she was gifting him. Celeste kept slowly taking a little more of him into her mouth with each stroke they made.

Celeste's hands were everywhere. She felt his chest, his abs, and the V cut of his waist. Finally, she put a hand on the lower part of his chest, guided him toward the couch where she was sitting, and urged him to sit and lay back. He did. She sat beside him, careful not to put any pressure on her knees, and leaned over. She slowly ramped up her pace, taking a little more of him into her mouth.

It didn't take long for the pressure to build within him. When he was close to his point of no return, he quickly untangled himself from her.

Celeste was so into giving him a blowjob that, at first, she didn't understand why he was stopping it.

Dillon helped guide her lithe body over, careful of her knees, and laid her on her back. He mounted her without hesitation and slid his hands up under her. He didn't take the time to guide his cock into her; he knew it would find its way into her with one or two hip thrusts. She was so hot and wet from their foreplay that he would no doubt slide deep within her.

Celeste moved her hand down and was about to guide him into her when he felt her opening and pushed deep into her vagina. Celeste's mouth opened, and she released a breathy moan of alarm as his girth stretched her and slid home perfectly.

"Oh, my fucking God. Dillon," she said in a semi-accusatory tone. She leaned her head forward and playfully bit into his shoulder as she drummed his shoulder with her fist. With a hitch of breathy air, she said, "I can barely contain you."

"You're perfect," he whispered.

Dillon slowly pulled out and then pushed forward to test how much of him she could take. His cock became lubricated even more with her wetness, making it easier for him to slide deeper into her. He quickened his pace as the pressure began to build within both bodies. His ramp-up time was already heightened from her earlier attentions; he quickly reached orgasm release mode. Celeste had pulled her legs up high, and Dillon had grabbed onto them to steady himself as he pumped steadily away into her like a jackhammer on a construction site.

At the point of ejaculation, he pulled out of Celeste. As he pulled out, her pussy erupted with her sexual liquid. It squirted all over Dillon's lower abdomen and crotch. Celeste quickly reached between her legs and rubbed her clit back and forth as though she were a DJ scratching records in a nightclub.

As Celeste's liquid speckled Dillon's body, he ejaculated thick streams of semen onto her waist and lower abdomen. He continued to jerk himself to completion throughout his final throes of ecstasy. They both stroked themselves till the last of their fluids dripped from their bodies, then Dillon crashed beside her on the couch.

"Jesus Christ, that was so goddamn intense," he said in a breathy whisper.

"It was, wasn't it?" Celeste asked, but it needed no answer. "I'm sorry I soaked you."

"Don't be; I don't mind. You drenched me. I soaked you. We're even."

They both gave a giddy laugh, then Dillon continued, "Sorry, but I didn't know if you're on birth control. I didn't want to be insensitive about the matter, but doing it this way is better than me getting you pregnant."

"Oh, I know. Don't worry about that. I'm glad one of us was thinking ahead because I sure the hell wasn't. I was so caught up in the moment. That was kind of hot… and by, *kind of*, I mean, it was fucking amazing."

"Talk about *coming* together. Holy Jesus," Dillon said.

"That was a righteous fuck, wasn't it? Never been nailed like that before," Celeste said. She paused, then said tentatively, "So… about that big, white elephant in the room. I'm a squirter."

"Oh, that's normal for you?"

"Not all of the time, but it's happened before. Why?"

"Oh, I just thought my technique was new to you, and I caused you to do that."

"It's been a long time, but yeah, you fucking did that to me."

"Well, that was sexy as hell. You think I might have a problem with that?" Dillon asked.

"The guys that it has happened with before do. Jesus, that makes me sound like a slut. Like, I'm screwing *so* many guys." She laughed at the thought, relaying to Dillon that she wasn't. "The guys like it at first, but most of the time, that's why they don't hang around. My waterworks and spraying everywhere become a nuisance to them."

"That's dumb. If given a chance, I would welcome a dousing from you every time we had sex."

"You saying you want to make love to me again?"

A devilish smile played upon his lips, and he nodded and glanced at her. "Oh yeah, I would love to make love to you again."

"When?" Celeste asked.

"How about…" He jokingly looked at his watch to pick a time later that afternoon but, in seeing the time, stood abruptly. "Oh, Jesus Christ.

Is it three o'clock already? Fucking hell. I'm sorry, Celeste, but I have to go."

He grabbed his T-shirt and pulled it on as Celeste said, a little dejected, "I know. Your three-thirty appointment with that couple. You told me. I didn't know it was that late though. I'm sorry if I made you late."

"I hate to run right after such a beautiful moment. You are so amazing and incredible, and your body, goddamn. When can we meet again?"

She smiled at his numerous compliments. "Why don't you call me later tonight, and we can plan something? I'll be around."

"Okay, I will. I'll do that," he promised as he slid on his underwear. He snatched up his jeans and was stepping into them when Celeste said, "You want to take a quick shower? Your clients will smell me on you or smell us and what we've been doing."

"I'm not worried about that. If they ask, I'll tell them it's a new cologne called *Celeste*." He said her name in a bad French accent; it made her smile. "I hate running, but I will call you soon. I promise." He took a step away, then double-stepped it back. "You want me to get you a cloth or something? Help clean you up or anything."

"Go. I'll take care of this," she said as she swept her hand down her body enticingly, indicating the glistening streams of sperm that dotted her skin. "Go meet your clients."

"Okay, I'll talk to you soon."

"You better. Bye."

He winked at her, "I will. I'll call you later tonight." Then he turned, stepped to her front door, and exited.

CHAPTER SEVEN

When Dillon Carmichael left, the front door closed harder than necessary for Celeste. The sound of it shutting seemed like he was purposely closing himself off from her. She immediately panicked as she looked down at what he'd deposited on her abdomen moments before. Even though he'd been courteous enough to ask if he could help clean her up, she had insisted that he meet his clients. Now, second thoughts were creeping in on her.

Why couldn't he have just called to cancel with them? It seemed like the moment we'd just shared wasn't important to him. Just cum on me and leave. Fuck, why do I let these things happen to me? I let *these things happen to me. Stupid.*

She wasn't immediately revolted by what had happened, just extremely disappointed in herself—and him. She was beginning to panic this was the last she would ever see of Dillon Carmichael.

She shook her head *no* to the thought, stood, and went to her bathroom down the hall as his semen began to slide down her skin. She spun and tore off a wad of toilet paper, wiped Dillon's residue from her body, pitched it in the toilet, and flushed the commode.

Since she was naked, she went ahead and stepped into the shower. This time she felt it was warranted only because she didn't want to go around all day with a cum glaze all over her body. She didn't mind so much that he'd ejaculated on her; she'd done him the same way. It was a good exchange.

Oh, my God, he gave me so much pleasure, she thought. *Take me to Orgasm City like that, and you can pretty much do anything to me.* She paused, the elation of the past moment fading. *But don't just fuck me and leave right after. That was an asshole thing to do; I don't care what you had on your schedule.*

She turned the water to the hottest setting that she could stand. She washed her hair once with shampoo and conditioner because she didn't feel like it was as dirty as her body, then she rinsed. Moving on to her body, she washed everywhere thoroughly twice and rinsed twice. As the warm water washed over her knees, the pain of the open wounds brought back the fear of the assault and attempted rape that threatened to flood her mind. Finally, taking several minutes just for herself, she stood again under the hot water, hoping it would take the roughed-up memory away from her thoughts.

She turned the water off, grabbed her towel, and wiped off as much water as possible before stepping out of the shower onto the bathroom floor mat. She hated puddles of water all around the bathroom. There was nothing like donning comfy socks and then stepping back into the bathroom to brush her teeth or grab her phone from the counter, but by doing so, stepping directly into that puddled area and ruining that fresh feel with water soaking into her socks. She hated a wet sock feeling. It was almost as bad as putting a shirt on backward. Almost.

Celeste dressed in Deadpool socks, faded red plaid lounge pants, and a Jurassic Park T-shirt featuring the famous wide-mouthed T-Rex with the words encircling his enormous head that begged anyone reading to SEND MORE TOURISTS.

She let her hair air dry. She had no plans to see anyone else today, so she didn't worry about applying makeup. All she was promised was a call from Dillon, so she didn't think they would see each other again today. From her earlier thoughts, she had almost convinced herself that Dillon wouldn't call her. She just moved to the couch, where for the past few days her thoughts had caused new feelings of desperation to overwhelm her.

Celeste didn't know if it was intuition, a sixth sense, or a general feeling, but the thought that she would never see Dillon again plagued her mind. Maybe the sex was something she shouldn't have allowed, not knowing how involved Dillon wanted or didn't want to be with her.

I made the first move. And three days after almost getting raped at that. What the hell is wrong with me? I'm the guilty one. But Jesus Christ, the sex was so fucking good. I guess I would rather beat myself up about being fucked or getting fucked rather than wish I had gotten fucked. It's a shitty feeling either way.

It felt like Dillon was gone for good and that he'd just taken her for a joyride to dampen her feelings. Even more, her attempted rape began to infiltrate her mind again. It was just little things at first, but the dam she had built up in her mind to hold that event at bay slowly broke apart. Finally, when the pressure was too much, the memory returned and destroyed the beautiful, passionate moment they had so recently shared.

She lay on the couch, mentally exhausted, for what seemed like hours, but when she looked at her phone again, only forty-five minutes had passed since her shower.

This is ridiculous. I have to do something about how I'm feeling. I have to pull my shit together and get over whatever's going on with me—having sex with someone so soon after my attack wasn't the wisest choice I've ever made. I have to talk to someone; that's apparent. It wasn't enough to talk to Dillon. It's evident I need to speak with someone else.

The memory of Dillon's advice when he gave her his number returned to her. Bits and pieces of what he'd said filtered through her mind.

I don't think you should go through this alone. I don't know how many friends you have you could approach to talk about what happened to you. I think you should… If you wanted to talk to someone, I would be willing to listen… But I think you need to talk it out, because I believe this will eat you up. Maybe even some sort of group therapy counseling might help.

The thought hit her hard. *Group therapy. Yeah, that's the ticket. I won't know anyone there, and I can begin to get some of this off my chest. Hear some other stories of what other women have been through. At least it will help pass the time until Dillon calls me again. That is, if he calls me again. Who knows?*

Suddenly energized, Celeste moved from her couch to her kitchen table, where her laptop sat open. She hit the power button and waited for it to boot up.

Once her computer was on, she opened an internet browser. She typed in several searches, including Group Therapy, Rape Victims Group Therapy, and Battered Women Group Therapy, along with her current city and state. Several suggestions came up, but the closest one was called Safe Haven.

The name connected with Celeste, and she read more about the group and what they did in the community. The more she read, the more she felt this was the group where she needed to start. She found the number for the coordinator of Safe Haven, entered it into her phone, then hit send to connect with the coordinator, Sylvia Bissell.

CHAPTER EIGHT

When Sean Asherton—the man parading as Dillon Carmichael—left Celeste's house, her front door closed faster and harder than he had intended. He quickly turned on his heels, almost reopened the door again and stuck his head in to apologize that he'd slammed the door on her by accident. It's not as if he was in a hurry; he had straight-up lied to Celeste that he had a client waiting for him. He was playing the game as he'd always played it.

Rule Number One: Always give yourself an out, he thought. *But I don't want an out. I want to be back in there on the couch with Celeste. I want to make love to her again and wrap her up in my arms. Jesus, I sound so sappy. A romantic at heart, I guess, if I know my true self.*

He was nearing his car when he stopped; he looked back toward the front door again and considered returning to her. It would be so easy to turn around and walk to the door. He could explain to her that even though they barely knew each other, she was more important than this meeting and that he had just canceled with his client until sometime next week. But then, he thought better of it and shook his head against the notion. He'd never done that before and didn't know how it would play out. He was playing it safe until he worked everything out with Thomas.

I have to talk to Thomas about this. I'll make it up to Celeste at a later date. I have to talk to Thomas about her and the game. God, he's not going to like it, but tough titties on him. It's been fun while it lasted, but I don't want to play this game anymore, not when Celeste is involved.

He turned back to his car, stepped into it, and cranked it up. Putting it in reverse, he exited her driveway and headed toward his and Thomas's house.

During the drive, Sean's mind was utterly consumed by Celeste. He kept grinning like an idiot schoolboy who had been on his first date and was now dwelling on that memory. And it wasn't entirely about seeing her naked and mentally reliving what it felt like to move within her. This time, he was focused on her smile, the memory of her amusing half-laugh, her sense of humor that had him smiling and laughing; it had been so long since a woman made him laugh out loud. He thought of the beauty of her hands, how she grasped her beer bottle—her pinky wrapping slightly around the bottom as she tilted it up to drink its contents. He loved the perfection of her manicured nails, the fact that she used very little make-up, how she unknowingly always swiped her hair around one of her ears—sometimes the right but mostly the left—and that she was the most stunning woman with which he'd had the pleasure to spend time with and been lucky enough to make love to.

Talk about being smitten, he thought. *She has my number.*

There were a host of other reasons he liked Celeste and why she drove him crazy in a good way; those drifted through his mind as well. But the main reason he wanted to be out of the game and with Celeste, the one reason that had just dawned on his mind, was that it was the first time he had been with a woman who didn't remind him of his mother. And that was a huge reason. He couldn't think of her right now. Didn't want to think of her. He pushed his mother's memory out of his head.

Sean reached for his cell lying in his seat and found Thomas Bonnomer's number. He was about to punch to connect when he thought better of it. If he had the nerve, he could tell Thomas what was bothering him and what he wanted to do. He could let that be it, spin this bitch around, and see Celeste. See if she wanted to spend more quality time with him today. This was the moment of reckoning for Sean; he thought about it very seriously but then decided against it. He pitched his phone into the passenger's seat and pressed the gas pedal harder to get home more quickly. He shook his head in frustration at himself and his decision.

The main reason he felt this way was that this was too big of a conversation to have via cell phone. It was just like breaking up with your significant other. If you were going to do the action, it should be done in person, face to face. Don't be a little bitch about it, taking the easy way out and telling them over the phone or in a text. Fucking man up, stand there in front of them and tell them to their face you don't want to be with them. That was what Sean was feeling now; he didn't want to be a little bitch, but he did need to hash this out with Thomas. It would happen as soon as he got to the house. Maybe it was too soon to even consider, but hopefully Celeste was going to become an essential part of his life.

When he pulled into the drive, his heart leapt with excitement at seeing Thomas's truck in its usual spot. He whipped into the driveway and killed the engine. He stepped out of his car, shut and locked his door, headed up the three stairs to the front door, and went inside.

The aroma of some Mexican food or another was ever-present.

Thomas must be making tacos, Sean thought.

In the foyer, he placed his keys and wallet on the little wooden table inside the doorway. He was gripped by a sudden panic over the argument he was sure would ensue.

Thomas's voice called out. "Sean? That you?"

Of course, it is, you idiot, he thought. *I'm the only other guy who has a key to this place.* Instead, he said, "Yeah. It's me."

"You hungry?" Thomas asked. "Making some quick tacos with Mexican rice."

Sean moved to the kitchen. He decided to play along as if nothing was going on right now, then get serious in a few minutes when the right moment came up.

He stayed silent. *Funny how we always wait for the right time,* Sean thought. *But the right time never presents itself in break-up situations like this. You might as well just come out with it.*

Entering the kitchen, he said, "No, I ate with Celeste earlier at Jasper's. Not too hungry right now."

"You mean you didn't make it with her to where you worked up an appetite." Thomas gave a deep chuckle.

"No, I made it with her," Thomas said, a little miffed. "I made it with her just fine. Was there ever a doubt I wouldn't?"

"Touchy, touchy."

"I made it with Celeste in several crazy ways. I'm just not hungry right now."

"You did?"

Sean nodded.

"Awesome! What is your final tally for this first session?"

"I don't know. I haven't calculated my points yet. My mind wasn't on the point system while I was fucking her."

"Why not?"

Here goes nothing, Sean thought, then said, "I am more or less into her, so..." He trailed off, feeling the conversation was moving into untested waters, and he didn't know how to approach the main crux of the discussion.

"Well, which is it?" Thomas asked. "Are you *more* into her or *less* into her?"

Sean gave Thomas an irritated breath through clenched teeth as well as a *fuck you* look. Thomas knew exactly what he meant. "What do you think? More," he admitted.

"I see," Thomas said as he turned his back to Sean and stirred the taco meat sauce bubbling in the pan. He added some spices, grabbed a handful of chopped peppers, and tossed them into the mix. Thomas was quiet for a long time.

Sean waited. He'd given him the news; he didn't know what else to say.

Finally, Thomas said, "Seems like there's more to this conversation that you're not telling me."

Here's my perfect opportunity. Time to drop the hammer, Sean thought, then he said, "Truthfully, I don't want to play this game anymore."

"I see," Thomas said again, then fell unnaturally silent.

Wanting to be done with this conversation, Sean blurted out what was on his mind. "This first time with Celeste did a number on me. I don't know; I felt something different with her than all the other girls I've played. I want out completely, you know, from playing this competition with you. If you want to continue with it, that's fine." It wasn't, of course, and he shook his head at even suggesting that, but he was speaking off the cuff. He wanted out. This game was wrong. He knew that. He'd always known it. They both knew it was wrong, but one day, they started and just continued to play.

He pushed their history out of his head and focused on the current conversation. Just as long as he could be free, that was the main thing right now. "You can find another competitor to play the game with you, but I can't do it anymore. I won't do it again. I'm out."

Sean couldn't tell what was going on with Thomas. He was still facing away and hadn't turned to him during the exchange. Thomas only stirred his meat sauce, but Sean saw his head shaking back and forth methodically. Sean had been friends with Thomas long enough to know that when that happened, there was a slow build to anger being mentally channeled behind his eyes and beneath his skin.

Thomas lifted his head from the saucepan, turned to where he was halfway speaking over his shoulder, and said in an even tone, "The game's not over, buddy. You dropping out before we know who the real winner is?"

"I don't care about that. You can be the man, Thomas. I don't care about getting more points than you because of what I did to some girl. I know, in the past, that we've had some close battles. But I'm done."

"So, you want out?" Thomas asked.

"Yeah. I was hoping to stop playing. Well, not *hoping*; I'm just letting you know I'm stopping the game, at least from my side. I want to go out with Celeste and not worry it will be over after two or three more dates. I'm done. I quit."

"We have way too much invested in it."

"Invested? No, we don't."

"Yes. We do. We have so much *time* invested in this little game. A lot of fucking time. Ever since that night we got drunk at Bowen's Landing; it was all a joke, with us telling stories about our past and jokingly creating this game. You want to throw that time away. *Our* time."

"You make it sound like we're like..." He didn't want to use the word, but he tried it on for size, "... *dating*... or something. Like we are an item, or we have this special relationship, or something going on between us."

"Oh, we do, bud. We have an extraordinary relationship. We're partners in a unique crime. Multiple crimes, as it turns out. We take turns heightening women's emotions by them almost being raped so the partner in crime, the *wingman*,"—he threw a hand over, indicating Sean—"can score some sweet pussy. Cut through all that lame-ass bullshit with women. We've tagged some major ass doing it this way rather than just chatting them up at some fucking bar. Yeah, we have an extraordinary relationship. And now, because you got your dick sucked from some pretty chick, you want to end this shit with me. I don't fucking think so."

"Well, you better get used to it because Angel Domingo was the last fucking chick I'm going to fake-rape for you. I will try and keep something going with Celeste Baker for however long she will have me."

Thomas stood there, smiling at his comment.

"What?" Sean asked.

Thomas laughed, "That's really cute. What do you think, Celeste whatshername? Baker, is it? What would she think, say, or do if she was informed that what you two shared was all a big fucking lie? That you participated in her attempted rape just to fuck her good a couple of times."

"You wouldn't."

"We've played this rape game with random women for a long time, Sean," Thomas said. "There isn't much I won't do. If you don't finish this game with me, Angel, and Celeste, I'll find a way to make sure she knows how fake you are to her in this beginning relationship you two have going."

"Are you stupid? She would go straight to the police with that information. You would go to jail."

"And so would you," Thomas said.

"You're bluffing," Sean said.

"Am I?" he said, shrugging.

Sean stood there dumbstruck. He didn't have the mental capacity to try and figure out what Thomas was threatening. It would be the worst idea ever hatched from his nimrod brain.

Thomas continued, "I never thought it would come to this, but since you're playing hardball, I can play hardball too."

"What do you mean?"

Thomas was already pulling his cell phone from his back pocket. He tapped some buttons and slid his fingers across its screen; then, he tapped the screen again. Thomas flipped his phone around to face Sean.

Sean naturally reached for it, but Thomas pulled the phone away. "I'm not handing over my phone. Just watch."

Sean dropped his hands again, then turned his focus to the screen. He heard the panicked screams from a woman on the video playing. The outcries were familiar to him. Once he processed what he was watching, a terrifying feeling bubbled up inside him. He knew immediately what this was.

In the video, he saw himself in an alleyway on top of a woman. It was Angel Domingo, the latest woman he had sexually assaulted, so Thomas could step in, stop, and fight him, and be the hero to this woman.

The video was filmed from around another corner—Sean's eight o'clock—where Thomas was waiting for the perfect moment to rush in and save the day.

The panicked feeling within him bloomed even more, and he became nauseous. Watching himself threaten her with their knife and slice the buttons on her clothes, manhandle her, slap her, even punch her—

He closed his eyes and turned his head away from the brutality. "Turn it off."

"What's the matter? You don't like to watch? You're not into voyeurism?" Thomas chuckled at the look on Sean's face, but flipped the phone back to himself and killed the video. He swiped a few times to get it back to the main screen, then shoved it in his back pocket.

"You filmed that? How could you?"

"Hey, we're pretty good friends, but the way all this happened and we hatched this game, I had no idea how long you might want to do this. And if you decided to bitch out on me or threaten to turn me in, I needed insurance. I believe I have it too."

"You're such an asshole."

"Maybe; but I'm protecting my ass. And that's not the only one. I have videos of all the other women you've assaulted. A nice little sexual assault collection featuring Sean Asherton."

"Where are they?"

"Oh, no. You don't think I'm just going to hand them over to you, do you? They're my insurance policy. Don't worry about them. They're on a jump drive, safely hidden away in a place where no one will find them. I'm the only one who knows where they are."

Thomas turned back to his taco sauce, then having a second thought, he turned back to Sean and said in an even, calculated voice, "Do you think I'm bluffing now?"

"But if you give that to the police, you'd be in just as much trouble as me for filming it."

"No. I can send it anonymously. I know you would probably bitch up and tattle-tale on me. But do you think they would even look at me twice when they have all these videos of all the women you've assaulted? I'll play dumb to filming them. I'll claim I found the jump drive. All the evidence would be on you, Sean."

Sean knew Thomas had him to a certain extent. It was too big of a gamble for him to push this issue. "You're such a dick."

"That's *Big Dick* to you, buddy. And you're a pussy for wanting to leave in the middle of our game and break up the good thing we have going. No one *ever* fucking leaves me." Thomas thought for a moment; he turned and faced Sean. "I'll tell you what I'll do to make this even more interesting; you have to beat me this one last time. Beat me, be the man, and you can step away. And I, in return, will keep quiet about the whole situation. You can go live happily ever after with your fucking Celeste bitch."

"Why do I have to beat you? Why is that so important to you?"

"To keep you honest with the game and to me. You could claim a certain amount of low points and say…" Thomas lowered his voice and took on a fake, pouty voice, "Aww, oh shit, it wasn't in the cards this time. You the man, Thomas; you win." He dropped the charade and continued, "If I keep you honest, you'll be trying to get the highest points. If you don't, we will continue playing the game with some other bitches. But I'll tell you this. I gained an ass load of points this go around with

Angel. Emphasis on the ass. Angel let me do all sorts of crazy shit to her tattooed body, and she loved every minute of it. I got to tie her up and choke her out as I was fucking her deep. She was a freak of nature, that one. She even begged for more too. So, you have your work cut out for you, my man. Better get busy tapping that ass and plugging that pussy, 'cause the game is still on."

"How do I know you're telling me the truth about all that? You could admit to all these high points in our point system, and then I'll constantly be trying to one-up you for the rest of my life."

"Haven't we always been honest about tallying our points?" Thomas asked.

"Sure; I mean, I have."

"And I have too. Why would we change now? I trust you. You trust me. At least on the point system."

Sean thought everything out for a few moments. "I don't think either of us will ever trust each other again. There is no trust between us now."

"Whose fault is that?"

Sean didn't have it in him to argue this subject anymore. He was tired of it; tired of the game and just wanted it to be over. Instead of answering Thomas's question, he said, "I'm going to do this just to beat you at your own game and because I want out fair and square. But I'm telling you, I have a horrible feeling about this."

"It's nothing a taco can't cure," Thomas said, smiling and holding up a spoonful of sauce. "You sure you don't want some? I have plenty."

"No, not after forcing me to continue in this shitty game we've been playing."

"The game *we're still playing*, right, Sean?" Thomas corrected.

"For now, I guess. Until I burn you with the point system."

"That's the spirit, Sean. That's what I love to hear."

CHAPTER NINE

Celeste Baker sat inside an old gymnasium belonging to Duke Street High School. She sat within a circular group with twelve other women. The women on either side of her were angled away, talking with others in the seats next to them.

Yeah, that's okay. Don't mind me. I'm just the new girl here, Celeste thought.

When she arrived, she had tentatively stepped into the gymnasium, unsure what to expect. A few of the women greeted her, and there was small talk. She met Sylvia briefly, and Sylvia was ecstatic to have her in the mix. Sylvia pointed to the refreshments table and told Celeste to get anything she wanted and to grab a seat; then, Sylvia turned to talk with another woman about the details of this afternoon's meeting.

Once Celeste had a coffee, she grabbed a seat. The other women settled in around her, but they either checked their social media, chatted with the others they knew better, or just sat in a trance, waiting for the show to start.

Duke Street High School had been closed for about two years. The state had released funds to allow a new—more significant—high school to be built a couple of miles away because there had been a higher influx of students in recent years. With it being closed down and only used at various times, an old, athletic smell had settled within at least this part of the gymnasium.

Celeste gazed over the women in the circular hub; they ranged from their twenties to—at best guess—their early fifties. The women were from numerous different backgrounds; no one ethnicity dominated the group. Celeste was about to inspect the women again but noticed Sylvia checking her watch, waiting for the precise moment to start.

Sylvia looked up, raised her hand to distract the women from their conversations and phones, and said, "Hello, everyone." Her voice echoed a little louder in the gym. "If we could all settle, we can get started."

The twelve other women stopped conversing, straightened in their seats, and turned their attention to the speaker.

"For those of you who are new to the group, my name is Sylvia Bissell. I am the section leader and coordinator of this chapter of Safe Haven. At this facility, you will find that many women come from different abusive relationships. It's not just physical abuse; there is also mental and financial abuse. I want you to know that everyone *here* is here because they are going through, or have gone through, something traumatic. If you are new today, and I see a couple of new faces, I urge you to speak up. Speak out about what is hurting you today. Don't remain a victim of what has happened to you. You raise your voice here, and telling your story begins your healing process. And if you speak up, I know it will encourage others who want to remain silent and invisible to speak up. You will be helping them heal. Because overall, that is what we all want this time to be: a time of healing. So, if we could go around the room and introduce ourselves and maybe tell one interesting thing about ourselves, that might ease everyone's nervousness about being here. It will help us all open up to each other. Can we start with you, Gabriella?"

"Of course. We always do," Gabriella said and added a small laugh. "Hi, everyone. My name is Gabriella Santana."

Everyone but Celeste said in unison, "Hello, Gabriella."

Gabriella smiled and continued, "Or you can call me Gabby if you like that better. I answer to both. I know a lot of you have heard my story. I won't repeat it now; I'll allow the newcomers to speak. I'll be happy to share my story again if any new ladies want to hear it. I don't mind talking about it. It would be better to let some new ones get some healing time in. I'm still healing. Things are so much better than they were. I have also taken steps to go back to school. I am focused on psychology and everything that goes with becoming a counselor, like Sylvia here. She has been mentoring me and pointing me in the right direction." Gabby smiled and looked around the room.

Everyone in the room clapped at the news.

"I think that's wonderful, Gabby," Sylvia said, then added, "Bravo."

As the applause died, Gabby continued, "Well, ever since I've come here and sat under your teaching, I've grown and just recently realized that I want to do what you do. I want to help people, mainly women, because you have helped me so much."

Celeste saw Gabby nod as she looked at the floor in the center of the circle. She appeared to be checking her mind to ensure she'd said everything she needed. Finally, she nodded again, looked up, and around at the other ladies. "That's all from me for now. But stay tuned. There's more to come."

"Excellent, Gabby," Sylvia said. "Thank you for sharing that with the group. That is spectacular news. Okay, Cynthia."

"Hey, everyone, my name is Cynthia Barnes."

Again, everyone chimed, "Hello, Cynthia."

Celeste, almost getting the hang of the way this meeting was going, also said, "Hello, Cynthia," but she started a half-step after all the other women. The word 'Cynthia' was stated after everybody finished the two-word sentence, and it hung out there as an echo, and a few women turned briefly to Celeste.

Celeste threw her hand up in a half-wave and muttered a pitiful apology for being so out of sync with the group.

Cynthia continued as though there hadn't been an interruption. "I like to…."

Celeste's mind drifted to her own thoughts.

Jesus Christ, I screwed the pooch right out of the gate on that one, didn't I? Does it help you to talk it out to a bunch of strangers? Jesus, why did I even decide to come here? The attack only happened a few days ago. It seems so long ago, but not enough time has passed to share with these women. Wouldn't giving myself some time to deal with it first be better than just coming in here and spilling my guts to all these girls? What the hell was I thinking?

"Celeste?" Sylvia asked.

Her spoken name caught Celeste off guard, and she realized the head honcho was talking to her. She came out of her blank, open-mouthed, dazed look and glanced at the host.

Sylvia looked down at the clipboard in her hands, double-checking to ensure she had the correct name. "Am I saying that right? Celeste Baker, isn't it?"

Celeste glanced around the circle at the women already staring back at her. She looked to Sylvia again. "Ah, yes, that's me. Hi, I'm Celeste Baker."

"Hello, Celeste," the group said in unison.

Celeste gave a nervous little laugh and a quick wave of her hand. "Um, hi. You caught me off guard. I was sort of… reliving what happened to me a few days ago. So… sorry."

"What did happen to you?" Sylvia asked, pouncing on the end of Celeste's statement, finding it might be a perfect segue into today's group therapy.

"Well, I wasn't raped, thank God for small favors, am I right?" Realizing this was a weird thing to say, Celeste quickly continued. "But I was *almost* raped. Got a real shiner from it. You can barely see it now, but the cut is still there." She threw an index finger to her face and pointed out the cut high on her cheek.

"I almost got stabbed, and my knees got pretty fucked up. I mean," Celeste coughed, then said, "Um, messed up. It was pretty terrifying, actually. I haven't slept much the past few nights because that man kept invading my dreams and followed through with what he did in the alleyway there… you know, in my dreams. But luckily, he didn't get me then. So that's a good thing, I guess."

"Well, that is certainly great news. Would you like to go ahead and share your full story with the rest of us?" Sylvia prompted.

Celeste wasn't expecting to go first; that was the last thing on her mind. "I don't want to intrude. I've never done this sort of thing before. I don't know what to do. I certainly don't want to impose on anyone coming here longer than me."

Sylvia held out a hand to stop the excuses, and in a soothing voice said, "Celeste, it's okay. I know you're scared. Everyone here is or has been scared like you the first time they came to one of these open meetings. They can be a little intimidating, but I can assure you, no one here will have a problem if you tell your story first. This is a safe place. This is *Safe* Haven, after all. Tell us your story."

Celeste looked around the room at the expectant, smiling faces. A few of the ladies nodded to let Celeste know it was okay for her to speak her mind, and a few more even started clapping their hands in unison and chanting Celeste's name. "Celeste. Celeste. Celeste. Celeste."

"Okay-okay-okay," Sylvia said, motioning with both hands for the women to settle. "Let's not put too much pressure on Celeste. She may not be ready to relive those moments quite yet."

"No, it's okay. I don't mind starting if everyone's cool with it. I just thought everyone would introduce themselves before confession time happened." Celeste looked around the room one last time.

All the women waited expectantly for Celeste to continue. Feeling encouraged by her warm welcome, Celeste was hopeful this might be some good therapy. A thought even drifted through her mind that she wished she'd come to group therapy sooner. She took a moment to focus on where in the story to start, then said, "Well, the whole situation caught me off guard. Guess it always happens that way. I was guilted into being nice to some homeless guy who seemed down on his luck. I gave him some money to help him out, and he suddenly pulled a knife on me and forced me into an alleyway."

Celeste continued with her story, filling in as much detail as she could remember. She told them of the knife he'd shown her, about the intricate detail of it, and how proud he seemed of it. She shared how vile his words were and how they cut deep into her psyche, even though she didn't repeat any phrases. She told them of the horror she felt in the initial assault and the vulnerability she experienced when her clothes were ripped open. She told them about the anguish of knowing he was about to force himself into her body, and the genuine relief when her savior pulled the attacker off her. She zoned out as she relived the event again, staring into the middle distance of the circle, not looking at any of them, just focusing on getting her story out in the open. She glanced to her left or right to make quick eye contact with some of the women, but she always returned her attention to the floor as she confessed her horrific story.

Once Celeste finished telling her nightmare, she came out of her focused area on the floor and looked around the room again. Glancing at each woman, she didn't know what reaction to expect. A little applause, maybe, or head nods of approval that she had been brave enough to share her story. But what she saw were confused faces. Some women stared blankly at her. Others were looking between her and another woman sitting on the other side of the circle. She couldn't read what their faces were relaying to her because she had never done this before. All Celeste knew was it was an adverse reaction to what she should be receiving.

Celeste followed the women's gazes and focused on the woman who sat directly opposite her. This woman had kept to herself and focused intently on her phone before the session began.

She was beautiful and alluring. The word 'badass' came to Celeste's mind. She wore a lot of black, dark jeans and a rock band T-shirt that proclaimed her love for the band, Tool. Black low-cut leather boots and a black leather jacket—now hanging on the back of her chair. A Goth vibe radiated from her. She wore lots of dark eye makeup and black fingernail polish. The woman had unique, tattooed sleeve artwork covering both arms to set off this look. It was the kind of tattoo work that was ingeniously thought out. This chick took her time with the message her tattooed sleeves were saying, and they blended entirely up and down both of her arms. She looked bad as hell, intimidating. Her face was set in a cold, hard, accusatory look directly at Celeste. Her eyebrows were twisted in confusion and her mouth set in disapproval.

Pissed was the word that came to Celeste's mind.

Celeste looked back at the leader of this pack for guidance on what to do next.

"Did... I... did I say something wrong?" Celeste asked.

Sylvia was about to answer her with a calm reply.

"You kidding me?" spat the tattooed chick.

Celeste looked back to the woman in dark attire across from her. She was leaning forward now.

Celeste was taken aback by her verbal attack. "I'm sorry. What?"

The dark woman said again, as though speaking to a slow-minded child, "I said… Are. You. Fucking. Kidding. Me? Did you hear me *that* time?"

Celeste used her hand, tapped herself on her chest, and asked, "You talking to me?"

"You're damn right. I'm talking to you. I'm looking right at you, aren't I?"

Sylvia held one hand out to the tattooed woman and one over to Celeste to calm the apparent beginning quarrel. "Angel, please. Let's give Celeste a moment, and we can all get to the bottom of this."

"Get to the bottom of what?" Celeste asked. "I don't understand."

Angel ignored Sylvia's request and held her black-nailed finger up to Sylvia to silence her, then she swung it toward Celeste and pointed accusingly at her. "You think you can just come in here and retell someone else's story? Have you ever been here before? When did you hear *me* tell *my* story? Did you think you could just copy it, put your little spin on it, and recite it? What is that? Verbal plagiarism? You trying to get attention or something?"

"Angel, please," Sylvia snapped, trying to add calmness to the situation. "Let me handle this!"

Sylvia's firmness took some of the fire out of Angel's accusations, but not all of it. She continued but in a lower voice. "That was low. Even I wouldn't stoop that low, and I'm a big-time bitch."

Shocked almost into speechlessness, Celeste looked back at Sylvia and said, "I… I don't understand."

Angel wasn't through. She turned to Sylvia. "What kind of battered women, rape help clinic are you running here, *Sylvia*?" Angel stood, snapped up her oversized purse, and looped it over her head. The bag's strap hung diagonally across her body. She turned again and jerked her leather jacket off the back of the chair. She huffed under her breath as she turned back to the group and said, "Having someone come in here and rehash the same fucking story that happened to me." She addressed Sylvia again. "If this is the type of help you're running in this joint, count me out. Take me off your attendance sheet. I won't be back."

Angel turned in place, then kicked the front part of the seat so it slid a reasonable distance across the polished gym floor. Angel flung open the gym door; its click and release were loud. The door squealed open as Angel walked through, then slowly closed behind her.

Silence poured into the room as the door's echo faded. The heads of each woman turned to the others for the correct reaction they should put on their faces from what had ensued.

Sylvia began, "I am deeply sorry that this happened."

"What *did* just happen?" Celeste asked.

Cynthia Barnes, sitting beside Celeste, leaned over and said, "I'm not a regular. I come here when I can. A few weeks ago, Angel was the first-timer and told her story. Your story is amazingly similar to what she told us. I mean, very similar down to the details of the chain etching on the knife and the color of it, the camouflage jacket, and the guy—a good Samaritan who stopped the attacker. The guy also lent Angel his jacket and offered his phone number to check on her. It was a little weird how closely your stories related. Not saying you copied hers, but I understand why Angel is so upset."

"Well, I didn't steal her story to get sympathy from anyone here. There are much easier ways to get attention. Whatever *Angel* is accusing me of would take too much time and energy. I have much better things to do with my time and life than that." Celeste turned and addressed the group. "Is that what all of you think I did?"

The question came at the wrong time, and the women's faces were caught with different looks from the situation.

Sylvia was still trying to figure out what had just happened. There was a delay with her answering for the group. "Of course not."

Celeste didn't believe Sylvia's words. Their looks said it all. "Oh, wow. Unbelievable." She stood abruptly. "If all I'm going to get is an accusation from all of you, and you don't believe my story at face value, then this was a huge mistake and a bad waste of judgment on my part."

Sylvia stood and said, "Celeste, please. I think this is all a misunderstanding."

"Save it, Sylvia," Celeste agreed. "You know, I misunderstood you to say this was a *safe* place and that I might find help at *Safe Haven*. Coming here was nothing but a waste of my time. I regressed in my situation."

Just as Angel had done, Celeste also kicked the seat of her chair in frustration to get it out of her way. It slid nicely across the gym floor.

"There," she said, pointing to the chair and her action; she turned back to the women. "That's me copying Angel." She moved to the double gym doors and pushed one side of them open. Again, the door's loud click and squeaking protest accompanied her exit. She kept walking and never looked back.

CHAPTER TEN

Celeste was sitting in a booth at the Skyline Diner, trying to calm her seething spirit. She needed something bad to eat; she craved it, as she had when she was out with Dillon. Comfort food was one of the main things to help her through life's disappointments. And the situation a few days ago, plus the shit moment that just happened, was a significant disappointment. She only ate crap food when something bad happened to her or when she was ultra-worried about something.

Angel Whatever-the-fuck-her-last-name-is. Who is she to accuse me of copying her story? It happened to me. *Did they even think that maybe that bitch who stormed out copied* my *story from me?* She shook her head. *No, that was a stupid notion. My incident just happened, and hers was a few weeks ago. It was already told to those ladies. Whatever. It doesn't matter because I'm never returning to Safe Haven again.*

She was sitting near the back, nursing some hot coffee, surrounded by the different aromas wafting her way from the kitchen area. A mixture of steaming fries, scrambled eggs, sausage, cheeseburgers, and buttered biscuits. That was the beautiful aroma of comfort food.

Her phone vibrated from within her purse. She retrieved it and glanced at the number. She didn't have the number programmed in her phone, but she recognized it as the digits belonging to Sylvia Bissell from when they had talked earlier.

"What the hell does she want?" Celeste asked her phone. *She probably had to end the meeting early tonight because of the big blow-up, and she's trying to find out if she can help save me. Yeah, don't worry yourself over little me, Sylvia. I'll get through everything just fine without you and your fucking group therapy.*

The waiter—a guy who looked younger than the legal age for public work—came and took her order: a ham and cheese melt with steak fries. Then he retreated to input it into the kitchen.

Celeste had just taken a long sip of her coffee when a large item banged off the wooden backing of the booth seat across from her. There was a hint of black as the thing dropped onto the seat itself. The loud sound startled Celeste, and she jerked back from the rim of her coffee cup. Across the small table, the tattooed Goth chick from the group meeting slid into the seat uninvited next to the purse she'd just flung into the booth.

As Angel settled, she asked, "Mind if I join you?" The voice had a haughty air behind it, a bit of seething mixed with a reluctance that she had to be here and have this conversation with Celeste.

Celeste was immediately on edge and lowered her cup to its saucer. She sat back in her seat, leaning away from the woman. She had no idea who she was and what she would do or say, but goddamn it, she wasn't going to be a victim of her bullshit. Not after today's fiasco in the gym, not after Barry Sloan's bullshit in court earlier this week, and certainly not after her attempted rape.

Celeste held her hands up to protest her seating herself without permission. "Yes, I do mind," Celeste said. "This is my table."

"Put your hands down," Angel said. "You're not going to do anything. You don't have any reason to be upset. On the other hand, I am very disturbed at what I heard today in *my* fucking support group."

"It's not your support group. You didn't start it; you're not running it." *The nerve of this bitch.* They stared each other down, neither one blinking, then Celeste asked, "What do you want me to say? If you're looking for an apology, you can forget—"

"How about you tell me why the fuck you stole my story? That story is personal to me. You always verbally plagiarizing people?"

"Get a new term; you used that one back at the gym. I don't know you. I had never seen you before until I came to Safe Haven."

"You sure about that, bitch?"

"Can you please stop calling me *bitch*? My name is Celeste. How would I know your story? I've never met you!"

"You sure about that, cupcake?" Angel said, picking the first word she could think of other than 'bitch' to call her.

"Do you know something I don't?" Celeste asked.

"You tell me?"

"Tell you what?" Celeste's voice was taking on an edge. She was close to losing it with this woman. She wanted to lean over the table and give her a bitch slap from hell. But she remained motionless, waiting for Angel to make the first move.

"Why is your story the same as mine?" Angel asked.

"I've never heard your goddamn story, so how the fuck could I know?" Celeste growled. *Yeah, light this bitch up. I'm not going to contend with her and continue taking it on the chin verbally,* she thought. *I can fight too.* "That is if yours is the same as mine. How do I know *you're* not making all this shit up to gain attention?"

That accusation seemed to squelch the fight in Angel. "I'm not doing this to gain attention."

"Well, I'm not either. As I told the group after you left, why would I take time out of my busy day to memorize all the details about your stupid story to tell it at some group therapy meeting? That's dumb. There are so many other creative ways to get attention. Why don't you tell me your story so we can both stand on the same page?"

A look crossed Angel's face. She clearly hadn't thought it through before firing on all cylinders at Celeste. "All right. That's a good point. I'll tell you."

"Great. I'm *soooo* looking forward to story time with you."

The waiter returned with Celeste's ham and cheese plate with steak fries. She noticed the cook hadn't skimped on the steak fries, which made Celeste inwardly happy. She popped one into her mouth. It was borderline hot and had the perfect amount of salt.

At least one good thing is happening for me this week, Celeste thought.

As Celeste ate her dinner, Angel began her tale. Her story was pretty similar to what Celeste had told the group. A man in a camouflage jacket sat shaking a cup filled with a few coins. Angel had stopped, dug a few dollar bills from her jeans pocket, and stuffed them into the cup. Before she could walk away, the man stood quickly, pulled a knife on her, stuck it into her side, and forced her down an alleyway he was seated near. Angel further explained that she went into the alleyway to give herself time to figure out when to fight back with a surprise attack rather than get shanked on the street. To Celeste, it sounded like it was in a different area than where she was attacked. Angel explained this alleyway was rarely used, but it was a shortcut from a small parking area to the back of the Main Street Shoppes.

Angel said, "Guess he thought he could rape me quick and be gone before anyone came through there."

Angel explained her assailant was a bit smoother than the vile abruptness of Celeste's attacker. Angel's guy told her not to make any quick moves because he said she might get cut. Instead of ripping her clothes, he started cutting the buttons from her button-up shirt. He slipped the knife between the cups of her bra and sliced the fabric that held them together. At one time, Angel fought back as Celeste had done, but Angel couldn't knock the blade free from his hand. Angel said she was gut-punched and slapped in the face, then eventually punched to kill that fight within her. When all her clothes had been sliced enough for him to "get at my goods"—as Angel put it—that's when the stranger came along. The two men had a swift and hardcore battle. It looked like it could've been pulled straight from the movies.

As Angel explained how the fight went down, the word 'choreographed' came to Celeste's mind. She thought back to how clean the fight was between the two guys involved in her assault. 'Choreographed' was a term that hadn't previously registered with Celeste at the time of her attack; she hadn't latched on to it then with everything that had happened.

Angel said the new guy got the best of her attacker who then ran off. Angel's guardian helped her, lent her his jacket to help cover her up, and walked her to her Jeep. He was a gentleman of the highest order, a knight in shining armor, so kind and attentive, her savior. Talk about calling the police was turned down, then he quickly scribbled his name and phone number on a scrap piece of paper and told her she could call him if she ever needed to vent or talk to someone about what happened. Angel said she would consider it, then got in her Jeep and drove away. Where Celeste had gotten angry with her rescuer, Angel more or less sloughed it off and mentally told herself she was strong enough to get through this attack alone. Because, after all, she hadn't actually been raped.

"Okay," Celeste said with a defeated breath of air, "I have to admit, our stories are quite similar, but I promise you I've never heard you tell it. And the story I told in the meeting is exactly how it happened to me a few days ago. I still have a barely bruised and cut eye to prove it. See." She pointed.

Angel acknowledged it and nodded.

"And you should see my knees. They are fucked big time. There has to be something more to what has happened to us?"

"What are you thinking?" Angel asked. Her pissy attitude had abated during her story, as though telling it, with Celeste listening intently, was helping calm her spirit. She was warming to Celeste, and the realization that they may be linked in some odd way was coming through.

"I don't know," Celeste said. "Hear me out. Go with me on this weird and crazy thought process of mine. Do these two guys know each other? Is the same guy going around trying to rape women, you know, like a serial rapist?"

"I'm with you," Angel said, "But how does this guy know to be in the exact place where our assaults happened? This savior guy comes around and interrupts our attacker just as he's about to shove his dick into us. It can't be a coincidence that these incidents happen similarly, can it?"

"I've never really thought about it until just now," Celeste said.

"Guess I should've considered that before I jumped down your throat during the meeting."

"That would've been appreciated," Celeste said with a sheepish smile. "Truce? At least till we figure all this out?"

"Truce," Angel said. "But after we figure all this out, I'm not going to go back to being mad at you. I'm sorry I went ape shit on you back at Safe Haven and then here. I was really fucking pissed."

Celeste shook her head. "I was pissed about you also. I thought you were going to kick my ass in front of everybody back at the meeting."

"That wasn't my best moment. Sorry."

"Forget about all that. No harm done." Celeste laughed as she relived the zestiest of Angel's demeanor. She pushed her plate to the center of the table. "Want some?" She rolled her fingers open toward comfort food goodness, presenting them to the woman across the table.

"Really?" Angel asked hesitantly. "You don't mind?"

Celeste shook her head. "Not at all; go ahead."

"Awesome." Angel reached and snagged a fry and popped it into her mouth. "Thanks. Oh, wow, these are good."

Celeste eyed Angel as she chewed. "You're the type of person who is very passionate about events that happen in your world." Celeste grabbed a steak fry, slid it through a dollop of ketchup, and shoved it in her mouth.

"I am."

"Very passionate." Celeste smiled, then asked, "So, did you call him?"

"Who?"

"The good guy in your—for lack of any better words—*life event.*"

"Oh, him," Angel said, disgust tainting her voice. "Yeah, I called him. The next day actually."

"You called him?" Celeste asked. She was a little surprised even though she'd done it.

"Well, I didn't know there was another incident like mine until tonight, so nothing seemed fishy or weird about this whole scenario."

"I see your point, but why him instead of coming to the group?"

Angel leaned forward and folded her arms on the table. She lowered her voice slightly and said, "Okay, I'm going to level with you. I'm going to tell you something about me, and if you ever repeat it, I will hunt you down and literally kick your ass."

Celeste was slightly startled at her statement, and her eyes widened in conjunction with Angel's threat. She couldn't gauge if she was joking or not. "Okay. What's this big secret?"

"Look at me."

Celeste did. "I see you. What about you?"

"No, look at me. I'm the type of person who doesn't let shit get me down, no matter how bad it gets. I'm a badass to the core of my being, or I try to look as much like a badass as possible. The clothes I wear, these bitchin' tattoos—it's all a fucking act." Angel started laughing at her phrasing.

"What's so funny?" Celeste asked.

Angel's laughter died away, but she continued to smile in amusement at herself. "I always attack first. Defend my territory. For lack of a better phrase, because I hate the song, I come in like a wrecking ball, then sift through the rubble after I demolish everything. I approach problems guns blazing. I'm like, kill them all, let God sort them out type of person; always have been. That's just me; take it or leave it. But really, I'm not as hardcore as I make myself out to be. I'm just upholding an image."

Angel paused, not knowing if she wanted to venture farther with a part of herself, but then gave a 'what the fuck' shrug of her shoulders. "And, big secret here, even though it may be TMI… I love the hell out of sex and love being pumped hard by some hot stud. I even love being choked hard and tied down. Bondage sex… makes me horny as hell. But when someone I don't know pulls a knife and forces themselves on me and possibly *in* me, someone I do not consent to, it does something to me on the inside. I needed someone to talk to and didn't want to talk to other women in group therapy. Women can be so judgy sometimes. I wanted someone who was there, who experienced it with me but wasn't connected to anything. He was a separate entity, or so I thought. Someone who seemed like he gave a shit about what had happened to me to a certain extent, I guess."

"I understand. I get it. It was the same with me," Celeste said, nodding. "So, what happened?"

"What, with Aaron?" Angel asked.

An instantaneous grim chill, as though someone had walked up behind Celeste and slid an ice-cold beer down the length of her bare back, caused Celeste's eyes to widen in alarm. She sat up straighter and looked over at Angel in sudden fear.

Angel was confused by Celeste's abrupt movement and the look on her face. "What?" she asked.

"His name is *Aaron*?" Celeste asked.

"Yeah, Aaron Brakefield. Why?"

"Uh, I don't know, but I suddenly have a big hunch about something."

"Well, spit it out. Don't keep me in suspense."

Celeste said, "I think it's odd that Dillon used the name *Aaron* when we were out on our first date."

At the sound of the word 'Dillon,' Angel looked up at Celeste as though she were a fortune teller who had just read the grimmest news in the crystal ball or the cards that lay before her.

"Did you say *Dillon*?" Angel asked.

"Yeah, why?"

"Because when I met Aaron for the first time, he asked me to talk about the attack to get it out of my system. He said, 'Tell me what you're really feeling. Pretend I'm the guy who attacked you. Pretend I'm, oh, I don't know… let's say his name is *Dillon*, for instance.' Did he ever say anything like that?

"He said the exact same thing to me," Celeste confirmed. "Except *Dillon* used the name *Aaron* when suggesting I open up to him about my attacker."

"Fuck me. Are you serious?"

Celeste and Angel thought about that for a moment; then, they started speaking almost simultaneously, just ahead of Angel, but they said the same three-word sentence: "They're working together."

Angel slapped the table, reacting to this eureka moment between them. It sounded loud in the small diner. The silverware rattled and clinked together. She leaned forward and hiss-whispered, "Motherfucker."

"Why would they do that?" Celeste asked, but she received no answer.

Angel and Celeste sat there in wide-eyed wonder. They couldn't wrap their minds around the possibility.

Finally, Angel said, "Whatever they're doing, it's one huge, fucked up game they're playing. They're messing with our emotions!"

"I don't know how Dillon could do that to me," Celeste said. "That is if he's doing the same as Aaron did to you. And it seems likely that he is. He sounded so honest."

"Wait," Angel said. "You *called* Dillon like I called Aaron? You didn't tell me that."

"Oh, right, I guess I didn't."

"So, we both called our knight in shining armor." Angel thought about her statement for a few moments. "Let me guess. You guys went back to your house, not his. You had sex with him, didn't you?"

"Yeah, I did. I guess that was their plan all along. Running back over all this in my mind, I've had this nagging feeling that even though the conversation over lunch was great, he was so courteous, and the sex was fucking amazing but there was a slight *fakeness* to it. I kept hoping that fakeness would turn into something real."

"Yeah. It was the same for me, too," Angel said. "Perfect moments, but they didn't entirely feel genuine. I can understand your use of the word *fakeness*."

"Okay, so it's not the same guy who saved each of us as we originally thought," Celeste said. She turned abruptly to her purse and pulled out the piece of paper that held Dillon Carmichael's name and phone number. She slid it over the table as Angel popped two more fries into her mouth.

Angel picked up the fragment of paper to study the name and phone number closer. "Yeah, it can't be the same guy. I think we determined that already because this handwriting is different." Angel dropped the paper Celeste had given her, grabbed her oversized purse, and rifled through it. In her small wallet, she finally found the paper with Aaron's name and number penned on it; it was tucked between a few dollar bills. She jerked it out, happy she'd found it. "Ha, here is it. Little bitch was hiding from me." She dropped the scrap of paper on the table, placed her dark-painted, slightly chipped index fingernail on it, and pushed it across the table's surface for Celeste to inspect.

Picking it up, Celeste studied it for a moment, then looked up again. "Huh, that's interesting. Something else jumped out at me about your story, and I was wondering if you could describe it to me again in better detail."

"What's that?" Angel asked, taking another ketchup-covered fry from the plate. "These are so good."

"Tell me about the knife he pulled and used on you."

"Why do you want to know about the knife?"

"From what we've said in our stories, we've mentioned the knife, and the chain etching; just want to know if it's the same knife or two different ones."

"Okay, well, it was one of those basic blades that fold up, or it looked like it could. I think it was the kind that has a little lever for your thumb to go on to flip it open real quick. Guys think they're so badass with shit like that."

She dropped her voice into a dumb-sounding redneck voice, giving a few shallow swipes in front of her, "I'm gonna cut the shit out of you, motherfucker." She dropped the act, gave a laugh, and shook her head.

"So lame. I didn't even see him open it. It was out of his pocket and at my side. I know he didn't use his other hand to help open it, because his other arm held me tight. Anyway, it was just your regular blade. Um, a dark blade, now that I think about it. But it looked extremely sharp. Maybe serrated, I can't remember exactly."

"What about the handle? Did you get a good look at the handle? It had those chain etchings on it, right?"

"Yeah, he showed it to me," Angel said. "He was damn proud of it. Like it was the next best thing compared to his dick. Maybe he looked at it like it was a second dick. Men are fucking obsessed with weird shit like that. I think the handle had a brownish, or maybe blackish, hue, a little bit of gold. It's been a few weeks since it happened. It did have chain etchings wrapping around the handle and the top part of the blade. Not like a real chain. It was just the way it was designed."

"A chain. I thought you touched on that when you told me your story." Celeste said.

"Why do you ask?"

"I think it's the same blade. My attacker threatened me with a chain-wrapped knife also. Either that, or they're using two different but identical blades. When I fought him, I was lucky enough to dislodge it from his hand. It flew off somewhere in that back alleyway."

"Ooh, you go, Michelle Yeoh, kicking ass, taking names. Wait!" Angel froze in mid-chew of the last few fries she'd eaten. It looked like the epiphany lightbulb flipped on inside Angel's mind and was burning bright with an idea. "You think the knife could still be down there in the alleyway?" Angel asked.

"I don't know; it could be," Celeste said, a look of sudden hopefulness crossing her face. "It's been three to four days now. Surely he's thought of going back down there and looking for it." Even though her answer was negative, she was getting excited.

Angel was getting pumped as well. "We could get lucky. It would have their fingerprints on it. Take that shit to the police."

"Hell yeah." A new fire was kindling inside Celeste. "I don't know what good it will do, but it may help us in the future."

"You know, Aaron's fingerprints are the only ones that'll be on it," Angel said.

Celeste shook her head, "I don't know; maybe Dillon's prints will be on it as well since it's a knife they both used. Well, that *we think* they both used. They may have the same type of knife; there could be two knives. Let's hope it's just one knife, and they take turns each time they attack a new girl. That is if we're right about this hunch, you know?"

"What are we waiting on? Let's go."

"I'm waiting on you to finish my steak fries," Celeste said, smiling.

"Well, I'm waiting for you to pay for this food," Angel joked.

"I'm going to," Celeste said as she rummaged in her purse for her wallet. She pulled out her debit card and grabbed the check. "Will you ride with me to the... you know, to the site?"

"Sure, if you're cool with me doing so."

"It would be a relief to have you there. I don't think I can even step back into that alleyway by myself. But if you're there, maybe I can drum up the courage."

"We can talk about it on the way," Angel encouraged. "If you feel like you can't, once we get there, then I can do it alone."

"You'd do that for me?" Celeste asked.

"Of course. We have to get to the bottom of this. But it's not just for you. I'll be doing it for us. I'm not getting my hopes up. The knife may already be gone. Dillon or Aaron may have already come back around for it. Somebody else could've already found it. But let's go check it out."

"Sounds good to me."

Celeste and Angel slid from their booth and headed to the register near the front doors to pay. In a few short minutes, they would hopefully find another small piece to this big, crazy puzzle they were piecing together.

CHAPTER ELEVEN

Sean cracked the door to his room and came out as quietly as possible. He was thirsty and headed to the kitchen to get a beer or soda; he didn't know what he was in the mood for until he saw it.

The smell of Thomas's Mexican cuisine was still in the air but had faded.

Sean didn't realize he was doing such a goofy tip-toe movement—so as not to disturb Thomas in his bedroom—until he broke from the hallway into the living room. Thomas wasn't in his room as expected; he was seated on the couch reading a book. It was too late; Thomas had already frozen in mid-sip, peering over the top of his coffee cup and noticing Sean's over-the-top, cartoony walk.

Sean abruptly brought his weird walk back to a normal one again.

Before taking his sip of coffee, Thomas lowered his cup just enough to ask, "What the fuck are you doing creeping around the house like that?"

"Oh, hey, Thomas. I was going to get a drink."

Thomas busted out with a little sarcastic chuckle at Sean's crazy movements. "Okay, but why the theatrics? Just go get it." He gave a half-laugh snicker that trailed off, took another sip, then set his coffee cup on the table in front of him. "You're not bothering me."

Sean saw Thomas reading a bluish-colored book with a cow on the front cover. The big-screen television was on, but the sound was muted. A basketball game was on, but Sean took no notice of who was playing.

He continued into the kitchen quietly but mentally kicked himself for the embarrassing charade that just happened.

At the refrigerator, he opened the door, looked in, chose a can of Sprite, popped the top, and guzzled half the can. It felt so good going down.

"Fuck," he whispered to himself. "I looked like such an idiot just now. What the hell am I going to do? He's got me in a bind."

"You say something?" Thomas said from the other room.

"No."

"Could've sworn you did."

"Nope, nothing to you. Just talking to myself in here."

There was an underlying tension between them now. To Sean, it seemed like Thomas was enjoying the little magnifying glass he had Sean under. *Thomas has me doing some out-of-character shit,* Sean thought. *Well, it's not going to last for long. Wonder what he would do if I pressed the issue with him and told him to either let me out or go to the police with the names of all the women we've played our game with. Fuck, they would string us up in the center of town if I did that. I'm not that good of a gambler to bluff him like that; I would cave. And he's got all that evidence on me, too. Jesus, I just want out. Maybe I'll call Celeste and see if we can do something later. I could be with her; forget the game stuff for a while. Just spend some time with Celeste and clear my mind of this shit. But if I do that, Thomas will want to know point systems and what crazy sex we had, when we may not even have sex next time. I swear, he gets off on all that. I've got to get out.*

He turned, moved back through the living room, and headed to his room again.

"Hey, man," Thomas said, stopping him before he got to the hallway.

Sean stopped and turned to Thomas, saying nothing.

"You still mad at me?" he asked.

"Ahh, no, man. Not at all. Why do you ask?"

"Just checking to see if it's still good between us."

"Sure; yeah, don't worry about that. We're solid."

"Good, 'cause I would hate to know you're harboring any shitty feelings toward me just because I still want to play the game."

"No, I'm good. It's all good. I'll be seeing Celeste soon, and I'll fuck the shit out of her in a bunch of crazy ways. Get a bunch of points and blow your score out of the goddamn water, then move on with whatever relationship I can with Celeste."

"Cool. We'll have to double sometime."

Sean gave him a half-laugh and said, "Why would you even say that? We could never double, and you know that. You're not even seeing Angel anymore because you broke it off with her when it was obvious you two were perfect for each other. We should dump the game. You go back to Angel; I move on with Celeste." He paused for a moment, then said, "You can never meet Celeste. She knows your face, dumbass. You're her rapist."

"Whoa, whoa, whoa, I did not *rape* her. Don't ever accuse me of that shit." He smiled at Sean. "You saved her from getting raped, remember? So, have you tallied your points so far?"

"No, damn it. I haven't; not yet. Why are you so keyed up about my points? I know you're ahead and have your ending tally. I'll be closing in on your final number very soon."

"Yeah, right. Dude, you haven't even scored the second time with Celeste yet. You're dreaming, man, if you think you're going to surpass me this time—"

"Okay, Christian Grey. We'll see."

They smiled at each other. An understood truce was agreed upon with a smile. They both knew Sean was pissed at Thomas for making him continue with the game. Deep inside, Sean was plotting how to sever their relationship altogether. He had witnessed a side of Thomas Bonnomer he'd never seen before, and he didn't like it. But for now, he would continue acting the way he had done in the past, keep playing the game, and carry on like Thomas wanted him to. For now.

Thomas asked, "When are you hitting that next home run with Celeste?"

"I'm planning an impromptu outing. I'm in the mood for sushi tonight, and I'm going to spring that 'if you aren't doing anything tonight and want to hang out, I'll be at Irashiai at 7 pm' bullshit on her. I'm going to let her *come* to me," Sean said, letting the innuendo hit, hoping Thomas picked up on it.

"Nice. That one always works on the ladies."

"No sweat if she doesn't want to meet up tonight. I'll work my way into her pants another time." He inwardly cringed talking about Celeste like that. It wasn't his nature to talk dirty about women he was falling for. He was only doing it for Thomas's sake, so he wouldn't get suspicious while he tried to figure out alternative routes for his life.

"Yeah, that's a good plan with a great track record. That was your suggestion way back in the day. I've used that one several times too. Less threatening for women. We've picked up a lot of ass letting them come to us."

"What about the third time?"

"What about it?"

"What's the plan for that one?"

"I haven't even thought that far ahead. What's the fucking rush, man? This isn't chess. Relax; I'm on it. I have to see what happens on the second encounter to maneuver into a successful third date. I thought I had taught you that too. Quit rushing me."

"Just want to make sure you're still committed to our game."

"I'm going to get through the second meeting for now."

"Okay. Good luck, man. Let me know how it goes."

"Oh, it'll be going, that's for sure." They were silent for a moment. Sean took another long swig of his Sprite, thinking Thomas was going to say something else, but he noticed his head had lowered, and he was reading again from his book. Then a thought came to Sean from nowhere. He didn't know why he'd thought about it but figured it was because his mind was thinking ahead, as you did in chess, to finagle a way out of his current rock-and-hard place scenario. "Oh, by the way," Sean said, grabbing Thomas's attention again.

"Yeah," Thomas said, dragging his eyes away from the page he was reading.

"Since I'm going to be kicking your ass in the contest for the last time, I'm going to need to get my knife back from you."

"I already gave that back to you. Didn't I?" Thomas asked.

"No, you certainly did not give it back."

"Huh, I thought I did."

"You thought wrong. Where is it?"

"It's in the camo jacket. I'll get it for you. Calm your tits."

"Like, go get it now."

"Dude, I'm reading. I'll get it to you in a few."

"No. You'll get it for me now, asshole. If I'm going to continue to play the game, you're going to get my dad's knife. You don't get to make all the fucking rules of this game. Go get it. Now!"

"Okay, Jesus fucking Christ," Thomas said, slapping his book shut and kicking his legs off the couch. "Calm down."

"Damn right," Sean said, then took a seat on the edge of the couch, fuming. He swiped his hands through his hair and drank his Sprite while he waited for Thomas to retrieve the knife.

Thomas walked down the short hallway to the coat rack by the door. He shoved his hand into the right-hand pocket of the camouflage jacket and fished around, but nothing was inside.

A slight panic flared out from the center of his body.

He grabbed the jacket, pulled the left side around, and shoved his hand down inside its pocket in case he had accidentally placed it there for some crazy reason. It was empty as well.

More panic seized his body. *Where the fuck was it?*

He searched all the pockets of the jacket, but they were also empty. Thomas stood there, frozen, and thought hard about where it might be. His mind drifted back to the alleyway, and the image of Celeste's hand hitting his wrist struck him like a sledgehammer. His neck snapped back, as though the memory of Celeste had punched the inside of his head. He saw the knife being dislodged from his hand and spinning off into another area of the back alleyway. He didn't remember where it went, but the sound of it hitting the ground and sliding into something metal rang out from his mind.

He was instantly afraid and stepped away from the coat rack. He turned and walked back into the living room, where Sean sat watching the muted basketball game.

Sean glanced at Thomas and said, "That's an odd look."

Thomas's head gave a little jerk as he surfaced from his deep thoughts and turned his attention to Sean. "I, um, don't have it."

"What, the knife?"

"Yeah."

"Where the hell is it?" Sean asked, a slight panic rising in his voice.

"Celeste knocked it out of my hand right before you came on the scene. I'd forgotten about it since that had never happened before. I guess it's still in the alleyway somewhere. I was so in the moment of the fight and playing my part that I never went—"

"Thomas! It's been three—no four fucking days—since the incident. How could you be so irresponsible? Get your ass in gear, get back down there, and retrieve it. It has our fingerprints on it. You never know who may find it and what they might do with it."

"Yeah, I'll get right on that," Thomas said but kept standing there.

"Like right fucking now, Thomas," Sean said and took a step toward Thomas. "You need to go now."

Thomas backed up a step or two. "I know. I was thinking."

"Yeah, well, time is of the essence. Get moving."

"God, I'm going, all right? Don't be such a dick."

"Me? Being a dick?" Sean was appalled at his accusation. "You're the one forcing me to continue playing this shitty game when I don't want to! You're the fucking dick in this situation. I can't believe you forgot about the knife. And after she knocked it out of your hand? And you don't think about it until now!"

He dropped his voice, "Fucking. Idiot." It wasn't that Sean didn't want Thomas to hear him; this news had just taken the wind out of him. To Thomas, he said, "You've gotten lazy. Go to the alleyway and get the knife; it links me to all the shit we've done over the past years."

Thomas said nothing but walked back down the hallway to the foyer table. He snatched his keys and wallet and shoved them into his pockets as he snagged the camo jacket from the coat rack. He slipped it on as he opened the front door, then slammed it behind him as he left.

The slamming door reminded Sean of how he'd left Celeste's house earlier that day, and that memory brought a deep regret that he hadn't stayed longer with her after they'd made love.

Sean returned to the basketball game, drained the rest of his Sprite, then crumpled the can, pretending it was Thomas's head.

Fucking idiot!

CHAPTER TWELVE

When Celeste and Angel arrived at the location where Celeste was nearly raped, Celeste parked in a small parking lot on the opposite side of the road, facing their destination. They were a few car lengths away from the alleyway opening. It was a self-conscious thing with Celeste not wanting to be anywhere near where the assault took place.

They sat there for a long moment; Angel waited, not saying a word. They both looked toward the alleyway entrance.

Finally, Angel said, "You know, I could go look for it myself, so you don't have to go back there. Then we could get the hell out of here."

After another long moment, Celeste said, "No, I can do this. I should be the one to do it. But I would love it if you came, too."

"Are you kidding me?" Angel said. "I wouldn't dare let you go into that alleyway alone. You let me know when you're ready."

The immediate sound of the driver's side door opening made Angel look in Celeste's direction.

"Now," Celeste said. She had already stepped out of the car and slammed the door on the heels of that single word.

"Well, shit. Give me a little bit of warning next time," Angel said, quickly opening her own door and stepping out. She closed her door and caught up with Celeste, who was already on the sidewalk and walking to the mouth of the alleyway like she was on a mission.

They were still on the opposite side of the street from the entrance. Angel thought Celeste was approaching it in a roundabout way. It looked like she was going to jaywalk by cutting directly across the street and straight into the alleyway.

When they both arrived at a position perpendicular to the opening again, Celeste stopped. An overwhelming fear gripped her body and mind. It wouldn't allow her to cross.

Again, Angel stood there beside her and looked on with Celeste. After a moment, Angel leaned in and said, "Hey, why don't you hold my hand as we do this? You can hold on to me as I take the steps across the street and into the alleyway." She paused for a moment and started snickering as a thought came to her. "We can pretend we're lovers. That would be kinda funny, wouldn't it?"

Celeste was still in her little world of painful memories, but she laughed slightly at Angel's suggestion. She didn't answer her, but she did slide her hand onto the other woman's arm, already positioned like a groomsman ready to walk a bridesmaid down the aisle.

Celeste stepped between the cars, her knees rubbing against the bumpers. She was headed straight out into the middle of the road without looking.

Angel had to jerk her back quickly in time for a vehicle to pass.

The driver blew its horn, and the car continued.

Angel shot the driver a middle finger salute. She looked both ways for them; finding it clear, they crossed to the other side.

With how Celeste acted, Angel half-expected her to stop at the entrance and go no further, but Celeste continued into the alley and down the corridor without hesitation. Right before she entered the alleyway, Angel heard Celeste take a deep breath, pull her shirt over her nose, and step forward. Angel thought she was psyching herself up, but as Angel entered, a step or two behind her, she realized Celeste knew this alleyway reeked with the stench of rotting food. She had prepared herself for that stench again. Realizing this too late, Angel was also hit with that ungodly smell.

"Oh, Jesus Christ, what is that?"

Celeste didn't answer but walked with a hurried step. "Here," she said as she took a hard left—the building on their left cut at a ninety-degree angle. There were two heavy-duty trash cans sitting close to the wall.

"Those weren't here before," Celeste said through the shirt that covered her nose and mouth. She walked about fifteen feet further into that space. "Right here is where he tried... to, um... tried to—"

Celeste couldn't finish; she couldn't bring herself to say that four-letter word. She looked down and stared at the area. She saw where she'd been dragged backward; there was still a hint of blood on the asphalt from her knees being ripped open. Her body shivered in phantom pain as she relived the event.

Knowing Celeste wanted to find the knife and get the hell out of this place, Angel stepped over to her into the spot where she was currently standing. "So, you were here, right?" she said, facing her.

Celeste was taken aback at first but then realized what Angel was doing.

"Yeah."

"So, the knife was in his right hand, and you hit him with your right or left hand?"

"My right."

"So, if you hit him here and it went flying, then..." Angel pointed and then moved in the direction she was pointing. She continued with her previous thought where she had trailed off. "That would mean it would've landed somewhere over here."

Celeste followed.

Angel was now holding her shirt over her mouth and nose. She kicked a few waterlogged cardboard boxes out of her way. They sagged inward.

"I remember the knife hitting something metal," Celeste prompted.

They moved a little further away from where the assault had taken place. Two more heavy-duty trash cans were there. Angel looked down at their base and saw they were made of a metallic material.

"Hey Celeste, I think it may be under here," Angel said as she moved the trash can away from the wall. She grimaced at having to touch the filthy containers.

Nothing.

"Fuck," Angel said. "I just knew it would be under this one."

"What about the other one?"

"Fifty-fifty shot. It has to be."

Celeste moved over and helped Angel manhandle the second trash can away.

"Bingo," Angel said as the trash can moved enough to reveal the open-bladed knife.

"You're kidding?" Celeste said unbelievingly. She thought her attacker would've already returned for it, or someone else would've found it.

"See for yourself."

Celeste smiled down at the evidence, even though her body was afraid of it. She saw the open, dark metal knife with brownish-blackish chain highlights that wrapped the length of the handle. The chain etching also ran the top ridge of the blade. It was the same piece used in both of their assaults. It was a well-made and beautiful knife. Celeste and Angel could not understand why the man hadn't returned to retrieve it.

"You have a tissue or something? I don't want to mess up the fingerprints with mine if we decide to have the police or someone dust it for prints."

"Wait. Shouldn't we call the police and let them handle it?"

Angel looked down at the knife glaring back up at them. "I don't know. I don't think so. I think there's too big of a chance that Aaron, or maybe even Dillon, would come back down here looking for it."

"It's been a number of days. If he hasn't come by now…" Celeste's words faded away.

"It's too big of a chance to leave it. Besides, I would bet the cops could say we planted it here because you never reported being attacked. You suddenly calling the cops and telling them of the sexual assault that happened three to four days ago, and the perpetrator left his knife down here for that long? I think they would consider this a fishy story, even though you would be telling the truth."

"Sure. I see your point," Celeste said, and she flipped open her purse and rifled through it for something to put the knife into to protect the evidence. She found a small pack with a few tissues still in it and figured it might be best to pick it up with one of those, as Angel had suggested.

Celeste handed Angel the tissues. "We might need to pick it up with one of those. You know, preserve the evidence."

Angel took the tissues from Celeste and held them while Celeste continued looking in her purse for something better.

"Wait. Will this work?" Celeste asked as she held up a small plastic bag. It was the bag Celeste used for her essential oils.

"Yeah, that'll work. That's pretty much perfect."

Celeste peeled apart the bag seal and dumped the vials back into her purse. She handed the bag over to Angel, who had stooped to retrieve the knife.

Angel inverted the bag, using it like a glove. She picked up the knife, leaving the blade open, then flipped it inside out, capturing it inside. She resealed the bag, turned to Celeste, then held the knife up between them at eye level. "Got these two sons of a bitches, now. This has to be the same knife used in my assault. It can't be a coincidence that we were both assaulted by two different people, both owning the same type of knife. They have to be working together. We got those shitheads now."

"Yeah. Let's get out of here before someone else comes back here."

"Yeah, we'll figure out what our next steps are going to be."

❧

When they were back at Celeste's Crosstrek, they sat there for a moment in silence, looking back toward the alleyway from which they had come. They were both a little surprised that they had even found the knife. A new, relaxed relief had come over them both. Mentally, they knew they weren't imagining things; a new reality had set in.

Celeste said, "So what should we do now?"

"Not quite sure, to be honest with you. Do you know anyone at a police department? A friend or a relative who could try to get fingerprints off it? If they get a decent one, maybe they could run it through the fingerprint database, see if these assholes have a record."

"Is that how they do it?"

"I don't know," Angel said. "I do binge-watch a lot of *Criminal Minds*, *FBI*, *NCIS*, and those other acronym shows. It's the way they do it, so I guess. I can't be too far off, can I? Most of the time, they don't solve crimes easily with fingerprints; that's boring TV. Even though that is the most basic of all criminal mistakes. Criminals aren't that stupid anymore. At least, not on those shows."

"But we're talking about Dillon and Aaron," Celeste prompted.

"That we are. They might not be as bright as they think they are. Not retrieving their knife was really dumb." Angel looked at the knife in the bag again, then lowered it to her lap, wrapped the rest of the plastic carefully around it, and handed it over to Celeste.

"And not wearing gloves during an assault," Celeste said, taking it. She placed it in her handbag.

Angel continued, "The way those shows are written these days, they solve the crime in much cleverer ways." She screwed up her face as she considered her choice of words. "More clever?"

"I know what you meant."

"Yeah, it would be crazy cool if we could get this thing analyzed."

Celeste said, "But if we did that, it would be in the police's hands. And I think we should figure out everything we can about these assholes and deal with them ourselves somehow."

"Yeah?" Angel asked, a little shocked at Celeste's words. "I would've never pegged you as a chick out for vengeance, but I like where your head's at right now. What're you thinking?"

"If we give this over to the police, we run the risk of an investigation trailing off into weeks, if not months, when we know exactly what's going on; or close to it. The investigation could go cold after so long or just get lost in the shuffle of police paperwork. Also, I don't want it to get out that I was assaulted. I'm protective of what people think of me."

"Me too," Angel agreed.

"I'm also protective of what's done to my body. And I may not be showing it outwardly, but I'm pretty pissed about everything that has happened in the past few days. And I've got a huge score to settle with those assholes who did this to us."

Throughout this exchange, Angel had turned and watched Celeste's mannerisms intently. "Sure. You're right about that." She turned away and looked back out the windshield once again.

A flash of various greens caught Angel's eye right before a big truck passed on the road in front of her. Her heart dropped to her stomach at the sight of that green, and fear engulfed that void. After the truck cleared her vision, she took a longer look at the green hues to ensure she didn't imagine anything. The green hues that made up a man's camouflage jacket looked familiar to her.

"Fucking hell!" Angel exclaimed.

"What?" Celeste asked, jerking her head up, tearing her gaze away from the knife that rested at the top of her purse. Angel was looking out the car window and in the direction of the alleyway. Celeste turned in the direction she was looking.

"I don't want to alarm you," Angel said, "But that's Aaron right there."

"Where?" Celeste asked, but she was looking everywhere except near the alleyway opening.

Angel triple-pumped her pointing finger against the window as she said, "Right. Fucking. There."

Celeste finally honed in on the figure in the camouflage jacket, and her blood ran cold. Her heart started beating faster as she stared ahead at the figure. She was suddenly back in the alleyway in her mind, with Aaron standing over her, pawing at her body. She had to focus hard on calming herself. "Oh my God!" she whispered.

Angel's anger softened. She turned to Celeste. "I don't want to say anything."

Celeste was locked in on the figure. Her eyes were staring at him, but they looked more like they weren't seeing anything in front of her. She sounded as though she were talking to herself, as if trying to convince herself that what she said had not happened. "That's… that's the guy who… who tried to rape me."

"I know; I had a feeling since we think these guys are working together."

Celeste looked away. "I'll be all right. Just give me a moment."

"Of course. Why the fuck is Aaron here? He told me he was moving; should've been gone weeks ago. They're playing us both as we've already figured out. They use the same knife. It's the same camouflage jacket. There's probably more to their little outfit we haven't figured out yet. But we don't need to. We know just enough. What kind of game are they playing?" Angel asked.

Celeste replied, "The worst fucking game imaginable, especially for a woman."

Celeste looked forward again. She and Angel both fell silent and stared as Aaron neared the alleyway they had just left.

Aaron pulled out his phone and glanced at it. Pretending to tap out a text or find a number, he glanced up and down the sidewalk. He waited for a couple holding hands to pass, then he quickly moved into the alleyway and put the phone to his ear.

"What do you make of that?"

"He's trying to play it cool," Celeste said. "That's pretty much what he did the day he assaulted me—checked to see if the coast was clear. But this time," she said, holding out the plastic bag that held the encapsulated knife, "he's going to try and find this."

"He's not going to have any luck."

"Yeah, 'cause we have it now."

"Aren't you glad we took it now instead of waiting on the police?"

Celeste nodded.

"Talk about your perfect timing," Angel said. "That was close."

Angel abruptly grabbed the car handle and said, "I'm going to talk to him."

Celeste instantly snapped her hand over and seized Angel's arm. "No, wait. Don't do that. He'll get suspicious if he sees you in this area."

"No. He won't suspect anything. I happen to be walking around down here, and we just happen to bump into each other."

"I don't think it's wise to do that. We should wait and think this out."

"I gotta see what this fuckface is up to. He doesn't come into our lives and do whatever the hell he and this Dillon guy did to us and get away with it. I have to try and milk him for information. What is it you said, wanting to get all the intel we can and deal with these assholes ourselves? This is me dealing with him, to a certain extent."

"I still don't think it's wise. Not without thinking it through; there isn't time to do that. We need to play it safe."

"Not this time. If we're going to figure out what's going on and why they're doing this, we both have to be assertive. I have to do this. I'd never forgive myself if I didn't at least try."

"Okay… if you have to. Just don't let him know you and I know each other."

"Who are you?" Angel asked with a slight smile to let Celeste know she was way ahead of her on not giving away any information now that they were partners in crime.

CHAPTER THIRTEEN

With a quick scan of the sidewalks and finding the coast clear, Thomas Bonnomer, AKA Aaron Brakefield, turned and quickly entered the alleyway. He tried not to look suspicious but felt he might be failing miserably. True, he was in a hurry; he had to find that goddamn knife. If he didn't, Sean was going to kill him. Well, maybe not kill him, but he would be majorly disappointed in him, and that was more than Thomas could bear. He hated disappointing people; they tended to leave him when that happened. Sean was already talking about leaving; their friendship would dissipate when he did. That always cut deep. He couldn't allow that to happen.

Sean's dad's knife wasn't expensive. Sure, it was different, a slightly rare make, but it could be found on the Internet if you looked hard enough. It had little or no monetary value, but its sentimental value for Sean was priceless.

I'll never know why we used that knife in the first place, Thomas thought. *If it's so special, why didn't we buy a new knife similar to it?*

Further down the alleyway, he turned the corner and stepped into the space where he'd forced Celeste up against the wall. He smiled, reliving the event over in his mind. He saw the fear in her wide, coffee-colored eyes and felt the panic he'd brought to her athletic body.

He relived the moment he stood before her, choking her against the wall. That right cross had surprised the fuck out of him, and it had knocked the knife out of his hand.

Bitch! She was a feisty one. I was too busy worrying about when Sean was going to show up. The asshole was fucking late. I was too distracted.

He saw it flash in his memory and caught the angle at which the knife left his hand. He stepped in that direction and judged the approximate area where the blade may have landed. He started there and kicked some water-logged cardboard boxes out of his way.

Nothing.

He moved in a circular pattern away from the vicinity of where the knife may have landed.

Thomas found two trash cans pulled away from the wall during his search.

What a dumbass. The asshole that took the trash out should know even back here, the cans would be better pushed up against the wall out of everyone's way.

Not wanting to touch them and get any grime on his hands, he kicked them back against the filthy wall, so he could look under them for the knife. He found nothing but asphalt, random soggy restaurant menus, and miscellaneous rotting food scraps.

"Fuck," he said under his breath. "Jesus, it reeks down here."

Thomas found an old broomstick leaning against the wall, the kind where one end had a metal twist formation, allowing it to screw into a replaceable mop head or a wide push broom. He used the handle to move some old empty boxes out of the way and lift a few wooden pallets, hoping the knife might have slid underneath. He used the mop handle to pilfer through anything the blade may have slid in or under, but he found nothing.

He checked and re-checked the area, but after a long, thorough, and exhaustive search, he found no hint of a knife.

"It's some motherfucker's lucky day," he muttered in disgust, thinking some pimple-faced busboy had come across it and pocketed it.

Probably the same asshole who pulled the trash cans away from the wall, he thought. *That's what I would've done. Someone must've found it; it has to be. God, I can't keep looking for the damn thing. It simply isn't here. Fuck, I have to tell Sean, and he's going to be royally pissed.*

Thomas spun and pitched the mop handle in a random direction. It bounced off the dirty wall and clattered to the pavement.

"Fuck!" he said a little louder, stormed out of that area, and moved back up the alleyway.

He was so deep in thought over the disappointment of not finding the knife, he didn't see the woman standing by the wall outside the alleyway. He'd just stepped back onto the sidewalk and headed back the way he'd come.

"Aaron?"

Hearing the name 'Aaron' didn't immediately jump out at Thomas because Sean and Thomas hardly ever used their aliases when talking to each other. Thomas kept walking at first, but something was familiar about the name; it was more the sound of the voice calling out that spiraled through his mental funk. He looked up, slightly confused.

The woman called again, "Aaron Brakefield?"

Thomas realized who was talking to him and his heart began trip-hammering inside his chest. Angel Domingo. This was the woman he had rescued from being fake-raped by Sean, the woman he'd slept with three times already. This was the woman he'd already broken up with because three rounds signaled the end of the game. He'd lied to her about moving out of town. He shouldn't even be here after what he'd told her a few days ago.

Shocked with the realization of how serious of a mistake this moment was, Thomas wheeled around faster than he'd wanted to. He knew guilt was painted all over his face, and he worked hard to tweak it into a look of pleasant surprise.

Angel waggled a finger at him. "I thought that was you." She was cool about it. There was an air of confidence in her movement. It was like she knew something he didn't. He didn't like it.

"Hey, Angel," Thomas said, trying to play it as cool as she was, but his nervousness was kicking in. There was a lot of shit on his shoulders right now.

"I was walking on that side of the sidewalk,"—Angel pointed across the street—"and I saw you duck into this alleyway. I didn't know if it was you, but I thought I would check it out. I'm so glad I did. Are you okay? You look frustrated."

"Oh, yeah. I'm good. Fine. Just focused on something, that's all."

"You can imagine my surprise, I'm sure." With a sly smile playing on her lips, Angel continued. "You didn't expect to ever see me again, did you?"

"Well, no. It's not that. I—"

"Or should I say, *I* wasn't expecting to see *you* again? What were you doing down there anyway?" She looked down the alleyway with fake interest.

He glanced guiltily down the alleyway again, then turned back and said, "I… um… I… was… looking for my, uh, wallet."

"Yeah?" Angel said, her voice rising a little with interest.

Is she faking interest, or is that a hint of sarcasm? Thomas thought with a dip of his eyebrows. He didn't like the sound of her insinuations.

"Yes," he said evenly and leveled his eyes on her. "I was looking for my wallet."

His sentence came out that time with a little more purpose. Not knowing where to go with this conversation, he rubbed his face in frustration. A slight pain erupted across his forehead from being punched in the eyebrow and high cheekbone area by Sean when they had their fake fight over Celeste a few days ago.

That's it, he thought. He pointed to it quickly and said, "I guess you noticed my head wound."

"There is a slight discoloration there, I guess," Angel said, downplaying whatever he was getting at. "Did you get into a fight or something?" she asked, a little fake concern coming out in her voice.

"I was in a fight, yeah. A guy was standing near this alleyway and got my attention when I walked past. The guy called me over, pulled a gun on me, and made me come with him down this alleyway. He took my wallet, car keys, you know, everything."

"No, I didn't know that. I haven't talked to you in a couple of weeks," Angel said, letting him know that she knew he was lying. She continued as though nothing had happened. "That must've been scary for you. I've been scared like that before. Did he rape you?"

"What?" he asked; her question had thrown him.

"You think it could've been the same guy who attacked me?"

"No. It wasn't him," Thomas realized what he'd just said. He verbally backpedaled. "I mean, it didn't look like him. I would've remembered 'cause I got a good look at the guy who attacked you that day."

"Your story sounds a lot like how that guy got me back into that alleyway across town, you know?"

"Yeah-yeah. I remember."

"I don't know why you couldn't fight him off like you fought that guy off me a few weeks ago. You kicked that guy's ass, you know, the one who assaulted me?"

"Yeah, well, it was a knife versus a gun, Angel. I sometimes choose not to fight if I think my life might be in danger. I chose not to fight this time because a car and some cash aren't worth taking a bullet for."

"But a girl you've never met *is* worth dying for?" Angel asked. She looked deep into his lying eyes and smiled.

"That day, I saw something I didn't like and reacted in the moment."

"Did you call the police or something?" Angel asked.

"No. I figured it wasn't a big deal since I wasn't injured. After he took my stuff, I thought he might have dropped the wallet and keys back here. I was taking a chance to try to find them, but no luck. He probably dropped them down into a sewer grate somewhere. Asshole. I'll never see those things again."

"I'm sorry to hear that. I hope you get everything cleared up before you move out of town. Shocked to see you around here, though. From what you told me, I thought you had already moved out of town weeks ago."

"It got pushed back a few weeks," Thomas lied immediately.

"Oh, wow, that's too bad. I know you wanted that job."

"I still have it. Just have to get down there to it."

"Well, it was good seeing you again," Angel said, lying herself. "I hope you get all this bad luck you've had sorted out, and have a safe trip to wherever you're going."

Thomas knew it was a bad idea, but after playing the good guy in the game for so long and not wanting to leave on a sour note, he couldn't help but say, "Maybe we could go out for drinks before I leave town." It was out of his mouth before he realized it, and he inwardly cringed at the response he knew would come.

❧

Angel's mind glitched, and she saw red instantly at his suggestion. Her mouth opened, and she was suddenly speaking. "That's a horrible idea. It would be a huge mistake. Are you kidding me, Aaron? You broke up with me, remember? You took a job out of town, if there really is a *job* you've been *hired to go do*." She air-quoted the emphasized words. "You said you were leaving close to *four* weeks ago. Yet here you are, magically standing in front of me. Is there even a job to get to, Aaron? Don't answer that because it's obvious there isn't, and I don't give a fuck anymore. Did you give me that bullshit line about a new job out of town so you wouldn't have to go out with me anymore? If you don't want me, just fucking tell me. Don't be a little bitch about it. Do you think I'm going to go out with you a few more times, get more attached to you so you can break up with me again if you *do* move? Do you think I'm going to let you worm your way back into my pants so you can get a little more of my sweet pussy? The answer isn't just no, Aaron; it's a big 'hell fucking no' from me. I don't want to get drinks with you, and I resent you for even asking."

Angel spun on her heels and headed up the sidewalk away from Celeste's SUV. She didn't want Aaron to see her with Celeste.

"Angel!" Thomas said, calling out to her.

Angel heard footsteps jogging up behind her, and she braced herself for anything physical.

Thomas said, "Look, I know you're angry with me."

Angel stopped and faced him abruptly, "I'm not angry with you. I'm fucking pissed off. I don't believe you when you say you were robbed. I don't believe you when you say you're moving to another city for an out-of-state job. Why can't you be honest with me? What kind of game are you playing with me?"

Instantly pissed at how this conversation had turned and knowing everything she spoke was the truth, Thomas shook his head as a condescending look became evident on his face. "I don't need this shit in my life."

"I don't fucking need you either, *Aaron*. I hope your car stalls out in the middle of nowhere on your way to the new job you don't have in the state you're never going to."

"Fuck you, bitch," Thomas said, turning away from her and heading back the way he'd come.

Angel turned and yelled after him, "You know I'm right, asshole." She was pissed and didn't give two shits if the other pedestrians on the sidewalk heard her.

Angel turned away from him and walked for a few seconds, still fuming. An idea hit her. As she walked, she glanced over her shoulder and saw that Aaron was still walking away from her. Making a quick choice, Angel dashed left to the road and stepped between two cars. Quickly checking the road both ways to see if the coast was clear, she ran across the street and slid between another set of parked cars. She stepped onto the sidewalk and walked back toward Celeste's Subaru. She was following Aaron at a distance, but now it was from across the street. She watched him as he strolled away, his head still shaking, obviously working out in his mind if there was anything else he wanted to say to her.

Aaron stopped mid-step and turned back to Angel.

Angel saw his abrupt movement and ducked behind a car. After a brief moment, Angel lifted her head enough to peek through the car's back passenger side window. She peered diagonally across and out the driver's side window to where Aaron stood in the middle of the sidewalk. He looked around as if she were going to be close enough for him to unload more of his thoughts or feelings onto her.

Had he looked around to talk to me? she wondered. *Had he wanted to get the last word in?*

Aaron looked away from the sidewalk and quickly scanned his surroundings.

Angel ducked back down behind the car she was hiding behind to ensure she wasn't seen. She gave it a few moments, then slowly lifted her head and peered over the lip of the car door and through the windows again.

She saw Aaron look back up the sidewalk. Not seeing her, he shrugged his shoulders and shook his head, then turned and headed back down the sidewalk again. Angel was immediately on the move and walked down the sidewalk toward Celeste's car again. Angel shuffled between the few people on the sidewalk and tried not to look suspicious. She didn't know if she was succeeding on that front, but as long as Aaron didn't notice her, she was good.

As she neared the Subaru, Celeste had a look on her face asking what the hell was going on.

Angel held up her finger to tell her to hold that thought and she would explain everything to her soon.

Angel walked past Celeste's car and followed Aaron for another fifty yards before turning down another connecting street. She moved behind another car for cover as she looked down the road Aaron was walking on. She saw Aaron step into his red Dodge pickup. It was the same truck he'd met her in the few times they had gone out. His truck was parked on that side of the building and in the second spot.

Aaron cranked his truck, pulled out of his parking place, and traveled to the end of the road that intersected Main Street. Seeing nothing was coming, he hung a right and headed back toward Celeste's car and the alleyway he'd just left.

From her hiding spot behind a car, Angel peered out as much as she dared, hoping she wouldn't be seen. As Aaron turned right, she ducked out of sight until he passed, then peered over the hood to get a bead on Aaron again. As he moved away, she stepped away from the car and headed back toward Celeste's car.

They had to follow him and find out where he lived. When she and Aaron had rendezvoused, he always came to her place. She quickened her steps to get back to Celeste but didn't want to draw attention to herself. She could still be spotted on the sidewalk in his sideview mirror if some fast-running movement caught his eye. She had to be careful, but she had to hurry as well.

Something about Aaron still wasn't sitting right with Angel. She wanted to find out exactly what it was. He hadn't been honest with her—they both knew that. She needed to find out the whole story, although she felt she had most of the story from her and Aaron's talk and what she and Celeste had discussed.

When Aaron's truck was far enough away to where he couldn't notice any abrupt movements, Angel sprinted to Celeste's car. She jumped into the passenger's side and asked, "Did you see that red truck drive by just a few seconds ago?"

"Yeah. It was a Dodge, wasn't it?"

"Right. Follow it, but don't let him see you tailing him. We're going to find out where he lives."

CHAPTER FOURTEEN

When Thomas arrived home, he stepped through the front door and placed his keys carefully on the foyer table. He stood there for a moment, absorbed in what had just happened between him and Angel; that conversation had plagued him the whole way home. Something wasn't right about it, but he couldn't figure out what it was.

"Thomas?" Sean asked from the living room.

Thomas looked up from his keys and down the small hallway into the living room. Sean was sitting on the couch with his arms draped over the cushions. Thomas could hear the faint sound of machine gun fire and explosions; Sean was watching an action movie. Sean's head was angled to where he looked down the hallway back at Thomas.

"You okay, man?" Sean asked.

"Yeah," he said, then, after a slight pause, added, "I think."

"You're not very convincing."

"I guess you're right."

Thomas shuffled up the hallway toward Sean, still lost in thought.

"I am right," Sean said. "You don't sound a hundred percent on any of the answers you just gave me. You find my dad's knife?"

Thomas grabbed both sides of the entrance, leaned in, then pushed himself back out again. He braced himself against Sean's reaction. "No, I didn't."

Sean jerked his feet off the coffee table and quickly pulled himself into a sitting position. It was rigid, his butt perched on the edge of the couch. "No? Why the hell not?"

Thomas stood there with a blank look on his face. "I have no idea."

"Fuck!" Sean said in disgust. He snatched his Cheerwine can from the coffee table, took a big tug, then set it down again. He'd gotten another drink from the fridge while Thomas was out looking for his knife. "I don't know why we didn't buy a new knife for this game."

"I've had that same thought myself," Thomas said.

"I can't believe you lost it."

"I'm sorry, Sean. I didn't do it on purpose."

"I know, I know. I wish you had thought to go back and get it after the initiation moment instead of meeting me further down the sidewalk. I don't want it getting into the wrong hands, that's all."

"I don't think it's gotten into the wrong hands."

"You don't know that. You can't know that. You don't even know where it is."

"I think some guy who works at one of those restaurants found it when he was taking out the trash."

"Oh, is that how it went down? A busboy found it."

"Probably. The worst-case scenario is that he saw it and kept it. It's not going to trace back to us."

"But it's my knife," Sean said. He thought for a moment. "No, the worst-case scenario would be Celeste traipsing back down to the alleyway, finding it, and figuring out that it belongs to us. I mean, *me*. Motherfucker!" Sean exclaimed. He stood and began pacing back and forth. He moved to the widescreen and back again. "Both of our fingerprints are on that knife. You know that, don't you?"

That little flicker of fear burning in the center of Thomas's chest since he'd come from the initiation site burned a little brighter. "I know. You're right. That would be the worst-case scenario."

Sean eyed Thomas for a moment. "What the hell is on your mind? You look like you're internalizing something. Like you have more information to share, but you're afraid to tell me. Did something else happen while you were down there in the alleyway? Were the police down there or something?"

"No. Nothing like that," Thomas said, sloughing off Sean's comment.

"Well, please tell me what this *nothing* was. If something seems out of place, you need to tell me."

Thomas zoned out again, lost in thought from the earlier confrontation with Angel.

Sean slapped his hands together in a single clap that sounded like a starter pistol at the beginning of a race. The sound startled Thomas from his thoughts back to the reality of the conversation.

"And he's back," Sean said aloud as he took a step closer to Thomas. "What… the fuck happened… down there… in the alleyway, Thomas?"

Thomas blurted, "Angel was there." He was still trying to wrap his mind around this fact.

The simple shock of the statement rendered Sean speechless for a few moments. He wasn't expecting this news. Finally, he said, "Angel? As in the Angel Domingo we've recently played the game with?"

"Yeah. *That* Angel. Is there any other?"

"And you didn't think to tell me this immediately when you got home?"

"I'm telling you now."

"Yeah, I had to drag it out of you. You probably would've kept that shit to yourself if I hadn't. Fuck, this is huge. You tell me exactly what happened. Don't leave me scrambling to mentally piece everything together. You tell me every goddamn detail that happened, now."

Thomas told Sean the whole story of getting to the alleyway, searching for the knife, not finding it, Angel standing at the mouth of the alleyway entrance, and their entire conversation.

"She knows," Sean blurted. It was like he couldn't wait for Thomas to finish explaining what had happened.

"What?" Thomas asked. He almost laughed aloud. "She doesn't know anything; that's ridiculous."

"Is it, Thomas? Is it really? I don't know how, but she knows."

"There's no way."

"Oh, there's a way!"

"Then how do you suspect she knows?" Thomas asked.

"I just said I don't know, Thomas. But you don't think it's a coincidence that Angel, the girl you saved from me, just happened to be walking past the alleyway where I just saved a chick who you assaulted at the same moment you were trying to find the knife you fucking lost? Do you think it's happenstance? She was watching the alleyway. She and Celeste, no doubt, were watching the alleyway." A bigger lightbulb brightened in his mind. "Oh, fuck! They arrived before you, canvassed the area, found the knife, and left. No wonder you couldn't find it."

"I don't believe that."

"Believe it, ass wipe."

"You really think so?"

"I fucking know it. I'd bet my goddamn balls on it."

"How would they meet?"

"Any number of ways. Uh, church… a… a…" Sean snapped his finger as it came to him in perfect clarity. "A help group. You know, where they sit together in a fucking circle and tell others what's bugging them and shit."

"Group therapy," Thomas corrected.

"Yeah, group therapy, smartass, or a help group, like I said. They met in a help group therapy session. I even suggested group therapy to Celeste if she felt like she couldn't deal with the trauma of this situation alone."

"I don't know. I think you're trying to box cobwebs."

"And I don't think you're opening your mind enough to the possibility that they are on to us."

"What? Are Celeste and Angel working together? No, I don't buy it, dude."

"Well, *dude*, I'm not waiting around. I'm calling her to book a date and question her to find out any information I can."

Sean grabbed his second phone from the coffee table; it was the burner phone he used while playing the game as Dillon. He searched under the B's for Baker and tapped the screen to connect. The only other number on the burner phone was Aaron Brakefield. It was for when Thomas Bonnomer needed to be reached if things in the game weren't going as planned. They had never been required to call each other on their burner phones. But they both knew how to play that character if they ever received a call on it.

"I still have my second go-round with Celeste. Maybe I can do both. We may have to call this game a no-winner."

"The fuck we are. If you're not going through to the second and third rendezvous—."

Sean held his finger up to quiet Thomas and said, "Her phone's ringing."

Thomas fell silent, but shook his head in disapproval at Sean's comment.

"Jesus, pick up the phone, goddamn it," Sean said, then his facial features abruptly changed.

Thomas heard a muffled voice come on the line. He couldn't determine what the voice on the other end was saying.

"Hey, Celeste," Sean paused, then, "I told you I would call." He shrugged his shoulders to Thomas, not knowing if that was the best way to approach this situation. "Me too. Listen, I was wondering if you were busy tonight?" He paused and listened to her reply; she sounded distracted. "Oh, well, that's too bad. I was in the mood for sushi tonight and thought it might be nice if you'd join me at Irashiai in a couple of hours."

Thomas watched Sean's mannerisms as he talked with Celeste, but he was shaking his head. Sean was going to meet Celeste over food and drinks when he thought there might be a problem with the game they were playing and the women they chose. He didn't like it.

"Celeste? Am I on speaker?" Sean waited to hear her answer, then, "I don't know, you just sounded distracted. I thought I lost you there for a minute."

Another slight pause, then, "Yeah, you can never be too careful."

Sean listened to her again, "Sushi? Tomorrow? Yeah, that sounds great. Let's say, maybe, 5:30. Is that good for you?"

Another pause, then, "What? My appointment? Oh, right, I forgot for a second. Yeah, it went okay. When we met, they hadn't decided which funds to use on any savings plans. They just had more loaded questions I had to answer. Maybe next time they'll be ready to get serious about their future."

He paused again, then, "So 5:30 tomorrow at Irashiai?"

He nodded, waited, then said, "Looking forward to it. Bye."

Sean punched the button to end the call, let his cell phone clatter to the coffee table, and muttered, "Fucking hell." It was as if that conversation had taken something out of him. He looked over at Thomas and said, "Now, that's how you play the game."

"Oh, yeah. You're such a player," Thomas said. "You just got a date with her. Anyone can do that."

Sean ignored Thomas's dig. "I'm going to get to the bottom of this and find out what's happening with these women."

"Like she's going to give up any information to you even if she does happen to know Angel."

"You don't know what I'm capable of."

Thomas pressed on, "Or if they've even met. Or if they even have the knife. Lots of scenarios here but no answers."

"And from what was said earlier, if they have met each other, you don't know what these bitches are capable of."

"Guess we'll just have to find out, won't we?"

"I guess so."

"You seem a little negative lately."

"You think?" Sean said, "I don't like these current competitors we're playing with now. They're making us do some crazy things. I don't feel like we're in control."

"We're in complete control," Thomas said. "We have to find out what they know, and then we'll be done with them. Then, we can move on to another set of fresh bitches. Start the game over again."

"I told you. I'm not playing the game after we finish this round. I'm fucking done, Thomas."

"If you beat me, right?" Thomas prompted.

"No. I'll be out when we finish this round. That's an affirmative. I don't care what you do with those videos. I don't think you're stupid enough to do anything with them. Things are getting extremely weird for me. I'm not going to chance getting caught. I can't believe we've played it this long, and now shit is going sideways. We may have to play some major defense to cover our tracks on this one."

"Sure. I guess so. Maybe."

"You know I'm right. Let's just put a pin in this conversation until after my sushi date. We'll see what I find out."

"Sure. Let me know when you know."

"Sounds good. And *you* let *me* know if you hear from *Angel*."

"She's not going to call me. She's too fucking pissed. She's done."

"Never hurts to be on your guard," Sean said, then grabbed his can of Cheerwine, drained the last of its contents, and headed for his bedroom down the hallway.

CHAPTER FIFTEEN

Celeste and Angel followed Aaron Brakefield as inconspicuously as possible to find out where he was going. As they drove, Angel told Celeste of the conversation between her and Aaron back at the mouth of the alleyway.

"There," Angel said, pointing. "He just turned right off this road into that neighborhood."

"I see him," Celeste said.

"He can't see you now, so punch it as fast as you can to get to that road. Make sure you slow down before you turn so your wheels don't squeal and give us away."

"I've got this, Thelma," Celeste said, referring to herself and Angel as the famous female criminal partners. Angel laughed. Celeste said, "I've seen enough movies to know how to tail someone."

Angel pointed again. "Wait-wait-wait. Pull over. He just turned into that driveway."

Celeste pulled over, but as she did so, she gave an audible gasp of air and said, "You've got to be shitting me!"

Angel glanced her way. A look of shock was on Celeste's face. "What's wrong?"

Celeste pointed and said, "That car. That Silver Charger with black accents in that same driveway. Who do you think it belongs to?"

"Dillon's, right?" Angel asked.

Celeste nodded, still looking at the vehicles in the driveway.

"No way. Dillon? The guy that saved you when you were attacked?"

"It's the same car Dillon met me in for lunch. The same one he drove when he followed me back to my place."

"They're roommates now, too?" Angel mused.

"I know. This whole scenario keeps getting weirder and weirder as we go along."

"And I feel it's going to get even crazier as we go forward, whatever we do."

Celeste and Angel were silent for a long while as they watched Aaron step out of his truck, move to the front door, and enter the house. Celeste broke the spell of palpable hatred that seemed to be growing within the vehicle. "What are we going to do about this?"

"They're playing one hell of a fucking game with us," Angel said. "We're going to fucking play them back. They want to play hardball; we're going to play some hardball, too. No one uses us and gets away with it, and we'll make damn sure they get that message."

"Okay. What do you have in mind?"

"I have no idea, but I'll think of something."

"No-no. *We'll* think of something. I'm involved in this too, you know? You're not going to be doing anything without my help."

"Agreed," Angel said, nodding.

Celeste and Angel sat in the idling car, fuming and watching Dillon's and Aaron's house. Their minds were working overtime. Each woman dwelt specifically on the man who had explicitly wronged them. Their minds were also working in unison on how they wanted to enact some type of revenge on them.

Both women were startled out of their thoughts when Celeste's phone started ringing. She grabbed her purse quickly, located her phone, and glanced at the screen. The number wasn't programmed in her phone, but she had seen it enough times to recognize the number.

"Fuck! It's Dillon."

"Silver Charger Dillion? Your savior, Dillon?"

"Yeah. Does he know we're out here?"

"I doubt it. There's no way Aaron saw us following him. Aaron doesn't know your car, does he?"

"I don't think so."

"Answer it. See what he wants."

"What do I say?"

"I don't know, but you have to answer it."

"Why?"

"Don't you see," Angel said, pointing to the house they were staking. "I would bet anything they just talked about *me*. Get it? He's probably calling you to see if you two can meet soon. He may know something's up. I don't know."

"With all I know now, I don't want to see him again. I'm not an actress. I have a horrible poker face. He's going to know something is up."

"See what he wants—deep breath. Act calm. Hurry before it goes to voicemail."

"Fuck," Celeste said under her breath. "Okay, here goes." She tapped the button to connect, then hit the button for the speaker, so Angel could hear and advise her silently on what to do and say.

"Hey, Dillon. What's up?" she said tentatively. She glanced at Angel and gave her a frantic look as though she didn't know any other way to begin talking to Dillon.

"I told you I would call," Dillon said from the phone's speaker.

"I see that. And it's appreciated. I can't say I haven't had a few thoughts that I might never see or hear from you again." She grimaced at Angel as though that might be too lame of a comment or that she might be overcompensating. Nothing like a clingy chick.

Angel gave her two thumbs up of encouragement to let her know she was on the right track.

"I'm glad you called," she lied.

Dillon said, "Me too. Listen, I was wondering if you were busy tonight?"

Celeste panicked and quickly said, "Oh, I don't know. I'm busy the rest of the day. I'm running some errands around town right now. Stuff I've put off for the past few days."

Angel was already shaking her head and motioned emphatically with her hands that this was the wrong thing to do.

"Oh, well, that's too bad. I was in the mood for sushi tonight and thought it might be nice if you'd join me at Irashiai in a couple of hours."

Celeste was paying too much attention to Angel's hand motion communications. She was distracted; Dillon's voice brought her back. "Celeste? Am I on speaker?"

Celeste panicked but told him the truth. "Uh… yeah. I'm just driving around town doing my errands. Why?"

Two more thumbs up and an emphatic head nod from Angel.

"I don't know. You just sounded distracted. I thought I lost you there for a minute."

Celeste said, "I'm driving. Trying to be safe."

Dillon again, "Yeah, you can never be too careful."

Celeste didn't know the best way to handle the sushi thing, but from Angel's excitement and thumbs-up hand motions, she knew she needed to accept his invitation though she didn't know why. She needed time to prepare herself before another encounter with Dillon knowing what she knew now.

Angel was exaggerating the mouthed word 'tomorrow.'

Celeste just went with it. "Hey Dillon, about sushi at that place you mentioned. I would love to join you, but I can't make it today. If you could hold off until tomorrow, I would love to join you for lunch or dinner. I'm just into some things and can't pull free."

A vigorous double thumbs up came from Angel.

"Sushi? Tomorrow? Yeah, that sounds great. Let's say, maybe, 5:30 pm. Is that good for you?"

The women listened to his reply. He seemed genuinely intrigued and excited.

"5:30 is perfect. Hey, how did your appointment go with that client?" She looked at Angel, who gave her a questioning look.

"What? My appointment?" Dillon said, "Oh, right, I forgot for a second. Yeah, it went okay. When we met, they hadn't decided which funds to use on any savings plans. They just had more loaded questions that I had to answer. Maybe next time they'll be ready."

Celeste said, "Yeah, maybe next time." Then, she shot a middle finger bird to the phone because she knew he was lying.

Angel snickered and looked away.

"So 5:30 tomorrow at Irashiai?"

"Yes, I'll be there.

"Looking forward to it. Bye."

"Me too. See you then."

Celeste ended the call and took a deep breath. "Goddamn."

Angel said, "And the award goes to Celeste Baker. Can't act, my ass." Angel broke into her serious version of Celeste. "Hey, how did your appointment go with that client?" She came out of Celeste mode. "He had no clue what was happening. Nice job, you."

"Wow. I can't believe I did that. Exactly why am I going on a date with him when we both know our attacks were faked for them to get intimate with us? That sounds so crazy to say."

"I think we need to continue playing their game, so they don't suspect we're playing them with our own game. I don't know why they're doing this. It seems like a lot of work to go through, but we're going to find out, and it's not going to be pretty for them."

"What are you going to do to them?"

"It's not what *I'm* going to do to them. It's what *we're* going to do to them. You said so yourself earlier. I want payback for what Aaron did to me and what Dillon did to you. I'm sure you want retribution for the humiliation they put you through. They took your dignity. *Our* dignity. I'm going to go out on a limb here and say it, and when I do, I know it's going to sound weird and crazy to say it like this, and you may disagree with me on it, but even though the sex was consensual, they raped us. It may not be the traditional sense of rape, but it was emotional. I'm not okay with that. It's how they went about everything—causing us to open up to them because of the circumstances of us being afraid because we were almost raped. An emotional trauma they put us through. It was a shitty thing to do, and we're going to take them by the balls and make them wish they had never fucked with us."

"And wished they had never *fucked us*," Celeste prompted. "I agree with you a hundred percent. But I am curious what you want to do to them."

"I have an idea, yeah, but it's extremely dark. I need to know if you are with me or against me?"

"Do you want to kill them?"

Angel didn't answer; her silence was the loudest yes. Their eyes met, and Celeste gave her a look that said she needed more to go on. "I am only interested in playing the game back with Aaron. You may be interested in getting back at Dillon. I don't know."

"But is what you are thinking of doing… will it allow them to do to anyone else what they did to us?"

"No. They will never be able to do anything remotely like what they did to us or any other woman out there ever again."

"What's your game plan?"

"First of all," Angel said, "let's get out of here. We need a few things before your big date with Dillon tomorrow."

Celeste put the car in drive again and made a U-turn in the middle of the neighborhood street.

"To where am I driving?"

"Right now, we're going shopping."

CHAPTER SIXTEEN

ANGEL INSTRUCTED CELESTE to drive to Cabela's hunting and fishing store.

"Cabela's? Are you serious?"

"Yeah. Just go with me on this. I'll explain it all soon enough."

"Okay. You've had more time to process everything since you were assaulted, so I'm sure you probably have a few crazy ideas in mind."

"That's true. And I plan to capitalize on them, too. But I didn't think it would come down to being able to go through with them until a while ago."

Celeste knew she was talking about Dillon and Aaron being partners in a shitty crime they had committed against them.

Like Celeste, Angel had always thought 'getting attacked' or 'raped' would never happen to her. The recent events had caused them to understand it could happen to *any* woman. And if it happened once, it could happen a second time. After the recent revelation in the neighborhood they just left, they were at Cabela's to make sure it would never happen to them a second time or a first time to any other woman. At least not from these two assholes.

When Celeste and Angel entered Cabela's, Angel grabbed a basket and handed it to Celeste to carry. There were a few items Angel knew she would buy and maybe a few other things she'd pick up on this shopping spree.

"What are you after?" Celeste asked.

"I'll show you as soon as I find them."

It took her a few minutes to look around the store to find the needed section.

"Ah, here we go."

The first item Angel picked out was a Klymit Roamer tarp that measured six-and-a-half by five feet. She grabbed two of them and added them to the basket.

"That doesn't look good."

Angel just shrugged her shoulders. "Just all part of my crazy ideas. They think they're going to get away with this. No, sir. Not on my watch." She moved on.

"Our watch." Celeste followed.

"Yes, our watch," Angel said. "But again, I'm not sure how far you're willing to go."

Celeste said nothing; she only followed and observed.

Looking around the store some more, Angel came to miscellaneous items in the fishing area. She checked out the items and zoned in on an assortment of red, green, and blue rubber bands. Offshore Angler Rubber Bands, to be exact. She grabbed three fifty-count bags and pitched them into the basket Celeste was holding.

"Rubber bands?"

"Yup. Those are more for me than you, but you can certainly use some of them once I tell you what I want them for."

"Sure. Okay."

They moved on.

In another section of the store, they came to a variety of self-defense weapons. Angel immediately grabbed an extendable baton. She had always wanted one of these for reasons she couldn't put into words, other than protection and that it looked bad as hell. The handle was about a foot long with two other steel rods stacked inside; Russian dolls of ass-kicking proportion. It was a weapon of hard steel that, when slung forward, extended out to a three-foot length. She looked the items over and grabbed the one that looked the most compact and the one that extended to the longest length. She chose the Smith and Wesson brand because it looked and felt the best to her.

"I may not have a gun, but I'm packing some heat. Don't mess with me, boys. I'll fuck you up." She laughed at what she'd said and remembered making fun of guys at the café earlier and how they think they are so badass when they have a knife, gun, or another weapon in their hands.

Celeste laughed and continued observing Angel in her element.

"And what are you going to do with that?"

"I have a few ideas."

Angel checked the price. "Goddamn, that's a lot. These things better work well," she said, shrugging her shoulders. "It's for a good cause. *Our* cause. Equipment for the game we're playing now."

"Okay," Celeste said, nodding. "I see where you're going with this."

Angel grabbed another one for Celeste and placed both in her basket. "One for me. One for you."

Angel moved down a few steps on the same aisle. Celeste followed. She found the mace self-defense spray. Angel looked over all the items and found the one that looked like it would fit in their hands perfectly and was small enough to fit in her shoulder bag so she could get to it quickly. The mace was housed in a light pink canister; the handle was made with a darker shade of pink. These models were the ones that supported breast cancer awareness.

"Save the ta-tas," Angel said, checking the price. "That's not too bad a price to help."

She grabbed two and dropped them in her basket.

"Mace?" Celeste asked.

"Oh, yeah, bring the tears to some asshole's eyes for starting shit with us—general protection from anyone. I should've already protected myself. We should arm ourselves when we go out. But it's also part of my plan."

Celeste glanced around their immediate vicinity, stepped closer to Angel, and lowered her voice. "I wish you would just come out and tell me your exact plan. I am getting some semblance of it, but I don't have a fully formulated master plan."

Angel smiled. "That's because I don't have a fully formulated master plan to share. I'm just thinking of things we might need as we go through this store. Besides, I don't want you to get cold feet about getting payback on these cunt nuggets before we even get started."

"I'm not getting cold feet—"

"Are you ready to go to the darkest of places on these guys? 'Cause I am."

"I have my share of dark thoughts on the matter, believe me. But I never thought an opportunity would ever present itself."

"Me either. I'm just going with my gut."

"Okay, I'll play along, but only if you promise to tell me your plan soon."

"Of course. I'm not going to leave you in the dark. I'll reveal my master plan when we get to my house."

"Good. That's all I need to know at this point."

Angel wasn't thinking or looking for tasers, but they were right next to the mace and caught her eye. "Fucking jackpot." She moved to them, looked through the different models, and chose the best one to work for her and Celeste. The flashlight/taser combo seemed like the most logical choice. She decided on a two-for-the-price-of-one package with a black and a pink one. Angel held it up to Celeste. "You good with the pink one? Because, you know, my color of choice is black, like my soul." She smiled again. She was having too much fun.

"Sure. I like the pink taser." Celeste laughed. "Never thought I would ever hear myself say that."

"Not a bad price for the two."

They continued walking around the store, looking at all the shelves and other items that might help them protect themselves in the future and with the loose planning of events that would play out soon.

They came across some racks with numerous fold-out blades like the one used in Celeste's and Angel's assaults. These knives weren't as beautiful or intricate as the knife with the chain-wrapped etchings, but there were some nice ones. Angel liked that knife they had found in the alleyway; it was pretty badass and beautiful at the same time. It was also the one she had been assaulted with several weeks before. But she knew she nor Celeste could never use it for personal protection, not after its history and what it had been used for.

Angel said, "I just realized you have their knife in your purse. You may need to put it somewhere else so Dillion doesn't see it in your purse when you go on your date."

"Quit calling it a date. With what I know about him and what they've done, I'm not too keen on this *dating* thing tomorrow."

"You're going to be fine. We're going to get through this."

"I'm getting the gist of things with this arsenal of items you have picked out."

"Part of it is to use on the guys, but part is for our protection. We need to keep you protected tomorrow in case anything happens."

"Nothing else better happen," Celeste said and grimaced. "I believe I would go bat-shit insane if I had to deal with another assault."

"No, that won't happen. I'm going to help make sure of that."

"I guess meeting you and knowing these things happen all the time to women helped put it in perspective for me. We need to protect ourselves from them, but there are also other assholes out there besides these shitheads we're dealing with. I will never be a victim a second time, and you won't either."

Angel focused again on the knives, as did Celeste. She wanted one straight from the package; she didn't want one with a vile history. Angel took her time and perused the multitude of options. She needed one that was easy for her to handle. Small and compact, but one long and sharp enough to cause real damage if she or Celeste were ever attacked again. It couldn't be too cumbersome or hard to open. The chain-etched knife now in their possession was a little too big for their hands. She saw a few promising possibilities, but there were other knives in the store. Some were more expensive and encapsulated in glass cases near the firearms.

Angel glanced across the aisle to one of the glass-enclosed gun and knife cases. A salesman was moving away from the case with a handful of papers. Angel was tempted to move to that store side and look at the knives under the glass but knew they would be more intricate in design, and with that, would have a much higher price tag.

Angel looked back at the knives in front of them. She smiled down at the blades and imagined being back in the alleyway where she was attacked. She imagined her attack again, but it had a different outcome this time. She saw herself grab her new knife from the front pocket of her handbag, then standing over her would-be rapist with the knife, her hand, and part of her forearm covered in blood. She shivered with retributive delight as she looked down on her sliced-up attacker. He had a surprised look on his face as he tried to hold the deep gash in his stomach together, his intestines bubbling out, fighting to push them back inside himself.

Then that vision was gone, and another replaced it. Her arm swiped again, a little higher this time. She saw her attacker fall and feebly try to hold the massive gash in his throat closed. He had very little luck as precious blood flowed out and down his frantic fingers, desperate to keep his neck wound closed.

She felt the counterfeit justice in her imagination trying to emerge and wanting to make her feel justified. But it was just a few wishful thoughts. It wasn't true.

Pointing at the knives, Angel said, "Pick one. One that is perfect for you."

"Okay."

Angel and Celeste each chose the knife they felt would work best for them. Both selections were CRKT flip knives, similar to the one used in their assaults. The handles were smaller, so they wouldn't be cumbersome in their grip. Each knife had a little more than a three-inch blade, and these were made with dark gray metal. Non-reflective. Sleek. Sexy.

"I could get used to this blade," Angel said. "I could practice taking it out, flipping it open, and train myself to give some quick jabs or shank moves that would catch my attacker off guard."

Celeste added, "It might be good if we learned where the vital points of the human body are, so if anyone messes with us, we could give them life-changing wounds."

"Possible *life-ending* wounds," Angel corrected. "I'm not playing around anymore."

"I see that."

"No one will ever get the jump on me again. Guaranteed. Yeah, this is the ticket. Hey, maybe if you and I learn some self-defense moves, we could put together self-defense classes for women only. Teach them not to hesitate or freeze if an attacker is present. What would you say about that?"

"I'm totally on board for that."

Angel and Celeste looked a little longer at several racks and shelves but didn't find other weapons they thought they might need. They left the area and slowly passed the rows of gun cabinets again. Angel's pace slowed even more as she glanced at the guns.

"C'mon, Angel. You don't need this yet," Celeste said. "Let's not get carried away. Maybe when we start self-defense classes. This is new territory for us. I'm not ready for that step yet."

"Yeah, you're right. But it doesn't hurt to look."

"Can I help you?" a voice asked.

Angel and Celeste had stopped and leaned over to look at the handguns in the case. Slightly startled, they straightened. With a bit of guilt at being caught doing something she shouldn't be doing, Celeste said, "Oh, uh, no. We're just looking."

The voice belonged to the salesman Angel had seen earlier. He'd circled back around and now stood before her, minus the paperwork. She hadn't even heard or seen him approach.

"Sorry, ma'am. I didn't mean to startle you." He held his hands out quickly and jokingly added—"Don't shoot!"—as though they had already purchased handguns and were currently packing heat. He laughed off his bad joke. "I wanted to offer my assistance and answer any questions you might have."

Celeste said, "Oh, I don't think we're ready for a gun."

Slightly stunned at her response, he said, "Uh, okay." He glanced down into the basket Celeste was holding, narrowing his eyes slightly as he gazed at the contents.

Celeste and Angel followed his eyes as he studied their basket. Celeste dropped the basket from the crook of her elbow to her hands, lowered it, and turned her body away from his prying eyes.

Nosy bastard, Celeste thought.

The salesman continued as though the basket contents were no big deal. "Well, from the looks of the items in your basket, I think you need a *single* self-defense piece."

"Maybe," Angel said.

"I'm afraid of guns," Celeste offered.

"I don't mean to pry, but did something happen to either of you?"

"We weren't raped, if that's what you're insinuating," Celeste snapped indignantly. There was a daring edge to her voice.

"Celeste," Angel said, calming her.

Even though she wasn't technically raped, she did feel like they had been violated due to the secrets they had discovered since their attacks. This salesman had struck a nerve with her.

"Maybe not," the man continued. "But it looks like you want to protect yourself if an encounter like that ever happens."

Celeste looked down at the basket's contents and nodded to his statement. "Yeah," she agreed and nodded at how it might look to the man. "It might be a little overkill. I don't know. We're just covering all our bases."

The man gave a 'come on down here' flare of his arm and left them as he said, "Follow me down to this other counter and let me recommend something to you. I'm not trying to sell you anything. Just a few options for you and your friend if you ever change your mind."

Angel and Celeste followed him to the next counter, feeling like he might change their minds about purchasing a gun.

When they arrived at the other counter, he continued. "Any of these guns here,"—he gave an "I caught a fish this big" motion with his hands and touched the top of the glass case. Resting his pinky fingers on the top of the counter, he continued, "These would be the most effective guns for you two to consider for self-defense. These are our brands of .380 caliber pistols. They have plenty of stopping power for whatever you need. Once you find the one that works best for you and practice at the range enough so you don't freeze up if you're ever attacked again, you would—"

Angel interrupted him. "We weren't attacked."

"Right." He snapped his fingers. "Sorry. I added the word 'again.' My bad. I'm trying to say using one of these single self-defense units here would cover all your bases rather than the eclectic arsenal you have in your basket there."

"I see. Those are nice guns," Celeste said. "I don't know if we're ready for that."

"I understand. Many people aren't. But the best way to get over a fear of guns is to go to a range, get some training, buy your own, get your concealed weapons permit, and learn to use it until it's a part of you. An extension of yourself. That fear will eventually go away, and it goes away faster than you might think. You never know when you might have to use one."

"We'll consider your suggestions, but I think we'll stick to these."

"Okay. Well, my name is Charles, but most people around here call me Scope." He chuckled at his nickname. "You know, like what's mounted on the top of a rifle."

Angel gave him a sarcastic half-smile, laughed, then said, "We know what a scope is."

Scope said, "Good, good. I'll be around if you change your mind."

"Thanks."

"You two have a great day now."

"We will."

Celeste and Angel left Scope's counter and moved to the front check-out area.

Angel half-expected to be grilled by the cashier about the items she was purchasing and what she planned on doing with them, but he only nodded at each item as he scanned the price.

The total was tallied, and Angel paid with cash. They took their bagged items and left.

Outside, Angel said, "Wow, that was easier than I thought. *Tomorrow* just got a whole lot more interesting."

"Yeah, it would if you would tell me what the hell is going on in that mind of yours."

"One more stop, and I'll tell you everything I'm thinking."

"Good. Because I am putting some pieces together, Angel, and this is getting extremely dark."

"Darker than what Dillion and Aaron did to us?"

Celeste raised her eyebrows and nodded in understanding, but she couldn't give her a definitive answer.

CHAPTER SEVENTEEN

After the shopping spree, Angel still hadn't revealed her master plan. They drove back to the Skyline Diner where they had their initial argument—or as Celeste would've said, "Angel had her bitchfest"—to pick up Angel's car. Angel told Celeste to follow her, which she did. It was about a twenty-minute drive out of the city of Silver Ridge. They crossed Half-Mile Bridge, then turned off the main two-lane road onto a narrow road that led to some outlying neighborhoods sprinkled around the lake. After parking their cars, they got out; Angel moved to Celeste's Crosstrek to help carry their shopping spree loot.

"Wow, you live here?" Celeste asked.

"I wish, but no. I am house- and cat-sitting for my friends, Mitch and Beverly Harrison. They're doing an adventure getaway in Colorado. They won't be back until around the fourteenth of this month. I have this whole place to myself. It's pretty great."

"Yes. It is. You said we were coming to your place, so I just assumed—"

"Well, it is *my* place until they get back. Sorry for the confusion. I'm not all there, with what we've learned today. I have an apartment across town. I just thought it would be easier to get my car real quick, then come here to discuss everything. It's secluded out here."

"It's beautiful. There's no other word for it."

Twilight had just started to fall over the lake. Tendrils of dark orange and deep purple hung low in the sky around the distant mountains. A few frogs droned away from their hidden places by the lake's shore. A white crane with its long wingspan flapped silently and low over the water, headed for a distant wading area on the other side of the lake. The lake was peaceful and still.

The Harrisons' two-story lake house was a decent size. A manicured lawn sloped down to the dock, where an expensive-looking boat was moored. It was quaint. Picturesque. Perfect.

"I could get used to this."

"I know. Me too. I'm always so psyched when Mitch and Beverly go out of town and need me to take care of their place, feed their two cats, and water their plants. Hang out and get paid a little for doing it. It's like taking a vacation without having to travel a long distance to get there and unwind."

"I'll bet."

"Come on. Let's get inside and talk about some things."

"Sure. I want to know what's on your mind and up your sleeve, although I have a good idea with everything you just purchased."

Inside the house, Angel didn't go through the motions of showing her around; there was no time, or so Angel thought. She dropped her carry-all bag on the counter but took the Cabela's bag of items and moved to the basement door. "Come down here."

"Okay. Should I be worried?"

Angel laughed, "No, not at all."

The basement area wasn't anything she had imagined. With Angel taking her to the basement, Celeste expected dim lighting with boxes and junk sitting around. To her surprise, it was refurbished. It had a small kitchen on one side and a living room area opposite it. But most of it was a wide-open space. There was plenty of room.

Angel slung the bag of weaponry up on the counter; the items rattled loudly, then settled into place.

The sound startled Celeste, and she turned to face Angel.

Angel was leaning on the table in the kitchen, looking intently at Celeste. "Here's the million-dollar question. How far are you willing to go?"

"Okay..."

"Because we've loosely skirted around the idea of killing Aaron and

Dillon, but now I need to know your deepest and truest feelings on the matter." Angel snagged the bag and pulled it in front of her. She reached in and grabbed the container housing the flashlight/taser combo pack.

"I knew you were going to say something like that."

"And?" She strung the word out, hoping to coax a straightforward answer out of Celeste. She fought with the packaging, and it finally ripped a little.

"If you're wondering if I have contemplated killing them, the answer is yes. I think about it all the time."

"Okay. That's a start."

"But thinking about it and actually crossing over that line and doing it are two different things. You think, hell yes, I want to fucking end them, but you never can fully rest in the fact you'll ever have to go there. Or, at least, I didn't. Or haven't. But to answer your question, yes, I have thought of lots of wicked ways to end their miserable existence. You never think that chance would come around. I thought the guy who assaulted me would never weave back into my life. Now, I find out he's linked to me through you. And the guy who sexually assaulted you is linked through me to you. It is a weird, wild, fucked up situation."

Angel finally managed to rip open the packaging. The two items spilled out onto the table. Angel grabbed the pink one and handed it over to Celeste. "Here's your pink taser." She grabbed hers and placed it to the side. "And a black one for me." She flipped the switch on it, and a blue light pulse flared out with an electric shock sound. "That's going to be a nice jolt to their system." Angel placed it to one side.

Angel looked up and locked eyes with Celeste. "Let me tell you how far I'm willing to go. I have no question in my mind I am going to end Aaron. That's just a fact, and it's going to happen soon. As in tomorrow, if all this goes down the way I'm thinking. And hopefully, I can do it with your help. We'll talk about your involvement soon. Right now, I'm telling you my side and how I feel about it. This game they're playing has to end. I know I'm not telling you anything you don't already know."

"True."

"I have no problems getting my hands dirty. Bloody is probably the better word here. There is no doubt Aaron will die for what he did to me. I need to know if you want in on this life-altering event to do the same with Dillion?"

Celeste was about to speak, but Angel held her hand up to stop her.

"Just think about that. Let me talk for a minute before you say anything."

"Okay. Sure."

"If I go through with ending Aaron, Dillon will go too. They are a malignant team that needs to be cut the fuck out and exterminated. I need to know you aren't going to rat me out, report me, or turn me over to the authorities." She held Celeste's gaze, but Celeste gave her nothing to go on. She was paying attention. "I need to know this secret is locked down between us. I'm talking about Fort Knox here. Area 51 secrecy. Even as secret as all the stuff that goes on behind the Vatican doors, or military secrecy."

"Angel."

Angel looked up, her hands still twirling as she tried to conjure a few other comparisons of how this info couldn't get out. "What?"

"I'm not going to rat you out. Who do you take me for? You think I would do that?"

"I don't know you. I mean, we're on the same page with all this, but we don't really know each other. We've only known each other less than twenty-four hours. I'm just supposed to take a chance on us going on the great adventure revenge spree and taking out two douche canoes and assuming you're not going to go to the police when, and if, your conscience gets the better of you when you can't deal with the guilt."

"I wouldn't do that."

"You say you won't, but I have nothing but your word."

"And my word is solid. My word is true. When I say I won't do something, I won't. And when I say I will, you have my full backing. I will follow through. What about you? How am I supposed to know you won't flip this whole scenario back on me, and I get blamed for what you plan on doing after it's done? We are both taking a huge risk."

"I know. I know. We've only been talking for half a day, but it feels like our history with these two takes us back even further than that. How crazy is that?"

"It's big-time crazy. I know what you mean."

Angel grabbed the baton package and worked to open it.

Celeste said, "One of the hardest things about being assaulted." She volleyed for a better word. She called it what it was. "Raped. One of the most important things taken from us is the ability to trust. If you do this, you will have to trust me and what I said earlier. If you get caught, it won't be because I turned you in. But if I'm being honest with myself, I couldn't let you do this alone. I would feel horrible if I didn't help. It's part of my healing too."

"I don't want you to feel like I'm roping you into something you wouldn't normally do."

"You're right. I wouldn't normally do this or have thoughts like this. I'm not someone who ever wants to harm another person. But this situation has changed everything, so if we enter into this... *partnership*? Is that what this will be? I'm not planning on harming anyone other than these two. I'm not going to get caught up in this situation and start killing people. I won't enjoy the killing side of revenge."

"I know that. Who said anything about us harming more people? You think you're going to become a serial killer or something because you take out one vile person?" Angel laughed.

"Well, yeah. I don't know how all that works and its effects on a person after the deeds are done."

Angel laughed some more. "Not like that. You're an upstanding citizen. A beautiful woman who happened to get a raw deal. Me too. We're resetting the score, so to speak. Or settling the score. Leveling the playing field. Drawing a line in the sand. Whatever buzz phrase you want to use, we're doing it. Some might say it will be an uneven playing field because they will die, and we won't. But I always say if the punishment fits the crime, they deserve it."

"I get it. I know what you mean. I have been fighting these thoughts ever since it happened."

"I know I've had a lot more time than you to dwell on this," Angel said. "And I eventually came to the truth that if an opportunity ever presented itself, I was going to jump at the chance to off my rapist. There is no way I'm going to sit by and let him use me in the worst way. And here's another thought. There's no way Aaron and Dillon just started this game with me, and then you were the second victim of this *assault game*—what the fuck-ever you want to call it. I would bet money they have done this before to numerous women. How many other women are out there now dealing with the grief, the hurt, the pain of being assaulted, having sex with their savior of the attack, him fucking her, and leaving after he's had his way with her? How many do you think they've played this game with?"

"Far too many."

"Agree. My conscience won't let me go another day without doing something that stops this game cold. Don't you have thoughts like this going on in your head?"

"Of course," Celeste said. "My life since my assault has been nothing but self-doubt, hurt, loathing of the guy who attacked me, and now, loathing of the guy I slept with, knowing he had a hand in it."

Angel said, "I've seen so many shows on television and true-crime shows where a violator will go to court, and the evidence was collected improperly, and they get off on some wild technicality like that. Sometimes, they don't even believe the woman when she claims rape. We have the knife with their fingerprints but don't even know if they would be admissible in court because of how it was collected. I'm not willing to go through all that just for them to go free, walk, and do it all over again. No need to go through that heartbreak. We know they're guilty, so why not prosecute them on our own?"

"I'm sure the defense would weasel something in there that there was no examination or pictures after the assault. And then there's that tidbit that each of us slept with the partner. It would be a major shit show I don't want to experience."

"Me either," Angel agreed.

"But my point is no one knows about this situation besides Aaron, Dillon, you, and me. If an investigation starts when they go missing, it won't lead back to us because no one but us four knows about the incident."

"True. What about Safe Harbor? Sylvia and her crew."

"Sure, they know our story, but they don't know their faces. It could be anyone that attacked us. We can't be linked to this crime. Well, maybe our cell phone numbers."

"Oh, yeah. Forgot about that. You think they're using their real cell phones to call us? Wouldn't that get confusing?"

"Honestly, I have no idea of their process, but we can look for their phones and maybe even a secondary phone when we meet up with them."

"Would they go to that much trouble?"

"I don't know. So, are you in this thing with me?" Angel asked.

"Still contemplating. Back to this situation. There are no cops involved; if they go missing, there will be no way to link them to us. We have no way of knowing if any of the other women have filed incident reports. Somehow, I doubt it. If they were like me when it happened, there was no evidence other than torn clothes and a shiner. The cops wouldn't have done anything because my attacker was long gone."

"Yeah, I see what you're saying. Say, what would you have done if someone told you about this incident, and how you would feel afterward?"

"I don't know."

Angel held her hand up. "But then, what if they told you all that wouldn't have happened if only the women before you had taken matters into their own hands—provided they knew who had done this—and had taken those men out of the equation? Would that have made you happy or disappointed?"

"Of course, that would've made me happy. I would've been thrilled I didn't have to take a ride on that emotional rollercoaster."

"I won't be able to tell the women who would've been molested, assaulted, and raped at the hands of these men because it would be impossible to know who they would be. But I will know there are women out there living a life free from sexual assault baggage because I took that pain from them before it happened."

"I see what you're saying. That's powerful."

"How much more powerful will it be for you after it happens? How will you be able to live your life better? Will it be better knowing you murdered—and helped murder—a couple of low-life rapists? Dealing with that grief? Or would it be harder to live your life knowing two men are out there raping women's bodies and minds when you could've stopped them? What would haunt you more?"

"Wow. You have a way with words."

"I'm just speaking the truth about this. It's a subject I get fired up about. I know I would sleep better at night knowing I had saved some women from the mental pain I'm dealing with on a daily basis. I don't know if I will ever be completely healed from what they've done to me, but I will not lose sleep over ending the lives of two evil and vile men."

Celeste moved to the chair where she'd placed her handbag. She opened it and retrieved her cell phone. As she scrolled through to her PayPal app, she asked, "Do you have PayPal?"

Angel squinted and pursed her lips, "Uh, yeah. What are you doing?"

"Your handle, please?"

Angel relayed the information to her.

Celeste did a search within PayPal and found Angel's profile as she moved to the Cabela's bag and withdrew the receipt inside. She checked the amount, then typed in an amount and submitted it to Angel. "There, I just sent you half the amount you spent. It's my share of these… self-defense weapons."

"You didn't have to do that," Angel said.

"I do. If we enter this partnership, we're splitting everything straight down the middle. No one does more than the other."

"Thanks."

"You're welcome. If we do this, and I am saying right here, right now, that I am, then I want to do this by the book. We have to know they are one hundred percent guilty. I mean, we already know they are, but before we…." Celeste paused, the word already feeling weird on her tongue. "*Murder* them, or end them, or take them out—whatever you want to call it—I want to know their story. I believe it will help me process everything after it's all over. One thing I wanted, and something I mentioned to Dillon before I knew he was in on the whole thing, was that I wanted my day in court with my rapist. If we can do that, I am with you one hundred and ten percent."

"I don't know how we'll do it," Angel said. "I just know it needs to be done. We can go about it any way you want. I can abide by what you want if you can comply with what I want. As long as I get to end Aaron. He may not have been the one who assaulted me, but he is the one who pulled the wool over my eyes as he masterfully infiltrated my emotions, broke down my guarded walls, and finally raped me. Aaron is mine."

"And Dillon is mine."

"I have your word that Aaron is mine."

"Of course. Do with Aaron what you want with him. I don't care. I won't stand in your way."

"And it's the same with Dillon, with you. I won't interfere with you."

"So, since you have thought about this more than me, where will this confrontation happen?"

Angel reached for one of the wrapped tarp packages and pulled it apart. She pulled the tarp from its plastic packaging. "I say we do it right here."

Celeste looked at the tarp, then glanced over to the open area, then back to Angel. "Okay, what do you propose we do?"

"I thought you'd never ask," Angel said, then she smiled.

PART II

~~UN~~NECESSARY ROUGHNESS

CHAPTER EIGHTEEN

Celeste Baker had been nervous since she agreed to meet Dillon for sushi. She was relieved she had almost a day to prepare herself for whatever weird questions she knew Dillon would ask. She had also thought of a few questions to surprise him. She would do so as long as they wouldn't give away that she and Angel knew each other, or that she knew a game was being played between them, and that Aaron and Dillon weren't their real names.

As it was with Jasper's Ale House, once Celeste entered Irashiai Sushi Pub, the hostess told her that her Dillon was already seated.

Damn, Celeste thought. *He makes it a habit of always getting here ahead of me. Let me guess; he's probably already ordered a beer for me too. I'm seeing more and more of how they're playing this game. Ever the thoughtful contestant.*

As Celeste followed the hostess to Dillon, she glanced at the faces of the people who were seated and wondered if they had plans in the works that were as fucked up as what she and Angel had discussed. The other thought going through her mind was whether she could go through with those plans. Talking about it and doing it when the time came were two different things. Only time would tell.

The hostess led Celeste to a two-person tabletop where Dillon was already nursing a Stella Artois. Another chilled bottle was placed near the plate where Celeste was to be seated.

Not in too much of a rush, are we? Celeste thought when she saw the bottle, then said, "Thank you," to the hostess.

Seeing that Celeste was in the right place, the hostess exited quickly.

"Hey, Celeste," Dillon said. He was all smiles. He stood, grabbed the cloth napkin already in his lap, reached out, and gave her a quick hug. He leaned in to kiss her cheek, but she turned her head in time to intercept his lips with hers.

We're going to see who plays this game best.

"Ooooh, nice. I like that."

"Me too," she lied. *I'm going to keep him on his toes.*

He stepped past her and pulled her chair out for her.

"Thank you," she said as she sat. "Such a gentleman. I like that about you."

"I'll always be a gentleman to you, Celeste." He sat and spread his napkin across one leg again.

Fucking liar, she thought but smiled at his statement. *I have to focus and not think of their game. Just trust Angel in what she said she was going to do. I have to play him the way they've been playing us. Stay focused, but I can't overdo it the way Dillon is.*

"I'm so glad we could meet again," Dillon said. "Didn't know if you wanted to see me again after our last rendezvous."

That statement struck her funny. "Why do you say that? Why wouldn't I?"

He gave her a sheepish look. "I don't know. I don't get many second dates. It's great to get a second chance to make my first impression with you."

Oh, God! Celeste thought. *So pathetic. Is this what today is going to be about?*

She dropped her head and her voice and played her victim card. "It's great to have a friend to go out with and grab a bite to eat. You know, someone I can *trust*."

On the word 'trust,' she looked at him to get his reaction.

He had just taken a sip of his beer. He paused, swallowed hard, nodded his head as he stared briefly at its label, then smiled and turned back to her. "Good, Celeste. I want you to trust me. It's a crazy world out there, and you've been through a lot. I guess I want to be there for you in any way you need me."

"Well, I appreciate it so much," she said, continuing her lie. "Yesterday was pretty special. You don't know how much you helped me. Maybe we could do it again sometime. That is if you wanted to do that again with me."

"Well, uh, yeah. I mean, there's no pressure to do so, but if you want to, I would love to experience that with you again. It was extraordinary the first time. I know the second time can be just as good or even better if that is at all possible."

They looked at each other, and their eyes locked. They both knew the moment between them had been remarkable, magical. Celeste saw something going on behind his eyes. There was a truthfulness to his look, or at least she thought there was. It was confusing to her.

Am I wrong about what Angel and I are going to do?

❧

Sean Asherton was battling within himself to come completely clean with Celeste. To tell her that he wasn't Dillon Carmichael. He just talked about trust and honesty. How could he tell any of that to her now? It wasn't the right time.

Would there ever be a right time? I'm just now gaining her trust. If I drop this heavy load of information on her, I'll lose her forever. Would it be any different once she falls in love with me? If *she falls in love with me. I may have to keep this shit to myself forever. Just distance myself from this lifestyle.*

He wanted to beg her to leave with him now and forget he ever knew Aaron Brakefield, AKA Thomas Bonnomer. But he knew if he did, she would demand an explanation, and he could never tell her about this horrendous and fucked up part of his life.

Why did I ever let Thomas talk me into playing this shitty, ridiculous game? There isn't a word that works well enough to convey how horrible it is.

He would have to sever this part of his life and try to forget it. He had to keep playing along until he could see his way clear of it and Thomas.

He saw Celeste's smile fade; a little sadness settled across her face.

He was about to ask what was on her mind, but before he could, the sadness was gone, and a bright smile invaded her lips. She turned to him and said, "I don't know how it could get any better, but I'm willing to give it a second round."

Sean smiled back. He hoped his inward negativity toward Thomas didn't come across in his smile. He felt that part of his life was subconsciously screaming out loud and clear to her.

"Maybe we could go to your house after dinner this time?" she suggested. She was looking at him with hope-filled eyes. There was a wanting there, but there was something else he couldn't place.

Fuck. That is entirely out of the realm of possibility.

He glanced down at his plate, froze at her suggestion, and then chuckled.

"What?" she asked, curiosity playing into her voice.

"Oh, I was going to say that I would love for you to come by my house and let me show you around, but it's going to have to be another time. I've had such a crazy week that I've let everything go. I haven't had time to clean up. There's no way I would let you come by with it such a wreck. I'm not a pig. It's just… I would hate for you to see the place as it is now."

"Oh, good. For a second, I thought you would tell me your big secret."

"Big secret?" Dillon asked as a guilty heat broke over his body and a sheen of sweat dotted his forehead. *She knows.*

"Yeah," Celeste said. "You know, that you're married, and your wife wouldn't like you bringing over your new girlfriend."

He laughed long and hard at her statement. It was a relief laugh. "No, no wife. Nothing like that."

"Nothing like that, but *something*, right?" Celeste asked.

Dillon panicked. His laugh trailed off, and he instantly became serious. "Absolutely not. No secrets."

The waiter came to their table.

Celeste quickly glanced down at her menu again. "Oh shit, I haven't even decided. I have no idea what to order."

Sean leaned forward and held out his hand to calm her. He asked, "Would you trust me to order for us?"

"Oh, sure. I guess," she said. Relief was in her voice now. "That'd be even better."

"Great. You will love this." He turned to the waiter and said, "For starters, we'll have a bowl of edamame, and then we'll share a Double Punch and a Black Dragon roll. We may order another roll or two later, but this will be a good start for now."

The waiter gave a quick bow and retreated to put in their order.

"I hope those rolls aren't the ones topped with real raw fish. I'm a lightweight when it comes to sushi."

"No, it's *fake* raw fish." Then he smiled at his wee joke.

Celeste caught what he had said and his little joke. "Ha, ha."

"Don't worry. You'll be able to handle this. I hope you like eel. The Black Dragon is topped with eel."

Celeste stopped and glared at him.

"By the look on your face, I'd say you're not pleased with what I ordered."

"Doesn't sound appetizing in the least."

"Will you at least try it before you judge it? I have a feeling you're going to love it. Just give it a chance."

"Okay. I'll try it, but I can't say I'll love it."

"If you don't, you have the Double Crunch roll to fall back on. It's a one-two punch to your taste buds. You'll love it. Trust me."

CHAPTER NINETEEN

Angel Domingo was focused, but she was nervous and scared beneath her mission intent. As she had briefly explained to Celeste yesterday, she wasn't as badass as her outer exterior, clothes, and actions made her seem. She felt inept at going up against Aaron Brakefield. It was a ballsy move, especially after her inner bitch came out at him yesterday near the alleyway where Celeste was assaulted. Angel had this underlying feeling that Aaron would see through everything she would say to him. There was no other way around this. It was something that had to be done. And she was going to follow through for herself, Celeste, and all the other women that came before them.

She had the weapons she and Celeste had bought yesterday, and they were in the best location she could think to put them. Her stun gun and mace canister were in a special compartment in her shoulder bag where she could get to them quickly and easily if shit went sideways.

Since there was a slight chill in the air, she wore the bitching leather jacket that helped solidify her badass look. It did help a little to be wearing her battle armor. The baton was up the right arm sleeve of her jacket. As long as she held her arm parallel to the floor, it wouldn't slip out. When the time was right, all Angel had to do was lower her arm and let it slide down the inside of her sleeve into her hand. Once it was in her grasp, she would give it a quick flick of her wrist to extend it out, and the ballgame would be on.

Who needs a concussion? she asked herself and smiled.

She had practiced the move so many times last night and this morning. She was ready for Aaron.

She drove around the neighborhood twice before building the nerve to follow their devised plan. Once she approached Aaron's house and rang the doorbell, there was no turning back. She would be committed to the full extent of this play. But time was of the essence; this had to be done.

Finally, she thought about the initial attack against her a few weeks ago from the guy who was now out with Celeste. A seething hatred began to build within her again. She thought of what they did to her and then switched roles, doing the same to Celeste. It was all just a big, fun game to them. That thought and the narrowing window of time caused her to put their plan into action.

Angel pulled into Aaron's driveway. She parked behind his red truck. It would be difficult for him to take off if things didn't go as she'd hoped. She wasn't worried about Dillon returning as he was currently out with Celeste. They both knew Dillon wouldn't chance bringing Celeste back here to his place and have Celeste meet Aaron, her rapist; no way.

She killed the engine, looped her bag over her head, double-checked the baton to see if it was in its rightful place up her sleeve, opened her car door, stepped out, then gently closed the door so as not to alert Aaron—or the neighbors—that he had company. She moved to the front door. She breathed deeply with every step, psyching herself up while mentally calming herself.

On the porch, she pressed the doorbell. After a few more concentrated breaths to still herself and put on her game face, she focused on the reaction of shock she knew would come when Aaron opened the door.

She heard footsteps approaching from inside. Knowing he would check the peephole to see who was on the porch before he opened the door, she gave her body a half-turn away to conceal her identity until he opened the door.

The footsteps inside stopped. There was a slight pause, and she figured Aaron was looking out the peephole as expected.

Angel smiled when she heard the latches being unlocked. She turned to the door and saw the doorknob turn; the door swung inward away from her.

And there it was, Angel thought. *He has such a confused look on his face.* It looked as though he didn't know what was going on.

"Angel?" Aaron asked.

"Yeah, Aaron, it's me."

"I see that," he said, still reeling at her standing before him. "What—what—why are you *here*?"

Angel launched her predetermined, practiced speech. "Look, I know what this looks like, me not knowing where you live, yet I'm here all the same."

"Yeah, I was going to ask about that."

She drilled forward, taking over the conversation, "To be honest with you, after our argument on the sidewalk in town yesterday, I immediately started feeling guilty and ashamed for what I had said. I just wanted to apologize to you, and the only way I knew to do that was to follow you when you left downtown, you know, where your wallet was stolen."

"You… you followed me home?"

"Yeah. Sorry about that. I know it doesn't look very good on my part. But when we dated, *briefly*, if you can even call it that, you never invited me to your place, so I didn't know where you lived. I assure you, I'm not stalking you, if that's what you're thinking now."

"That was close to twenty-four hours ago," Aaron said.

"I know. I started to drop by yesterday and couldn't get up the courage. Even today, I've been driving around the neighborhood trying to get up the nerve to come to apologize to you."

"Don't worry about it, Angel. It's nothing."

That statement pissed her off. *It was something, you asshole.* She kept her anger in check but added more urgency, "No, I feel like I owe you more." She took a deep breath, faking her nervousness. She shook her hand, the one that didn't have a baton up her sleeve. "Good God, I'm so nervous. This was so hard for me to do. Come up here and ring your doorbell. Do you have any whiskey? I need a good stiff one to calm my nerves."

"Whiskey? You want alcohol?"

She cocked her head to him inquisitively and added a hint of seduction in her eyes. "Yeah. You know. A toast to our old times. Well, not *too old of times*, but maybe we could toast to our not-too-distant past."

"I don't know," Aaron said. He stood implacable in the doorway and glanced out at the street.

Angel saw Aaron's inwardly guarded nervousness. She knew he was wondering about Dillon—Sean (his real name)—and when he would return. She saw a reaction on his face, probably when he realized her car was directly behind his. She remained poker-faced—Little Miss Innocent.

We know your secret, Thomas, she thought, calling him mentally by his real name. "Oh, come on, Aaron, just one little drink for old-times sake. You owe me that much," she said playfully.

Aaron seemed to come out of a thought process he was meticulously going over in the back of his mind. He looked at her more directly now.

"Okay," he said. "One drink, and then you have to go. It's too hard for us to say goodbye. We keep meeting, and it's becoming way awkward for us."

"That's entirely my fault. I made it, um…" She paused to find the right word. "…*weird* yesterday. I'm so sorry about that. I don't want our argument returning and giving us any bad karma because of the misunderstanding about you moving."

"Sure," Aaron said. "C'mon." He gave her the same arm flourish Scope had given her in Cabela's yesterday. "Whiskey's in the kitchen. Let's drink to the good times between us."

"That sounds great," Angel said, giving him a little bit of fake relief in her voice. She turned and scanned the neighborhood to see if anyone was walking by or sitting on their porch. All seemed quiet and clear of prying eyes. She turned, followed Aaron inside, and closed the door. She twisted the lock on the door handle as well.

Angel was about to lower her arm to let the baton slide free into her hand, but then she noticed the foyer and the hallway were too narrow. There wasn't enough room to give a good swing unless she came down right on top of his head. But she just wanted to knock him unconscious; she didn't want to kill him. She still had unfinished business to sort out with this asshole. She couldn't move the baton down to her hand because he could look back at any moment and ask what she was holding in her hand.

Angel noticed he was already halfway down the short hallway, and she quickened her pace to catch up to him. She was careful not to alert him with a hurried shuffling of her footsteps. She didn't want him to think she was charging him.

As she moved to catch up, she noticed how together everything looked. Coats and jackets still hung on the coat rack; she saw the camouflage jacket in particular. Knick-knacks sat on the foyer table. Wall art and some enlarged photographs still hung on the walls.

Angel already knew he had been lying about everything. *There was no moving to another town or city. If so, why weren't there moving boxes in different packed stages? It's because there was no move in Aaron's or Dillon's futures.* There was no need to bring any of that up again.

She told herself to do what she needed to do and get out.

They soon passed through the hallway opening into the living room. Aaron was ahead of her, moving toward the kitchen. This room had plenty of space for what Angel wanted to do.

This is it, Angel thought and moved toward him. *The moment of truth.* She slowly lowered her arm.

Aaron was right there facing away from her. The baton slid down and out of her sleeve. She caught it and gave it a sharp up and downward snap of her wrist as if trying to pop a catch in her elbow. The baton extended out. Aaron's ears pricked at the sound, and he turned to Angel, but she was already rotating at the waist and drawing her arm into a backswing. Aaron's eyes widened as Angel came around. His mouth flew open in shock as the baton entered his vision field. He flinched away from the swing so the blow wouldn't connect. He was half-successful. The rod caught him on the top left side of the head above his eye. He continued in the direction he was turning and corkscrewed himself downward as the blow dropped him to the hardwoods.

His body hit the floor, but the blow to his head was not hard enough to put him out. He rolled away and rose in a crouch. "You fucking kidding me, Angel? I knew you were up to something."

But Angel was already on him again, flinging herself at him desperately, coming in with another hit that promised to put him unconscious.

He flung his arm up and blocked most of the weight of the blow. Her arm rotated hard at the wrist and still swung downward, the baton's tip catching him in the top part of the head for the second time. He threw his other arm over and connected with her forearm. It was enough to palsy her arm and make her drop the baton. It clattered on the hardwood floor in the living room.

The loud drumming of the baton settled to stillness.

Aaron rose to his feet, and they both looked down at the baton.

Angel wanted to dart in and snatch it up again, but it was closer to Aaron's feet.

Aaron's brows furrowed in confusion as his mind searched for what the strange thing might be. When his mind registered it was a baton, his head swiveled up to meet her matching gaze. Their heads rotated to meet each other, and their eyes locked. The expressions on their faces were extreme opposites. Immediate guilt had washed over Angel's face, while Aaron's features had changed to utter shock at first, then to aggressive anger.

CHAPTER TWENTY

The waiter returned with their bowl of edamame, placed it in the center of their table, and then retreated.

Dillon grabbed the soy sauce and poured a little over the bean pods for extra flavoring. He grabbed one and began to pop the beans out one by one into his mouth. "Go ahead. Try some," he said as he grabbed another one from the bowl. "They're good. Best appetizer ever."

Celeste grabbed one and followed suit. She put the pod to her lips, tasted the soy sauce and salt on the beans themselves, and popped a couple into her mouth. She nodded as she chewed. "They are good."

"Told you," Dillon said. He grabbed another and shelled it as he watched her fight, shelling the last bean. "You don't do much sushi, do you?"

"Hardly ever. I've had sushi before. It's just not a delicacy I love."

"Well, if you're going to hang out with me, you better learn to love it quick," Dillon joked and smiled at the look on Celeste's face.

Celeste's hint of slight shock began to creep out on her face.

"I'm kidding about the sushi thing, but if you didn't want that to eat, you could've said something yesterday. We didn't have to come here. We could've worked out another location."

"No, that wasn't necessary. You said you had a strong pull to come here, so I wasn't going to come between you and your almighty sushi." She smiled back at him, letting him know her sarcasm game was strong.

"I appreciate that. It's been a while since I've had any. I hope you like what I ordered for us."

"If it's anything like this edamame, then I'm sure I will because these," she said, holding up another bean, "are tasty so far, so it's a good sign the rest will be too."

He plucked another bean from the pile. He continued to watch her as he shelled it. After he popped the beans into his mouth, he asked, "So, what did you do yesterday?"

"Yesterday?" she asked, beginning to panic. She wasn't expecting that question. She didn't want to tell him what she had done and how things had unfolded. Her mind began to bat around all the recent thoughts she'd been thinking about. She settled on "Nothing." She knew he would call her bluff on that simple answer because she had done a lot of stuff.

"Oh, come on now. You had to have done something. Didn't you go shopping or something like that?"

"Oh, right, I did," she lied. *Angel and I had an excellent discussion while we did it too.* "I thought you meant anything else besides my shopping."

He jumped in on the heels of her statement. "Well, did you?"

"No," she said almost too quickly. She looked over at him, but he didn't seem alerted by her quick answer. He was busy shelling another edamame bean.

"What did *you* do?" Celeste asked him, putting the imaginary interrogation light back on him. "Did you do anything exciting?"

"No," he said, pitching a few more beans in his mouth.

"You didn't meet any friends to hang out with last night?"

Dillon looked up at Celeste. A look of confusion worked across his face; then it was gone. He shook his head, but there was a blankness to his expression. Celeste could see that his mind was working something out.

He asked, "Why do you ask?"

"Well, you said yourself that you were moving soon, right?"

"Uh-huh," he said.

"So, I figured you might've gone out with some close friends since you won't be around that much longer. Thought you might get together with *him* and play some games?" The upward inflection of her voice made it sound like it was a question.

"Excuse me?" he asked. "What did you say?"

"Huh? Oh, I was saying that I thought you might get together with them, you know, your friends, and play some games. Or something like that."

"Oh. I thought you said something else," he said, eyebrows dipped in confusion. He took a moment wondering about her words, then asked, "To what games are you referring?"

"I don't know, whatever games friends play when they're moving away. Beer pong, for one. That's always a fun one. And, well, some bars have a trivia night; you could've done that." *That's stupid. He wouldn't play trivia.* "Or you could've gone to a bar and watched a game. And, well, that's all the games I can come up with. Maybe conversation and shots." She smiled sheepishly, as though maybe it was a dumb idea he might get together with friends for one last soirée.

"I see. That's a good idea, but I stayed in last night and got some much needed rest."

"You have a move coming up soon, so I guess that was best. You're probably going to need it."

"Yeah," he said.

Dillon fell silent for a time and continued to shell more beans.

Celeste noticed the quiet playing out between them and wondered if Dillon noticed it too. She said nothing to change it. She had plenty of things on her mind as well.

While they sat in the growing silence, the waiter returned with their main courses. Dillon slid the edamame bowl out of the way so the waiter could slide the two sushi trays in the middle between them. The waiter indicated the first tray closest to Dillon with an open upturned palm and announced, "Your Double Punch entree." He swung his open palm over to the other tray and said, "Your Black Dragon roll." He pulled his hand away, clasped it behind his back, and asked, "Will there be anything else?"

Dillon answered, "No. I believe that covers it for now. Thank you."

The waiter said, "Very well then. Enjoy." He stepped backward away from them, turned on his heels, and retreated.

Dillon poured some soy sauce from the bottle into his small dipping tray; then, he poured some into Celeste's tray. He slid his chopsticks from their paper sheath and snapped them apart. He grabbed a pinch of the wasabi, added it to the soy sauce, then stirred it with his chopsticks. He did the same for Celeste again and said, "The wasabi adds a little more spiciness to it, but I didn't add as much to yours as I did mine. I don't know if you'll like it, but at least try it."

"I'm sure it's delicious," Celeste said and continued to observe him.

Dillon grabbed an end piece from the Black Dragon roll, dipped a small section of it carefully into the soy and wasabi combination, then slid it into his mouth. He closed his eyes and chewed slowly. A look of bliss came over his face as he relished the morsel. He finally opened his eyes as he swallowed. Dillon noticed Celeste was still sitting there, just staring at him. "Something wrong?" he asked.

Celeste smiled and shook her head, "No, I was watching you enjoy this sushi. I was interested in how carefully you prep everything."

"I do love my sushi. You don't just eat it; you experience it."

"I can tell," she said, nodding. She grabbed her chopsticks and prepared them as Dillon had done. Before she partook of a morsel of her own, she asked, "Is something else on your mind?"

He reached over the table to get a piece of the Double Punch roll. He pulled his arm back and rested his forearm on the table. "Why do you ask?"

"You're just quieter now than before. Thought something might be on your mind."

"Sorry," he said, nodding his head. "To be honest, I have been beating myself up about something."

"Oh?" she asked.

Dillon continued, "Yes, and while I dare to admit it, I've been thinking that I owe you an apology."

Celeste didn't understand what apology he meant, but her mind immediately went to his abrupt leaving after sex. *That's right. You should apologize for that. It was a cruel thing to do to me, and it was right after you came all over me.* She bluffed instead. "Apologize? For what?"

"I shouldn't have left you so abruptly.

She played dumb. "But you had your appointment."

He held his hands up to stop her before she could kill this moment of confession he was offering. He pressed forward, "I know I said I had an appointment, but I should've canceled it right then and there. It wasn't right for me to leave you after the amazing moment we shared. At the risk of sounding trite, it was such a beautiful and magical moment. I wish I could go back to that moment and redo my actions. I should've stayed. I wanted to stay. I wanted to make love to you over and over and over again. I may be overwhelming you by saying this, and I don't mean to; I'm stating facts and my true and honest feelings. And by saying this now, there is no pressure for you to reciprocate those feelings. I mean, after all, we did meet under the most bizarre of consequences. Anyway, I'm rambling. Sorry. I wanted to set the record straight and get that off my chest. I should've canceled the meeting. I regret now that I didn't. I am genuinely sorry. It will never happen again. I can promise you that. I honestly just wanted to spend the rest of the day with you."

She was all of a sudden scared, but she couldn't exactly pinpoint what frightened her. She felt it had to do with the subject matter she and Angel had learned. There might have been a bit of truth in his statement, but it wasn't complete honesty, because of what she and Angel had already figured out with this game.

Are Angel and I utterly wrong about this game? Were we grasping at anything to make sense of our confusion? Did we invent answers? Celeste was confused. He sounded so honest and truthful just now. *Do Angel and I have the wrong information about him? About Aaron?*

He tried again, "Is there any way we could start over again? Not completely, mind you. Maybe forget my lack of thoughtfulness to you at that time. That was so wrong of me, and I wish I could take that back and spend the rest of the afternoon with you."

"Of course," she said. Even though she answered without hesitation, there were reservations that her intuition was telling her he wasn't being honest with her.

"Good, because I would love nothing more."

Celeste gave him a playful smile and worked the chopsticks as best she could. She grabbed one of the end pieces of the Double Punch roll.

She dipped it into her soy sauce as Dillon had done and slowly moved it to her mouth. She almost dropped it but, at the last minute, snagged it before it dropped off the end of the chopsticks.

"Bravo," Dillon said. "Well done."

Now Celeste knew why the look of ecstasy had crossed Dillon's face. To her surprise, it was delicious, and she immediately loved it.

As she chewed, Dillon asked, "Did you happen to go to any group therapy last night?"

Celeste stopped and glanced up at him mid-chew. A deer in the headlights moment as she stared blankly at him. He was staring intently at her. *Is he trying to read my facial expressions?* She didn't know how to answer him, so she played it off by holding up a finger as she chewed a few more times.

"Oh, sorry," Dillon said.

Taking the time to chew gave her enough time to form an answer, although she felt as if Dillon could see guilt washing over her face. She thought she took too much time to find an answer and swallowed the sushi too quickly. She finally found her voice as she grabbed her beer. "Um, no," she lied and tilted her drink back. She swallowed and set her beer down again. "No group therapy for me, at least, not yet anyway. Why do you ask?"

"Oh, I don't know," he said, looking at her. To Celeste, it looked as though he were staring at her to see if there were any tell-tale signs that she might be lying to him. He reached over and glanced down long enough to chopstick another piece of the Double Punch roll, then looked at her face again. He held it in his chopsticks for a moment and said, "Since I'm not a counselor, I didn't know if I had helped you with my weird philosophy, psychology, and suggestion of using me as the verbal punching bag."

He gently dipped the sushi piece into the sauce and then took it in. He closed his eyes for a moment and relished the taste again. Celeste was about to answer him on that, but he began talking again. "I also thought if you had found some sort of group therapy, there might've been someone you connected with and hit it off."

He knows, she thought. *Jesus Christ, he and Aaron know. They figured out that Angel and I have met, but he has no proof because he's fishing for it. I have to keep him as far away from what I did yesterday. He doesn't care about me at all. That GI Joe power play earlier about wanting to start over and what happened between us is just him trying to keep me close to extract information from me. But, oh Jesus, he sounded so truthful earlier. Doesn't matter now. What Angel and I have planned is going to happen. I hope whatever's happening with her and Aaron is going down right now as she planned.*

Celeste snagged a section of the Black Dragon roll and dipped it hard into the sauce. The rice soaked up a good bit of it. She paused long enough to say, "No. No group therapy and no new friends either, other than you." She popped the soy and wasabi piece into her mouth and bit down. The acrid and salty taste of the soy sauce with the added bit of Wasabi filled her mouth. She didn't gag or cough, but there was hardly any other taste except a mouthful of soy sauce. *Jesus Christ, no wonder he only dips a small portion of the sauce at one time.* She chewed quickly, reached for her beer, and took a long drag.

Dillon continued, "It would also mean if you found someone to counsel you, you might not need me anymore."

Her hand went to his. She held it tight. Even though the sentiment was there, it was all fake. It was a way of giving him a false sense of security while she figured out what to say and do.

If he is saying shit to me that isn't true, I'll follow up with physical actions that aren't true.

Dillon didn't realize the slow-build effect his questions were having on Celeste. "That's good," he said of the hand-holding. "I like that. Group therapy could be helpful if you're still having trouble with it. Don't ever rule it out."

Oh, he's good. He's really good. He's played this game longer than Angel and me and has all the angles worked out. I'm competing mentally with a pro in this game he's invented.

Celeste set her beer bottle down harder than she had anticipated.

Dillon looked up at her but didn't see an outward look of anger on her face. He continued questioning her. "Did you go back to where the incident happened last night?"

Celeste looked up with genuine amazement, "What the hell is this?" she demanded.

"What?" he said, a little confusion beginning to play on his face.

"Why am I suddenly getting this weird, third-degree interrogation from you?"

"I wasn't aware I was giving you the third degree, but if these questions bother you, then I can stop." The statement was free from any sarcasm, malice, or hateful intent.

Dillon's words set Celeste off even more. She continued, barely taking time to decipher the intent of his statement. "For the last time, I didn't go to group therapy. And no, I didn't meet any new friends. How could I if I didn't even go to any group therapy in the first place? And no, I didn't go back to where I was almost raped. Why would I? I'm trying to forget this incident happened to me, but you keep drudging it up. I thought maybe tonight we would talk about ourselves, but I see that's not going to happen. Why the hell are you grilling me? I did some shopping, grabbed a bite to eat, went home, watched TV, and then crashed out. Are you one of these boyfriends, provided we ever get that fucking far, that keeps tabs on their girlfriend twenty-four-seven, where they feel like they are in prison rather than a relationship, because if you are, then I want no part of you or whatever this is becoming for us."

Dillon sat there in stunned silence. He had no comeback.

Celeste seemed to come out of her temporary upset funk. She saw the shocked look on Dillon's face. She was confused as it seemed like an honest enough look of astonishment. *I can't play this game. I am failing at this... this... whatever the fuck I'm doing with him. I know too much, and his comments and answers confuse me. He's been playing this game longer than Angel and I have been playing it. So yeah, he has the upper hand in this conversation. He knows the correct facial expressions to give me. But he still doesn't know what we have planned for him. How could he?* Her shoulders slumped, and she took a deep breath. "Fuck." Then, she said, "I'm sorry."

"No. Don't apologize. I mean no harm. Honest. I was trying to make conversation."

"Sounded like it was a twenty-question interrogation. And we were only up to the third question."

He gave a half-amused laugh. "Just trying to show you I'm concerned about you."

You sure about that, Cupcake? she thought, thinking back to when she and Angel had it out about their duplicate stories. *I'm on to your game, asshole.* Out loud, Celeste said, "Felt more like you were grilling me for information."

"No. God no. I want to ensure you have what you need to overcome that life-moment thing you're going through. If you can call it that."

"I'm getting through it," Celeste promised. "I'm getting through it in my own way."

"Fair enough," Dillon said. "Okay, how about this? No more questions about what happened to you unless you need or want to talk about it. Whenever you do, don't hesitate to bring it up. That way, I'll know it's clear to ask questions about it, and you won't feel like I'm grilling you. Does that work?"

She continued playing the victim for the sake of this game between them. "Thank you. I'm just trying to forget the incident. It would help not to talk about it for a while. Guess I feel differently now than when it happened and what I said about it, you know? I'm getting on with my life."

"Sure. It's not a problem. Please, don't be afraid to bring the subject up, as I'm here to help you heal as best I can."

Oh, Jesus Christ, Celeste thought. *I can't believe how two-faced you are in this. You're so far gone; you don't even realize you're doing it.*

CHAPTER TWENTY-ONE

***Fuck!* Angel shouted** inside her mind. At first, she saw Aaron was frozen in confusion, but it quickly changed to anger. *There's still time!* she thought.

She dropped to the ground and grabbed the baton. She stood and turned as she came back around to clock Aaron out.

But Aaron was right there, already in a forward movement. His arm came down with a crushing blow as Angel came across. There was no contest. The pain was immense, and she could do nothing but drop the club again.

Aaron immediately seized her striking arm, grabbed her by the throat with the other hand, and violently pulled her close to him. He shouted into her face. "What the fuck is this? The fuck do you think you were trying to do? I knew you were up to something, you fucking bitch!" On the word 'bitch,' he shoved her backward into the couch.

The shove was hard, and the couch stopped her cold, but she was too top-heavy and folded backward and rotated over the back of the couch and into the horizontal cushions on the other side. She rolled over the cushions and dropped the short distance to the floor.

Aaron immediately grabbed the black thing lying where Angel was forced to drop it. He picked it up and quickly examined it. He hadn't known exactly what it was when he'd first looked at it near their feet. The look on Angel's face told him it wasn't a good thing. It looked like a weapon at first glance, but now, studying it over, he realized what it was.

"A police baton? You fucking kidding me, Angel?"

He looked diagonally over the couch cushions and saw her head rise above them. He saw utter fear in her eyes. They both knew she had fucked up. There was a little hope that spiraled through Aaron's body. He was going to bag this bitch and save her until Sean arrived home from his date. Then he and Sean would figure out what to do with her together.

Angel was quiet. She said nothing. The fear of being attacked again was seizing her up. This time it seemed like if he caught her, rather than make love the way they had when they were involved, he might actually rape her. Or kill her. Or rape her, then kill her. Or he would kill her and then rape her. Either scenario wasn't good.

"Answer me!" Aaron shouted.

Aaron's yell brought Angel back around to the immediate terror that was happening.

He circled the couch.

Angel ducked underneath the coffee table that was high enough for her to slither beneath.

Aaron rounded the couch. He came in swinging the baton at her lower body—the only area he could reach. The club landed high on her thigh, and a rich, dull pain bloomed where he had planted it, a charley horse from hell. She pulled her leg under as part of her body moved out to the other side of the coffee table.

"What the hell did you think you would do with this?" He was screaming his questions at her. "Bash my brains in? Huh?" He was becoming unraveled.

That's where you're going to make your mistake, Angel thought.

"Answer me, you bitch! What did you think you were going to do with this piece of shit?"

He stepped to the left of the coffee table and swung the baton down, aiming at Angel's head.

Instinct caught up with Angel, and she pulled her arms up to defend herself. As she did so, her arm caught the leg of the coffee table, and it slid it up to where it covered her face.

The baton crashed down on the corner of the table. A couple pieces of wood splintered off.

Aaron was pissed. He grabbed the coffee table with both hands and jerked it up from where Angel lay hidden beneath. He pitched it as hard as he could to a corner of the room. Glass shattered as a part connected with a window.

With Angel lying completely exposed with nowhere to hide, she knew she had to do something immediately, or that dull throbbing in her head would be a splitting headache.

Her purse lay at her side—still attached to her as she always looped it over her shoulder and across her body. Her hand fell onto its strap near the purse itself.

Of course, she thought excitedly.

She grabbed the strap and pulled her purse closer. She shoved her hand inside it as Aaron rounded back to her. He loomed over her, breathing heavily. She felt around as stealthily as she could.

"I want some goddamn answers, and you're going to damn well give them to me even if I have to beat the ever-loving-fuck out of you for them."

Angel said nothing but gazed up at his anger-emblazoned face.

Aaron's head moved to her purse, and he noticed a minimal hand movement. He noticed that it was on the inside of her bag.

"What the hell are you doing?" he asked, anger gone and replaced by dreaded curiosity. He knew something terrible was going on inside that purse.

Angel's hand stopped, then moved as though clutching something inside her bag.

Aaron's eyes moved back to Angel's face, which had already changed. The fear was gone, and a hint of amusement had replaced it. She gave him a sly smile. Aaron didn't like her fucking smile and was determined to wipe it from her face. He raised the baton and brought it down, but as he did so, she jerked her hand from her bag and sat up quickly into him. As she did so, she shoved her fist into his crotch and pressed the button.

Aaron froze in mid-swing and started to convulse. He folded over and jittered uncontrollably as 2,400,000 volts of Angel's new Ergo Stun Gun were transferred into his cock and balls. Angel held it there as long as she could, a satisfaction swelling in her body. She wasn't going to be the one who stopped the electrocution. She was having too much fun.

Aaron was the one who stopped the assault on his nether regions. He folded over from the voltage, fell away from her stun gun, and dropped to the hardwood flooring.

Angel had to force herself to release the trigger button on the stun gun. She stood quickly and kicked the baton out of his hands. She almost reached down to pick it up but didn't know if any voltage was still coursing through the heavy steel. Realizing it had a rubberized handle, she felt it was safe to pick up.

Aaron's body jittered a time or two, along with some matching moans. When Angel decided to pick up the baton again, he slowly sat up and looked around the room. His arms moved like he wanted to get up, but it was as though he'd forgotten how to use them, a baby figuring out what each appendage does.

"Stay down," Angel said, "or I'll give you something worse to moan about."

He looked at her sideways as his head lulled to one side. "Fuck you," he stammered.

Angel was standing over him with her baton in her right hand. She didn't like his two-word comeback. "No, it's going to be *Celeste* and me who's fucking you."

At the sound of the word 'Celeste,' Aaron's eyes leaped with the dawning revelation of what Sean had said to him earlier.

Angel raised her new baton out to her side. "And I can assure you, you're not going to enjoy it one fucking bit." She swung with a snap of her hips as she brought the rod into the side of his head, sending him into a dark unconsciousness.

CHAPTER TWENTY-TWO

"So, since you're so embarrassed about having me over to your house," Celeste began, guiding the subject back to what might happen after this meal. "Or to your apartment, studio flat, or wherever it is you call home, would you like to come back to my place again? Remember, I've already cleaned. It's ready for guests." She felt it was a stupid ploy to get him focused back on her, but she was sure that hinting about his chances of having sex again was a big motivator.

Celeste had called Dillon on it, and she knew he couldn't argue with her. "I'm sorry, Celeste," he said. "Now isn't the best time to go to my place."

"So, you have a *place*. I bet it's nice," she said, giving him a hard time. "When *will be* the best time, huh?" she asked, raising an eyebrow. Even though she asked the question, in the back of her mind, she knew nothing could ever work out between them. The lie of what he and his roommate did to her, Angel, and the other women, could never be forgiven. But she had to continue playing this game a little longer.

"I don't know," he said. "But trust me, there will be a time. Soon. Very soon. I promise."

"Or will you be moving out of town sooner than expected?"

"Who's grilling who, now?" Dillon asked. He shook his head against his question. "Listen, I haven't wanted to say this so soon because nothing is carved in stone, but I've been thinking of staying around here."

"What?" Celeste asked. Confusion sprouted on her face. "But your company and your job."

"Yeah, I know. I may not be moving after all," he admitted truthfully. "I have to see if I can find something around here with equal or better pay. Or at least something that rivals my current pay situation so I could get out of this thing with my company."

Celeste took that statement in but didn't know if she believed him. *He's lying again,* she thought. *There is no way he's going to change his life just for me, and even if he did, I couldn't knowingly be a part of it with what he and his friend do in their spare time.* "Oh… well… that's great." She smiled to let him know she wasn't going to make a big deal about this, at least for now.

"You don't sound like it's great."

"No, it is. It's just that you're moving one minute, and the next, you're not. It almost feels like you told me that so you wouldn't have to develop a relationship with me."

"What?"

That had slipped out; she realized it too late. She pressed on, hoping to pull him away from her knowledge about the game. "I don't know what to think or believe anymore. I had a nice time with you yesterday, but then you dropped the shitty news on me you're not going to be around, so naturally, any fun we're having, I know that it won't or can't last. Now, you tell me that those plans might have changed. If we happen to go out in another day or two, or a week from now, will *your moving away* be back on? And don't get me started on the fact you chose your appointment over me right after you doused me with yourself. Jesus, Dillon. It's a lot to process."

"I've already apologized about that. What more do I have to say? You can't know how awful I still feel about it. How I felt the moment I left. If I could relive yesterday over again, I would do it in a heartbeat, but this time, I would stay. And for the record, we doused each other, remember?"

"But I didn't leave. You did."

A visual embarrassment crossed his face; he looked down at his hands and fiddled with the napkin in his lap.

Celeste didn't care how he felt; she had feelings, too, so she pressed on. "Now, I get news you might not be moving at all. If that's true, I thought you would've told me as soon as I arrived for dinner. I don't know what to think anymore, but I'm protecting myself, so I won't get hurt, because I've been falling pretty hard for you since we first met." She smiled at how truthful her argument spilled out of her. She took a moment to pat herself on the back because she was playing the hell out of this game.

"I'm sorry," Dillon said again. "It's all I know to say. And yeah, you're right. It's a lot to process with what you've been through."

She flashed a look at him. "What I've been through has nothing to do with whether or not you're telling me the truth about moving. I already know I'm getting in too deep with you from what happened between us. I barely know you. Now, I'm trying to guard my heart, yet here I sit on another date with you. So, forgive me if I'm not cutting backflips with this news."

He nodded to her reasoning. "I get it. The bottom line is, I like you, Celeste Baker." Dillon looked her in the eyes. "Like, a lot. Enough to change my current situation so I can be with you."

Celeste's eyebrows dipped, and her head snapped back slightly. She wasn't expecting those words to be spoken.

Dillon realized he'd just let out some deep personal feelings. "Oh, wow, that just popped out. Sorry. I know that might put some undue pressure on you. Please don't feel like you have to reciprocate in any way."

"I don't, but did you mean that? What you just said."

"Every word. I'm not trying to take it back. I want to express more, but I know it might be too soon. I don't want to scare you away."

Celeste smiled on the outside, but on the inside, her mind was lit up and zinging with questions. She managed to say, "How about we do this? Let's table this subject for now and let whatever happens between us progress naturally, instead of all the maybes or maybe nots."

Dillon gave a relieved breath of air. "I like that. That sounds good to me."

"And how about, for now, you pay the bill? Not that you're paying for my meal as though we're on a date. But since I paid last time, you can cover it today. So there will be no undue pressure on either of us. We'll see how the rest of tonight pans out and the next few weeks."

"Of course," he said. "I would *love* to treat you to our meal."

Love? Celeste thought. *That is the second time he has used the word* love. *A little too soon to be dropping that word on me. Am I reading into things? Did he emphasize that word on purpose, or was it a slip of the tongue?*

Dillon threw up his hand to snag the waiter's attention. The waiter immediately came over to their table.

"Was everything to your liking?" the waiter asked.

"Of course. I was going to get the bill. We'll be leaving soon."

"Certainly. Right away." He grabbed his waiter's pad, flipped through the tickets, snagged the one for their table, and pulled it from his stack. He quickly and precisely laid the ticket in the leather holder he held in his apron, then turned it with a flourish and placed it in front of Dillon. As Dillon picked it up and looked at the bill, the waiter gathered their dishes in a balanced heap. Before he stepped away with the dirty dishes, Dillon whipped out his wallet, grabbed his bank card, and stuck it in the upper plastic area of the leather folder. He spun it back to the waiter and held it up for him to take it on his departure.

In the few seconds it took for Dillon to flip open his wallet, grab his card and deposit it into the holder, Celeste had enough time to see the plastic housing of his driver's license cover. She read the name on the card—

ASHERTON, SEAN WYATT

A fearful heat began to radiate from the center of her chest and emanate outward. Dillon Carmichael wasn't even his real name. This moment suddenly felt alien to her. He hadn't even been honest with her about his name, so everything about him was completely fake.

Seeing his real name in print on an actual government-issued card made this situation and the game they were playing more real than ever. She knew her and Angel's imaginations weren't playing tricks on them. Dillon—Sean Wyatt Asherton—was a dishonest, maniacal man. They were playing the worst game imaginable, and she realized she was scared.

Everything he'd just said couldn't be taken seriously. She was sitting in the presence of a rapist. This beautiful man had everything going for him. Why would someone like him play an emotionally crippling game with her and other women before her? Seeing this truth made her body lurch with trepidation.

She glanced briefly at his bank card hooked into the clear plastic at the top of the holder before he closed it and handed it off to the waiter. There were only a few seconds to read it, but it said:

SEAN W. ASHERTON

Secondary proof that he was a fake.

She immediately glanced at Dillon, who was looking up at the waiter taking the ticket holder. She quickly glanced away.

They were quiet for a moment. Dillon noticed the silence as he snagged his beer once more. He seemed confused by it. He looked at Celeste more directly. "What's wrong?"

Celeste had time to control her emotion. Fear was still causing her heart to knock around in her chest. She turned her head his way. "Nothing," she lied. "Why?"

"I don't know. You seem to have suddenly grown ultra-quiet."

Her face relaxed, and a smile crept in at the corners of her mouth. "Sorry. I was thinking about the last time we finished a meal and met at my house. A lot happened during that time." *Oh, that was close,* she thought. *I have to focus on not giving myself away.*

"Do you regret any of it?"

Note to self. To get the interrogation lighting off me, just to change the subject to sex.

"Oh, no. It was stunning, beautiful, arousing, mind-blowing, and very erotic. I've never come that hard before in my life."

He was skeptical of her facial expressions. The fear was gone now. "It was pretty amazing, wasn't it?" he asked.

Celeste nodded and smiled at him, then she winked. A wink that hinted at more sexual deviancy between them. He returned the wink, relaying the same message.

The waiter returned with the leather bill holder and handed it to Dillon. When he looked away from her again and opened the bill holder, Celeste's smile faded quickly. Dillon added a tip and signed his name. After he'd signed his first name—Sean—he stopped in the upswing of the 'A' of his last name. He saw his real name on his bank card and realized he wasn't signing his name as 'Dillon.' He quickly covered the name on his card, then glanced up guiltily at Celeste.

Celeste looked away, pretending she hadn't seen anything.

Fuck! Celeste thought.

Her body was still engulfed in the heat of fear, as though she were a peeping Tom looking in on Sean as she stood fingering herself outside his window. She picked up her beer and played it cool. As she drank, she glanced back to Dillon and asked, "What?"

Dillon didn't say anything at first.

She pressed, "Is something wrong?"

"No. Nothing's wrong. Just thinking of something, that's all." Dillon hurriedly signed his last name and returned his bank card to his wallet. As he did so, he saw the name on his license and shook his head at the small mistake he'd allowed to happen.

"Good," she said. "You ready then?"

"Yeah, let's get out of here."

CHAPTER TWENTY-THREE

"You seem distracted," Dillon said.

"Huh?" Celeste said as she came out of her head again.

They were standing at her kitchen bar as they had yesterday afternoon. This time, they were kicking back shots of Jägermeister. Celeste realized she had gone deep inside her head as they were both standing there holding shot glasses, waiting for her to toast to *whatever* before they threw them back.

Celeste shook her head and focused on the reality of the moment. "Sorry." She thought quickly. "I'm trying to decide whether I should let… *whatever we are…* go as far as I did last time. That wasn't wise of me."

"I think you decided what's going to happen when you invited me here from the restaurant again."

Oh, really. Is that the way you see it? Just because I invited you here does not mean you'll be getting into my pants again. Far from it.

"For what it's worth," Dillion said, bringing her back. "I'm glad you let it go as far as it did."

"I'm sure you are."

He held his shot glass a little higher. "How about we toast to giving into temptation?" He gave her a seductive smile.

"Ha. Funny."

"I'm serious. I'm hoping you let it go that far again this time and even further."

"I'll just bet you are," she said, letting some sly seduction tinge her words. The beer from the restaurant and the two shots they had killed were working, which was good. What she felt on the inside was a lot more sarcastic and hateful, but she managed to keep her tone seductive enough to where Dillon didn't notice.

"Well, how about we drink to letting whatever happens happen?"

"Okay, I can drink to that."

They clinked glasses and tossed them back, both grimacing at the bite of the strong licorice taste.

"Truth be told," Dillon said, "I'm crushing on you hard."

"I know," she said, moving away from the bar area and into the living room. She had to put some distance between them. Another shot or two might have her doing things she knew should never happen again. *Will never happen again.* As she came to the back of the couch, she thought, *Where the fuck is Angel?*

Dillon moved closer as he lowered his voice. "I'm hoping we can be as intimate as we were last time." He stopped next to her, swiped a strand of hair back over her ear, and pulled her attention to his face. "I want to worship your body, Celeste. I want to caress every beautiful curve you possess."

He gently stroked her back and looked into her eyes with those sparkling pools of blue that always made her just a little nervous.

She glanced down at her hands clutching the back of the couch. She was in a vulnerable spot. Vulnerable with her senses muddled and vulnerable if Sean suddenly didn't like her pushing him away. *Could he be as aggressive as her rapist from the alleyway? Where the fuck is Angel!* She wanted him in a way, and she hated herself for it. But because of what she knew, she knew they would never make love again. A part of her was deeply disappointed by that because it had been so damn good.

He moved in closer and whispered into her ear, "If you let it happen again, this time I'm not going to take off afterward. No appointments. No other places to go. Today, I'm all yours. All I want to do is focus on you for as long as you will let me."

His breathy whispers tickled her ear and sent gooseflesh down her arms. She found herself tilting her face up to him. She was torn. She knew this was wrong because of what she knew had happened before. It had all been a ploy to get into her pants. The worst trick imaginable for sex.

Celeste knew their secret, but it was the truth she felt he was speaking now. She knew it was all part of the game but felt that, at this moment, there was something more to his words. She didn't know exactly what to do, so she did nothing.

And that was making a choice.

She closed her eyes and gave in to temptation. Their lips touched softly, and passion ignited between them again. He turned into her. Their bodies were as close as they could get. They were sliding and grinding against each other as they started to remove their clothes again.

Dillon worked his way behind Celeste. He slid his left hand under her arm to her breasts. His right hand moved down, and he unsnapped and unzipped her pants. He took a few moments to pull her pants from her hips and let them fall to the floor. Then his hand was inside her panties, massaging her womanhood. He gently caressed her clit with the fingers of his right hand as he pulled her back into his chest with his left. He showered her neck with kisses and buried his head in her hair.

All the while, Celeste loved and hated what she allowed to happen to her. Her head automatically shook back and forth to this physical contact, though she didn't voice what was happening inside her thoughts. Her mind was pulled in both directions, trying to enjoy this ecstasy and knowing it was wrong because of what she knew about him. She was random points on an imaginary sex game board.

Dillon moved his left hand from her left breast up under her arm and around her neck. He added gentle pressure to her neck to indicate he wanted to bend her over onto the couch so he could enter her from behind.

Celeste allowed herself to bend at the waist but shook her head during this action the whole time. *What the hell am I doing?*

But then, when Dillon pulled his fingers from inside her, grabbed hold of her right hip, and slid his left hand from her neck down to her left hip, her mind jolted on her. One second, she was in the middle of her living room; the next, she found herself in the alleyway again, at the point of the attack.

It was the grip. Dillon's hands were in the same place as Aaron's hands when he had seized her in the alleyway. Instantly, she relived the embarrassment of being stripped naked. She felt the uneven pavement under her as she relived the abrupt, harsh backward jerk and felt the raggedness of her knees being shredded across that coarse pavement. She felt the mounting fear and anticipation of being raped; the possibility of her vagina—or even her ass, depending on which orifice he chose to fuck—being torn as he dry-thrust his girth deep within her. It was more than her mind could take, and the moment was over.

She shuddered. Her head snapped up, and she said, "No." She looked across the room at her and Dillon's reflection on the mirrored surface of the widescreen.

"What?" Dillon asked, not immediately understanding.

Celeste began to raise back up into a standing position, "I said, NO! Not this fucking time."

Dillon didn't fully understand and put his hand on the back of her neck to hold her down over the couch. He wasn't forceful; it was just a gentle coaxing. "What do you mean, Celeste?"

Celeste pushed back with more force. She turned at her waist and came up and around with an elbow. It didn't connect with him, but it told Dillon she meant business. "I said no, and I mean no, goddamn it!"

Dillon backed away quickly to give her room, "Okay, okay." He stooped to pull up his pants. Celeste did the same.

There was a rustle behind them, then a voice.

"No means no, motherfucker!"

The noise and abrupt movement caused them to jerk to attention and look behind them.

Angel was there, and she rushed at Dillon with her baton club extended, aiming at his face.

Dillon had enough time to throw his head down and his hands up for cover. "Oh, Jesus Christ, what the fu—" was all he could get out of his mouth.

The baton smacked the back of his head, and he crumpled under the dull, throbbing pain that spiraled outward and around his head from the impact.

Angel lowered her body, came in with her left hand, jammed it into his right pectoral muscle, and pulled the trigger on the stun gun.

The last thing Dillon saw was Angel bending at the waist as her arching arm crossed his field of vision, then an abrupt and instantaneous rich pain and darkness flooded his body.

Dillon's body erupted in uncontrollable jolts of electrocution, and he jittered like a fish out of water on Celeste's living room floor.

"You hear me, you piece of shit?!" Angel yelled again. "No means no, motherfucker!"

Angel stood again and swiped a couple of strands of hair out of her face. "God damn, that felt good. Hey, sorry I'm late. Things didn't go as planned with Aaron at first. Hey, new rule. No one goes anywhere or does anything by themselves anymore. We do everything together, as a team."

By this time, Celeste was completely dressed again. "Okay. Deal. What happened? Are you all right?"

"I'm fine. I'll tell you about it later." Angel looked down at Dillon again. "See, I told you I'd be ready for him when you two got back from your date. You didn't believe me, did you?"

"I didn't know what to think. I didn't see your car," Celeste admitted. "I did wonder when you were going to show yourself. It didn't dawn on me till now that you probably parked around the corner or down the street."

"I never show all my cards unless I'm ending a game. Here," Angel said, handing the baton to Celeste. "You good to watch him until I move my car around?"

"Sure. I guess."

"I may need you to move your car out of the garage so I can pull mine into it. We can get him loaded in the trunk with Aaron without anyone seeing. That's what I did when I was at their house."

"You got Aaron into your car by yourself?"

"He's tied up nice and tight. He's not going anywhere."

"What if he wakes up?"

"He's out cold, sleeping like a little bitch baby, or he was when I last checked on him. But we need to do all this quickly and get over to the lake house before these two assholes wake up."

"Go," Celeste said. "I'll watch him."

"Okay." Angel handed the baton over to Celeste. She reached into her oversized bag and pulled out some zip ties. "Zip tie this bitch. Knock his ass out again if he begins to wake up. Please don't take any chances with him. Be back as soon as I can," She turned away and was about to leave but then spun back to Celeste. "You were going to let him fuck you again? That wasn't part of the plan?"

"I know. I don't know what the hell I was doing or thinking. I didn't know where you were. I was just playing the game so he wouldn't get suspicious. But for the record, I wasn't going to let him fuck me again."

"It sure didn't look like that from where I was standing."

Celeste was about to spar verbally with a comeback but saw Angel smiling. She relented. She lifted her hands, pointed to her head, and wound her hand and fingers around in opposite directions. "I know, it's fucked up in here."

"I'm just checking on you. Are you still good to go through with everything we discussed?"

"Oh, hell yeah! Definitely."

"Okay," Angel said. "I want you to be one hundred percent sure. I didn't know if you still had feelings for this guy. That would make it crazy complicated for you."

"No. I'm all *game* to continue."

"All right. I'm going to get my car."

"Okay," Celeste said. "Whatever you say. Thanks for helping me get over this situation."

"What are friends for?"

"Friends." It was an indifferent statement. Celeste hadn't even thought about that subject, but she knew Angel was right.

"I know we had a rocky beginning, but we are friends now. Or you are in my book. Besides, I'm not just helping you. You're helping me. It happened to me, too, remember?"

"I know."

"Be back in a few," Angel said, then turned and left to get her car. Over her shoulder, she added. "Tie that bitch up."

Celeste did so.

CHAPTER TWENTY-FOUR

Celeste and Angel stood inside Mitch Harrison's lake house basement, waiting for their two captives to awaken.

Angel was standing between Dillon and Aaron, one on either side of her; both men were naked. They were seated in chairs on opposite sides but were facing each other. Their arms were pulled back and lashed with rope to the single supports that held up the backs of their chairs. Angel had found and retrieved the ropes from her friend's discarded boat supplies in the garage part of the refurbished basement.

Angel was a bit antsy to start interrogating these two pricks about everything they had done. "You don't have any smelling salts, do you?" she asked as she looked over her shoulder at Celeste. Angel knew it was a dumb question. Nobody carried around smelling salts on their person and could pull them out on a whim.

Celeste was standing behind Angel, staring through the basement window blinds framed in the center of the wall. It was the only window with the blinds scrolled open. Celeste marveled at the peaceful night that had slowly fallen over the lake. The water was calm, and moonlight shimmered off its dark, reflective surface. Celeste didn't say anything at first. She stared transfixed at the half-moon slowly rising out of the eastern mountain range in the distance. She wanted a few more minutes of this tranquil view before she looked back at the tableau they had set up behind her.

Celeste chuckled at Angel's posed question, but no joy existed. "No, no smelling salts here." She was pondering the same thing Angel was thinking. *Yeah, let's get this show on the road and finished.*

Angel knew this was a crazy weird situation for Celeste; it was for her as well. She said gently, "Close those blinds. We don't know if any neighbors could be looking in with binoculars or even a telescope. We have to be careful."

Celeste continued to peer out the basement window. Night had fallen, but she could still see the backyard down to the pier. She took a mental picture.

This lake house had been constructed in such a way that the foundation was three to four feet lower than the backyard elevation. The bottom of the basement windows and backyard were about the same level. When Celeste stared out the window, she already had a low vantage point that looked out over the neatly trimmed grass and down the slight slope of the backyard to the dock where Mitch Harrison's Bayliner was moored.

The timing of everything couldn't be more perfect, Celeste thought and hugged herself tighter as a shiver ran through her. *I hope her friend's plans don't fall through and they return home before the appointed date. We would be royally fucked. I'm taking everything with Angel on faith.* That thought seemed to jolt her back to the moment here with Angel and the two assholes they had just kidnapped.

Thinking again of what Angel had asked her, she laughed and continued with the earlier reply, "No smelling salts, but I have some essential oils. We could see if that brings them back around."

Angel said, "It's worth a try."

Celeste took in the last vestige of the lake view, then scrolled the blinds shut. She moved her handbag to a small, square table in the little kitchen area to her right. Opening her bag to get the oils, she asked, "You sure your friends aren't coming back any time soon?"

"Yes, I'm positive. They called me three days ago and told me they had touched down safely and that Colorado was amazing. Mitch and Beverly are backpacking through the Maroon Bells and doing a horseback riding tour through Brown's Creek Park. They won't be back until the fourteenth. We have plenty of time. Quit worrying about that aspect of this plan."

Celeste returned to her purse for the oils, then stopped and looked at Angel. "You know, that was brilliant about backing the car into their garage to load Dillon's body into your car. I can't believe you knocked Aaron out and parked with him in your trunk down the street. That was a big gamble."

"It wasn't smart at all. It was stupid of me." Angel stepped between the two bound men and moved to the table on the other side of them. She double-checked the items that had been placed there. She turned away from the evidence and leaned against the table. "Aaron could've woken up and started beating on the trunk. If someone had been walking their dog and had heard that, we might not be here right now."

"Well, he didn't wake up, and as far as we know, no one knows what we've done. At least, we hope not. Jesus Christ, would you listen to me… *us*. We're talking so casually about this like it's something we always do. That's not normal, is it?"

"I don't know, Celeste. But I think we have to talk about it. It took work and extreme mental focus to make sure we didn't leave any trace of ourselves in their house. I mean, it's not anything *you* have to worry about… *you* were never at their house. Dillon was only at yours. I did a thorough wipe-down of their house because I was there. I was careful not to touch anything, but I wiped down much more than I should have to be sure. I don't know what someone will think when seeing where that coffee table broke the window. I cleaned all the glass up and put the table back in its place in front of the couch. Who knows? It may or may not raise some suspicions and questions later on."

"You sure it was wise to leave their cars in their driveway?"

"Don't know. I've never done anything like this before. I figured people would start looking for these guys later if their cars remained in their driveway. It would look more normal for their cars to be there than if we had driven them elsewhere and left them for someone to find. I wasn't up to the task of trying to figure out how to get rid of two cars. That would be damn near impossible. I had a gut feeling it was better to leave them parked at their house. It would be more of a mystery if everything remained as normal as possible and looked as though they had just up and disappeared like they had gone on a trip, you know?"

"You think anyone saw us returning Dillon's car from my house?" Celeste asked.

"There's always that possibility, but wearing our ball caps low on our heads and stuffing our hair up into the hat itself probably kept any nosy neighbors from being able to identify us, or at least we hope it did, right?"

"Yeah, that was a smart move. You really know how to cover up a crime."

"I got all those suggestions from those TV crime shows I've watched and all the horror books I've read. I hope we thought of everything."

Talking about what they had done made Celeste feel better about their cover-ups. She finally looked down and began to pilfer through her purse's contents. "Okay," she said. "I'm just still a little scared about what we talked about doing." She paused again, then said, "Are we really going to go through with what we said we would do in the car and on the phone yesterday?"

Angel glanced over at Celeste and saw her pawing through her belongings as she finished speaking her questions. She moved over and knelt in front of her. "I am," Angel said. "I'm ready to take this as far as we need. I don't know what's going to happen. I have ideas of what I want to do to these two assholes. We've already talked about some of those ideas. But I'm not going to do anything until I am sure what we think they did is true. If you have any reservations about continuing on this course with me, you can step out now. I will not fault you in any way for it. I want you to have a clear conscience if we step into the realm we discussed. Once we go there, there is no turning back."

Celeste nodded, conveying to Angel she understood, then looked down into her lap.

"But if you stay," Angel continued, placing a gentle hand under Celeste's chin and tilting her head up so they could see eye to eye as she finished her thoughts. "We are in this together one hundred percent. If we get away with it, we get away with it. If we get caught, we get caught. And if *I* get caught, I will never say anything that you were involved. I know we both have trust issues because of what these two assholes have done to us and others, but believe me when I tell you: I promise I will never rat you out. I hope, and I trust, you to do the same for me."

"Yes, of course."

"But so help me, God," Angel added, "if you double-cross me, our friendship is over, and I will come after you with everything I have whenever I get a chance. But I will not give someone a tip and blame you for what we are going to do. Is that fair?"

"Yes," Celeste said weakly, then more firmly. "Yes, it is."

"Does that sound fair?" Angel asked again, wanting Celeste to be more confident about what she agreed to.

"Yes, it does. It's very fair."

"So, I ask you now, are you with me one hundred percent?"

"Yes, I am. One hundred and ten percent."

"Good, because I cannot do this alone. I need all the help I can get with these two."

To further ease Angel's mind that she was on board with their decision, Celeste held up three small vials and asked, "Citrus Bliss, Peppermint, or Melaleuca?"

"Melaleuca? What the hell does that smell like?"

"It's not my favorite scent. So, it might be the best to wake them up."

She unscrewed the lid and walked over to the two men strapped into their chairs. The top of the bottle had a small roller ball that would transfer the scent when rolled across the skin's surface. She quickly moved it back and forth over the top lip of both restrained men.

Celeste and Angel stood near the table and waited, but the men weren't coming around. For a split second, Celeste began to think they both might be dead and only sitting up because they were lashed to chairs, but then she saw their chests barely moving. Their breathing was shallow.

Celeste went to them again and rolled the scent on top of their lips a second time for good measure.

After a few seconds, the men began to come around.

"Oh, wow. I can't believe that's working." Celeste said. "Yet another reason to use dōTERRA."

CHAPTER TWENTY-FIVE

SEAN ASHERTON WAS the first to come around. When he squinted his eyes, the sight before him shocked him to full attention in the chair where he sat; there was a startled influx of air. A strong scent assaulted Sean's nose.

Thomas Bonnomer sat before Sean completely naked; his arms were pulled back to the sides of his chair, and from what Sean could gather, they were tied with… something.

Sean wriggled his nose, then snorted, trying to get the scent out of his nostrils. "Oh, Jesus, what the fuck is that smell?" He closed his eyes against the scent.

Sean tried to lean forward and bend at the waist as a wave of nausea washed over him. He felt he was going to hurl at any moment. He swallowed the queasiness and took some deep breaths through his mouth, so he wouldn't have to smell the awful scent. He realized he couldn't bend at the waist because he was sitting in the same position. When he glanced down, he saw he was completely naked as well. He tried to move his feet, but his ankles were lashed to the chair legs. His feet drummed against a cool plastic that coated the floor. Horror wrapped his body in a dread-filled blanket. He searched the floor quickly and saw it was a large square piece of gray plastic that was duct-taped together in several places. With that realization, trepidation shuddered through his body as an intense panic set in. He started hyperventilating. He had seen too many movies where plastic-wrapped floors meant blood was about to be spilled.

ණ

Thomas Bonnomer's head also began to move. It lulled to the side and back before rolling forward and jerking him awake. He squinted and began to look around. The squinting wasn't due to any bright lights in the room; he was just confused as to where he was and why his head hurt.

Thomas realized he was in a decent-sized room by the looks of it. Minimal accouterments made up this space. To his left was a couch with two reading chairs and a mediocre entertainment center with a big-screen television. The most alarming thing he saw was the two women leaning against a long table. Both women stood with their arms folded across their chests, faces set in grim determination.

ණ

Sean pulled on his bindings in a frightened panic. He searched the room for anything that might help him get loose. On his left, against the far wall, was a small kitchen area with a table, four chairs, a refrigerator, a stove, and countertop space with cupboards. There was a regular door directly behind Thomas that led somewhere.

Outside to a backyard, possibly? Sean thought.

The shade mounted at the top of the door had been pulled down over the window, so he couldn't see what was beyond it.

The wall on Sean's left had three windows. Each window had its blinds drawn.

"Not a good sign. Not a good sign," Sean whispered to himself.

His mind was working fast but wasn't coming up with any solutions. He looked to his right. There was a set of stairs against the far wall that went up from this area to a second floor.

We're in a basement. We have to be, Sean thought as he looked to his far right and a little over his shoulder. He saw a single door that led off into another room.

ණ

Thomas's mind was foggy; he tried to think. *Still hazy from what? Was I hit on the head?* He couldn't remember, but his head was throbbing like a son of a bitch; a heavy pounding with each heartbeat. Thomas looked away from the women and ahead of him. His gaze rested on Sean, seated in a mirror image of himself. He became rigid in his seat as a huge, invisible vat of fear poured into his body and began filling him up. He stared at Sean, who had an 'oh, fuck' look painted on his face, the same look that he, himself, now wore. He saw Sean frantically working his wrists and ankles within their bindings, then Sean finally resigned himself and stopped.

They looked over at the two women standing sentinel over them.

Without hesitation, Sean got right to the point and began begging for his life. He couldn't talk fast enough. "Celeste, whatever you're thinking about doing, I beg of you to please reconsider. Please, for the love of God, don't go through with what you're thinking of doing."

Celeste ignored his pleas to release him. "Now that you two assholes are awake, we can begin. I, Celeste Baker, call this court hearing to order."

This line of dialogue wasn't what either Sean or Thomas were expecting.

"Say what?" Thomas asked for both of them. He gave a half-laugh, as though what Celeste said was utterly ridiculous, even in their grim situation.

Celeste focused on Thomas and said, "This court hearing is now in session. The honorable judges Baker and Domingo presiding. Today's case is Baker and Domingo vs. *Sean* Asherton and *Thomas* Bonnomer."

Thomas, not realizing that Celeste and Angel knew more than he did and currently not caving to the fact they already knew their actual names, asked with laced sarcasm, "Who the fuck is Sean Asherton and Thomas Bonnomer?"

Celeste and Angel both turned in his direction and gave him an appalling look. Angel said, "Oh, that's right; how could I forget that? I'm supposed to call you both by your code names: Dillon Carmichael and Aaron Brakefield, because you're still playing your fucked up game with us, aren't you?"

"Those are our names," Thomas said, adding a little pissiness with his reply. "And *game*? What game are you talking about?"

Angel jumped in to help the two men out so they would all be on the same level playing field. She turned quickly to the table behind them, plucked two cards from its surface, and turned back to them. "Okay, you two, just cut the bullshit because we both know everything. For the sake of these courtroom proceedings, you will henceforth be referred to as…" She held up Dillon's license and read it, facing him, "Sean Asherton." She looked at the picture, then turned it around to face him. "That's you in the picture there, correct?"

Angel had him; he couldn't say otherwise. "Yes."

She looked at the license in her other hand and turned in Thomas's direction. She read the name printed on its surface. "And you are Thomas Bonnomer, correct?"

Thomas remained implacable.

"Yes," Sean said. "His name is Thomas Bonnomer."

"Shut the fuck up, Dillon."

Angel cast an evil smile at Thomas. She spun and gave an approving nod to Sean, then handed the cards to Celeste.

"But that's not my name," Thomas said, still trying to bluff. "That's not *his* name."

"Shut up, Thomas," Sean said. "They know. I told you yesterday they knew when you came back from trying to find my knife."

"So, it is your knife?" Celeste asked.

"Yeah, it's my knife," Sean said, a little dejected for having sprung a leak and sharing information.

"It was his dad's knife," Thomas corrected.

"Shut the fuck up, Thomas," Sean said and tried to throw a kick or punch in his direction, but it looked silly as his hands and feet were currently tied down.

"We'll talk about the knife later," Angel said. She turned to the table again and picked up two more IDs with different names. "These are your fake IDs with your aliases' names on them; Aaron Brakefield"—she pointed to Thomas—"and Dillon Carmichael." She pointed at Sean. "Why do you two need fake IDs?"

Neither man answered. They didn't have a decent comeback, and to tell the truth would be to admit they had them made for the game they played.

Angel handed all four cards to Celeste.

Celeste took the cards and said, "May I enter into evidence Exhibits A and B: Thomas Bonnomer's real license and fake ID?" She emphasized the word as if that would help them see there was no use in playing that name card any longer. She continued with another question. "And Exhibits C and D: Sean Asherton's real license and fake ID?" Celeste stood between them and held her arms at length to show them their licenses. She glanced over at Sean and said, "This is where you fucked up a little bit, when we went for sushi. But I think you already know this. You should've replaced your real license with your fake ID. Also, your bank card still has your real name, which didn't help you either."

"Celeste, please," Sean began. "Let me explain. Please."

"Save it," Celeste ordered. "For fairness, you will have a chance to tell your side of the story. After all, this is a courtroom setting, and it is only fair, even though neither of you deserve it. But Angel and I both want a clear conscience."

Imitating a judge's answer as best she could from the crime and courtroom dramas she'd seen on TV, Angel continued without worrying about Sean's pleadings, "I will accept these four exhibits. You may proceed."

Celeste continued, "We will, from this point, on be referring to you as,"—she pointed to Sean—"Sean Asherton. No more *Dillon* in your future." Celeste pointed to Thomas with his license. "And to you as Thomas Bonnomer. No more *Aaron* in yours either."

Celeste returned to the table and replaced all four licenses where Angel had picked them up. She picked up the two pieces of paper and turned back to the men, and said, "Since these two pieces of paper have the names Dillon Carmichael and Aaron Brakefield written on them with a phone number to each of your secondary cell phones, we can only assume these are the code names you chose for your role in this rape game you two play and to which you probably wanted to be referred to while playing that game. We will go with your real names, Sean and Thomas; that will be easier for everyone."

The men said nothing. Everything was coming at them in full force. They didn't know where to begin explaining what these two women now knew was true.

Celeste continued but was speaking more to Angel. "May I enter into evidence Exhibits E through J? This would be the two pieces of paper containing the alias names and phone numbers written on them and four phones. Two belong to Sean Asherton, and two belong to Thomas Bonnomer. The alias phone numbers are written on pieces of paper and match each man's secondary phone. From this point on, I will refer to the secondary phones as their burner phones."

Angel said, "I will allow the six pieces of evidence to be entered into these court proceedings. Did I say that right?"

Celeste turned and smiled at Angel, who was playing along with this pretend game of being in court. "Yes, Your Honor. That was perfect. Thank you for asking."

Angel smiled back at Celeste, proud she was doing this right. She continued to study the two men Celeste had built her case against. She glanced over to Sean and saw his lips mouth the word 'fuck' to himself as he mentally beat himself up for being called out on the real and fake names. As suspected, they were guilty, and he had just proved it another way.

Thomas shook his head and said, "What the fuck is going on?" He was still trying to throw them off, but he wasn't getting an answer. He tried again, "I don't know what the fuck you're talking about."

Celeste said, "The crimes against both of you are false representation, lying, attempted rape, *rape*." She emphasized the word, making it hard to ignore.

Both men looked at her in astonishment and said, "What?"

Celeste repeated the word, emphasizing it so there would be no question this was the main reason they were tied up in this situation. "I said, *rape*."

Thomas protested, "You can't put us on trial for rape! We didn't rape either of you." He felt funny saying the words 'put us on trial' as he didn't feel like this was a trial. He had no idea what this was.

Celeste said firmly, "It was rape whether you think it was or not."

A thought came to Sean, and he was talking before he even realized it. "Might I remind you of what you said the day I helped you in the alleyway? I wanted to call the cops for you because of the assault, but you said, 'no,' and you were very emphatic about it. You even told me, and I quote, 'I wasn't raped. It was close, but you stopped that. The cops won't have anything to go on. I want to go home, take a shower, go to sleep, and forget it happened.'" He immediately felt like shit for saying it, but he was pissed he was tied up and at the mercy of these two women.

Sean remembered the moment he had a chance to get out of this game forever. The moment was right after he left Celeste, right after their beautiful shared moment of ecstasy. He closed his eyes to that moment and relived it in his mind. The closing of her front door seemed to jolt him in his chair. The prolonged, abrupt harshness echoed out again in his mind. He also closed his mind to trying to reason with Celeste about almost being raped versus actually being raped. He knew she was right in her argument.

Celeste paused where she was and whipped her head around toward him. If looks could kill, he would instantly be dead. She was seething. "You're going to sit there and presume to tell me what constitutes rape and what doesn't? Your and Thomas's setup was all a ruse, but if you think about it, I mean, really concentrate on the subject, you just admitted to it being rape because you're the one who suggested calling the cops after the attack, indicating it was rape."

Thomas fired back from his tiny prison. "You're splitting hairs. It's not fucking rape if both parties are consenting and both of you very much consented to fucking us both."

And there it was, Sean thought. *The admission of guilt. Way to go, Thomas. No playing any more games. They have the ammunition they need now.*

Angel couldn't help getting involved. She lunged diagonally across in front of Celeste and punched Thomas in the center of the mouth with a sucker punch out of nowhere. Thomas saw the punch coming, but he could only move his head back so far to try to evade her extending reach. She came across and rocked his head back. His head bounced forward again, and his lip began to bleed. "And you're not a goddamn woman who knows what it fucking feels like to be on the receiving end of something so hideous, you piece of shit!"

"Oooh, Jesus Christ, bitch. You split my fucking lip."

"That's not all I'm going to split, you cunt. I was fucking raped by you"—she jabbed a finger hard into his chest—"whether you two want to believe it was or not. And Sean"—she turned and threw a finger in his direction—"attempted to rape me. The same thing happened to Celeste, and even though we were consenting adults about it after the fact, it was the fucking circumstances surrounding it all"—she threw a circular hand motion up above her head—"that made it fucking rape. There are no gray areas here, asshole. It was rape, plain and simple. Don't try to weasel your way out of these charges we have set against you."

Celeste stepped forward, placed a hand on Angel's shoulder, and gently pulled her away. "Angel, there will be time for you to question both of them, especially Thomas. Let's get their full side of the story, and then we can judge them accordingly."

"Oh, you can bet your ass I'm going to place some fucking judgment. I can guaran-damn-tee that." She looked down on Thomas as though he were nothing; her fear was gone. "You just wait and see, motherfucker."

"I know, we both will, but right now, court is in session. Remember?"

Angel stepped back and took her place but said nothing more. She didn't have to. Her eyes were stating everything she was thinking. She was livid and anxious, ready to get started.

Celeste gathered her thoughts. "Now, where were we?"

Angel said, "You were listing the shitty crimes these assholes committed against us."

"Oh, right. Yes. Attempted rape, *rape*"—she emphasized it again even more, then continued—"playing with our emotions, fucking with our psyche, and overall being two of the biggest douchebags we have ever met."

"That's not a crime," Thomas shot back as he spat built-up blood onto the plastic tarp beneath his tied feet.

"Oh, it's a major crime against women," Celeste said. "It happens all the time. All men need to stop doing that shit to us."

Thomas sat back in his chair again as his mind started to work. He asked, "Why are we on gray plastic?"

Angel said, "This is my friend's house. I'm house-sitting for them. I don't want to get any blood on their beautiful floor if it comes to that. It might be hard to clean up and harder to explain."

Sean asked, "What the hell is going on here? Where are we? Why are we tied up? And the big question on our minds is, why the fuck are we naked?"

Angel stepped forward, wanting to be part of these fake court proceedings. "We all know the hard answer to that. We were exposed when you raped us, so now we're exposing you and the game you've been playing. Everything is going to be out in the open." She glanced at his midsection and snorted as though what was between his legs was the most pitiful thing she'd ever seen.

Celeste was immediately on the heels of Angel's statement. "*Were* playing... *were* playing on us. They won't be playing their game anymore after tonight, remember?"

"Right," Angel said, realizing 'were' was the better word to use. "We'll see how they like being vulnerable and used."

Thomas was still thinking about the plastic. He looked up and over at Angel. "What are you going to do with us?"

Angel avoided the question and said, "We're curious about a few things."

"Yeah, like, why do you play this game between the two of you?" Celeste asked. "We genuinely want to know. 'Cause to me, it seems like a whole lot of trouble to go through."

Angel spoke again, "Yeah, you both are beautiful men. Good looking enough if you played your cards right and I saw you in a bar, I might be inclined to go home with you for a one-night stand. You know, a good night of banging."

Thomas said nothing. He was slowly shaking his head back and forth, silently seething.

Celeste chimed in, "So why the run-around with having one of you go through the motions of nearly raping us and the other one saving us?

It makes no goddamn sense. We both have no idea why you would even put a woman through something like that."

Thomas was tired of playing the innocent. He wanted this question session to be over. He said reluctantly, "It's just something we do for fun. A way to get an adrenaline high. We have no idea what the woman is going to do or if we're going to get hurt in the process or not. But the high."

"Well, it's a shitty fucking game," Celeste said. "If you didn't know that before, I think you know now. Because we're playing along now, we're going to show you what good contestants we are. Make you realize that going up against a couple of bitches in a game like this, you're going to lose, and you're going to lose big. You're going to get so much more than you bargained for."

Celeste turned away from the staring contest between Angel and Sean and picked up her plastic ziplock bag from the table. She turned back to the two men. She held on to the top of the bag and dropped the contents that had been rolled up into what looked like a giant plastic cigar. The contents of the bag unraveled. The knife with chain etching across the top of the blade and wrapped around the handle hung before them.

Celeste glanced between the two men as she turned the knife in each direction so they could see it perfectly for a moment. She turned to Sean, "You say this knife is yours?"

Sean glanced from the knife to Thomas, "Nice going, shithead. I told you they knew about the knife and that we were working together." He looked back up to Celeste, "Yeah, I own it. It's my dad's knife. What of it?" He couldn't bear to look her in the eyes; he just stared at the knife.

Celeste stated to everyone, "I would like to enter into evidence Exhibit K. Let the record reflect this knife belongs to Sean Asherton."

"Oh, Jesus fucking Christ, will you stop with the damn courtroom proceedings lingo bullshit," Sean said. "It's driving me fucking nuts."

"No, I won't stop," Celeste said evenly. "This is our court, and we will conduct this hearing the way we want. We're playing our little game now, and you will play along with us, just like we played along with your rape game. I told you once that I would have my day in court. Today is that day, and you and Thomas are on trial."

Playing along with Celeste, Angel said, "I will allow Exhibit K into evidence. The record now reflects an admittance of guilt from Sean Asherton."

"Thank you, Your Honor," Celeste said. She turned her attention back to the two men. "Start talking—one of you. Either of you, I don't care which one it is. We have posed the question to each of you, but we have yet to hear an answer. Now the interrogation starts, and we're asking the questions, and you're going to fucking answer them, or parts of your anatomy will be taken from your body, and you will never get them back."

Both men were quiet. They eyed each other for a moment, mentally trying to figure out who would talk first.

Celeste continued speaking without getting upset. She calmly repeated the main question to which she and Angel wanted an answer. "Why do you play this rape game with women?"

"Hmmph," Sean said. "That question should go to Thomas. He's the one that started playing it first. But it wasn't a game back when he was in high school. That was real life."

"Don't fucking blame me, asshole," Thomas said.

Angel and Celeste turned to Thomas and waited. Thomas was looking straight ahead, boring a hole of hatred into Sean.

"Thomas?" Celeste coaxed. "You want to tell us about it?"

"No, not really."

Celeste regrouped. She opened the ziplock freezer bag, retrieved the knife from within, and held it up in front of Thomas. "My bad. I meant to say it as a statement, not a question. You *will* tell us about it. So, start talking, or I'll slide this blade under each of your fingernails until you give us a bedtime story. And if we don't get what I think is the fucking truth, I'm going to start my manicure session, and I'm going to go deep."

Thomas looked at Sean and shook his head. "How could you? You know I don't like re-living that part of my life."

"I don't think you have a choice in the matter, Thomas," Sean said. "Just fucking tell them."

Thomas began. "It all started with two bitches."

The word 'bitches' pissed Angel and Celeste off, but they said nothing as they didn't want to deter him from opening up to them.

"It was early in my senior year, and I was going home late that day, an hour later as it happened to be, since I had to stay in detention for making a fucking dart with a long pin, an eraser, and some paper folded into a star, you know, like the dart had four fins to make it fly really well. I didn't know it would fly as well as it did until I zinged it at Matt Mahafery, and it caught him high on the back of his thigh, like right in the bottom of his ass cheek. You know what that son-of-a-bitch did?"

"Kept it?" Celeste asked, assuming the obvious answer. She continued to fiddle with the knife, keeping it present to remind him she had the upper hand in this forced confession.

"That's right," Thomas said. "He kept it. He wouldn't give it back. That asshole turned it in to the principal, Dr. Jacobson. Yeah, *doctor,* can you believe that shit… he has a *doctor* attached to his name, and he has a job as a principal. Dr. Jacobson called me into his office and gave me the third-degree bullshit about how I could've put someone's eye out with it. I wanted to tell him I wasn't aiming it at his eye; I was aiming it at his big ass. One that I couldn't miss. But I didn't say that. The dart was sitting in the center of his desk as we discussed the matter. I wanted to grab it and throw it in his fucking face."

Thomas looked up at them to see if they were still with him on the subject.

Angel and Celeste both shifted their weight, refolded their arms over their chests, and gave him a 'keep-going-this-is-good-shit-but-not-the-shit-we-want-to hear' look. This story was just off the wall enough to be the actual truth.

Thomas turned back toward Sean, although he wasn't looking directly at him. To everyone else in the room, it looked as though Thomas was going somewhere in his mind that he didn't want to go. The situation caused him to make a mental shift. He turned his head like he was trying to pop his neck vertebra; nothing snapped, and he leveled his head again. Then Thomas looked like he was staring at some far-off distant place as though a small portal had opened up, and he could see the memory playing out, watching himself go through the motions in that distant memory.

CHAPTER TWENTY-SIX

Thomas Bonnomer left the detention classroom shortly after 4:00 p.m. and made his way to the back entrance of the school. He often went that way because he lived about four blocks to the west of the school, and it was easier to cut down behind the stadium and across the two practice fields to get to his home beyond the school grounds.

The main playing field, the stadium bleachers, and the two practice fields were devoid of life by this time. There wasn't any football or cheerleading practice; everyone had already gone home for the day. If anything, it was weight day, and all the football jocks would be in the gym working out to get their swole on.

Those assholes, *Thomas thought.* They were always lifting and pumping, trying to be better than the next football player so they could make the perfect play and look good doing it. Too much fucking work. I hate those fuckers.

He made his way down along one side of the stadium. As he walked, he fished his iPod and headphones out of his backpack and unraveled them. He was about to shove the earbuds into his ears when he heard faint voices from underneath the bleachers.

Thomas stopped short and craned his head to listen.

Yes, it was voices; it sounded like a guy and a girl.

He smiled, shoved the iPod and headphones back into his book bag, and crept to the corner of the stadium where the voices were the strongest.

Thomas realized that he was out in the open and knew he had to conduct himself as though he were hanging out there instead of looking as though he were creeping around trying to break into the enclosure underneath the bleachers. If any of the staff saw him, they could make a judgment call and report him again; he would have to waste another hour of his life in detention tomorrow.

He was standing by the door that led underneath the enclosed stadium bleachers. It was where all the main electrical breakers and switches were to turn on the field lights. It was also where all the equipment was kept to groom the grass of the football fields, the chalk materials to mark the lines on the field before Friday night's big games, and where Coach Morris kept a lot of the sporting equipment for gym classes. Very few people had keys to this place. The door was always locked, and a big red sign had been attached to it that stated: FACULTY AND STAFF ONLY - NO ONE ELSE PERMITTED.

Yeah, right, *Thomas thought.* No one is permitted except the couple getting it on inside this storage room. And me. Oh damn, what if it's Coach Morris and another teacher? If it is, and I get caught, I'm probably going to get expelled. Ha, it'll be worth it just to see the look on their faces. If it's not, and it's just some punk and his girl, I'll probably get my ass kicked over this. *He shrugged his shoulders.* Seeing a hoochie momma getting fucked hard still might be worth the ass beating.

His mind was made up. He nonchalantly looked in every direction to see if any faculty or staff were watching him. Seeing no one, he carefully and silently rotated the doorknob and pulled it open.

As soon as he opened the door to the storage room, he saw a spillage of late afternoon sunlight pour into the doorway of this under-the-stadium chamber.

Thomas half-expected to hear whoever was down here shout out in alarm, and the show he hadn't even got to see yet would be over. He slipped inside as quickly and quietly as possible. He closed the door behind himself, cutting off that slash of light so he wouldn't give himself away. He was also happy not to hear a hinge squeal that would've alerted the couple that they were not alone. He turned the doorknob again, shut the door so the latch wouldn't click loudly, and then quietly released it.

Hell yeah, *Thomas said, mentally high-fiving himself at how quiet he had been.* I'm a fucking ninja, bitches.

Thomas stood in the dim lights under this stadium area and listened intently. His heart was pounding at the possibility and thrill of seeing two people having sex. There was a certain amount of anticipation of him getting his ass kicked because he knew he would be caught watching—and most likely be labeled a peeping Tom—but he didn't care. He was still pissed at Matt Mahafery for turning his ass in over that stupid dart he'd made and having to stay for detention.

If you didn't want anyone watching you fucking some chick, *Thomas thought,* you should've locked the door behind yourself, you dumb son of a bitch, whoever you are.

The small clip of distant voices and laughter he'd heard earlier wasn't as far away now; it had taken on a more distressful quality. Thomas's brows furrowed in confusion as he listened.

"I said no, Greg, and I mean no. Quit trying to fingerbang me. I'm really not in the mood now."

Oh, shit! *Thomas thought.* That was Rebecca LaGrande. What the fuck?

"C'mon, Becca, why not?" a guy replied in disappointed protest. He was beginning to pout. "I worked crazy hard to make a copy of my dad's keys to bring you down here. You're the one who said you wanted to do it someplace weird. You can't get any weirder than here under the stadium."

Holy shit. That's Coach Morris's son, Greg, *Thomas thought again.* He's a big son-of-a-bitch. If he finds me hovering around down here eavesdropping, he will royally fuck me over.

Greg went into a high falsetto and mimicked her, "C'mon, Greg, it'll be fun. Don't tell me where you're going to take me. Find somewhere that's, like, you know, crazy weird where we can do it."

"Stop it, Greg. I didn't say it like that. I don't talk like that," Rebecca said.

Greg shot back. "That was exactly how you said it."

"Now you're just being an asshole." There was a lot of hurt in Rebecca's voice.

Thomas stood there deciding if he should leave as silently as he'd come or help Rebecca out. This chick was dating a human tater-tot, and he had no clue how to conduct himself around women properly. Or should I watch how badly this dude fucks this girl over for not going through with what she initially agreed upon? *He'd never seen a couple having sex other than pictures in some porno magazines he had pilfered from his dad's stash or the numerous videos he'd pulled up online or watched on video when his parents were away.*

But a fucking rape? Are you kidding me? To witness that… oh shit. I don't know if I could look on and just let that happen. Not to Rebecca, that girl's hot, but she doesn't deserve that.

"I'm *being mean," Greg's sarcasm was thick. "Fuck you, Becca. You're the one being mean by not giving it up. I have a good mind to rape you right here and now and take your fucking pussy since you're not giving it up freely as you promised. How would that be? Would that be weird enough for you?"*

Her voice took on a little edge of panic. "Stop it!"

"I asked you a question. Would that be a fucking weird enough for you?"

"I said, stop it!" Rebecca shouted at him.

His voice became louder. "And I asked you a goddamn question. Would that be a little fucking weird?"

The crisp slap echoed throughout this confined space under the bleachers. Thomas knew the look of shock suddenly painted upon his face and the 'oh' his mouth was changed into was the same look that was pasted on Greg Morris's face. It was almost as if Rebecca had slapped him and Greg simultaneously.

There was a moment when nothing happened. Time seemed to slow down, extend, or grow to stand still and draw out into a long moment of anticipation. During that time, Thomas knew Greg was weighing his options. He could take the defeat of the simple and abrupt slap, save face, and leave disappointed. Or he could stop the presses, apologize, and see if she wanted to go somewhere, share a Coke, and talk about their misunderstanding. Or he could just—

Another slap and an audible gasp of pain from Rebecca answered Thomas's quandary.

Or you can just rape her, *Thomas thought.* Guess you're going to take that pussy like you said you would.

"Ooooh, fuck, Greg. Quit it!" Rebecca snapped.

There was a quick tearing of cloth.

"What the hell are you doing?" Rebecca asked.

Thomas heard open slaps of protest against Greg's arms, or that's what he imagined the sounds to be in his mind.

"Quit asking dumb fucking questions, Rebecca. Is this the part of the

role-playing game you wanted me to do? I get you down here, you refuse the possibility of sex, then I rape *you." The word 'rape' was over-emphasized. "Is that all part of the excitement? All part of this weird fucking fetish you have with sex?"*

"What? No! Stop it, Greg. Get the fuck off me!"

I can't just stand by and let this happen to her. I'm sure he's going to fuck me up pretty badly. *Thomas reached for the handle of a bat from the fifty-five-gallon drum full of sports equipment standing near him. He grabbed it and quietly pulled one out. He was surprised that he'd picked up a cricket bat instead of a baseball bat.* Okay, a cricket bat will work just fine. I hope you can save my ass. *He gripped the cricket bat in both hands as he looked at the smooth wood grain and how it was made.* Let's see how weird I can make this interruption for you, Greg.

Thomas moved down the short hallway to the alcove Greg and Rebecca were in. He held the bat out in front of him as though it were a crucifix. He looked more like Van Helsing in the castle of the Count, ready to battle with an ancient bloodsucker, than a teenage kid out to defend the innocence of a cheerleader from the cornerback of his school's football team.

Greg was towering over Rebecca, blocking her view of her savior quietly sneaking up behind them. Thomas raised the cricket stick with both hands as though it were a wooden stake, as though he were about to give the final impalement to Dracula in his coffin. He stabbed down and caught Greg in the lower back with the fat end of the bat with a hard blow.

As soon as he made contact, Thomas shouted at Greg, "Hey, asshole! What the fuck do you think you're doing to her?"

Greg was more startled than Rebecca because he was about to slide his dick home. Greg immediately thought it was some teacher, faculty member, or maybe even his father who had come down here for some crazy reason. It was as though someone had snapped his bare ass with the towel—as all the football teammates do, grab-assing as they get ready before or after practice—and stung him into an immediate standing position. He quickly pulled up his pants, fastened them, and zipped them up.

He rattled off some lame excuses, "I'm sorry we were here. We were just trying to find a place with a little privacy." Glancing up, Greg finally realized it wasn't a teacher but another classmate, although he couldn't tell which one as Thomas's face was draped in shadow. "Hey… who are you?"

"Thomas?" Rebecca said, recognizing him from their Literature class. "Oh, thank God."

"Bonnomer? Is that you?"

"Yeah, it's me, dickhead. And from what I heard, it sounded like she wanted you to stop a long time ago."

"What's going on in here is between us. A nosy little shithead like yourself shouldn't be snooping around in other people's business."

"When it comes to the shitty way you were treating Rebecca, I'll stick my nose in as far as I fucking feel like, cunt nugget."

"That's funny, Bonnomer. You'll look even funnier when I punch your fucking nose out the back of your skull."

Thomas knew that Greg would and could do it too. He had to strike first before Greg had a chance to get to him. He was standing with the handle of the bat across his chest. The handle was in his right hand, and the bat's sweet spot was in his left.

"Take your best shot, jizz biscuit," Thomas admonished, hoping to God that whatever he was going to do would be a better move than what Greg might do to him.

Greg pulled a fist back to charge and connect with Thomas, but as he did so, Thomas stepped in and shoved the bat forward with his right hand. That bat end struck Greg in the center of his stomach and packed the same punch as a real fist. Thomas's hand pulled back to the neck of the cricket bat, and he pulled up hard as Greg doubled over from the punch to his gut. The flat, sweet spot of the cricket bat clocked Greg in the center of his face, broke his nose, and bloodied his lips as Thomas swung upward through his headspace.

Greg's head whipped back; he folded backward and crumpled to the ground. He rolled over and stood quickly. He staggered back away from Thomas to put a little distance between them. He shook his head fiercely to clear his mind.

From Thomas's point of view, that action looked like a mistake. Greg faltered, but he didn't go down. He looked like he was about to collapse, but he was fighting against a blackout. The hit had almost turned his lights out.

Greg took a moment to feel his nose and winced at the pain. He looked at the blood on his fingers, then glanced over to judge where Thomas was standing. His eyes narrowed, widened, then narrowed again. It was as though he were seeing double or trying to figure out his depth perception that had been jarred. Finally, getting his wits about him, he charged Thomas.

While Greg tested his nose, Thomas had already brought the bat back across his chest and held each end as before. Thomas pushed forward again when Greg charged him. The bat caught Greg across the chest. Thomas pushed him back as hard as he could, but Greg was strong, a regular attendee at the gym. Greg shoved Thomas up against the shelving. Cans and small equipment fell off because of the hard shove against them.

Thomas knew if he didn't do something soon, his lights would go out quickly. Then, something passed through Thomas that scared him. He didn't know where it came from or what it was, but a temporary possession lit up inside him like a panicked heat. A rage ignited and filled him up. Thomas jerked the bat down and away from where it made contact with Greg's chest, ripping it from Greg's grasp. He turned to the side and came back around, swinging the bat as hard as possible within the confined space. The bat found its mark, and Greg dropped quickly with each blow that rained upon him. Greg yelled all sorts of expletives and pleas.

Thomas knew that one of them would end up being put in the hospital, and he knew it wouldn't be him.

It was Rebecca who stopped the beatdown before the situation escalated further.

She ran up and stood between Greg and Thomas as he pulled back into a backswing to come in from the side and into Greg's ribs.

Thomas was already coming down with his forward swing when he saw Rebecca jump in front of Greg.

Rebecca held up her hands to shield herself as she began yelling, "Thomas! Stop!" It was a ballsy move on her part, knowing the thin blade of the cricket bat could've split her skull open.

Thomas was able to stop the swing inches from her outstretched hands. The possession—that fucked up heat deep inside him—sizzled out with the heart-felt panic that he'd almost fucked up Rebecca's beautiful face.

"You're protecting him?" Thomas said in dismay as he lowered the weapon to his side. "He was going to rape you."

"No! God no. Not protecting him. I don't want you to kill him." She looked down at Greg, groaning on the floor. "He deserves it, but I don't want

your life or mine messed up with any police questioning us, although that is one way to beat his ass down. Good God, you looked possessed. The cops will probably come around asking questions."

"Yeah, probably." Thomas looked from Greg to Rebecca. "You okay, though?"

"Yeah. I'm okay."

Thomas gave her a disbelieving look.

Rebecca confessed, "Okay, I'm scared shitless."

"You're going to be okay now," Thomas said. "I'll make sure of it. Do you mind if I walk you home?"

"I'd like that very much."

"Good, just let me do one other thing."

Thomas leaned the bat against one of the iron-gray shelves holding equipment. He stooped to Greg's level, pulled him up by the shirt collar, and looked into his eyes. Thomas slapped Greg's face, then snapped his fingers to get him to focus on him and what he had to say. "I'm only going to say this one time, asshole. Hear me and comprehend what I'm telling you. Don't ever come near Rebecca LaGrande or me ever again. Do you understand? Nod your head if you understand what I'm saying."

Greg nodded. It was weak but enough for Thomas to continue.

"If you try to talk to her or come after me and beat me up because of what happened here, I will fucking kill you, no questions asked. This is your only warning. I will be prepared for you and any of your boys. Rebecca is off-limits to you and your football cronies. As of right now, you two are not dating. You just broke up. Just stay away from us, and all this can be put behind us. Do you understand what I am just now telling you?"

Greg nodded again.

"I need a verbal response of acknowledgment, Dickcheese. Say, 'Yes, I understand you, Mr. Bonnomer.'"

"Yes. I understand you… Mr. Bonn-Bonnomer."

"Good boy. We're going to go now. I suggest you stay here until we are long gone."

Greg nodded, then Thomas released him. Greg sunk back down to the concrete floor.

Thomas stepped away from Greg, adding, "Piece of shit." Then he moved over to Rebecca.

"Are we just going to leave him here?" she asked.

"I'm only concerned about you. And after what he did to you, I don't know why you're so concerned with him."

"I'm not. It just seems wrong to leave him there."

"If I didn't come along when I did, do you think he would've helped you after he'd raped you?"

That question alone put everything in perspective for Rebecca. She shook her head. "No, probably not."

"You're damn right. He would've left you there, gone to find his boys, had some beers, and then he would've been right back with you tomorrow at eight o'clock chatting you up at your locker as though nothing had ever happened."

"You do have a point there."

"I do have some smarts about me," Thomas said.

Rebecca smiled as they exited from beneath the bleachers and closed the door behind them.

CHAPTER TWENTY-SEVEN

"Let me stop you right there, Thomas," Angel said. She was getting a little perturbed that this story took so long to tell. She could've dealt with the Cliff Notes version. She didn't care about his detailed account of every damn thing. "This story is all fine and good, but that still doesn't tell me why you and Sean do what you do with your little fucking rape game."

"Well, I am getting to that point if you fucking bitches would be a little patient. Where's the fire? Are you expecting company? It *would* be bizarre if anybody else came by and you had a couple of naked guys tied up down here. You're the one who asked me to tell you. So I'm telling you. You didn't tell me to condense it down. You want to hear my story or not?"

Angel ignored his arrogance but said, "I get where your story is going. You walked her home. You offered to meet her anytime for a coffee or a light meal. Just give her a chance to talk about almost being raped as you did with me. Like Sean did with Celeste. Anything to gain her trust."

"No, that's not it at all. When I walked her home, she invited me inside because her parents wouldn't be home until after eight. She said my *rescuing her*"—there was a flair of attitude when he said it—"had turned her on. She was ultra-horny. She needed me to help her out with that, so I did what any teenage male my age would've done. For the next three hours, I fucked her silly. And I'm not talking about putting on clown masks while we did it, either. No, we fucked in almost every way possible. How's that for being weird?"

"Great. Just like you planned. She repaid you in sex for saving her ass. Lucky you."

"Yeah, it was a monumental, memorable day in my life."

"Has that ever happened to you, or you, Sean, during your game? Getting laid right after a girl was fake raped by the other person. Did either one of you ever get as lucky as Thomas did after saving Rebecca?"

"Never happened to me," Sean said. "It's a delicate process."

"No, that was the only time," Thomas replied.

"Jesus, God, that seems like way too much work," Angel said. "Seems easier to chat up a girl in a bar, go to her house, bang her, leave her, and never call her again. That's usually the way it works, anyway. Do it that way, and you're off the hook for rape. You guys would still be the world's biggest assholes, as are the guys that fuck me and leave me, but I'm a big girl. You know, the one that is *not* the asshole, mind you. But you two. Adding those few extra steps makes you guys the godfathers of Assholeville.

Celeste asked, "Did that Greg Morris guy ever come around you or Rebecca?"

"No, that shithead was way too scared of me. I don't know why he would be. I was nothing compared to him back then. I just got lucky that day in both senses of the word. He avoided Rebecca like she had chlamydia or some other STD. She kept calling me to talk, and we got to know each other and eventually started dating. Guess she liked the sex too much."

Celeste asked, "How long did you and Rebecca date?"

"Most of my senior year."

Angel nodded more emphatically. "When and why did she break up with you?"

"How did you know that?"

"Because I'm a smart chick. I'm putting two and two together and coming up with why you're so fucked up in your head. Answer the goddamn question."

Thomas thought for a moment, swallowed hard, and then went deep into his mind, where he had buried the hurt of his breakup with Rebecca. He finally began to speak.

ര

"Hey, what's wrong?" Thomas asked. "You seem a little different today. Not like yourself. You're kinda quiet."

"I'm all right," Rebecca lied. "Just have some things on my mind."

"Like what? Did I do something?"

She shook her head a little too quickly but said nothing. She looked off straight ahead and locked in on something in the distance. It was as though focusing on it would keep her from turning and looking at him directly. She looked like she wanted to say something but either was afraid of his reaction or didn't know how to say it.

"But?" Thomas said, drawing the word out longer and making the inflection come out as a question.

Rebecca broke her gaze and looked over at him, confused. "What?"

"Well, something has your mind going crazy. Talk to me about it. Whatever it is, it's okay."

"School's almost out," she said.

"Yeah. Just a couple more weeks."

"Have you thought about what you'll do after you graduate?"

"Some," Thomas said. "Why do you ask?"

"Just curious."

"But?" He drew the word out again, making it another question; he hoped to coax more information from her. She looked over at him again. Thomas smiled back.

Rebecca gave a little laugh, then looked off into the distance again. "I'm serious. What are your plans?" She didn't look at him but waited for him to answer.

Thomas looked out into the distance to try and see what she had honed in on. "Honestly, I have entertained the idea of heading off to Penn State with you after graduation."

Rebecca jerked her head back to him so fast that the motion of her movement pulled his attention back toward her. Her eyebrows were dipped in confusion, or maybe that was anger. Her look caught him off guard, and his face changed to confusion. He could tell she wasn't pleased, but he had no idea why. He continued speaking but the news of this surprise—as he had hoped—wasn't enjoyable since her face showed disappointment.

"I know you have your heart set on Penn State, so I applied myself because I have no idea what I want to do. But I know you're the only direction I have in my life now, so going there with you seems like the best idea. But now I'm confused at your reaction because it tells me I made a huge mistake in doing that."

"You never said anything about going to Penn State or college," Rebecca blurted. "I don't want you to go to Penn State with me."

The words felt like a hard punch to his psyche; they stung him deeply. It took him a while to find his voice. "Why not? We've been dating for a few months now. I thought you would be thrilled. I thought that might be a safe bet for my life. I thought it would be a nice surprise to tell you when I got accepted."

"I just need some time away from everything."

"You want some time? Just let me know. You want to go out with your girlfriends? Go. Have fun. You can do that, you know. I'm not keeping you from anything."

"I know, Thomas, but..." Her shoulders slumped in defeat.

"But what? Just tell me what you want."

"I don't want to be tied to anyone right now."

"How is me going to the same college tying you down? It's not like I'm asking you to marry me, move in together, or anything like that."

She blurted out again, "I don't want to date you anymore."

Thomas had just turned in her direction when she said that phrase. She had not indicated that anything was troubling her mind, and now the moment's epiphany hit him full force. It took him an extended moment to process exactly what she had said. He froze in mid-turn as the blow of those seven words obliterated something within his being. It was as if time had stopped altogether.

"Thomas?" she questioned, then placed a hand on his shoulder.

Time seemed to restart; it began spinning at the regular speed again.

Thomas realized her hand was on her shoulder. Why is it there? Why would she even touch me if she didn't want to date me anymore? *Thomas rotated his shoulder and sloughed her hand away. He turned, faced forward again, and slid a short distance away from her.*

Anger was building up inside him, and he fought hard to harness it. It was that rage ramp-up that he had experienced during the beatdown with Greg Morris. He managed to say, "Why? What's the real reason?"

Rebecca turned away from him again and placed her hands on her lap. She picked at a troublesome cuticle on one of her manicured nails. She pulled the little piece of skin from her thumb and rubbed it smooth. She looked up and out again at the thing she'd locked onto earlier and said, "Here lately, it seems that I've been dating you because of what you did for me in the Room."

Many times, after their initial discussions of when he had rescued her from Greg Morris's clutches, the area where the event had happened was referred to as 'the Room.'

Thomas looked over at her with slack-jawed surprise. He asked, "What?"

"Recently, I've felt like I have to have sex with you because you expect it. You know, because you saved me, I have to always give it up."

"I have never demanded sex from you," Thomas said emphatically.

"I know."

"I'm not like that Greg Morris asshole, and I resent the implication that you're comparing me to him."

"I didn't mean it like that."

"I would never force you to have sex with me," he said, driving his point home even farther.

"I know that. You've been the most understanding boyfriend I have ever been with."

"Except for now. I do not understand what you're telling me." He repeated her reason under his breath. "Don't want to date me because you feel like you owe me sex."

"Exactly,"

"You're the one who threw yourself on me that day. Wanting me to fuck you in so many ways because of me beating Greg up after saving you. You said that it turned you on. It was your fault. Fuck! I should've let Greg rape you that day and saved myself all this fucking heartache." It was out of his mouth before he realized he'd said it. He blew out a frustrated breath, then said, "Fuck. Sorry. I didn't mean that."

Now it was Rebecca's turn to be surprised. It was also her turn to be emphatic. "It's funny how one little sentence can solidify in my mind the reason for not wanting to date you anymore. You could've said anything but that."

"Really. Truly. I'm so sorry for saying that. I'm just upset. I didn't mean it, Becca."

"No, you meant it, Thomas. I do not doubt that you meant every word of it. Even though you inwardly killed me just now with your choice of words, I hope you are successful and that you find new happiness somewhere down the line with someone else. Have a nice life, asshole."

CHAPTER TWENTY-EIGHT

The women waited for Thomas to continue with more of his story, but he was done. He slowly came out of his funk. It was as though that memory he was locked on so intently had finally faded away, and he could no longer see it clearly. He blinked, and the tears brimming in his eyes eventually fell. He shook his head slightly and said, "Then Rebecca stood and walked out of my life forever." He motioned like he wanted to wipe the tears from his face, but he couldn't move his hands because they were still tied to his chair.

"Boo-motherfucking-hoo," Angel said. "And because you love this Rebecca chick so much, and because she broke your heart so bad, and because she devastated your life so completely, *you* have to rape women to get back at Rebecca. All these women in your past relationships are Rebecca LeGrande."

Thomas nodded as though he had never understood why he played the game but had just been convinced of his actions. "In a way, yeah. Maybe. I don't know. Haven't you ever been crushed by a true love that's pissed you off?"

"Oh, hell yeah. Plenty of times," Angel shot back. "But you don't see me going around taking my rape revenge out on men because of failed love like you do on us women. I go to the gym and work out. I do hour-long aerobics workout sessions to clear my head. I spend some time with the punching bag and pretend the bag is the guy that I'm so pissed off at. I don't keep that shit buried inside me."

"I do that too," Celeste said, then turned to look at Sean. It was as though she were talking to herself and convincing herself of what she was saying. "True love comes along every once in a blue moon. You have to be thankful that you had that time together with that person, but if she's not happy… you let them go and hope that someday that love comes your way again by another person."

Sean bowed his head. He knew she was saying that to him. She was talking about them.

"Yeah," Angel agreed. "Doing what you did to all those other women and us, true love is so far from you. Karma has a way of keeping that at bay from guys who make douchey moves like you. I doubt you will ever find anything resembling true love again."

"What the hell is that supposed to mean?" Thomas asked.

Angel continued, ignoring his question. "So, you replay this beginning meeting of Rebecca out on all these other women as a way of finding a perfect true love again?"

Thomas looked up at Angel with a tear-streaked face. He didn't like being made fun of. His face changed as anger replaced his sadness of lost love. "No. I've given up on true love altogether. I'm just trying to get back at Rebecca by hurting all these other women I *can* get to."

"So that's your reason for playing this game? Save a girl from almost being raped to sweep her off her feet and be the perfect gentleman, bang her a few times and get her to think you two are an item, and then crush those feelings the way Rebecca LaGrande devastated you by breaking up with them first and leaving?"

"Yeah, that is it completely. I don't give a fuck about women in general, and the harder I can fuck them, use them, and hurt them by the time I'm finished with them, the better."

"Well, just know I am the last girl you will ever do that to."

"You keep saying that, but you won't answer me. What the fuck do you mean by that?"

Both women turned away from Thomas and placed their interrogation gaze on Sean.

Since Sean had heard Thomas's sob story numerous times, he had been paying more attention to Celeste and Angel and to the questions they were asking him. He saw them harnessing the rage that was seething just beneath the calm outward demeanors they were showing them. He had no idea if he would ever get out of this chair, out of this situation, or if this basement room would be where he would breathe his final breath. These ropes were extremely tight. One thing he did know was that the longer he talked, the longer he would be alive. He just might be able to worm his way out of this situation.

They continued to stare at Sean, letting the moment's seriousness soak into his body. Sean felt their eyes on him. "What?" he asked.

"You tell us," Celeste said.

"Tell you what, Celeste?"

Celeste said, "You've been quiet for a long time. We've heard Thomas's side of the story and we accept his answer. It all makes sense, but, at the same time, I have difficulty understanding his thought process."

Angel said, "Yeah, me too. How are you involved? I mean, from the looks between you two, I would've thought you were the one who was in charge—and maybe you are—but I would've bet you were the one with his fucked up view of women and a bad relationship gone awry. You seem like *you* would've involved *him* in this little caper you two do."

"Who says I didn't have a bad relationship with women?"

Angel and Celeste both shrugged their shoulders.

"If anything, my experience is probably worse," Sean admitted.

Angel and Celeste raised their eyebrows with interest, glanced at each other, then back to Sean.

"Enlighten us. Open our eyes, as Thomas did, to your side of the story."

"What do you want to know?" Sean asked softly.

"Everything. Like why and how did you get tied up playing this *game* with Thomas? How did you two meet? How did this rape game begin between the two of you?"

"If you want me to start from the beginning, we would have to start with my mother."

Angel said, "And there it is. Relationship complications with your mother. Is this the other bitch Thomas was talking about when he said 'two bitches' earlier?"

Sean shrugged his shoulders and nodded.

"What, was she too possessive? Did she not give you enough love? Did she give you too much love? What, did she rape you? Have sex with you? I knew it was something like that."

"You don't know anything, Angel. No, my mother was the perfect mother to me. She was just a bad wife to my father."

Celeste couldn't help but say, "Maybe your dad was a bad husband to your mom. Ever thought of that? Why don't people own up to their shortcomings?"

Angel looked over at Celeste. She was staring at Sean but nodded her approval.

"As it turns out," Sean said, "My dad was the perfect dad to me and a good husband to my mom. It was my *mom* who was the *whore*."

Celeste and Angel exchanged inquisitive glances again.

Sean didn't go inward on himself like Thomas had when he talked about his past. Instead, he continued to speak freely, glancing between the two women and Thomas casually.

CHAPTER TWENTY-NINE

Cut school, *the devil side of Sean's conscience said to him.* What's one day going to hurt? You've been a good little boy and had excellent attendance this whole school year. But you're a senior now; time to be an adult. Cutting one day of school doesn't make you irresponsible.

Those were the thoughts plaguing Sean's mind throughout his morning classes. He didn't want to be in school today for some damn reason, so at lunch, he listened to his devil side and snuck out, grabbed his bike from the rack near the side entrances, and rode home to play video games.

Once there, Sean realized that playing hooky was much more boring than he'd thought. No other players were online to fight or shoot because none of his friends had cut school as he had. He had to play against the computer, and that was lame. The computer was always a smart ass. Nine times out of ten, the computer won.

Fucker, *Sean thought of his gaming system.*

He finally got tired of that bullshit. Maybe someone would be online in a couple of hours, and he could take out his pent-up aggression on them.

He tried reading a few comic books—Spawn, X-Men, Ghost Rider, Daredevil—but realized he'd already read them several times. Instead, he just looked at the pictures and wished he could draw as well as some of the featured artists.

Sean pitched them aside and thought for a moment. Wonder what Ricky's doing today after school? It's almost time for school to let out anyway. *He grabbed his phone and texted Ricky McClure.*

SA: Hey man, what U doin' after school? Can I come over?
RM: Where R U, dude? U R not N class.
SA: Playin' hooky.
RM: No way. U didn't invite me?
SA: I should've. Believe me. It's so stale hangin' out at the house alone. Nothing going on.
RM: After school. Come by whenever. I B there by 3:30.
SA: 10-4.

Sean texted his mom and dad on a joint feed.

SA: Hey, guys. I am going by Ricky's house after school today. I wanted to let U know where I would be. Love you. S.

Caroline Asherton, Sean's mom, texted back immediately.

CA: Okay. Be careful. Remember, it's a school night. Don't stay too long.

Sean never received a message from his dad.

With renewed excitement, he grabbed one of the few novels on his bookshelf and settled on his bed to read to pass the time until it was time to go to Ricky's. Shortly into the third chapter, sleep washed over him, and he slept hard.

Harsh voices awakened him. He looked at his bedside clock and saw the green numerals read 6:47 p.m.

What the hell? *He thought.* How long did I sleep? Do Mom and Dad even know I'm here? Did they look in my room when they got in?

He replayed everything in his mind. He'd been careful so as not to get caught. He hid his bike in the shrubs in the side yard. He used his house key to enter but locked the door behind himself. He had closed his bedroom door as he always did for privacy. Today, he'd played his video games with minimal sound, so he could hear either of his parents if they had come home early.

Sean reached for his cell phone and saw only one call from his mother and one text from Ricky from the earlier feed. The new text from him was from about an hour ago.

RM: Yo bitch! Thought U were coming over after school. Where U at, dawg?

He was about to text Ricky back and then listen to his mother's voicemail, but another raised voice from the other room—he thought it was his mother's—snagged his attention.

That was odd, *he thought.* Mom and Dad hardly ever fight. They don't say a lot to each other nowadays. It must be something crazy wrong.

He slowly opened his bedroom door and peeked out. The voices became louder with the open door. No one was in the hallway.

"How many?" his dad asked, his voice echoing down the hallway.

"How many what?" his mom asked in return.

"You know what I'm asking."

"Be specific, Dustin. *How many times have I* fucked around *on you? Or how many men have I fucked around on you* with*? Or, even better, how many times have I fucked* each man *that I have been fucking around on you with?"*

"You're such a fucking whore," his dad said, much too calmly. Something was beginning to bubble underneath the surface of that statement.

"Did that make you feel better?" Caroline asked. "Are you trying to get a rise out of me? That word doesn't bother me. Yes, I am a whore, if you want to label me. And I love every minute of being a whore."

What? *Sean thought in dismay. This was news to him as well as his dad.* That's not her. I can't imagine mom being a— *He couldn't even think of that word and his mother in the same sentence, but it had intrigued him to give movement to his feet. He ventured down the hallway to the outside of the living room entrance. He stood there for a moment listening to his mother's vent, then peeked around the corner into the living room.*

Caroline continued, "Because the men I've been with worshipped my body. I felt their love, or-or lust, or whatever they had for me during our time together. And I can't get enough. That's why I'm in the gym every day… working on my muscle tone… slimming down, so I am the most sought-after piece of ass in this town. Someone has to fulfill my needs, Dustin; you certainly aren't doing it. You made me this way, asshole, because I certainly don't get any love or attention from you here at home.

"To begin with, you're hardly ever here anyway, and when you are, you're still mentally unavailable. In your mind, you're always at the office thinking of ways to make some more goddamn money. I, frankly, don't care about the money." She fell silent for a moment, composed herself, then came at him again with a calmer tone. "You know, I have my intuitions about you. And my intuition says that you're fucking around on me behind my back."

"No. I'm not a whore like you, Caroline," Dustin said. "I spend so much time working to support you, Sean, and our nice life. I work, so you don't have to. I see now that my hard work is going toward things that allow me to unknowingly *pimp you out to all the assholes in this city. I mean, that is about the size of it. Right, Caroline?"*

"If you pimped me out, we would be making much more money than you make as a stock trader. A fuck-*ton more. Emphasis on the word 'fuck' because I have been doing a lot of it, and I have loved every orgasm given to me."*

Sean stood there looking through the living room doorway, stunned and mesmerized by his parent's argument. Oh, shit! Mom is going off. Not the woman Dad and I have known. *With the last cut down his mother had bestowed upon Dustin, Sean would've thought his dad would've slapped her, punched her, or something, but he was holding it together pretty well. The only thing Dustin did was turn away from her as though her words hadn't affected him. He stuck his hands in his pockets.*

"So, I'll ask you again. How many?" Dustin said.

Sean saw that his dad was looking off toward him, but he was focused on something sitting on the bookshelf near the living room door. Sean could see the mounting anger underneath his calm demeanor. His dad's jaws flexed as he stood solemnly, waiting for her answer.

"I never kept track of that," Caroline said.

"Then come up with a fucking number?"

"Why? Who cares how many men it was? Who cares how many times I fucked each of those men? Who cares h—"

"How many, Caroline?" Dustin said, raising his voice. As he did so, he looked back over his shoulder at her. "Come up with a goddamn number."

She yelled back, "I don't know. Let's say thirty-two. How does that number suit you?"

Dustin looked away and back to the thing on the bookshelf. He nodded, considering her answer. "Suits me just fine." He pulled his right hand out of his pocket.

Sean saw the item and knew it was his dad's pocketknife.

Dustin flicked it open with his thumb as he closed his eyes to steel himself. Then he whispered to himself, "Thirty-two it is then."

Sean was close enough to hear his father's words, and the epiphany hit hard in his mind. He knew his dad's plan. He saw the knife in his dad's tight grip, the blade extending out the bottom of his fist. Sean almost yelled out for him to stop, but the cry of appeal to spare his mother's life or scream of warning to his mom to run—he didn't know which—just stuck in his throat.

Dustin opened his eyes, and he turned on Caroline. His arm came up quickly and flashed down without any pause or warning to his wife.

Caroline only had time to form an 'oh' with her mouth before Dustin hit her in the chest with a hammer fist stabbing and wrapped his other arm around her lower back to pull her close.

"That's one!" Dustin shouted with rising vehemence.

The blade stabbed into the center of her chest was the exclamation point on that yelled word. Dustin held her tight as he looked deep into her eyes.

He jerked his arm away; a single stream of her blood fell from its sharp tip as his arm arched back over his head again. There was a slight hesitation, then another quick flash of movement, and another fist hammer blow stabbed the knife deep into her chest again.

"Two," Dustin said, his eyes flashing with bloodlust happiness.

Two? *Sean thought.* Oh, Christ Almighty. He's counting up to thirty-two—.

"Three," Dustin shouted. He jerked the blade out and up again as Caroline found her voice and cried out.

Sean looked on in rapt horror as his dad's hand rose and fell again. He couldn't see his mother's chest because his father's back was the only thing visible as he towered over her.

"Four!"

His mother's face, now etched in unimaginable horror, changed slightly each time the knife was driven home. Then, Caroline's head lolled to the side, and her eyes fell upon the living room doorway. Sean saw her looking at him. His head was low to the floor, peeking out from around the doorjamb, watching in horror. Their eyes locked on each other for a brief moment.

Caroline's right arm dangled limply at her side, but she tried to raise it toward her son.

Caroline whispered, "Sean."

Sean didn't hear her call out to him, but he listened to her voice in his mind as his name played out on her lips.

The knife entered her again as Dustin yelled, "Six!" Her arm dropped feebly; then, his dad rotated her head away, blocking her face from Sean.

Then, with some energy reserve, his mother flung herself away, turned from his father and ran or instead tried to run. She stumbled, fell to her knees, and sprawled on the floor.

Dustin was upon her, raining down blow after blow into her back, releasing all his anger and pent-up aggression into her with each stab.

"Seven!"

"Eight!"

"Nine!"

As Sean looked on, tears slowly began to form. The tears pooled in his eyes for the longest time, building upon his eyelashes, causing the figure straddling his mom to blur into an amoeba-looking form.

"Seventeen!"

"Eighteen!"

"Nineteen!"

Finally, the brimming tears were too much for his eyelids to hold, and they dropped away, giving him a clear view of his dad stepping aside to flip his mom over as he plunged his knife into her body over and over and over again, all the while yelling each consecutive number down into her face. His arm was now a continuous blur, casting off red swatches of blood like it was magic.

"Twenty-eight!"

"Twenty-nine!"

"Thirty!"

"Thirty-one!"

As Sean looked on in horror, his mind began to tune out his dad's number yells. He was hearing them, but in Sean's mind, he was seeing his dad's body clear one moment, then blur into some otherworldly form as tears built up again; then, as his tears dropped free, his dad morphed back into himself.

Finally, his dad, his voice ragged and hoarse, yelled—"Thirty-two!"—straight into his wife's face as he plunged the knife into her body one last time.

Sean saw his dad try to stand, but his fatigued muscles failed him. He crumpled to the ground, then tried again. Getting his feet under him, he finally stood and swayed like a drunk man trying to take straightforward steps. Then Sean saw his dad stagger around as though he were going to go to his bedroom. Sean knew his dad would see him, and as far as his dad was concerned, Sean wasn't even home yet.

I shouldn't even be here, *Sean thought.*

His father turned in his direction, but not before Sean threw himself out of the doorway and out of sight as Dustin came around.

There was an audible squeak as Sean moved into an area of the hallway that didn't even have floorboards underneath the carpet. Sean closed his eyes against the tell-tale noise and shook his head.

"Fuck," Sean mouthed to himself.

"Sean?" his dad asked. "You here?" Sheer fear had consumed his dad's voice.

Sean heard his father's footsteps stumbling toward the hallway entrance. Sean was already moving back toward his room. Luckily the hallway floor didn't squeak anymore as he moved to his destination.

Sean thought, What the fuck am I supposed to do when I get to my room? He's going to kill me, too, if he knows I saw that whole fucking shit show.

Sean cut the corner to his room and swung the door almost closed a couple of seconds before Dustin turned into the hallway. He slipped under his bed as fast and quietly as he could.

"Sean?" Dustin asked in the empty hallway. He strained to hear anything at all. "You here, buddy?" He waited, but no answer came.

Sean heard his dad moving to his bedroom door in a rush; then his bedroom door swung open. The door gave an audible duh-duh-duh-duh sound as it connected to the doorstop.

"Shit," Dustin said in a low voice to himself.

Sean could tell that some relief had replaced the initial fear. "I must be hearing things after what I did. I would've hated for Sean to have seen that."

Dustin left Sean's bedroom door open and stumbled to the master bedroom.

A few moments later, pushing himself as far back under his bed as he could, Sean heard the shower in his parent's bedroom turn on.

What the fuck is he doing? *Sean thought.*

Sean didn't dare slide out from where he was hiding to investigate. Intuition told him that Dustin was getting cleaned up. But thousands of thoughts and questions were assaulting his mind on what he would do. As he lay there underneath his bed waiting, he mentally prepared himself for what he would do.

Eventually, he heard the shower turn off, but as his dad dried off, he began to whistle.

How the fuck can he be so calm after what he's done? *Sean thought.*

To Sean, it seemed like it was taking his dad forever to do whatever he was doing there. While waiting, he pulled out his phone and ensured it was on silent mode. He didn't want it going off at any time while his dad was in the house and giving him away. That's when he saw the conversation feed with Ricky again. He punched through to the feed. He re-read Ricky's text and texted him back.

SA: Hey...sorry I didn't come by. Fell asleep wastin' time. Could I crash there 2nite? Need a change of pace. U think your mom and dad would care?

A few seconds later, Ricky texted back.

RM: It's a school night, but I'm game if U R. Dad's watching the game. Mom works late, so she's not gonna give a shit.

SA: Tks, bro. U R a lifesaver. I will bike over soon. 4 reals this time.

RM: NP.

Sean heard Dustin coming back down the hallway by the sound of his whistle getting louder. He clicked his phone off and covered it so there wouldn't be a glow shining out from under his bed. A lump of panic rose in his throat, thinking his dad, for whatever reason, would come back into his room, flip his comforter up and smile at him from his crouch, but Dustin passed by, heading back to the living room.

What the hell are you doing, Dad? Was Mom right? Are you going to meet someone? Or are you going back to work? *That's when it hit Sean.* He's planning on staying away and letting someone else find her. Or me. That way, he will be less likely to look like the culprit. He's distancing himself from what he did. Is he planning on pinning this on me? Shit just ain't gonna happen, Dad. Good thing I texted them earlier today that I would be at Ricky's house.

A loud crash rocked the front area of the house. Sean had no idea what was going on, but he stayed hidden. More random sounds of wood breaking followed another loud sound of broken glass—more and more sounds of furniture destruction and glass shattering.

Dad's losing it, *Sean thought.*

Sean lay underneath his bed, flinching at the hurricane of destruction that was blowing throughout the living room and kitchen. There was no sound besides glass and furniture being broken down, and thumps that could've been books tossed about.

The destruction went pretty quickly, then Sean heard the door that led to the garage open. He heard his dad's SUV start up as the garage door scrolled back. He listened to his dad back up and leave; the garage door closed again.

Sean slid out from beneath his bed and moved to his door. He was leery of being tricked by his dad, faking that he'd left, then somehow, he would magically be standing there smiling at him with that amused 'I gotcha' look on his face, but since Dustin had driven away, there was no way he'd be here.

Sean crept to his bedroom door, slid into the hallway, and moved to the living room entrance.

Sean's eyes widened in surprise when he saw the living room's utter destruction. Most of the bookshelves had been cleared; books were strewn in all directions on the floor. Picture frames and knick-knacks had also been smashed and tossed in all areas of this room. There was no particular organization to this attack on this room—just utter devastation.

That's what Dad probably used to destroy everything so quickly, *he thought, looking at the baseball bat near his mother's feet.* He made it look like a random burglary that ended with an attack on Mom. Smart. But you're still not going to pin this shit on me, Dad.

Sean grabbed his phone to call— Who? *he thought.* Who am I going to call?

That's when he saw the text indicator notifying him that he had one new text message. He hadn't felt or heard it because he'd recently turned it to silent mode. He touched the screen to move to the text bubble window. It was from his dad. It sat in the dual message window he'd sent to his parents earlier that day. His dad had sent him a reply message close to two minutes ago. It read:

DA: Hey, son...I was in a meeting earlier. Saw this and thought I had responded. I see now that I hadn't. Yes, as your mom said...don't stay out too long. It is a school night. You can hang out longer on the weekend. Be home by 9:00 pm.

"Fuck you, Dad," Sean said aloud. "Not coming home and being the one who has to find my mom like this. Are you kidding me? Hell no!

Sean took his time constructing the message and texted him back.

SA: Spending the night here at Ricky's tonight. I already talked with mom earlier today. She said it was okay. I checked with her since I didn't hear anything from you earlier. Don't work too hard. See you tomorrow after school.

"Try that on for size, asshole," Sean muttered. "Two can play your little game."

Sean turned his phone off because he wasn't going to play a texting game with his dad. He was done for the moment.

Get my bookbag and some clothes for school tomorrow, and get the fuck out. Let someone else find Mom first.

Sean's eyes gravitated to his mother. The sight of her lifeless body caused something to break apart inside of him. Grief bloomed, hot and explosive. He stood there trembling as it spread out from the center of his being. Tears poured out of his eyes again, and he mourned his mother. He couldn't take his eyes off her limp body, so he just stood there, dejected and alone.

He couldn't remember how long he stood there and cried, but eventually, the tears dried up, and he wiped his eyes. As the sorrow faded to a dull ache, ever-present within him, it slowly took on the form of anger. It began to needle at him, then festered until it infected his psyche.

Sean glanced around the room, mentally double-checking everything. Out of his harbored anger, a thought hit him. He took the time to dwell on it for a moment. Concluding, he picked up the baseball bat and went to the nearby front door, unlocked it, and opened it. He locked the door again, stepped outside and pulled it shut.

Locked outside his house, he brought the baseball bat down on the handle a few times, bending and warping the handle. He stepped back and kicked the area near the doorknob like a SWAT team member. It collapsed a little. He kicked again, and the door frame buckled, swung inward, and banged off the inside wall.

Standing on the inside again, Sean dropped the bat back into the area his dad had dropped it and said, "C'mon, Dad, use your head. Why is everything destroyed in our house, but the whole house is locked up? Have to make it look believable, dumbass. I can't believe I'm helping clear you in Mom's murder. You can say she fucked us over by fucking these other guys she's been with. Guess I feel a little betrayed too. But all I have is you now."

Before he left, he stepped to his mom's body and knelt by her side. He looked her body over once and then back to her face. The tears threatened to pour forth again, but he forced the sorrow deep within him, and more of the anger and hate of what she'd done returned.

Her body was devastated. He knew thirty-two brutal stab wounds had been inflicted. He saw that his dad had not used the bat on her; there was no blood on it. Using the bat was to help make the room look like a burglary.

He looked down at the handle of the blade sticking out of the center of his mom's chest. It was the knife he'd always coveted, the one he'd seen on his dad's bureau many times. He had handled it several times, checking out the handle and blade. Fantastic chain etchings wrapped back around the knife's handle. It was cool as hell and so badass. He reached out for it and hesitated; his hand hovered over the blade.

"Do this, and you're committing yourself to this as much as your dad," *the angel side of his conscience said.*

"But what if your dad tries to pin this shit on you?" *the devil's voice said, speaking up.* Maybe this is your bargaining chip with the police a little way down the road.

Sean's angel voice spoke again. "Get out, Sean. Leave things the way they are. You've already entangled yourself enough."

The devil voice told him what he wanted to hear. "You've always liked and wanted this knife. Who's going to know? When your dad hears or finds out there's no murder weapon, do you think he'll ask you for it back? Take what you've always wanted. It's your knife now; you found it. Too bad it's sticking out of your mom's chest. Who's going to know? The police will say the killer was smart, taking his blade so as not to get caught. Lack of evidence and all that shit, you know?"

His hand hovered, almost touching the beautifully crafted handle.

"Do it!" *the devil voice screamed.*

And with that, Sean wrapped his fingers around the handle and pulled up on the knife. The blade was plunged deep and was stuck firmly in his mother's sternum. Caroline's body lifted slightly as he pulled up harder. He finally jerked hard away, and the blade slid free with the tiniest scraping sound of steel on bone and a slight hint of suction.

Caroline, being pulled a little way off the ground, dropped back to the floor. Her head lulled to the side and lay still.

Sean went to his bathroom, carefully holding a hand under the open knife to catch any blood droplets that fell. If the police found the slightest hint of blood anywhere else in the house, they could figure out that Sean—or somebody else—was in here when the crime occurred or even say that he was the one who staged this whole tableau.

Not me, people, *Sean thought.* I have an alibi. Talk to my dad about this. Check our phone records. You'll see that I was never here.

Sean took his time washing the knife. He made sure no blood was anywhere else on the knife. With a clean washcloth from the linen closet, he dried off the blade, closed it, wrapped his new prize, and put it in his jacket pocket. He grabbed his duffle bag, stuffed in some school clothes for tomorrow, and grabbed his backpack of schoolbooks. He left the house as it was with whatever lights his dad had left on. He stepped to the side yard, grabbed his bike from its hiding place in the shrubs, and peddled off to Ricky McClure's house. He left his mom's body to cool even more as she waited for someone to find her corpse.

CHAPTER THIRTY

Sean was quiet for a long time as he sat there still. It looked as though the story had taken a lot out of him.

To get him to continue talking, Angel asked, "So, who found your mom?"

"Dad. He eventually went home, called 911, and the police came."

"When?" Celeste asked, "How long?"

"Sometime before lunch the next day. Two cops came to my school. The lady in the office called over the intercom, asking me to come to the office. When I got there and saw the two officers, I started to panic. I thought they were there to pick me up, take me to jail, or whatever cops do when they know someone's a suspect. But instead, they calmed me down, told me what happened, and said they were taking me to meet my dad."

Angel asked, "What happened to your dad?"

"Nothing. He got off scot-free. The cops had no murder weapon because, of course, *I* had it." He laughed at how lucky he and his dad had been. "It was right there in my pocket the whole time. Because I had an alibi, I wasn't a suspect or anything. They didn't even check my pockets for anything. I was a kid whose mom had been killed ruthlessly due to a random break-in. Nothing was out of the ordinary with my dad's schedule. He always worked long hours. I spent the night at my friend's house. Ricky even testified that I had been with him since early that afternoon of the day before. It was a pretty cut-and-dry case. A cold case now."

"But your dad," Celeste commented. "He had to know you had the knife."

"Oh, *he* knew. I made sure he knew."

"Did you guys ever talk about it?" Angel asked.

"Once. And only briefly."

Celeste asked, "What did the conversation entail?"

"It was shortly after everything had calmed down, and life had progressed back to normal. He just gave me a simple thank you for taking the knife and keeping it safe. The fucker even asked for it back. Can you believe that shit? I laughed in his face as I pulled it from my pocket and showed it to him. I told him it was mine now and that if there were ever any rockiness between us, the police would get my testimony. He was reticent after that because he knew he was walking around a free man because of me. We had an understanding.

"I told him it had been in my pocket the whole time. He got so fucking pissed at me for being so careless. He called me stupid. I reminded him of how stupid he was when I told him I was the one who gave the little addition of busting in the front door to make it look like a real break-in. Jesus, if you're going to be a criminal, cover all your fucking bases.

"The cops looked at my dad as a suspect because he found her. And spouses are usually looked at first in homicide investigations. I'm lucky they only dug through his phone records, but they didn't see any red flags. If they had just checked mine and read my texts, they might have seen that I didn't make it to Ricky's house on the day my mom was killed until later in the day. If they had dug deeper, they might have gotten suspicious enough to ask me different questions. If that had happened, I would've ratted my dad out so goddamn quick. But, uh, it didn't come to that."

Celeste blew a disgusted breath from her mouth, then asked, "You think it's fair for him to be going around without paying for murdering your mom?"

"I was… confused. I acted on impulse back then. I was upset that Mom was dead. I was pissed at what she did. I was mad at him for killing her; I still am. But later that year, after I graduated, moved out, and got a place of my own, I had time to think about it more openly and not as a one-sided, biased opinion, you know, with my dad's presence always lingering to sway my thoughts toward him. I finally realized that my mom was the one to blame. She's the one who broke our hearts. She had betrayed the family's trust, my dad, and ultimately me. The consequences that followed are her fault."

"You can't be serious?" Celeste asked.

"Afraid so. Look, it's not like my dad's a serial killer, you know. He doesn't have an addiction to offing people and should be stopped. He's not a bad man. He was wronged. He dealt with that offense. He just had to teach mom a hard knocks life lesson."

Sean saw the looks on their faces. "Oh, don't get me wrong, I hate my dad with a passion for taking my mom out like he did, but I understand why he did it. *Caroline…*" Sean said with much disdain, "… *my mother…* betrayed my dad's commitment to her. And she betrayed me by basically walking out on him. She walked out on me. Walked out on our family."

Angel looked at Celeste and said, "You see, this is what is wrong with the world today. So many assholes out there with the wrong mental capacity focused on the wrong thing."

Sean said, "She wasn't your mother, *Angel*, so you didn't experience the hurt of what my dad and I felt."

"You think your mom deserved what she got?" Celeste asked.

"Hell, yes, she deserved it. She betrayed us. We trusted her, and she's out and about fucking every other man in town. Not being faithful. Just going around being the town whore like it's a normal thing. God, I hated her for that."

Celeste stepped closer to him, got down on his level, and said, "Has it ever crossed your fucked up mind that maybe you two shitheads didn't give her the love and attention she needed or deserved? Have you ever thought that maybe the reason she turned her back on you is that you and your dad turned your back on her first?"

"You saying it's all our fault?"

"Not saying that at all. Just offering a suggestion that it could be a reason. You seem very one-sided in your thought process."

"You seem to be one-sided in yours," Sean shot back, grasping at comeback lines.

Angel saw that this back-and-forth was getting them nowhere. She asked, "Did you and your dad really believe that your mom was going around screwing thirty-two men?"

"Right," Celeste agreed. "That's what I was thinking. I have no doubt she was sleeping around, true. But thirty-two? There's no way. She was trying to get through to your dad. Wake him up that he was losing her. Not the best way to reason with him, but I'm sure it was a desperate ploy. You know it's not entirely a bad thing to be a whore."

Sean's eyes flashed with hatred toward Celeste. "You don't know what the hell you're talking about." He turned to Angel and gave her an icy stare. "Either of you. You weren't there."

Celeste waited for a few seconds as his glaring eyes returned to her again. She stood again and moved away.

"Where's your dad now?" Angel asked.

A cold, palpable silence, then, "Somewhere. I don't know. I don't talk to him much anymore. I don't keep tabs on him."

"I don't believe this line of dialogue with you," Angel said. "You are so off-kilter in your head; it's ridiculous. I'm not cheering on your mom's actions, but she didn't deserve that. No woman deserves that."

A single bark of laughter burst from Sean's mouth, "Well, we'll just have to agree to disagree on that."

"So… why is that knife so special to you?" Angel asked.

"I don't know. I've just always thought it was a cool piece of hardware. Maybe if the cops or detectives had frisked me, they would've found it. If that had happened, they might have become suspicious of the knife, taken it as evidence, and maybe solved the case by blaming me. If that had happened, I would've turned around and blamed my dad. It just didn't go down like that. I consider this knife my lucky charm. It's got me through some hard scrapes in life."

Angel was quiet for a few moments, letting the confession settle. She took turns looking between the two men. Finally, she asked Sean, "How did you and *Heartbreak Ridge* over here meet?"

Thomas answered for Sean, "Sort of a chance meeting, really."

"Aww, true love in the making," Celeste said.

Sean began, "It was about a year or two after I moved out of the house with Dad. Maybe my second year of college. I sort of went into a depression state. I was down at Bowen's Landing. It's a bar on Silver Ridge Lake."

"I know the place. I've been there a few times."

"Yeah?"

"Uh, yeah. We're not far from there."

"Really?"

"Yeah, Silver Ridge Lake is right out that window." Angel pointed to the middle window that Celeste had been looking out before the men had awakened.

Sean looked toward the window as though he could see through the blinds and down to the water's edge.

"Other side of the lake, though," Angel said to help Sean get his bearings on where he was. "The south side."

"Oh, I see. Good to know," Sean said, nodding, "I was drinking a few beers at a table alone."

Thomas cut in with a snide breath of laughter. "Yeah, he looked like the saddest sap just sitting there with three empty bottles pushed to the side. He had that knife in one hand, spinning it in front of everybody. He was working something over in his mind. I had to know this guy's story, so I bought two beers and placed one in front of him."

CHAPTER THIRTY-ONE

Sean sat in a booth at Bowen's Landing by himself. He was staring at his dad's knife; the tip of it was touching down on the table's surface. He held the other end of the handle perpendicular to the table with his index finger and spun the handle with his middle finger. It turned, the point grooving a small circular divot into the wooden surface. He had mesmerized himself into a trance as the different color bar lights winked off sections of the blade's darkened surface.

Sean had already drunk three beers; he'd just set the third bottle aside. Peanut shells and their dust had been swept away near the bottles, leaving the surface in front of him clean.

Gretchen Wilson's "Redneck Woman" was playing in the background. It was just loud enough to further lull him into reliving his memories. Now and then, there was an outburst from other bar patrons who were watching one of the games on the big screens nearby. Other groups burst out in laughter at someone's humorous tale that was being told.

An uncapped beer bottle entered Sean's field of vision directly in front of his spinning knife.

Sean blinked and shook his head slightly at this visual interruption. He angled his head, looked up from his trance, and saw a man standing near the edge of his table, holding his own beer. The man took a swig off his bottle, then stared back at Sean.

"What's this for?" Sean asked the stranger.

"It's for you to drink," the man said, smiling. "A man sitting there twiddling a knife like you are can only mean one of two things."

"And what's that?"

"Either he's contemplating murdering someone, or he's thinking about the person he's already killed."

"What?" Sean said in alarm.

The guy leaned over, set his beer on the table, and placed his hands on the table's edges. He looked around conspiratorially, then faced Sean again; he leaned in a little closer and said, "I'll tell you about the person I *killed if you'll tell me who* you *killed."*

Sean's head jerked back as though he'd been punched, and he looked at the man's serious face with a shocked look of his own. "What the fuck kind of statement is that?"

The man couldn't contain his seriousness for long and burst out with a chuckle. He grabbed his beer bottle and stood again. "I'm fucking with you, man. I'm just fuckin' around. Calm down, dude. It was a joke." The new guy took a long pull of his beer and chuckled a few more times at his cleverness. He tipped the end of his beer toward the empty seat and asked, "You mind if I sit?"

The weirdness of this whole conversation was starting to dissipate, but Sean wasn't entirely sure of this new guy's motives. He wanted to be alone and think. A new thought formed in his head, a way to get rid of the man. Sean gave him the typical double open-handed halt signal and said frankly, "Look, if this is your idea of a good pick-up line, then you're going to be lonely for a very long time. If you're trying to pick me up, it won't work because I'm not into guys." He thought of other words that might have been more offensive to this guy, but he wasn't one to use them. "You might as well take your beer and give it to someone else looking for a boyfriend."

The man laughed out loud at this statement. He turned away and scanned the bar again, then turned back to Sean, his laughter changing into a chuckle. "That's funny, man. I am not into guys, either. I have no interest in men other than sharing a beer with you. Maybe make a new friend in the process. And you look like someone who needs a friend right now."

Sean gave him the courtesy of a half-laugh, which seemed to ease the tension between them. He nodded. "Okay, sure. Sorry about that. Never been hit on by a guy, so I wasn't sure how to handle it. Have a seat."

The man slid into the booth and said, "My name is Thomas. Thomas Bonnomer." He held out a sideways fist.

Sean placed his knife on the table, then bumped Thomas's knuckles. "How's it going, Thomas, Thomas Bonnomer?"

Gretchen Wilson finished singing about how refined a redneck woman she was, then Rascal Flatts started singing "These Days."

"Not too bad." He took another swig of beer, leaned forward, and said, "I bet you the next round of beers, my story will be sadder and more depressing than yours."

Sean laughed. "I doubt it very seriously."

"You willing to make that bet?" Thomas asked.

"That's not much of a bet. A round of beers."

"I'll tell you my sad story if you tell me yours."

Sean thought about it for a second, then said, "No, I can't do that."

Thomas replied, "You have to talk to someone. It might as well be me. I'm your new best friend."

"I don't know you."

"I told you; I'm Thomas Bonnomer."

"But that doesn't mean I know you." Sean looked down at his knife, stuck it back into the little groove he'd made earlier, and began spinning it again.

"Telling your troubles to a stranger might make it easier."

"Sure, but I can't tell you my story."

"Ooooh, I'm even more intrigued. Why not?" Thomas asked innocently, "Does it have something to do with that knife you're playing with?"

Sean looked up at Thomas with a guilty and horrified look. He closed the knife and quickly shoved it into his pocket.

"It does, doesn't it?" Thomas asked.

Sean started to slide out of the booth seat, but Thomas's hand covered his and held it in place. "Please, don't go."

Overcome with the touch from Thomas and the possibility that he could still be trying to pick him up, Sean jerked his hand away. "You sure you aren't into dudes?"

Thomas moved his hand away from Sean but didn't answer his question. "Sorry. Um, hey, listen. I'm not going to rat you out. I promise. No matter *what was done with that knife or who was hurt by it. I don't give a fuck about that. Just looking to hear an interesting story. I have one of my own if you want to hear it."*

Sean still wasn't convinced that this guy wasn't gay, but the soft-spoken plea was just enough to keep him from sliding the rest of the way from his seat and heading to the bathroom, home, or anywhere other than here.

Thomas continued, "How about this? How about I tell you my story, and if you're up to trusting me with your story once I'm finished, then I would be all ears to listen. Either way, if both stories are told, the one with the least-saddest *story, I think that's the best word, buys the next round."*

"I think I can manage that, but I'm not promising anything," Sean said.

"Okay."

*Sean slid back into a more relaxed position, and Thomas launched into a detailed account of his escapades with Rebecca LaGrande and how their relationship turned into a relation-*shit.

By the time Thomas had relayed his whole story, they had already ordered two more beers each. Because of the booze and the free-flowing conversation about Rebecca LaGrande, it didn't take much coaxing for Thomas to convince Sean to give a detailed account of his mother's murder by his father's hand.

"Holy fuck!" Thomas said in a long-whispered tone. "That's effed up. You're right; yours is a sadder story. Drinks are on me." He held his hand to the bombshell waitress who came over, gathered their empty bottles, and took their order for two more beers. She sashayed away, and they both watched her ass as she did so.

"She's working that ass for a big tip, isn't she?" Thomas asked.

"Yeah. And I've got a big fucking tip for her. Right on the end of my dick."

Through his laughter, Thomas managed to say, "Yeah. That's where mine is too."

Sean joined in with his laughter at the raunchy innuendos coming naturally between them. They looked at the waitress leaning on the bar; her ass stuck out toward them as if she were secretly inviting them to dock their cocks in her. The waitress glanced back at them quickly, caught them staring, and what their eyes were feasting on. Sean and Thomas looked away quicker than she had looked at them, but they had been caught.

Some old-school Dwight Yoakam was playing now, but the conversation had grown to fill that musical void. More laughter from a group off to their left. Cheers and jeers sounded out from the guys watching a game. A few high fives clapped together—a sound of a glass shattering near the bar.

"Would you do her?" Sean asked.

"What, her?" Thomas said, regarding the waitress. "Oh, hell yeah. I'd fuck her in a heartbeat, but I don't want anything more than that with her. I don't want a relationship with her. Not ready for that shit in my life again."

They glanced her way and became quiet as she sidled back to them. They watched as her bombshell of a body swayed and bounced in all the right places. She said nothing as she set their beers in front of them.

Thomas pitched a ten-dollar bill up on her round serving tray and said, "Here, this is for the beers. Keep the change." He threw another ten on her tray next to the other ten, "And this is for us admiring your body. You caught us looking. Figured we might as well pay since you cold busted our ass looking at your dangerous curves."

An alluring smile broke out over her face. "That's very sweet. The only two gentlemen here at Bowen's Landing tonight. No one has ever done that for me before. But I see so many looking. You're a real sweetheart." The waitress leaned down, grabbed his chin, and held it firmly as she kissed the side of his face. "Just for that, feel free to look me over the rest of the night." The waitress stood again, smiled at Thomas, then winked at Sean. "Let me know if you two need anything else, and I will be happy to serve you." She moved away, giving a little more bump and sway of her hips as she went, knowing they were still watching.

"Oh, we'll let you know," Thomas said as she left their table. He glanced over his shoulder to get one last look at her ass as she walked away. When she was out of earshot and attending to another table, Thomas turned back to Sean and said, "Fucking whore."

"Why did you do that?" Sean asked.

"What? Tip her for the look?"

"Yeah."

"Oh, you never know where that might lead," Thomas said. "She was working her body for tip money. I've done that a time or two before, and it's got me laid a few times. Other times it's gotten me some pretty heavy make-out sessions with a few waitresses after they had knocked off after their shifts.

It's always worth pitching a few bucks their way. But, yeah, I wouldn't mind going a couple of rounds with Hot Tits there."

Two women started singing karaoke somewhere on the far side of Bowen's Landing. It was a terrible rendition of "Summer Nights" from the classic movie, Grease.

"Wish there was a way to cut through all the bullshit of picking up a girl at the bar and just fuck her," Sean asked.

"You can," Thomas said. He gave a snide laugh at the idea that just popped into his head. "You could just rape her." It was more or less a joke, but he toyed with the idea in his mind.

Sean looked at Thomas as though he'd lost his mind. "I'm not looking to go to jail, dude."

"Neither am I, but… let's say, what if I raped her?" Thomas said, and then a look crossed his face.

Sean saw his mind was working overtime. "Then you would go to jail. Obviously."

"No, I mean, wait." Thomas paused for a moment as an epiphany worked its way clear into his head. It bounced between what happened with him, Rebecca LeGrande, and Greg Morris. He sat at attention as his wild idea formed. He continued talking a little bit faster as the brainstorming idea came to fruition in his mind, "What if… just go with me on this… hear me out, what if I proceed to do all the pre-rape stuff?"

"What?"

"You know, attack her, rip her clothes a little, or off, you know, shit like that, and then you jump in right before I commit the crime. You know, go balls deep in her sweet spot. If you did that, you would be a fucking superhero for saving her. She would probably go down on you right then and there."

Sean laughed. It was a ridiculous idea. "I doubt she would go down on me right then." He upended his beer and took a swallow. Considered it. "Maybe. That's fucked up, though." He tilted his beer bottle toward the bombshell waitress and said, "You want to fake-rape her *to see if* I *can get some action? You'd do that for me? You barely know me."*

"Or you do it for me to see if I can get some. And no, not that bitch whore waitress over there. Are you crazy? She knows what we look like. Either of us does anything toward her, she could nail us because she's seen us here,

and we've had a conversation with her. And if she can ID me, she can sure as hell ID you. No, this would have to be some random bitch who has never seen either of us. You want to try it to see if it works?"

"Dude, you're talking crazy. There's no way that would work. It would end up backfiring on you, big time. I'm not going to fake-rape some chick to see if she'll give you a quick and easy fuck."

"I'll do it for you,. man. My new friend. It could be like an initiation of our new friendship. You know, my new wingman."

"Wingman?" Sean said, chuckling. "A wingman is supposed to help a friend get a piece of ass, not barely rape a chick to see if they can get laid. I don't know, man, that's the craziest fucking idea I've ever heard."

"I swear to you, it would work. I bet you five hundred dollars that we could get so much pussy if we did it. It would be ridiculous."

"But I don't want a relationship right now," Sean said.

"I don't either, but I would love some easy pussy. So tired of acting all interested in the shit they're interested in. I just want to fuck them and leave them."

"But I'm not the type of guy who could do that. I can't hit a girl and bruise her up."

"Jesus Christ, what are you talking about?" Thomas asked. "Hitting and bruising? Who said anything about that?"

"Isn't that what rape is?"

"Yeah, maybe for the big-league boys who do it just because they want to be in control over something. I'm talking about just giving a hint of rape to some chick. Rip a few clothes, manhandle her enough for her to think you're going to beat the shit out of her, and give her some crazy verbal threats. By that time, you would be there and pull me off her; then you would fuck me up big time. Get it?"

Sean gave Thomas a disbelieving look. He wasn't convinced.

Thomas said, "Yeah, I said it. You hit me. Save the hits for me. We could figure out a rapid but effective fight scene that makes me look like a punk ass bitch and makes you look like Bruce Lee, Jet Li, or one of those fucking Lee boys. Kick my ass a little, then I run off, but you can't catch me, conveniently, because you have to play Mr. Affection to her and wrap her all up in the fake compassion. You'd be like her knight in shining armor. I swear, she would fuck you that day for saving her, or at least within a few days of the event. And you aren't doing anything to her but having sex because she would consent to it."

"Seems like a doable idea. Cold-blooded, uh, fucked up, but very doable. I can't believe I am considering doing this with you."

"I swear to you it would fucking work. It would be a way to get back at the bitches who fucked our emotions up."

"Ha. Yeah."

"It would have to be at a different time because I'm too buzzed to do anything right now. The lucky woman would probably be able to kick my ass if we tried anything tonight."

"I think by tomorrow afternoon rolls around, after we wake up and deal with our hangovers, this idea will have dissipated from our minds when we remember this conversation. We'll realize how ridiculous this idea is and laugh it off."

"I don't know," Thomas said. "Maybe. Can I get your number? Maybe we can meet for a late lunch and see whether we remember this idea. If not, perhaps we can get some good food without *beers this time.*

"Sure," Sean said. "My number is—"

CHAPTER THIRTY-TWO

A PALPABLE SILENCE stretched over the basement room after Thomas and Sean finished their origin story. The mood in the basement was somber, bleak, and quiet. The men had confessed, and it seemed they wanted to tell their story in some strange way. Not that they were completely sorry, but there was an air of shame for what they had done. More so from Sean than from Thomas.

Celeste was the first to break the tension. Understanding how the game started, she said, "I see now why you two hate women so much."

"It came down to that weird chance meeting," Angel said. "If Thomas hadn't gotten detention or had left for home a different way, he would've never crossed paths with Rebecca, and this game would've probably never been sparked in his mind."

Celeste mused, "He definitely wouldn't have been heartbroken by Rebecca, which was the beginning of that secret hate."

Angel said, "And if Sean hadn't played hooky, he wouldn't have been there when his mother was murdered. He would have never known of her promiscuity. He never would've taken the knife, and his dad might be in prison today if Sean hadn't taken the murder weapon."

"Rebecca LeGrande would've still been raped, though," Celeste said. The statement hung in the air. She took a moment to let it settle. "And now, thinking about that and the game that came out of it, maybe it would've been better if she had been raped."

"Celeste."

"I know, it sounds so bad to even say. I just mean that this game would've never been hatched… or invented… and all those women before us wouldn't be dealing with the repercussions of their game."

Angel traded looks between the men. "I think we all know that what we're doing here today is us *dealing with the repercussions of their game* in the best way we know how. We're doing what we're doing for ourselves and for all those other women who came before. We've gotten to the root of the problem. I think we all know what needs to happen next."

If, for some reason, Sean and Thomas thought they were getting out of this situation, they now knew the chance of escape looked worse. The news dropped onto them like a load-bearing beam stacked too heavy with weight. The reality of the moment came crashing into their beings, and panic in both men caused them to sit up a little higher and straighter in their chairs. Their legs automatically closed inward as they tried to cross themselves to cover and protect their privates, as though Angel's verbal threat was enough to lop off their appendages.

Even though Thomas knew what she meant, the spreading panic in his body made him ask, "What the fuck's that supposed to mean?"

"I'll tell you what it means," Celeste said, cutting in. "You two have been harping about getting pussy and this maniacal game for most of the night now, so because you want it so bad, we're going to take your manhood from you and give you a pussy of your own."

Thomas and Sean's assholes clenched together a little tighter—if that was at all possible—and the mental hurt of just imagining their privates being extracted from them caused them to flex their lower bodies in attention even more.

"No!" Sean screamed, and tears burst from his eyes. He began to shake his head back and forth. "No-no-no-no-no! Please! I'm begging of you, Celeste. All… all of this was-was just a game," he stammered.

Thomas said, "Calm down, Sean. They're fucking with us. They're just trying to scare us. They're not going to castrate us." Even though it came out as a statement, there was an extreme inflection of a question in his voice.

Angel turned to him and shot back, "You think we're playing, Thomas? You guys played us so well and did a great job of nailing us in the first half, but this, right here, this is the halftime show. The second half is just starting. It's our turn now to play our game. We made our play when we brought you here. We're going to end you two shitheads and your fucked up game that you have played on so many women for so many years."

"No! Please, I beg of you," Sean said, continuing to plead. He looked beseechingly between Celeste and Angel, more to Celeste since they had developed more of a relationship in the past few days. "You won. Okay. You won. Please, just let us go. Let *me* go. I don't care about Thomas. I'll never play the game again. I've already told Thomas that I was out."

Celeste turned and moved to Sean. She put her hands on Sean's chair and leaned down into his face. "I know," she said, searching his beautiful blue eyes. "You won't be able to play your game ever again because you won't have the right equipment to do so."

Sean was terrified, and tears continued to flow in rivers down his face. It looked like he was losing a significant part of himself, the most crucial part. He wasn't thinking right when he asked, "What are you going to do to me, I mean, *us*?" He swallowed hard and tried again. "I mean, how are you going to do it?'

Celeste finally answered Sean's question and Thomas's broken-record plea that he'd been asking since the beginning of this rendezvous. "I don't know what Angel plans on doing to Thomas, but I'll tell you what I'm going to do to you."

"Finally! Some answers," Thomas said from behind Celeste. He looked up at Angel. "I've been asking you two bitches that question the whole fucking night."

Celeste moved to the table and picked up Sean's knife from where it lay among the pieces of evidence. To Thomas, she said, "I'd watch whom you call a bitch." She turned to Sean to answer his earlier question and moved to him in a slow deliberate walk. "I have a knife. It's not going to take that long." She leaned down into his face as she brought the knife up into his line of sight.

Sean's head began to shake back and forth. He shut his eyes again with his dad's blade now so close to his face. So many times, he'd taunted women with that same knife. Full-circle Karma moment. Seeing the knife now wasn't as cool as he used to think. It was a thing of nightmares. Crushing dread overcame his body, and he hung his head to avoid its gaze.

Taking up the eerie and creepy threat Celeste had started, Angel stepped toward Thomas and leaned down into his face. "Hey Thomas, have you ever seen the rubber band watermelon challenge videos?"

"Rubber band? Watermelon challenge?" Thomas asked to make sure he heard her right. He searched his mind for the meaning of her statement and shook his head. "Uh, no... no. What-what the hell is that?"

Sean knew exactly what she was talking about. He'd seen a few videos and had an idea of where Angel was going with this line of questioning, but he didn't know exactly what she would do. *If it's what I'm thinking, surely, she won't go that far. We don't deserve anything that harsh.*

Angel continued, "It's just what it sounds like. In these videos, people see how many rubber bands it takes to split a watermelon in two." She held up her finger, indicating for him to hold any further questions. She pulled her cell phone from her back pocket. "I'll show you. It's better if you see a visual than for me to try and explain it, although I think you get the gist of what I'm saying."

Thomas shrugged and shook his head, then looked over to Sean for any other clue to help him understand.

Sean just shook his head sadly. The look of fear on his face told Thomas that the subject of what Angel was talking about wasn't good.

She swiped and tapped a few times on her iPhone. "Here we go." Angel tapped for the video to begin playing. The sound started, then stopped as she touched the play bar on the video. Angel slid her finger over near the two-minute mark in the video, hit play again, then turned her phone around for Thomas to view the video.

The video showed a close-up of a watermelon sitting in a hot pink bowl on a small table with a white and blue checkered tablecloth. The watermelon already had numerous rubber bands stretched around its middle. The hands of two figures were already in motion, stretching another rubber band and placing it around the watermelon's center with the others.

The figure on the left was in black shorts, a gray short-sleeved T-shirt, gray socks, and safety glasses. On the right, his partner was wearing long black pants with flip-flops and a white shirt with a bow tie; he also wore a white jacket that reminded Thomas of a chef jacket or a lab coat. The two guys were so jumpy with each stretch and placement of a new rubber band; they acted as if it was going to split open at any moment.

The video changed to a wider shot capturing the action from the left character's four o'clock; it was recorded from his back right side.

The characters in the video sounded as though they had Russian accents. They were laughing goofily as they placed three more rubber bands. As they were stretching the fourth rubber band over the watermelon, the middle of it suddenly gave away as the numerous rubber bands pulled in on themselves. The watermelon disintegrated into two halves. The top half of the melon exploded upward about two to three feet, and the insides of the melon streamed out away from the rubber bands. Startled by the sudden eruption, the two boys turned their heads as they jumped backward and fell out over their lawn chairs to escape the small explosion that had just scared the hell out of them. They both burst into brays of hideous laughter.

Their goofy laughs faded as Angel pulled the viewing screen away from Thomas's eyes and back to her face. Their laughter was cut short as she tapped the screen and stopped the video. She tapped her phone a few more times and swiped some other screens away; then, she turned off her phone. She placed it back in her back pocket and stared back at Thomas.

Having forgotten her threat for a moment as he watched the entertaining video, Thomas asked, "So what's the big fucking deal about that rubber band watermelon challenge?"

"You still don't get it?" Angel asked in surprise.

"Get what?"

Angel turned away abruptly, grabbed her backpack from the floor, then spun back to Thomas and slammed it down on the table. "Goddamn it, some of you men are so fucking stupid. We always have to spell everything out for you assholes."

She unzipped her bag, pulled out three plastic bags of regular-sized rubber bands, and slapped them down on the table beside him.

Angel continued, grabbing one of the bags and turning to face him.

She held the bag of rubber bands up in front of him. "What I'm saying is this, *dumbass*. I have exactly three bags worth of rubber bands. The count in each bag is fifty, give or take a few. We're going to see how many rubber bands it will take before your cock and balls are emasculated from your piece of shit body. Is that clear enough for you to understand?"

A wash of color drained from Thomas's face as the thought of the watermelon challenge replayed again in his mind, but this time, he saw his man goods wrapped tightly in green, red, and blue rubber bands rather than around a watermelon. In less than three seconds, Thomas went from a cocky asshole to a blubbering beggar. "No, God. Please, Angel," he started; he continued with random pleas as tears began to run down his face.

Angel continued, "But I'm not a total bitch, Thomas. If your manhood and fun sack can withstand all three bags of rubber bands and it *doesn't* rip your dick off—and I would be shocked if that happens—I will allow you to keep your family jewels. But I highly doubt that it won't happen. They are going to be mine."

Thomas's begging and blubbering were growing louder and more ridiculous with each word he spoke.

A crisp slap rang out. "Shut up!" Angel shouted.

Thomas did so, but his annoying mewling couldn't be turned off.

"You stripped Celeste and me of our dignity, our confidence, of our self-respect when you and Sean started playing your little rape game with us. Don't start trying to work your way in on our sensitive side for us to let you go. Our sensitive side toughened up when we discovered what you did to us and who knows how many other women before us. You're going to have to take this play like a man. Just like we took your plays like women. We played your game; now you're going to play ours."

Thomas tried to sit up even higher in his seat and began to squirm as though he had to piss badly. He started begging again for the safety of his private sector.

Angel tore open the bag of rubber bands she was holding, dumped them onto the table, then pitched the empty bag over her shoulder. She chose one of the rubber bands from the pile and toyed with it by stretching it a little as she prepared to strap it to him. She thumbed one stretched part of the rubber band with her finger; it gave a nice twang, so she strummed it a few more times. With disappointment painting a new look on her face, she said, "Oh shit, that will not do. These rubber bands are just a tad too big. Or it could be that you are just a tad too small. If I put this around your twig and berries, it won't be tight enough to do any damage."

Thomas looked at her with a pissed-off stare of hatred. His head began to shake with vehemence as he stared at her.

"What are you going to do?" Celeste asked. She'd been watching this whole exchange quietly from the sidelines without interference. She moved away from her place near Sean and replaced the knife back on the table from where she had snatched it earlier. "Do we need to go get a different brand?"

"No, there's not enough time. We're going to get this show on the road." Angel gave a little flash of her hands and finger and held it up for Thomas to see. "I'm just going to loop it and make it half the size, which, in turn, will make it much tighter. Problem solved. I'm sure it will take fewer rubber bands to complete the task."

"Jesus—God—NO!" Thomas screamed. "Please!" He yelled like a little kid throwing a tantrum in the supermarket. "I'm begging you to please don't do this!"

"Shut up, Thomas, or I'll slap the shit out of you again. You don't get to beg, because it's not going to do you any good." Angel pulled a chair over to Thomas and sat in front of him. "I thought this type of thing turned you on, Thomas. What's wrong? Why aren't you hard right now? Bet if I were tied up in front of you, you would have a raging hard-on, wouldn't you?"

Thomas was seething and pissed off. He snapped at her, "Fuck yeah. I've had you tied up before, remember? I fucked every one of your holes. And you loved it. I would love to have you tied up again. I would make you my little bitch sex slave. I'd rope you up and fuck every hole you have numerous times until you were raw and bleeding."

The look on Angel's face changed to unbridled anger, but she didn't lash out at him. There were just a few seconds when Celeste and Sean didn't know what she was going to do.

On the other hand, Thomas knew he'd fucked up and said the wrong thing by letting his anger get the best of him. If he'd had any chance to talk his way free with Angel, that door had just closed and was now locked down tight. He knew he was doomed to the fate she had promised him.

In a low whisper that only Thomas could hear, Angel said, "You shouldn't have said that to me." She leaned quickly into Thomas. Her hands shot forward as she stretched the double-looped rubber band wide and slipped it over his penis and up under his scrotum. She set it as far back on his taint as she could and then released it. The rubber band rolled off her fingers and onto his skin. It reversed direction when it hit his skin, rolled backward a short distance, and then held fast around the center of his manhood.

Thomas screamed as some pubic hairs he hadn't groomed lately intertwined in the rolling strands.

"Aww, damn, I bet that did hurt," Angel said. "Get used to it because you have an ass-load of rubber bands and pain to go." She reached over, grabbed another one from the table, looped it again, stretched it high like the other one, and released it. The rubber band rolled off her fingers and slid onto Thomas's skin. Again, it reversed direction, entangling pubic hair into it as it rolled to a stop near the first one. The double-looped rubber bands were extremely tight and began to dig into his skin and cut off his circulation.

"That's two. Wonder how many rubber bands it's going to take?" Angel mused. "Let's add number three to the pile, shall we? Sit back and get used to this. It's going to be a long night."

The pressure was already starting to build around his testicles, and they slowly began to turn a bright shade of red.

"Jesus! God, take them off. Please, take them off," Thomas begged.

"Why? You and Sean wanted us to play your game, so that is what we're doing." She looped another one over his junk and snapped it into place. This caused Thomas to sit up and pay attention. "Your game isn't so fun now, is it? This is what happens when you fuck with women's emotions. You manipulated us into having sex with you and Sean."

"You did it of your own free will, bitch," Thomas spat between clenched teeth. "No one forced you to fuck us."

The snap of another effectively placed slap came out of nowhere, and an 'oh shit' look was pasted on everyone's face except Angel's.

Now Angel was seething with hatred. "You want to fuck with me, bitch?" She leaned down and thumped Thomas's nut sack with her middle finger. There was a thick, fleshy, solid sound like a farmer checking to see if a cantaloupe was ripe.

"God fucking damn it!" Thomas yelled. "Don't do that."

"I'll do whatever the *fuck* I *want* to do. You taught me that taking anything that doesn't belong to you is okay. You took my pussy, so I'm going to take your fucking dick. Do you understand? This is going to happen. And I will draw it out as long as I want so it is as painful as I can make it."

His attitude pissed her off, and she grabbed five to six rubber bands and dropped them into her lap. She took one, doubled it, stretched the band, and placed it with the others. She grabbed another one, looped it, stretched it, and snapped it into place. She did this for all the rubber bands she had snagged.

All the while she was placing them, the pressure in Thomas's scrotum and penis was building. The bright red was dimming and changing to a deepening purple.

Thomas gritted his teeth against the pain and mumbled unintelligible words and phrases while Angel continued her devious work.

Sean looked over at Celeste, who was looking at Angel, who was slowly getting her vengeance for being raped. He watched Celeste's eyes slowly widen in horror at the unspeakable atrocity Angel was reaping upon Thomas.

"Celeste," he said in a gentle whisper. He said it as loud as he dared. He tried to get her attention without Angel hearing him. He didn't want Angel's vengeance coming down on him too.

She didn't turn to him. She was too mesmerized by what she was seeing.

Sean tried again, a little louder this time. "Celeste."

Celeste finally turned to him. Her widened eyes slowly returned to a focused stare as she locked onto him.

"I know I have no right to ask this of you, but I am begging you. I am begging you to forgive me for everything I did to you. I am pleading with you to give me a second chance."

Celeste looked away and back at Angel and her actions.

Thomas was leaning over with his head looking down into his lap. He was rocking back and forth, bracing himself against the pain.

Knowing he didn't have much time, Sean began talking faster, urgent. Words began pouring out of his mouth. "Celeste, please, just listen to me and know I am telling you the truth. From the time we met in the alleyway, from when I helped you and walked you to your car, to the few conversations we had on the phone and over the amazing lunch and dinner we shared. Finally, the first beautiful moment we made love, I need you to know that I was slowly being changed from playing the game as I always have done to wanting to get out of playing it completely. I even went to Thomas and told him I wanted out. I told him I wanted to quit playing the game."

Celeste looked over at Sean again. "Really? You did that?"

"Yes." A spark of hope.

"You wanted to quit playing this fucked up game you two created?"

"Yes, you can ask him."

"Okay, let's see what Thomas has to say about that. That is, if he can talk through the agony he appears to be in." She turned to Thomas. "Thomas?"

Thomas slowly looked up as though her voice had broken through his aura of torment. His face was a mask of unimaginable hurt. Sweat had popped out on his forehead and had dampened the hair that had matted to his forehead; some hair had fallen over his eyes. His face was slightly red from how tense his body had seized up trying to adapt to his agony.

Celeste asked, "Did Sean come to you and tell you he wanted to quit the game at any time since you attacked me in the alleyway? Did he tell you he wanted out?"

Thomas locked in on Celeste for a moment; then his head wavered as he turned to look at Sean.

Celeste, Sean, and Angel saw something going on behind his eyes. The wheels were turning over in his mind. He gritted his teeth and set his face in determination.

Sean gave him a flare of his eyes and a head gesture toward Celeste for him to back up his story. But Thomas was taking too long. Time was of the essence. Sean commanded, "Tell her the truth, Thomas. Tell her what I told you."

In a slow, deliberated speech, Thomas turned back to Celeste and said, "Yeah, Sean talked to me about you. But he said *you* reminded *him* of his whore of a *mother,* and because he hated *her* so much for what she did to *him* and his *dad*, he said he would use and abuse *you* for as long as he could. That's what he told me."

"YOU LIAR!" Sean yelled. "You fucking tell her the truth!"

Thomas, barely able to talk through his pain, continued, "He said *he* was going to turn *you* into the slut his *mom* was. Oh, he had plans for you."

"Celeste, you cannot believe him. He's lying. He told me he would go to the police if I stopped. He said he would tell you what we had done. I didn't know what to do. I had to keep playing the game in his eyes, but I wasn't playing the game. I was biding my time until I could figure a way out of this with him. I knew if you found out, we would be over. I wanted to put this shitty part of my life behind me. There was nothing I could do about what I had done in the past. I was going to get out. Working on getting out. I would start a new life with you if you would have me."

"And you think that's right? You don't think I need to know your past? The *real* you?"

"It's not the real me—just something I do with Thomas. Or rather, *did.* We all have certain things in our life that we can't or won't share with another mate. I couldn't share this with you. With anyone."

"You're right, because you deserve to pay for what you did."

"And if you continue to go through with what you two are doing to Thomas, and if you don't have a change of heart about what you are doing to me, when you start to date someone else, would you tell them about this night?"

"Don't you fucking dare play that card with me. Don't you dare try to guilt me into letting you go. This is not the same thing."

"It is too the same thing. Sort of."

"No, Sean, it isn't. This is not something that Angel and I do on a regular basis."

"You can't answer the question because you wouldn't tell the next guy if it's not me."

"Shut up. I'm not answering the question because it is irrelevant to this situation. You two are going to pay, and you're going to pay big."

As Celeste argued with Sean, her mind contemplated the men's relationship. She was more apt to believe Sean than Thomas. She knew Sean wasn't just blowing smoke up her ass; there was some semblance of honesty to what he said. But it wasn't a great idea to pull Thomas in on it. If Thomas were going down, he would take Sean down with him. She thought quickly about how to get the truth out of him, if only a subtle version. "If you're lying and Sean did opt out of the game—and I have no reason to believe either of you—why wouldn't you let him quit?"

Thomas had been looking on through leaky eyes. Pain-filled tears had started to run. Through clenched teeth and the unbearable pain, he said, "*Nobody*, and I mean, *nobody,* ever leaves me unless I want them out of my life."

That phrase froze Sean and the women where they stood.

A flicker of a thought lit in Celeste's mind. It brightened, and she asked, "Is that what happened to Rebecca LeGrande?"

CHAPTER THIRTY-THREE

Celeste's last question caused a look of guilt to cross Thomas's face.

Ever since they had told their origin story of the game, something about Rebecca LeGrande remained to needle Celeste. Something about it was peculiar and didn't ring true. Maybe it was how Thomas had told his side of the story, but it continued to plague her mind. Thomas's recent statement pulled that forming thought to the forefront of her mind, and everything clicked instantly.

"What?" Thomas asked as he looked up at Celeste.

"I just asked you, what happened to Rebecca LeGrande?"

An incredulous tone filled Thomas's voice as he asked, "What makes you think something happened to her?"

"At the beginning of your story, when you asked Sean about his knife, you said that you would tell him about the person *you* killed if he told you about the person *he* killed. Not knowing that his story involved his mom being murdered with that knife and thinking it was an interesting way to start a conversation, you felt you could at least tell the breakup part of your story."

"Oh, shit," Angel said, realizing Celeste's implication. She looked over to Thomas. If it were possible to detest anyone more than she currently abhorred Thomas, a new lower opinion of him had just formed in her head.

Thomas gave them a simplistic grin. It boasted of nothing but didn't relieve them of Celeste's accusation. He said, "I believe we have a detective in our midst."

"You son of a bitch," Sean said from his seat across the room. He sat staring at Thomas with renewed wide-eyed wonder.

Celeste glanced his way; she could tell Sean didn't even know about this detail. He thought Rebecca had just broken up with Thomas, and that was it. No, there was more to this story. She turned back to Thomas and continued, "You killed her, didn't you?"

"I admit to nothing. I went to college there at Penn State, but she never made it. Thought we might bump into each other and that she might reconsider our relationship once we were there, but I never saw her."

"You're a liar," Celeste said.

"She never made it?" Angel asked on the heels of Celeste's comment.

Sean knew Angel had him with that statement.

Angel said, "It's funny that you don't deny it, which is the same as an admission of guilt."

"Where's her body, Thomas?" Celeste asked.

Through clenched teeth, and as spittle shot from his tight lips, he said, "I will talk no further of Rebecca LeGrande, no matter how much fucking torture you put me through. Peel my fingernails from my hands? Go ahead." He held his fingers to them as much as he could, bound to the chair. It was an invitation for them to get started. "She made her choice."

"And apparently, you made yours," Celeste said, driving the point home even more that Thomas had done something unspeakable to Rebecca.

A slight smirk from Thomas told them he still had information about her, but he was through talking about the subject. He sat there looking straight ahead toward Sean, but he wasn't looking *at* him. He was staring at that far-off place again. A seething hatred for all of them had been added to the pool of agony in which he was submerged.

Regarding Thomas's earlier comment, Angel said, "And I'm continuing to make *my* move." Angel considered what Celeste had said. "I hate to break it to you, Thomas, but like Rebecca LeGrande left *you*... your *dick* is about to leave your body in an even worse break-up. Happy trails, motherfucker." Angel continued to strap rubber bands to his midsection. She had committed to this long haul.

Thomas looked down again at his bulging scrotum sack. It looked as though it were going to explode at any second. The pressure around everything was unbelievable, and agony enveloped his body.

Celeste turned to Sean, "So you are telling the truth."

"Yes. I am. I promise you; I am."

"Why did you want to quit playing the game?"

A slight relief filled Sean's body. It seemed like a chink in Celeste's armor, and he'd found it. That little question told him that she'd felt the same as he did. He prattled off his thoughts to her without any regard for censoring himself. "Because the bottom line is, I fell in love with you. Or maybe it's that I'm *falling* in love with you. I fell harder for you than I have ever fallen for anyone in my life."

"Plleeeaaaassssse," Angel said as another rubber band tightened and nestled in deep with the others.

Celeste was dumbfounded. She knew there was some memorable exchange between her and Sean. There had been intense initial feelings for Sean, but those had been wiped entirely away when the news came to her and Angel that it was all a ruse. She didn't like being made a fool. She didn't like people using her. She didn't like that she had been chosen randomly to be an unknowing participant in this fake-rape game. She didn't like that she was a victim. She didn't like that she had been mentally raped, as though the act had taken place. She didn't like being physically raped; that was precisely what it felt like, even though she had been consenting with her savior after the fact. To find out that they were victims being tricked into sex filled with empty emotions and fake feelings, it was as though they had been raped altogether on the day of the incident. She felt like she had been used, abused, and pitched away without regard for her emotional or mental feelings. There was no ounce of forgiveness in her. She had been hurt too deeply. What these two assholes were doing was wrong, and she and Angel felt justified in ending these two guys' reign of terror on unsuspecting women everywhere.

The word love came back to the forefront of her conscience. She had been surprised to hear that word—love—coming from Sean. It was unfathomable for her to comprehend, just like their game. She felt he was saying phrases to get out of this situation. She laughed outright. The laughter seemed out of place with Thomas's unintelligible mumbling and groveling, which were becoming louder with each rubber band Angel stretched and snapped into place.

Celeste's laughter died, and she finally spoke. "You don't love me, Sean. There is no fucking way. Not after playing the game as long as you and Thomas have been playing it. I'm not such an amazing person that I will change your mind and habit of numerous years doing this shit. You all of a sudden want to stop? It just doesn't happen like that. I'm not stupid." She turned away from him for a moment and toward the windows. Tears were on the verge of flowing off her hardened game face, and she didn't want Sean to see any weakness in her.

"That's where you're wrong, Celeste. It does happen; it did for me. You have such a low opinion of yourself, which is partly my fault. You looked down on yourself, but what I did made that worse, and I am sorry. That is something I had hated to hear from you. You downing yourself, you know, the few times you did that when we were together. True, I have been playing the game for a while now, but that's over. I have wanted out for a long time now."

"Then just get out!" Celeste yelled as she wheeled back around on him. She was instantly pissed and began to cry. Tears from her inward hurt and the pain for the other women who had unknowingly been forced to play this game. "Don't continue to play the fucking game and abuse and terrify women as though they are going to get raped. Do you have any idea of the emotional trauma you have put on all those women you've mentally raped? Do you?"

Sean hung his head in shame. "I know. I know. I see that now. I mean, I knew it all along. But I know."

"I don't think you do, because if you did, you would've stopped long ago. No, scratch that. You would've never started this sicko game in the beginning. Even if I could fathom building up enough compassion to where I let you go, do you think for a second that I would want anything to do with you, knowing what I know now about you?"

"No. Probably not."

"You're goddamn right, *probably not.* It's a big fucking no. It's the most enormous fucking no I have ever given in my life. You and Thomas will never leave here alive, that I can promise. Even if you promised to be a good little boy and were the nicest guy on the face of this earth and the best gentleman to every woman you came in contact with from here on out, it's not enough. It's not enough because where is the justice for all the other women who came before Angel and myself? Huh?"

Sean's head and body were pulled back as far from Celeste as he could. Celeste was ultra-close to him now; her fingers curled as she released her pent-up anger on him.

"Where is it?" Celeste shouted.

"I-I don't… I don't know," Sean stammered.

"I'll tell you where," Celeste stated firmly. "It's right in front of Thomas"—she pointed at him—"and right in front of you. It's Angel and myself. We are the justice for all those women that came before us. What you and Thomas did to all those women was so ungodly and morally wrong on so many levels. You two are so mentally fucked up. Angel and I are the ones that are going to cut the evil out of the world, and we're going to start with you."

Celeste was only seeing red now. She turned and snatched the knife back up from the table behind her. She rounded on Sean and pointed his dad's knife into his face.

"Then, after we finish with you two, we're going to hunt down your dad, and we're going to figure out a punishment that goes along with his crime of murdering your mother."

Angel was too focused on Thomas, but she interjected without looking their way. "Something dealing with thirty-two sounds good to me since he likes that number so much."

Celeste went for Sean. Her hand shot down into his crotch, and she grabbed the fullest handful of his penis and scrotum that she could grip and pulled it away from his body. She looked like a butcher with a chicken in one hand, holding it ready to drop the cleaver to sever its head. She brought the knife in from the side and placed it on the side of his scrotum at the deepest part of his inner thigh.

Sean's body went rigid. His muscles seized up as tight as they could with the wrappings around his hands and feet. The sharp edge of his father's knife felt cool against his privates' soft, tender underside, and it had him screaming out for mercy. "Wait-wait-wait! Please! Please! God! Stop! Stop! Stop!"

Celeste stopped.

Sean took a deep breath, then whispered in a breathy anxious pant, "Celeste. Wait, please, tell me. Please remember how good it was between us. Please think back to when we made love. You have to remember how perfect it was between us. I know it was good for you. I don't say that with an air of arrogance. It was amazing because it was the best sex I've ever had. We can have more of those moments. Please give me a chance to prove that I am not as bad as I have made myself out to be."

Celeste looked him in the eyes and said, "We can't go back because I could never trust you. And after this incident, you would never trust me. It would be a horrible relationship knowing what we both know now. My conscience is clear. My mind is made up. This has to be done. This is for all those other women and me."

Celeste broke eye contact with him and looked down into his lap. She pushed hard on the knife as she jerked up vertically and then pulled up diagonally toward his belly button. Blood erupted from the laceration and shot in numerous directions.

Righteous agony erupted throughout Sean's body, and his screams were loud, long, and not of this earth.

Celeste quickly switched hands with what she was holding in each. She grabbed the handful of meat she had again and moved the blade down into the crevice between his inner thigh and scrotum but on the other side. She choked back a wave of nausea as she did so. She mirrored her first ruthless cut, pushing down hard as she dragged up sharply with a vicious swipe that intersected the first. Blood sprayed and splattered everywhere, erupting from the nasty slices. It caught her, mainly on each of her forearms. The two significant cuts weren't enough to where his manhood was solely hers. She hadn't tucked the blade far enough under him to slice all of his manhood free; it was still attached somewhere underneath.

"Fuck," Celeste said, but no one heard her; Sean's screams crescendoed throughout the basement of this lake house.

She turned the blade over and placed it underneath the last small remaining section of skin; then she pulled away as she sliced one last time upward. The last strands of flesh slapped back to her new prize. Celeste was immediately hit with the visual of eating a fried chicken leg, the veins snapping back at her when she pulled the meat from the bone. This elicited a disgusting shiver within her.

The blood geyser shot off toward Thomas as though Sean was ejaculating blood rather than semen. The red liquid pitter-pattered the filmy gray tarp Angel and Celeste had been wise enough to put underneath them.

Sean's screams subsided, but his whole body was steeped in agony. His body was going into shock from the instant trauma. His anger came out in verbal diarrhea. "Oh. You. Fucking. Bitch!" Sean managed to say each word, building to a high-pitched squeal. Spittle sprayed from his mouth with each word. "I… can't believe… you… you cut… everything…" Sean's eyes fluttered, and his head bobbed. He was losing consciousness.

Celeste leaned down and slapped him hard to bring him back to alertness. She wasn't done. She lifted her other hand, still clutching his severed man meat, up in front of his face. Her voice was filled with vehemence. "I. Fucking. Win. You. Fucking. Lose."

Sean's eyes fluttered again, this time with regret. He squirmed in shock, winced, then said, "We could've… been beautiful… together. I would've been… the best thing… ever happened… to you. I… loved… you."

A wave of guilt washed through her at the mention of love. It had been good from that one moment in time between them, but she could never have had a good and honest relationship with him, knowing what he and Thomas had done to so many women. She turned hard again, letting that guilt pass through her. It vanished faster than she expected. She allowed what Sean and Thomas had done to return to the surface of her mind.

Anger flared in Sean's eyes, but it was a wave of half-assed anger. His body was shutting down as his life's liquid quickly drained. His body was like a condemned building. The imaginary foreman within was going through, flipping the breakers off for the last time.

Sean didn't have the energy to argue with Celeste anymore. All he could say was a whisper, and only Celeste heard it. "You won this round." Then Sean's eyes drooped but remained half-opened, staring at nothing in particular.

Celeste stood there, still leaning down in his face, searching his half-closed eyes. Her eyes narrowed and dipped in confusion at what she thought was the oddest last statement.

A sharp shrill cry from Thomas snapped Celeste out of the moment.

"Oh, Jesus Christ!" Angel said as she stood abruptly. Her chair slid away across the blood-coated plastic tarp.

"Fuck!" Thomas exclaimed, the word drawn out in length.

"You son-of-a-bitch!"

"What?" Celeste asked in sudden alarm as she turned away, distracted from what she had just done to Sean. "What is it?"

Angel turned, and Celeste saw a slash of blood splatter across her face. Angel threw a hand back down toward his crotch. "His testicle exploded like a goddamn zit. Fucking hell! It was like one of those fucking fast-food ketchup packets that shoots off if too much pressure is added. Shot off and hit me in the fucking face. You're such a piece of shit. I got your number, you fucking twat. I'll fix you."

Angel grabbed seven rubber bands at once. She hooked six of them around her left pinky to hold them close. She didn't know how many more his man-meat could take, but she was going to find out quickly enough. The single one she held, she looped it as she'd done all the others and snapped it around Thomas's ever-tightening mid-section.

"That's the last time you'll shoot off on me, asshole."

Thomas's eyes bulged as the dull pain in his groin spread to all areas of his body. His mouth opened and closed like a fish chewing on something invisible. He indicated to the women in the room that he wanted something to bite down on because the pain was excruciating. He wanted it, but they weren't going to give him anything to quell the agony. He shook his head against the torture as Angel bent forward and placed another looped rubber band around his junk. His eyes were leaking; he silently cried against the immense knot of pain attached to his middle. His feet tapped out an irregular beat on the plastic beneath him.

Angel looped another rubber band near the last one.

Through his irregular breathing, he managed to say, "Just… just kill me… now."

"Oh, you're going to die, motherfucker. Both of you," Angel said, stretching another band on top of all the others. "You're both going to bleed out. You will be forgotten. You will not be mourned. No one will shed a tear for you. Rebecca didn't. Your family hasn't. Sean only had tears for himself. Celeste and I certainly won't shed any tears that this world is losing you. In a way, you two have already been forgotten."

Angel inverted another rubber band, pulled it wide, slipped it over his bulging junk, and snapped it into place.

"Oh Jesus," Thomas managed to say in a frightened panic. He looked down at his dark red and ungodly purple mid-section. It now looked like a deformity that no doctor could manage to heal.

Angel said, "Oh my God, is this it? Is this actually going to work?" Excited curiosity was in her voice as though she didn't know what to expect.

Thomas's upper body shook involuntarily with the pain. His feet were tied down, and his arms could go nowhere, but they shook and flopped uselessly in their bindings. He could bend slightly at the waist and lean back in his chair. His fingers clenched and unclenched as he worked through the agony in his crotch.

"Can it take one more? Let's try and see."

Angel double-wrapped another one, looped it around, and stretched it near the others. She pulled it extra wide and then released the bands simultaneously. Angel jerked her head and hands back quickly; she didn't want any of his blood to shoot off into her face again. She sat back as though she were playing some kid's game that if it caved in or exploded on your turn, you lost.

The bands snapped around his engorged penis and scrotum, and as they did, there was a sick, wet suction noise as though someone were bending up a shovelful of damp earth. The audible slurp grew louder as the rubber bands shifted toward the intersection of Thomas's legs. As they rotated backward, his cock and scrotum were pushed forward as the pressure of the rubber bands dug in even tighter, cut more profoundly, and severed Thomas from his most prized possession. The rubber bands tightened like a cluster of miniature snakes trying to wriggle free.

His manhood didn't explode away as the watermelon did in the video because it was made of a different substance; it more or less rotated out on itself. The blood gushed forth from other rips in the skin of his split midsection, causing the rubber bands to spring, snap, and readjust into a tighter bloody knot and tighten deeper within him. Although Thomas's manhood wasn't completely severed from his body, it was close enough because the shifting rubber bands knotted up on the veins and last pieces of tender flesh. The wad of twisted rubber bands and minced meat dangled by a few threads of red tissue. No operation or gifted doctors would ever be able to fix the wreckage Angel had reaped upon him, even if Angel released Thomas back into the world with his devastating crotch.

An air raid siren of a screech burst from Thomas's throat as he looked down at the hideousness between his legs. "Jesus Christ… that is. That… that's fucked up," Thomas managed to say through ragged breaths. "You bitches… are fucking… crazy." His voice took on another high-pitched wail but of a different timbre.

"Guess who made us that way?" Celeste asked.

Thomas had no comeback. He pleaded, "Just kill me… right here and now."

"No," Celeste said. "You're going to bleed out. Angel and I will wait. We've got nothing but time."

Angel was staring down at Aaron's devastated crotch with a frowning look of disgust. "You know what's disappointing about this whole experiment?"

Thomas's head bobbed up. He stared at her with a confused, tear-streaked face.

"Is that those rubber bands didn't separate you from the main root of the problem."

Aaron realized what she was going to do. He said, "No! No-no-no-no—"

But Angel was already reaching between his legs for the tight softball-sized mesh of bloody man meat. She latched on to it and gripped it tight. Blood squeezed out from the cluster like it was a sponge. She gave a quick jerk, pulling up and away.

The few tendrils of flesh still attached to Thomas pulled away with it but ripped free and snapped back.

Over the new anguished wails coming out of Thomas, Angel said in an elevated voice, "You don't get to keep these. They're mine now." She shook the softball-sized knot of flesh in his face as Celeste had done to Sean. "Now we're even, bitch."

Disgusted at what she held in her hand, she relaxed her grip and let it roll off the end of her fingers. It was mainly a ball of compressed rubber bands, so it bounced higher than she had expected. Angel watched as it splashed into the blood directly in front of Thomas. It quickly drum-rolled into stillness.

Celeste said, "Jesus Christ, I can't believe you did that. I can't believe I did what I did, either. We just castr—" But she didn't have the heart or the stomach to say it.

"These sons of a bitches deserved it," Angel said.

"Oh, I know. I didn't know I had it in me to do that."

"These guys brought this upon themselves. They started a game they couldn't finish."

"We win."

"Hell yes, we won. Game, set, and fucking match. We ended their game as well. We won't have to worry about any other women being played by these two." Angel turned and looked at Celeste, then said, "Um, Celeste?"

"Yeah?" Celeste said as she turned away from her locked gaze on Thomas's eviscerated mid-section.

"Why are you still holding *that*?"

Celeste looked down and saw Sean's limp meat in her hand. She was so focused on everything she'd done to Sean and what Angel had done to Thomas that it hadn't registered in her mind to release Sean's manhood. Realization hit her whole body, and she involuntarily shivered. It was Sean's penis, the same one that she had let slide deep between her legs. The one time they had made love, it had been good—no, better than good, it was amazing, perfect even. And she had loved it. But now, looking down at it clutched in her blood-drenched hand, she was revolted by it and wanted to be rid of it. Her arm spasmed, and she flung it away. It dropped closer to her than she wanted. It slapped down into a puddle of blood near Sean's feet. When it landed, it also bounced—more like flopped over—which caused one of the testicles to slide free from its home within his scrotum. It rolled in an awkward semi-circle and finally stopped.

"Disgusting," Angel said as she watched the movements of Sean's detached penis. "You've got bigger balls than I do. You really took it to him."

"Took it *from* him," Celeste corrected. She cleared her voice and said to Angel, "I don't think what I did to Sean is any worse than what you did to Thomas."

"Yeah, I guess. But that… that…" Angel couldn't find the words to describe her feelings.

"It was retribution," Celeste said.

"I guess that's the one word that sums up everything with what they did to us versus what we did to them. One thing about it is they're not going to be able to play their game anymore." Angel threw a hand up in the direction of both men's mangled midsections. "If the punishment fits the crime, then…"

"So, what are you saying?"

"I don't know," Angel mused. "Just putting it out there that we helped save each other. We could help save other women going through the same thing we did. You know, those other women at Safe Haven or other abuse self-help groups. I feel better knowing these two assholes won't be out on the streets preying on other women as they did us. I would be down to help other women fight the people they are suffering under."

"You have a point, but where do we go from here?"

"Well, first, we have to get rid of these assholes and cover our tracks. I want no way anyone could track these dick bags back to us or this house. I am here for another eleven days before my friends return from vacation, so I want to make damn sure this house is spotless."

They looked down at the puddles and rivulets of blood pooled all over the plastic-covered floor.

"That's going to be a major clean-up job in and of itself, but I helped make this mess; I'm here to help you through the rest of it."

"I'm glad you're just not planning on grabbing your purse and taking off," Angel said, more or less as a joke. But she was relieved that Celeste was on board as she was tonight. She would've bet Celeste wouldn't have gone through with it.

Celeste said, "I'm a bitch sometimes, but not that big of a bitch."

They stood there in the warm light of the basement, Angel on one side of the men and Celeste across from her, a mirror image. They took turns looking back and forth between the two men. The mewling from Thomas dwindled as his blood flow slowed. This caused him to lapse into an unconscious death, as Sean had done earlier.

When the men were finally silent, and the blood flow stopped, Celeste asked, "What are we going to do with their bodies?"

Angel said, "I've been thinking of that since we arrived yesterday. I knew we couldn't cut their junk off and release them to the world if they survived. I don't know if they would live or die with what we planned to do with them. But we know what happens when trauma comes to their little manly bits."

Angel walked around the two guys, making sure not to step in any blood puddles and track bloody footprints on the carpet on the opposite side of the room. She stopped at the window, stuck her finger into the louvered curtains, and spread them open. She peered across the leveled ground as Celeste had done at the beginning of this interrogation. She looked all the way down to the lakeside dock. She saw the boat attached to the pier. She thought for a moment, then turned away from the window and said, "Here's what we're going to do."

CHAPTER THIRTY-FOUR

Mitch Harrison—whom Angel was house and cat sitting for—was addicted to fishing and always had to have the top-of-the-line fishing boat to tool around Silver Ridge Lake. Every so often, Mitch would see a new Boston Whaler, Carolina Skiff, or Cobia and realize the new boat was slightly better than his current model. He could never suppress the urge to sell and upgrade to a new watercraft. This was why Angel was currently standing at the center console controls, steering a Bayliner Trophy T24CC through the darkness. The 300 HP Mercery engine screamed, propelling them into deeper waters.

Standing near Angel, Celeste squinted into the darkness and the onslaught of wind that whipped her and Angel's hair back horizontally. It felt great out here on the open water. It was great to fill her lungs with the refreshing lake air after breathing the coppery smell of blood during their lengthy aftermath clean-up in the Harrison's abode.

Being out on the lake would've felt even better if they weren't hauling two corpses during this nighttime ride. Celeste was nervous that a lake warden was patrolling the lake. If he came up beside them for any reason, there would be no way he wouldn't see the two men that were now clothed, wrapped in chains, and weighed down with cinderblocks.

Celeste turned away from the influx of wind and looked back at the two dead men that lay at the back near the engine. Celeste could see them by the white glow of the light attached to the boat's stern.

The chains that bound each man were wrapped twice around their feet, then up around their waists, and looped around and through their belt loops. Their hands were tied in with their waist loop. The chain continued, wrapped twice around their necks, then back down, and was padlocked to their wrist loops. A cinder block was also intertwined around the chain of each of the men.

Angel turned the boat, angling it to a different part of the lake. This movement caused Thomas's body to move slightly to the left as if he had shifted toward her. Celeste's heart leaped in her chest at the furtive movement.

Did he move, or did Angel's boat maneuvering cause him to shift?

She half expected Thomas to bend at the knees, fold at the waist, and sit up. A dreaded feeling infected her that he would lurch forward, grab onto her, step away, fall backward over the boat, drag her into the lake depths with his weighted body, and leave Angel unknowingly alone.

Celeste shook her head again and pushed back those unnerving thoughts that arose in her mind. She looked back at the two dead bodies. They were in the same position; they had shifted but hadn't moved anymore. She turned and raised her voice over the whipping winds and the engine whine and asked, "How far out are we going?"

Angel didn't take her eyes off whatever she was looking at in the darkness, but she angled her head and yelled sideways to Celeste, "The deepest area out here that I know of."

"How much farther?"

Answering her question by pulling back on the throttle, the boat's speed abruptly slowed. Angel said, "No farther. We're here."

She pulled the throttle up into neutral, causing the propellers to stop completely. The boat's bow dipped slightly as the watercraft rode out the wake that caught up with them. It leveled out, fell still, and floated as the engine idled.

Celeste said, "I don't understand why we didn't just dump them somewhere or bury them in the woods behind your friend's house."

Angel was doing a slow three-sixty turn around the boat, looking to see if any other vessels nearby might be observing what they were doing. "I think that's where we would've made our mistake. Dumping these dickless twats somewhere could lead right back to haunt us."

I already think they're haunting us, Celeste thought, remembering the movement she had imagined Thomas's body making.

Angel continued speaking as she scanned the dark surface of the lake. "Especially burying them on Mitch's property. If someone or some animal found these bodies buried in a grave behind his house, you can bet your ass the investigation would lead straight back to me or us. By dumping these two shitheads in the lake, if they ever resurface, hundreds of lake owners would have to be questioned. It would be nearly impossible to interview everyone around here or find everyone who visited this lake. If they ever find any part of these guys and do a major search to find more of their remains, it would be hard to pin it on us because we would be long gone. And even if they come around and do a door-to-door investigation, my friends Mitch and Beverly won't know anything about it. They would act naturally to any questions that come their way. But the chances of them doing an investigation and tracking this back to us are exponentially slim. At least, I think they are. I hope they are, anyway. This is the best plan I could come up with. Let's hope I'm right."

"You have no argument from me," Celeste said. "It makes a lot of sense."

Angel moved to the back of the boat near the two bodies. "And I wanted to get them out here in the middle of the lake, so it isn't closer to any certain part of the mainland. I want it to be as confusing as possible for someone to figure this mystery out, that is, if the mystery of these two guys ever comes up."

"Okay, I'm more on board with this plan now."

"Remind me never to swim in this lake ever again. Going to be gross for me to know there are decomposing bodies in this lake with my friends still swimming in it, but we have to do what we have to do. Come on, let's dump these losers and get back. I still want to do a second walk-through to ensure we took care of all the evidence. I will double and triple-clean the downstairs again before Mitch and Beverly return. I will make sure this doesn't come back to bite either of us in the ass."

Angel grabbed the chains wrapped around Sean's wrists, and Celeste grabbed his chained feet. She still couldn't shake the image of Thomas coming to life while they were en route to this destination.

Celeste and Angel heaved Sean's body up on the starboard side of the boat, and then with a slight push, they rolled him off into the water. They followed his body as it splashed down into his new resting place. There wasn't much light from the boat itself because they didn't want to draw attention to themselves out here this late at night. They watched as Sean sunk by what little light was shown from overhead.

Sean's body rotated through the light shining on the water's surface. His half-open-eyed frozen-agony stare spun toward them; it connected with both of them for the briefest of seconds. Then, just like a kidnapper wrapping a black bag over a victim's face, the dark currents of the Silver Ridge Lake wrapped around Sean's visage as he sunk quickly into deeper depths.

Celeste pulled away from the lake's surface. She couldn't help but think that Sean would begin to struggle, and like Houdini, miraculously maneuver his body out of his chains, swim to the surface, burst through the water, seize both of them by their shirt collars, and drag them, kicking and screaming, beneath the waves.

They rechecked their surroundings, then repeated the movements with Thomas and rolled him over the side. He splashed down and disappeared faster than Sean had.

Celeste and Angel waited a minute or two longer, making sure the bodies wouldn't pop back up around the boat because of trapped air or some buoyancy property they hadn't thought of. They just stood there silently, imagining these butchered corpses sinking to the bottom of the lakebed.

When Angel was satisfied they were gone for good, she and Celeste stepped back to the center console. Angel pushed the throttle forward, swung the boat in a wide half-circle, and headed back to the Harrisons' dock and the lake house.

CHAPTER THIRTY-FIVE

"Hello, everyone," Sylvia said as she waved a hand above her head to get everyone's attention. As the women of the group began to fall silent and turn her way, she dropped her hand to her lap and continued, "If we could all settle down, we can go ahead and get started with today's session."

The other women seated in a circle stopped conversing with whom they were sitting next to, straightened themselves, and turned their full attention to their host.

"As some of you may know, my name is Sylvia Bissell. I am the section leader and coordinator of this chapter for abused women. At Safe Haven, you will find many women from different abused relationships. I want you to know that everyone here is here because they are going through some traumatic event, whether physical, mental, or financial abuse. If you are new today, and I see that a couple of you are, I would urge you to speak up—"

A loud click of the latch in the gymnasium door diverted most of the women's attention, and they glanced in that direction or turned in their seats to see who was entering.

A squeal of unoiled hinges accompanied the late arrival of two other women.

Sylvia could do nothing but fall silent because of the noisy gym doors. She had lost the women's attention to that loud distraction.

I'm going to have to remember to talk to the custodian about that, Sylvia thought. *Those doors are simply awful.*

Sylvia quickly noted this on top of the folder and penned a massive star by it.

Celeste Baker and Angel Domingo entered through each side of the double doors—Celeste on the right and Angel on the left. As they approached, the doors clattered shut behind them.

All the women watched as they made their way to the curvature of the seated circle.

Wanting to get to the heart of this interruption, Sylvia immediately said, "Celeste? Angel? This is a delightful surprise. Please, grab a chair from against the wall, and we can continue today's session."

"That won't be necessary, Sylvia," Angel said. "We won't be staying for group therapy today."

Celeste added, "We don't want to step on any toes here, but we dropped by to give out some of our business cards in case anyone needs additional help."

Angel and Celeste began to walk in different directions around each side of the circular group. They both pulled thin business card holders from their back pockets, opened them, and pulled a few cards from within.

Angel continued, "We certainly don't want to take anyone away from the great work you do here. Everyone knows you have helped so many women in the past. But if any of you feel that talking isn't enough, you can blow off some steam and learn some self-defense. We will be teaching that and having our own counseling sessions."

Celeste chimed in, "You can call either of our numbers on these cards to set up a meeting with us. We can help you with a more physical approach to therapy to help you get through these tough times."

Angel and Celeste met on the opposite side of the circle and began handing out their cards.

"So, what is your angle?" Sylvia asked. "Are you passing yourself off as personal trainers or something?"

"Yes, that is the perfect way to put it," Celeste agreed. "Personal trainers." She handed her business card to another woman who accepted it and looked down at the information. "It's a more hands-on approach."

"Part of our offer is beginning self-defense classes to ensure a secondary sexual assault or rape will never happen. We know they do. We want to remedy this."

Sylvia's mouth had dropped open. She was appalled at the nerve of these two women who had barged into her talk session and begun discussing their new kind of therapy. This was her turf—her hallowed ground. She was the only one qualified here to help these women. She had gone to school and studied all the psychology classes and types of domestic abuse. They were treading on her sacred ground. Sylvia said, "Angel. Uh, Celeste, I don't think you two are qualified to treat these women. You simply don't have the credentials or a license to operate. What training do you have to teach this so-called self-defense?"

Celeste handed one of her cards to another woman in the group, then turned to Sylvia. "We were sexually assaulted and raped. That is license and credential enough to start what we want to do and help other women. No other school offers the kind of therapy we specialize in."

"You are simply not qualified," Sylvia snapped.

Angel turned to Sylvia. "With what we have been through recently, we are the two most qualified women in this room."

Sylvia began immediately, "Well, Angel, I don't think now is the best time to talk about this."

Angel's calm demeanor rose a little; she said, "I think it's the perfect time to *talk* about this. After all, that is what *you* are all about. *Talk*. Always talk it out. That's your world, your healing, and we're not taking your world away from you or this opportunity away from these women. Celeste and I are merely offering additional ways of handling every unique situation, which stemmed from your wisdom in this group. So, thank you for your enlightenment and for showing us the way to our healing. The kind of healing that worked best for us."

It was a nice compliment, and Sylvia put a hand to her collar and straightened it as she shuffled to get more comfortable in her seat. This also gave her time to think of a different approach to come back at these women verbally. "Well, sit down," Sylvia repeated, her interest piqued. She hadn't even remembered offering them a seat before. "I would like to discuss all this and hear what you two came up with. I believe I am an authority figure on what good therapy would be for Safe Haven women to go through. It might be something I might like to incorporate in my therapy teachings."

Celeste continued to smile and hand out their new business cards. She chimed in on the heels of Sylvia's statements. "We're not seeking anyone's approval other than our clients' healing. That will be approval enough. We're doing this to help women."

Angel said, "We're giving them a chance to fight back so they won't be victims. Our new self-defense therapy is still being worked through. Not every detail is in place. We are just beginning."

Sylvia found herself nodding, "Oh, yes. Yes, of course. I see."

Celeste ignored Sylvia and addressed the rest of the women. "Please don't think we are stepping on Sylvia's toes or what she is doing here. She is doing great work in this community. Simply the best. Please continue working with her. But if you need any additional help or resources, please call either of the phone numbers on our business cards. We can meet and discuss the best possible solution to help you almost any time."

Angel and Celeste finally met back where they had stood when they entered the room.

"Hey, Gabby," Angel said. "You're still here? Weren't you going to school to do what Sylvia does?"

Gabby was caught off guard and had no idea where her line of questioning was going. "Uh, yes." There was a guilty glance at Sylvia.

"When will you branch out and start your own Safe Haven? Different name, of course."

"Yes, of course. I don't know," she said in a wondering tone.

Celeste interjected, "You are ready. You don't need to finish school. If you want to help women, then help them."

"You don't need to wait," Angel added. "Just like we're not waiting. If you are scared to start your chapter, don't be, because you are more than ready. Just food for thought."

"Thanks," Gabby said. "I'll give it some thought."

"Thank you for your time, Sylvia," Celeste said and waved quickly.

"Ladies," Angel said with a slight nod. "Again, sorry to interrupt, but we have to leave. We look forward to talking with some of you soon."

Celeste added as they turned to leave, "Have a great talk therapy session with Sylvia. She is extremely good at what she does."

Angel couldn't help but think, *Yeah, but so are we—emphasis on the* extreme.

Angel and Celeste turned and moved away from the group. They hit the gymnasium doors simultaneously. The clack and squeal of the doors opening continued to capture the women's attention. The doors finally squeaked shut with a loud click of the latch; then, everything fell silent again.

Sylvia was frustrated and angry. She tried to gather her thoughts about what she was saying to the group before Angel and Celeste had so rudely interrupted her session.

❧

Paula Rainey, a first-timer to this Safe Haven therapy session, sat quietly and tried to look invisible as she watched the tennis match discussion between the three women. She thought the two ladies who had arrived late seemed confident in how they carried themselves and spoke.

She thought, *If they have gone through their problems and have started this new treatment and come out as confident as they looked, maybe I need to look into what they are offering. It's as though they know exactly what they want to say and do.*

Paula wanted to be that powerful, but she had no idea what she would say to the group whenever it was her turn to speak. Paula studied the navy-blue business card with raised silver lettering as Sylvia blundered in the background.

The card read:

BRAKEFIELD/CARMICHAEL THERAPY SOLUTIONS
Women's Self-defense and Counseling

Paula didn't understand the business's title because the two women's first and last names were listed below the company. She would've thought the name of their company would be something like Baker/Domingo or

Domingo/Baker Therapy Solutions, but for whatever reason, they chose not to use their last names.

That's interesting, Paula thought. *Who cares about the title of the business? As long as the two women talked about helping me, that's all that mattered.*

Paula was more comfortable having a one-on-one or two-on-one discussion; there wasn't as much pressure. She felt it would be more conversational than group therapy. The word group in that two-word phrase seemed to make her nervous. It was like public speaking, and she loathed speaking in public. She'd rather die than get up in front of a bunch of people. There were more women here than she wanted to tell her embarrassing situation. Paula also felt like everyone in the room had secretly judged her since she'd sat down. And this was before she had even opened her mouth and told them her story. What would they do once they heard? Paula looked longingly at the door, then again at the business card. The card beckoned her to go to them.

I could catch them before they leave the parking lot.

Paula looked toward the door again.

Sylvia was speaking again, "Well, that was certainly interesting. I don't know what those two are up to. Until I can look into their business and find out exactly what their therapy is all about, it may be best to continue working with me. I will have more information about their *company* at the next meeting. Um, could I see one of their cards?" she asked the woman sitting next to her. The woman handed over the card, and Sylvia studied it and read, "Yes, Brakefield/Carmichael Therapy Solutions. I will have to see what their… *company* is all about." Sylvia used the word 'company' loosely and with some disdain because she couldn't develop a better word for it. "Now, to better acquaint ourselves with each other, why don't we just go around the room and introduce ourselves—"

Paula quietly stood and moved quickly toward the door. As she did so, her foot hit the chair and scraped across the floor. She inwardly cringed at the sound but kept walking. She didn't get far.

"Excuse me. Paula, is it?" Sylvia said, slightly startled at Paula's abrupt movement from the group.

Paula stopped mid-stride as though she were a teenager who had just been busted for sneaking in the back door after curfew. Paula turned back to Sylvia on the balls of her feet.

Sylvia asked slowly, "Where are you going? This meeting has already started."

It took a few moments for Paula to find her voice with thirteen pairs of eyes staring at her. She swallowed hard. She tried to speak but found her voice was clogged. Finally, she cleared her throat and added, "I'm not a big speaker. I don't like to talk in big groups. It, um, makes me nervous." Paula held up the recently received business card quickly. "I don't know what this is all about, but I feel it's more my style. Maybe. I don't know. But I have to go find out. Sorry."

Paula rotated away on the balls of her feet again and exited as quietly as she could, but the heavy steel door made that impossible. She cringed again as the door protested her escape.

She turned back to the group, shoulder up and a grimace on her face. "Sorry. Someone needs to fix these doors." Then she turned from the ladies and scurried out of the gym.

Relieved to be outside, Paula checked the first parking lot she came to and looked frantically around for the two women, but they were nowhere in sight. She started to panic as she moved around to the back parking lot. She thought she had waited too late inside to make her decision because she didn't see them. As she was about to turn away from the parking lot, she saw two bobbing heads stride over the roofs of parked cars. She entered the parking lot and realized it was the two ladies nearing a parked vehicle. She ran toward them.

"Hey!" Paula yelled just as Angel and Celeste pulled up on the Subaru's handles and opened the doors.

Angel and Celeste exchanged wary glances, then shut their doors again. They stepped to the front of the car, curious about what this woman wanted but realizing this would probably be their first client.

Paula had run to catch up with them, and she was a little out of breath by the time she reached them. "Sorry to… uh… stop you… I was trying to catch you… before you left." She stopped in front of them, bent slightly at the waist, and took a few deep breaths.

"You're from the group we just left, aren't you?" Celeste asked.

Paula nodded, "Yeah, today was going to be my first talk therapy session. Talk Therapy Session. That three-word phrase scares me to death."

"Bet Sylvia didn't like you leaving the group, did she?" Angel asked.

"No," Paula said with a little chuckle. "No, I don't think so. She seemed like a control freak if you want my true opinion."

Celeste and Angel glanced at each other and laughed along with Paula.

"Exactly what we've thought," Angel mused. "She's just protecting her turf. We didn't take any offense by it."

"So, why did you leave?" Celeste asked, getting right to the heart of this conversation.

"I wanted to talk to you two instead."

"If you had missed us, you could've called one of the numbers on the card. That's what they're there for."

Paula looked down at the business card still clutched in her hand. She face-palmed her forehead and mentally kicked herself for being so dumb in front of these incredible, confident, beautiful women. She shook her head and laughed. "That's only my first idiot moment of the day. I didn't even think about that. I was just so desperate to get to you." She took a few more deep breaths.

Angel and Celeste smiled at her semantics and waited to figure out what secrets she wanted to discuss.

Paula began, "I don't know what therapy you two are in, but I would like to discuss my problem with you rather than with that group. That is if you have the time."

Angel looked over to Celeste. She squinted against the sunlight's glare that pinged off a few parked cars behind Celeste's head. Celeste returned her gaze. They both nodded, then turned to face the woman again.

Angel said, "I think we have a little time on our hands to discuss your problem."

"What's your name?" Celeste asked.

"Paula?" she said in a mousey voice. It sounded like she was testing her voice to see if her name was enough for them to accept her as a client. Trying to emulate the women, she quickly repeated herself more confidently. "Paula Rainey."

Celeste held her hand to Paula; she accepted it, and they shook. "I'm Celeste Baker, and this is Angel Domingo." She motioned in Angel's direction, and they shook hands also.

Paula said, "It's great to meet you two."

"What's happening in your life that you need our help with?" Celeste asked.

Ashamed, Paula looked down at her hands, grasping her purse to herself as added protection, and said, "My husband drugs me and rapes me when I'm asleep."

Angel and Celeste's eyebrows dip with curious looks of skepticism. They asked in unison, "What?"

She looked at them more directly—a little more confidence playing on her face and in her voice. "My husband drugs me. And when I'm out… he… he rapes me."

They were quiet for a moment, then Angel said, "Forgive me, but how do you know this? Other than possibly feeling like you've had sex when you wake up."

Knowing this question would come up, Paula reached into her purse, grabbed three disks from a side pocket, and pulled them out. "Because I have proof." Her eyes began to tear up as emotional hurt broke out on her face. Her voice cracked, and she looked down, ashamed, "I have three DVDs worth of filmed episodes where he has done this to me. He filmed himself. I pulled these from a file on his computer. You can watch them if you need to see I'm telling the truth."

"Oh, Paula," Celeste said, moving to her, "come here." She pulled her into a tight hug.

Angel moved in and wrapped her arms around Paula and Celeste. They stood there in a tight cluster. It was a tight welcome hug that gave Paula's body the freedom to release her hurt. They stood there holding Paula while she wept.

Paula said, "It's not fair. It's just not fair. I wish there were a way to make him pay, you know. I mean, really pay for doing this to me."

Once the emotional episode drained from within her, the embrace slowly released.

Angel said, "I'm so sorry that happened to you."

"Thanks," Paula said, swiping her tears from her eyes.

Celeste and Angel turned to each other, and their eyes met. They both nodded; then, they looked back to Paula.

"It's not a question of us believing you, Paula," Celeste said. She reached in and lifted the woman's face to look into her eyes. "I know you think your story sounds unbelievable. But when you've been through what we've been through, we know an honest confession when we hear it. We see the hurt in your eyes and the pain on your face."

Angel turned to her and asked, "Are you hungry, Paula?"

"I guess, I mean, I could eat," Paula replied.

"Good," Celeste said. "We know a great little diner a few blocks from here where we could sit down and discuss your case in more detail. It's where Angel and I first worked out our differences a few days ago. We figured out how we could take care of our problems with the men that abused us. Would you like to grab some food and discuss it with us?"

"Sure. That sounds good to me."

"I believe we can help you, Paula," Angel said.

Celeste added, "We don't do this for everyone, but we have a special package that we only discuss with complicated cases."

"We call it our Platinum Package."

"It's more of a hands-on approach therapy."

"I don't know what that means," Paula said, "But I'm interested."

"Do you feel comfortable riding with us?" Angel asked. "We could always drop you back by your car when we're finished discussing your case."

"Oh, um, sure. You don't mind me riding with you?"

Angel shook her head, "Not at all. Hop in."

Paula stepped toward the back of the car, but Angel had already opened the front passenger's side door. "Oh no, Paula, you're the client. The client always rides shotgun."

Paula looked at the open door and smiled as she raised her eyebrow. "Oh, wow, I've never had this kind of attention before." She looked at Angel and then at Celeste.

Celeste gave her a friendly smile of approval and nodded encouragingly.

Paula stepped forward and took the passenger's seat.

Angel closed the door and moved to the back passenger's side door.

Angel and Celeste exchanged a smile over the top of the car. Angel winked at Celeste, and they stepped into the car together and closed the doors.

Celeste started her Crosstrek, backed out of her parking space, and moved to the exit. She turned out of the gymnasium parking lot and pointed her car toward the Skyline Diner. They knew they could help Paula with her current problem, provided she wanted to move forward with them in this new therapy they were offering.

And if she was, they knew Paula would gain closure to this horrific chapter of her life, just like they had done.

ACKNOWLEDGEMENTS

Lee Bagwell – Thank you, Lee, for letting me shoot ideas off the cuff with you, chiming in with honest feedback, and finding ways to make my stories more extraordinary. I value your input on anything, but your storycraft ideas are always brilliant. Thank you for working with me on most, if not all, of my stories. You are a badass through and through. But I am not telling you anything you don't already know.

Evan Bond—Thank you, Evan, for giving *These Bloody Games We Play* a beta read early on and for all your excellent story suggestions. Thank you for finding all the small details I missed while writing it. Also, as always, thank you for all the encouragement over the past years since we met through Instagram. Your friendship is invaluable to me. I appreciate you, all you do, and the advice you give.

Chris Cashon – Thank you, Chris, for helping me tweak this cover early on. I don't know everything about Photoshop yet, but I am learning. Thanks for helping me pull this cover together the way it should be. I appreciate all your help with my Photoshop needs over the past few years. I'll never forget it.

Heather Daughrity – I just wanted to say how grateful I am to have Heather as the final editor of this project. I am thankful that the content within the story didn't scare her away. In doing the final reading and editing of this story, I kept returning to its smooth readability. I am incredibly pleased with everything Heather did for this dark tale. I appreciate her character advice, the storyline inconsistencies she caught, her suggestions for writing a cleaner narrative, and her keen eye for catching all my grammatical mishaps. She enhanced my writing and helped make my story 100% stronger. If you have a manuscript that needs editing, contact Heather Daughrity. You and your readers will be happy you did and thank you for it. She is everything you would want or need in an editor.

William Gary – A special thank you to William, a retired detective with the Spartanburg Police Department, who is so generous with his time. He always makes himself available to help me to fine-tune my storylines to real-world situations. I have a great time discussing forensics with him.

Laurie Jones – It wouldn't feel right to put this book out without acknowledging my wife for all the hours she spent editing some of the early drafts of this story. You may not see yourself as an editor, but I loved all the nuances you added. I am thankful for the time you spent on it.

D.A. Schneider – Thank you for all your encouragement along this writing pathway we travel. As a fellow author who is always killing it in the publishing industry with your multiple-genre tales, you constantly inspire me. Thank you for taking an interest in my writing and for all the edits and suggestions you made early on for this crazy story.

Thank you to a few of my early Beta/ARC readers (those not listed above), for taking the time to read, review, and spotlight my work in your social media feeds. I appreciate you more than I can adequately express. Jay Bechtol, Patrick Delaney, Stephanie Evans, Beverly D. Laude, Shasta Mathews, Milt Theodossiou, Josette Thomas, and Matthew Vaughn. If I have left anyone off, it is not intentional.

FEMALE BETA READERS

I wanted to shine a specific spotlight on my female beta readers. I don't feel an acknowledgment in the back of a book is adequate praise for what they did, but I want them to know how appreciative I am of their time to read and pass along their thoughts. This book wouldn't be as good if they hadn't helped me with it. These superhero women readers are:

Samantha Hawkins
(please look up her book reviews here: @samanthas_shelf)

Laurie Jones

Corrina Morse
(please look up her book reviews on Facebook: *No (Re)Morse Reviews*)

Lauren Bayliss Schuldt

Photo Credit: Silas James Rowland of Rowland Film Co.
(www.rowlandfilm.co)

Photo Location: Sabal Studio, Greenville, SC

ABOUT THE AUTHOR

Wofford Lee Jones is a horror/thriller writer who loves coffee, a good book, and a great story. His love for horror grew from watching movies in the late 70s/early 80s. However, it was only in his twenties that he started reading horror. He enjoys art, drawing/painting, watching live theatre and movies, traveling, reading, book cover design, and supporting his fellow writers. He works as a designer at Yates Construction by day, but engineering is different from where his true passion lies. Nightly and on the weekends, he can be found with a hot cup of coffee, studiously banging out that next chilling tale. He always strives to keep it dark, disturbing, and a little bit creepy. Welcome to his darkness. He lives in Greenville, South Carolina, with his wife Laurie. He is working on his fifth and sixth books, a novel *Becoming Ally Winter*, and a collection of horror and thriller stories titled *Fatal Potions*. Stay tuned; there is more coming down the pike.

For more information about the author, please see www.woffordleejones.com. Consider signing up for his monthly newsletter. It comes out on the third of every month, and a free flash fiction story comes out on the eighteenth of each month for his subscribers.

Acclaim for
SOUL DREAMS

Soul Dreams is incredibly engaging and masterfully written. It is a wicked fresh take on possession horror filled with relatable characters and shocking twists.

—Kevin Woods

Jones creates a story that you just want to keep reading. He really does a great job at painting a picture that you can see, touch, smell, and hear.

—Alex Pearson

A fun ride with some cool thriller revenge moments and the battle within ourselves and our souls.

—Chad Farmer

This book left me shook.

—Alexandra Hernandez

Scared me to the end.

—Kim Fowler

A passionate portrayal of possession.
Jones takes readers on a journey that is at once haunting and heartbreaking. The juxtaposition between Edward McDaniel and Tyler Curtis' characters sets the stage for a horror novel that is both delightfully unsettling and psychologically gripping.

—M.K. Deppner author of *Photographs of October*

Rave Reviews for

OFF THE BEATEN PATH

Wow! Just wow! The sheer level of brutality in these stories was an absolutely pleasant surprise. Many of these stories were based on potentially real and possible scenarios, making them that much more terrifying!

—Joshua Marsella author of
Hymns from the Dirt **and** *Hunger for Death*

Jones is a masterful storyteller!

—Steve Hodgson

Full of fun, twisted stories, *Off the Beaten Path* is a great collection that's a little bit sci-fi, a little bit horror, with a lineup of stories guaranteed to turn your stomach.

—Patrick Delaney author of *Witch 13* **and**
Return to the House that Fell from the Sky

Raw stories that'll stick with you!

—Brian Coker

Jones does revenge better than anyone else. There are brutal moments here and gross ones, violence, and vengeance. But there are also moments of humor, love worth killing for, and maybe, once or twice, the feeling that people get exactly what they deserved.

—Heather Daughrity author of
Echoes of the Dead **and** *Knock, Knock*

Each story explores the aspects of the desperate and insane, while Jones builds the suspense to a satisfying and sometimes chaotic climax. With plenty of twisted imagery and bloody intensity, any horror fan will relish in the fun, gruesome tales told here.

—D.A. Schneider author of *Salvation*, **the** *Irish Black* **series and the** *Ghost Hunter Z* **trilogy**

Praise for

HELL NIGHT IN HOPEWELL

The amount of violence and carnage is mind-blowing in a deliciously dark way. I finished this one and let out a satisfied sigh. It's a good one.

—Heather Daughrity author of *Tales My Grandmother Told Me*

Jones has a particularly descriptive way of writing, and when the red stuff gets flowing and the violence reaches a fever pitch, he leaves no doubt that he is one of the most exciting (and possibly depraved!) writers in the game today.

—Kevin Woods

Hell Night in Hopewell was the perfect read for the Halloween season. It plays out like an old-school slasher, and I was delighted to sit back and enjoy the ride like I was watching a movie.

—Katheryn G. Owen

Jones has an incredible ability to paint a vivid picture of each carefully crafted scene and make you feel as though you are there. And trust me when I say Hopewell is not somewhere you want to be!

—Evan Bond author of *Getaway* **and** *Glowing Embers*

The way it goes wrong and the degree to which it goes wrong were completely unexpected. The relatable characters make the mayhem more painful, as no one is safe and anything can happen. And does.

—Jay Bechtol author of *The Great American Coward*

Jones' storytelling is tense and threatening. The reader is constantly teased by an impending horror, suspecting what may come next, only to be shocked by a twist far more horrifying than imagined.

—D.A. Schneider author of *Salvation* **and the** *Ghost Hunter Z* **trilogy**

Praise for
LETHAL DOSES

I'm a fan of Jones' stories.
They are usually dark, twisted, violent, and always horrifying.
Overall, there are more than thirty doses in this book, from the
micro to the full weekend bender. You are guaranteed to enjoy them.

—Jay Bechtol author of *The Great American Coward*

Jones never fails to deliver.
I love his writing. He is able to showcase his talent in *Lethal
Doses*, where you can easily see how wonderfully diverse his
writing really is. Each story is fully fleshed out, and ranges from
weird, silly, creepy/scary, to brutal and everything in between.

—Shasta Matthews

This collection shows off Jones' ability to draw you into his world
with entrancing descriptions along with twists and turns that leave
you scratching your head until it bleeds. Be prepared to exceed
the recommended dosage and OD on his top-notch storytelling.

—Lee Bagwell co-author of *Family Tradition*

Lethal Doses is a treasure trove of creepy stories not for the faint of
heart! The sheer variety of the stories, the twists and the turns each story
has in store, all of them well-written and brimming with originality,
make Jones' new collection an absorbing read you won't be able to
put down. I think the stories' length has a lot to do with it: each
story is exactly as long as needed, there are no fillers, and all stories
provide closure, with no cliffhangers, no outstanding questions.

—Milt Theodossiou

TRIGGER WARNINGS

As promised in the opening message, here are all the possible triggers that could affect a reader. These are in random order.

Coarse language
Sexual Assault
Rape
Assault and brutality (female and male)
Explicit sexual scenes
Castration
Emotional rape (female and male)
Emotional mind games (female and male)
Premeditated murder
Murder
Disposing of dead bodies

www.ingramcontent.com/pod-product-compliance
Lightning Source LLC
LaVergne TN
LVHW041113080826
845145LV00007B/1796

* 9 7 8 0 9 9 9 0 9 2 5 8 3 *